PRAISE FOR **BETWEEN EARTH AND SKY**

"The world sucks you in from the start, and the pacing yanks you along by the collar. *Black Sun* is instantly riveting from the beginning—Roanhorse is at the top of her game here."

—R.F. Kuang, bestselling author of *The Poppy War*

"Absolutely tremendous. Roanhorse knocks it out of the park again with an epic tale about duty and destiny that will sweep readers away and broaden the horizons of an entire genre."

—S. A. Chakraborty, nationally bestselling author of *The City of Brass*

"Engrossing and vibrant. *Black Sun* left me with my jaw on the floor."

—Tochi Oneybuchi, author of *Riot Baby*

"Readers are in for intricate worldbuilding, engrossing adventure, and stunning backdrops."

—*The Washington Post*

"The pages turn themselves. A beautifully crafted setting with complex character dynamics and layers of political intrigue? Perfection. Mark your calendars, this is the next big thing."

—*Kirkus Reviews*, starred review

"Roanhorse introduces an epic fantasy with vivid worldbuilding and exciting prose. Readers will be attracted to the story, in which there is no real right vs. wrong. Only inevitable change will draw out the heroes of this imaginative tale."

—*Library Journal*, starred review

"A razor-sharp examination of politics, generational trauma, and the path to redemption . . . Roanhorse strikes a perfect balance between powerful worldbuilding and rich thematic exploration as the protagonists struggle against their fates. Fantasy fans will be wowed."

—*Publishers Weekly*, starred review

"Bold, richly emotional, and expertly crafted, *Black Sun* shines brighter than even the highest expectations."

—*Shelf Awareness*, starred review

"A must-read for fans of N. K. Jemisin's epic fantasy and those who love George R. R. Martin's Song of Ice and Fire series but want more diverse worlds."

—*Booklist*

"Excellent plot machinations and stellar prose . . . an excellent second installment that adds even more detail and intrigue."

—*Kirkus Reviews*, starred review

"A great second entry in what is likely to be a stellar epic fantasy trilogy."

"[*Fevered Star*] sets up the promise of an explos

Tova

Tovasheh

Huecha

Obregi Mountains

The Meridian

Barach

Hokaia

Crescent Sea

Teek Territory

Lost Moth   Cuecola

City of Tova

Otsa

Tsay :
Golden Eagle Clan

Tovasheh River

Sun
Rock

Odo : Carrion Crow Clan

Titidi :
Water Strider Clan

The Maw

Eastern
Districts

KUN : Winged Serpent Clan

FEVERED STAR

BETWEEN EARTH AND SKY

BOOK TWO

REBECCA ROANHORSE

SAGA PRESS

LONDON SYDNEY **NEW YORK** TORONTO NEW DELHI

SAGA PRESS

AN IMPRINT OF SIMON & SCHUSTER, INC.

1230 AVENUE OF THE AMERICAS, NEW YORK, NEW YORK 10020

First Saga Press paperback edition March 2023

SAGA PRESS and colophon are trademarks of Simon & Schuster, Inc.

For information about special discounts for bulk purchases, please contact Simon & Schuster Special Sales at 1-866-506-1949 or business@simonandschuster.com.

The Simon & Schuster Speakers Bureau can bring authors to your live event. For more information or to book an event, contact the Simon & Schuster Speakers Bureau at 1-866-248-3049 or visit our website at www.simonspeakers.com.

Interior design by Michelle Marchese

Manufactured in the United States of America

10 9 8 7 6 5 4 3 2 1

Library of Congress Cataloging-in-Publication Data has been applied for.

ISBN 978-1-5344-3773-9
ISBN 978-1-5344-3774-6 (paperback)
ISBN 978-1-5344-3775-3 (ebook)

For Maya, the original #TeamBroCrow
This book would suck without you.

THE PEOPLE OF THE MERIDIAN

• THE OBREGI MOUNTAINS •

Serapio – *The Crow God Reborn*
Marcal – *Serapio's father*
Powageh – *Serapio's third tutor, a Knife*
~~Saaya – *Serapio's mother*~~
~~Paadeh – *Serapio's first tutor*~~
~~Eedi – *Serapio's second tutor, a Spearmaiden*~~

• CITY OF CUECOLA •

Balam – *Lord of the House of Seven, Patron of*
   the Crescent Sea, White Jaguar
Pech – *A merchant lord*
Tuun – *A merchant lord*
Sinik – *A merchant lord*
Keol – *Captain, sailor*
~~Callo – *First mate, sailor*~~

• CITY OF TOVA •

THE WATCHERS
Naranpa – *Sun Priest, Order of Oracles (hawaa)*
Iktan – *Priest of Knives, Order of Knives (tsiyo)*
~~Abah – *Priest of Succor, Order of the Healing Society (seegi)*~~
~~Haisan – *Priest of Records, Order of Historical Society (ta dissa)*~~
~~Kiutue – *Former Sun Priest*~~
~~Eche – *Dedicant, Order of Oracles*~~

• THE SKY MADE CLANS •

CARRION CROW
~~Yatliza – *Matron*~~
Ayawa – *Yatliza's consort*
Okoa – *Yatliza's son, Captain of the Shield*
Esa – *Yatliza's daughter, Matron*
Chaiya – *Former Captain of the Shield*
Maaka – *Leader of the Odohaa*
Feyou – *A healer*
Uuna – *A Shield*
Ituya – *A Shield*
Mataya
Juuna
Fress
Haalan
Kutssah – *A giant crow*
Benundah – *A giant crow*

WATER STRIDER
Ieyoue – *Matron*
Aishe
Zash
Tyode
Uncle Kuy
Omataya

GOLDEN EAGLE
Nuuma – *Matron*
Terzha – *Daughter of Nuuma*
Ziha – *Daughter of Nuuma*
Layat – *Advisor to the Matron*
Kuya
Suhtsee – *A giant golden eagle*

WINGED SERPENT
Peyana – *Matron*
Ahuat – *Captain of the Shield*

THE DRY EARTH (CLANLESS)

Denaochi – *Brother to Naranpa, Boss of the Lupine*

Sedaysa – *Boss of the Agave*

Pasko – *Boss of the Blackfire*

Amalq – *Boss of the Wildrose*

Zataya – *A witch*

Baaya – *A servant*

~~Akel – *Brother to Naranpa*~~

• CITY OF HOKAIA •

Daakun

SPEARMAIDENS

Seuq – *The leader of the Dreamwalkers*

Gwee – *A Dreamwalker*

Odae – *A Dreamwalker*

Asnod – *A Dreamwalker*

Naasut

• TEEK •

Xiala – *A sea captain*

Mahina

Alani

Teanni

You have arrived on earth
where your relatives, your kin, suffer hardships, endure
     affliction,
where it is hot, it is cold, it is windy.
It is a place of thirst, it is a place of hunger,
a place without pleasure, a place without joy,
a place of suffering, a place of fatigue, a place of torment.
O my little one, perhaps, for a brief time, you shall shine
     as the sun!

—*The Florentine Codex*, Book VI, 128V–151R

CHAPTER 1

> I have done great deeds both good and evil, and who is to judge
> me but the gods, and what shall they say to me but that I dared?
>
> —From *The Manual of the Dreamwalkers*,
> by Seuq, a spearmaiden

The sun had not yet risen on the first day after the new year's winter solstice, and it felt not at all as if an age had ended, but Balam knew better.

He left his home well before dawn, a purse of cacao, a small clay cup, a mirror, and an obsidian knife on the belt at his waist, and he walked. Normally, he would bring servants with him. A man to carry his purchases home, another to guard his person, although there were very few things he feared. But today he went alone.

He traveled the wide, spotless avenue that ran the length of Cuecola, past the still-sleeping market, and through the city gates. He walked past the farming village of Kuharan with its oval houses and thatched roofs, past the jail where'd he found the Teek woman, and into the surrounding jungle.

It had rained all night, and the air here was heavy and wet.

Water dripped from wide, notched leaves, and the ground was soft under his sandals. He had worn a long white cloak that fastened across his chest, and he had wrapped his hair in a matching white scarf. Jade hung from his ears and nose and encircled his wrists and ankles. He had also painted the top half of his face blue.

His destination was a small temple, one of many that had been abandoned after the Treaty of Hokaia had forbidden the worship of the jaguar god. The stone building had once been beautiful, colorfully painted and well-tended, but now it ran to decay. Cracks marred the wide steps, and the verdancy of the jungle had taken over much of its facade. He was careful not to disturb anything as he entered.

He made his way to the altar off the central courtyard. He was not a pious man, at least not in the way most people meant it, but he revered power, and here once had been a place of great power. He pressed his hands to the cold stone and bowed his head. He murmured a prayer that had not been heard in this place in three centuries. And then he sat on the steps, purse in hand, to wait.

It did not take long for the thief to arrive.

The man did not see Balam there, sitting so still in the shadows. The jaguar lord watched, curious, as the man walked the length of the courtyard, admiring the fading stone reliefs, the elegant decay. The thief carried a woven sack over one shoulder. He wore an unadorned white loincloth, and his black hair was cropped close to his head in an unfashionable bowl, but his face was handsome and young, and there was an intriguing audaciousness that glimmered in his eyes. It was that spark of impudence that had brought him to Balam's attention to begin with, and then to learn that he had access to the royal library, well, it had come together nicely.

"Welcome," he greeted the thief, standing to reveal himself.

The man startled. "Seven hells," he swore, glaring. "What kind of person sneaks around in a place like this?"

Balam smiled as he always did, mouth closed to hide a predator's teeth. "This is the house where my ancestors worshipped long ago."

"Well, it's eerie. I don't see why we couldn't have met in the city. Perhaps over a drink."

Balam lifted an elegant brow. "I was clear that this endeavor required the utmost secrecy. You have not told anyone of our meeting, have you?"

"No," the man said hastily. "I kept my word. Now you keep yours."

Balam motioned for the thief to ascend the stairs and join him in front of the altar. He hesitated, so Balam shook the purse of cacao in his hand. That seemed to dislodge the man's doubt, and he quickly climbed the steps.

"Did you have trouble entering the vault?" Balam asked.

"A few days of planning, a sweet word to the night guard. I don't think anyone has tried to break in before." The thief made a face as if he thought Balam a fool.

He ignored it. "May I see it?"

"This is the first time I've been hired to steal a book." The man drew a large bound manuscript from his bag and set it on the altar. "Is there a market for it? Might you have some friends who need a man with quick hands and soft feet?"

Reverently, Balam opened the cloth cover and unfolded the bark pages. They stretched out in a long continuous sheet of glyphs and phonetic symbols. He recognized the archaic language he had long studied, confirming that this was the knowledge he desired as his own.

"Can you understand it?" the thief asked, curious.

"Of course," Balam said absently. His mind was already focused on the writing before him, his eyes devouring the first page. *You hold before you the* Manual of the Dreamwalkers. *Those who eat of the godflesh and practice the spirit magic therein risk madness, as my sisters may attest from their cold tombs. But for those who do not fear, unfathomable power is yours.*

"What does it say?"

"Hmmm?"

"The book. What does it say?"

Balam brought his attention back to the present. He folded the pages into the book and closed it before giving the thief a wry look. "Do you wish to become a sorcerer?"

"Me?" The man laughed, leaning back against the altar. "I have no use for magic."

"There was once a time when thieves practiced shadow magic as part of their profession. It is said to run in their blood."

"Old superstition," he said, before spitting on the floor. "A sucker's endeavor, something for the feebleminded. I'll stay in the light of reason, thanks." He touched his fingers to a pendant around his neck, a small golden replica of the sun.

Balam's eyes flicked in irritation at the globule of spittle on the ancient stone floor. He ran a tongue around his teeth, as if clearing them of words better unspoken, and said instead, "And if I told you that even the Sun Priest's power was simply magic derived from the old gods?"

"I'd tell you that you were a fool, too, esteemed Lord." He bowed mockingly. "But it's none of my business why you want the book, truly. My only god is that which you hold in your hand."

The cacao. Balam gestured for the man to give him the sack. He did, and Balam slid the book back inside and set it at his own feet. In return, he handed the man the purse of cacao. The thief's eyes shone with greed as he opened it. Balam watched as the man mentally counted the sum. Possible futures flashed across his features: new jewels, the best drink, the most beautiful women.

Balam slipped his knife from its sheath. "There is one other thing I need from you."

"Name it," the man said, eyes still focused on his new wealth.

Balam calmly stepped forward and slid the knife into the man's belly. He jerked upward until he hit bone. The thief gasped, the purse falling from his hands. Cacao scattered across the stone floor, cascading down the altar steps. The thief beat feeble fists against Balam's chest. He ignored it, lifting the man to lay him on the altar. He stepped back and watched as that brazenness that he had admired drained from the thief's eyes.

Then he got to work, first collecting the fresh blood in his clay cup. When he had enough, he dipped his fingers into the bowl and painted vertical lines on the bottom half of his face. Then his palms and the soles of his feet. When he was ready, he placed the mirror on the ground and poured blood across its surface. He chanted the words to call forth the shadow. A circle opened before him as if reflecting off the mirror. The gateway was a bubbling darkness, frost sizzling and cracking along its boundaries. He hoped he was correct, and the thief's blood would ease his way through the shadow world and, if not, that the offering of the thief on the jaguar altar would make his ancestors look kindly upon his journey. He slung the sack over his shoulder, whispered his destination, and stepped into the darkness . . .

. . . and out into his own private rooms, gasping. He dropped the sack and collapsed. His skin was glazed with a thin layer of ice, and his breath puffed white before him. He dragged a nearby blanket from his bed and wrapped it around himself.

He lay there, shuddering, unable to do more until, finally, he began to thaw.

Once he felt himself, he made his way to an adjacent room where a steam bath already awaited him. He cleaned the blood and shadow from his skin and donned a simple pair of pants cut in the northern style. He called for a servant, who came immediately.

"I am not to be disturbed," he explained, as he arranged the table in front of him: an abalone shell, a brick of copal, a small wooden box, and, next to it, his new acquisition. "It is very important. Do you understand?"

"Of course, Lord."

"Not by anyone," Balam insisted. "The other lords, my mother, and certainly not my damnable cousin."

His cousin, who had once been called Tiniz but had kept the honorific Powageh as xir name since returning from Obregi, had been haunting his doorstep. Balam was not interested in what his cousin had to say, what case xe wished to plead on Saaya's son's behalf. Frankly, he thought his cousin compromised, addled by age and sentiment. Powageh had always loved Saaya to unhealthy extremes, and it seemed now xe had transferred xir affections to her son. Understandable, he supposed, if a bit shortsighted. Powageh had waxed on about guilt, of all things. How the boy didn't deserve his fate, how in the end Powageh had had second thoughts.

Balam had listened to his cousin that day as long as he could before exasperation forced his tongue. "Have you forgotten what we do here? We are breaking worlds, realigning the very course of the heavens. We manipulate powers not seen in three hundred years, no, a thousand. Against all odds, all reason, Saaya rebirthed a god, and now you wish to insult him with your mawkishness?"

"We raised him up only to die for our schemes."

"Would that the whole of humankind had such divine purpose!"

"But we did not even ask if it was what he wanted."

Balam had scoffed. "We made him a god, Cousin. He is not a maiden deciding which dress best suits her eyes. He was a weapon, and a fine one at that." And by now, he would have slain the Watchers, thrown the sun from its course over Tova, and ushered in a new era.

Yes, Serapio had done his part. Now it was time for Balam to do his.

He opened the book and began to read.

The dreaming minds of all human beings are open to you, but the dreams of the creatures—furred, finned, and feathered— will remain closed. They dream in a different world from ours.

"Well enough," he murmured. He had not thought to manipulate birds and beasts, anyway.

You may eat the godflesh whole, but it is better to make a tea of it. One cup may keep you in the dreamworld half the day and will exhaust you upon your return. It is best only to Walk when another spearmaiden can watch over your corporeal form.

Ah, yes. The spearmaidens who practiced this forbidden magic had always been paired. Well, that was not an option now. He read on.

It is best to begin with inquiry into the victim's mind. Once you are confident, you may begin to plant thoughts and desires and return again and again to cultivate their growth. You cannot kill outright in a dream, but you may convince the victim to harm themselves or others because their dream demands it. Beware! It is a delicate thing to manipulate minds. Do not get entangled.

7

He read all day and well into the night, not eating or sleeping, and his household did as instructed and did not disturb him. So many warnings of death and madness coupled with promises of power beyond imagining. Balam suspected the author had been quite mad herself by the time she committed the magic to writing. But the text was all that was left of the practice; no dreamwalkers were known to have survived the purge that came after the signing of the Treaty of Hokaia.

He would be the first in an era, and he was ready.

He lit the copal and fanned it until it burned steadily, filling the room with sacred smoke. He donned the regalia of his station, similar to what he had worn to the temple, but now his cloak was rare white jaguar skin, and he wore white shell around his neck and in his ears and nose. He extinguished the lanterns, leaving the room in semidarkness, the moon through high windows the only light.

He took the godflesh from the small wooden box he had set on the table. He ate a piece the size of his fingernail and settled himself onto the cushions to wait. He did not wait long. The dreamworld opened to him. He marveled at its beauty, and at its terror.

And Balam went hunting.

CHAPTER 2

> Within even the smallest act of love lives the potential for a
> miracle.
>
> —*The Obregi Book of Flowers*

The Odo Sedoh dreamed, and in his dreams, he was legion.

He was black-winged murder flying over a vast sea. He was
the bloodthirsty havoc of beak and talon. He was the stately
flock that wheeled over a city stained by injustice.

He became the shout of a thousand prayers on a thousand
lips. He became a prophecy of revenge. He became the blos-
soming shadow that engulfed a sun.

He was Crow who then became the slaughter.

Serapio screamed and screamed and screamed and—

*Gentle hands shook him, and his eyelids involuntarily flut-
tered open. But all was shadow, as it had been since he was
twelve. His nose filled with the scent of crows. He felt the rough
scratch of quills against his back. A voice called out concern for
the Odo Sedoh.*

I'm alive!

And then he was falling, falling . . . back into his dreams.

Dream morphed to memory, and memory took on shape and form.

He remembered speaking his true name under the black sun, and how it had shattered him.

He remembered that he had gone forward with staff and blade and become the whirlwind.

His remembered his hands had grown slick with blood, and his ears had filled with the cries of the dying. And standing amid the chaos he had wrought, he had exulted.

And then he remembered he had been thwarted. The Sun Priest who was his nemesis, her death his very purpose, was not there. She had been replaced by an impostor. Some fool wearing the mask and vestments of priesthood but lacking the essence of a god. The Odo Sedoh had slain the deceiver, his rage so dark that he barely registered the sweep of his knives separating neck and head.

And then the crow god had fled, and his body had begun to fail.

As it was meant to.

As was expected.

But there was one condition his creators had not foreseen. Something his mother had not anticipated, an occurrence for which his tutors had not planned. Serapio had made the small crows his friends. He had loved them and protected them. And in the moment of his death, those friends came to him with mutual love and monumental will and sacrificed themselves so that he might live. The southern sorcerers should have known the power of a sacrifice given with love, as such a sacrifice from his mother had been what tied the boy to her god so long ago. But perhaps they could not fathom that such small beings as crows were capable of so much love, and that a man whose deeds were as dark as his would deserve it.

CHAPTER 3

CITY OF TOVA (THE CROW ROOKERY)
YEAR 1 OF THE CROW

> Put not your faith in the gods of old. Their will is unknowable, their power fickle. They will abandon you when you least expect it.
>
> —*Exhortations for a Happy Life*

"Drink this."

Someone lifted Serapio's head, and liquid touched his lips.

Memories tumbled rootless and disordered, and he was twelve again, a clay cup sweet and cold in his hands, his mother smiling as she fed him poison. Her face morphed before him and became a skull, empty and leering. Her voice, the slap of running feet bound for flight.

Panic welled in his chest, choking, suffocating. A primal urge to get away rolled through his body, the need to stop what he knew came next.

He threw his arms wide, a shout on his tongue.

A man cried out, startled, as Serapio knocked him away. He dimly registered that whoever had cried out was not his mother, but instinct gripped him now, and all he knew was that he must survive. He hurled himself forward, colliding with the man, but the stranger was quick. Powerful arms encircled him and rolled him to the ground.

Only years of training kept Serapio from being pinned as he fought to stay off his back. His opponent was bigger than him, heavier, but that left gaps in his guard, space for Serapio to maneuver. He turned his shoulder and thrust his forearm into the man's throat. Distance opened between them, but before Serapio could move, a punch ripped across his jaw.

"Stop!" The shout was raw, hoarse.

Serapio's neck twisted with the impact, and he followed the momentum, rolling to his hands and knees. His face throbbed, and he felt unsteady, but he scrambled to a crouch. He tucked his chin, lifted his fists in defense, and listened for his opponent's next move.

None came. Instead, the man shouted, "I do not want to fight you! I am not your enemy!"

"Everyone is my enemy!" Serapio roared.

"Not! Me!" The stranger's breath came in gasps. "Not me."

"Even you."

Just as he had not hesitated to attack, he did not hesitate now. He had no weapons, no crowsight, and in this unfamiliar place, blindness put him at too great a disadvantage. He could not let the man get the upper hand again. Serapio reached for shadow, willed it to his fingertips. *Destroy!* he thought. *Devour!*

But the shadow did not come. Instead, pain, sharp enough to make him hiss, tore through his side. He collapsed into himself, body hunching instinctively around the agony.

"What is it?" The voice was concerned. "Is it your injury? What—" Feet shuffled closer.

"Stay away!" Serapio thrust out a hand to hold the man back. Confused, in pain, he demanded that the darkness answer his call.

Nothing.

Terror edged at his senses now. A helplessness he had not felt in a decade.

He dug deeper, desperately seeking the place where his god lived within him, that reassuring pool of shadow that had been with him since he was a child.

And found . . . nothing.

He was empty, a cupped hand that retained the shape of something precious it had once cradled but was now hollow.

He was a child, again. Alone, afraid. Waiting for the world to make sense, to become the god his mother had promised. He could not go back to that place. Small and weak. At the mercy of those who professed to love him but whose actions betrayed their selfish intentions. He grasped for something to fill his lack, something to anchor him, something he knew was true.

"Xiala," he whispered. Yes, he remembered her. She was solid and real in his mind. The ocean scent of her long coiling hair, the brash sound of her unapologetic laughter, the feel of her body moving beneath his touch. He clung to those memories and let her moor him to reality, a steady beacon to guide him to safer shores.

And crows. He remembered his crows.

He grabbed for the bag he always wore at his neck, but his star pollen was gone. A shivering fear clutched at his heart, but he could not believe his crows would abandon him as his god had. They were his oldest friends, his true companions. He flung his mind out, willing the crows to answer, and his world exploded.

Crows. There were crows everywhere. Small crows by the hundreds, of all different shapes and sizes and hues. They had not left him.

And even more, he sensed the giant crows, the great corvids of clan Carrion Crow.

"Benundah?"

I am here, Suneater. He recognized that voice in his head and almost wept to hear it.

"Benundah, what happened? Where am I?" He wanted to ask her why he could not feel his god, but he dared not, afraid of the answer.

You are safe. You are alive. Okoa has brought you to the rookery. It is our sacred home. Our nesting grounds far from humans.

"But I fought a man." Even now, he could sense the stranger before him. Waiting, watching, his breath coming rough and labored.

That is Okoa. He is a warrior of Carrion Crow, a crow son like yourself. You can trust him.

Serapio turned his face, listening for the telltale shifting of feet, the rustle of clothes. "Okoa?"

"How do you know me?"

He focused on the place from where the voice had come. "Why am I alive? Do you know?"

"Who were you talking to?"

Serapio shook his head. It was all wrong. This place, this person. Serapio himself. "Why am I alive?" he shouted. If things could only make sense.

Benundah answered: *The little ones have their own magic, and they used it to save you. It cost them dearly.*

The little ones? Grief shattered his heart. "I cannot accept this. Take it back. Tell them to take it back!"

It is too late for that, Suneater. They gave their lives freely. Do not dishonor them now with your refusal.

Shame burned him. He bowed his head. "I would not dishonor them, but I cannot accept their gift. I am . . . unworthy."

Whether you perceive yourself worthy or not is inconsequential. They loved you, and that is all that matters.

"Who are you talking to?" It was the man again, the one Benundah named Okoa.

Serapio's frustration flared. "Why am I here?"

"We came from Sun Rock. I thought you dead at first, but . . . Benundah knew. She is the one who chose the rookery. You said her name. Is that who you were talking to? Can you . . ." He could hear doubt in Okoa's voice. "Were you speaking to Benundah?"

"What do you want from me?"

"I . . . only to help. Only to do the right thing."

"Benundah says I should trust you."

"I am not your enemy."

"Then why did you attack me?"

"I did not." He sounded confused, offended. "I only offered you water."

Serapio tried to remember who had struck first, but it had happened so quickly, and he was not sure what had been real and what was a dream. He remembered dreaming of his mother and the panicked feeling of needing to fight, to not be helpless. The rest was unclear.

Perhaps Okoa had not attacked him after all. But that did not mean he could be trusted.

Serapio stood and whistled sharply. He felt the crows stir at his request, and they came to him on beating wings.

"I only need one," he whispered, and a single crow flew to his shoulder. He had only ever been able to use his crow vision when he was under the influence of star pollen, so he was not sure it would work now without it. But the gift of the small crows gave him a peculiar confidence, and he knew his friends were with him, and that this, of all his powers, would still be his.

He closed his eyes, the crow's eyes opened, and he could see.

They were in a round room, more ruin than dwelling, a gap in the wall so large he spied the snowcapped mountains beyond. The stone that was left bled shades of red and brown, rock worn dull and crumbling by the weather. Bands of orange and white curved through the darker rock, and the ground below his feet was loose pebbles and a fine sandy dirt. There was at least one more floor above them, but the wooden stairs that led upward had fallen to disrepair. A watery winter's light offered scant illumination, and the space felt both exposed and claustrophobic at the same time.

"Where is this place?" he asked.

"We are in the mountains west of Tova. I do not believe any human has set foot here in more than a hundred years." Okoa walked to the nearest wall and ran a black-gloved hand over the stone. His whole form was sheathed in black, his shirt thick quilted armor. "Someone once lived here. Someone once dedicated their life to caring for the crows."

"It is a monastery." The truth of it came to him all at once. "The mountains of Obregi are dotted with solitary buildings such as these that house devotees of the Obregi faith. This one must have been dedicated to the crow god at one time."

"Did Benundah tell you that?" Again, that doubt.

"She did not have to. I am familiar with such places."

He pushed thoughts of Obregi from his mind. If he let them linger, they became dark memories, and he worried that he would fall back into that lonely place that had taunted him earlier. Obregi was only neglect and loneliness. And his mother's death. And his father's disregard.

He had come far from there, he reminded himself. Always before, he had quieted such thoughts by summoning his purpose, his destiny. But now, when he tried, he faltered. Had he not fulfilled his destiny? Found his purpose on the blood-soaked ground of Sun Rock? If so, who was he now? And again, that question: *Why am I alive?*

"How is your wound?" Okoa gestured to Serapio's side.

He had almost forgotten it, he was so used to tolerating pain. He pressed a hand to it now and drew it away, surprised to find it sticky and wet. "It bleeds." Now that he had been made aware of the wound again, it was a fresh agony. He gritted his teeth, and the small bird on his shoulder cried out in sympathy.

"Let me help you."

Serapio stepped back.

Okoa raised his hands. "I will not hurt you. I swear it. If I wanted you dead, I've had my opportunity. Let me help you. Please, Odo Sedoh."

Odo Sedoh. Was he still the Odo Sedoh? It felt like a lie.

"My name is Serapio."

Okoa didn't acknowledge him, but he approached, palms showing, and Serapio let him come. He was not quite as tall as Serapio, but he was wider, and he gingerly slung Serapio's arm around his neck to help him over to a dugout fire waiting to be lit.

"I was about to make a fire before you woke up," Okoa explained, as he lowered him to sitting. "Heat some water to clean your wound." Serapio could see now there were strips of black cloth laid out, remnants of Okoa's undershirt, if he had to guess. The man busied himself with starting the fire. Once it was lit, he fed the flames until they blazed.

"I made a poultice earlier," he continued. "Wild lettuce, sage. I was lucky to find that much at this time of year. We learn basic field medicine at the war college, but I am a poor healer. It is not improving." He glanced at Serapio. "How is your face?"

Serapio touched a hand to his cheek, puzzled.

"It is not my way to hit a man already injured, but I thought you might kill me. You're deceptively strong." He said that last with a smile.

His face was still warm from Okoa's earlier punch, but it was nothing. "It is forgotten," he assured him. "How long did I sleep?"

"A day, perhaps two? But not well. Your dreams were troubled." Okoa's voice was low under the crackling of the fire, his face pinched in concentration as he worked.

"I believe . . ." Okoa drifted off, seeming to battle with himself. Finally, he spoke again. "I don't believe the sun has truly set or risen since the Convergence. I don't know what that means."

There was a hint of accusation in his voice that pleased Serapio. He knew what it meant.

"The crow god challenges the sun." Serapio said it with conviction, and now the absence of his god made sense. It still unsettled him. He could not contemplate it without tendrils of panic tightening his chest, but at least there was a reason for it, one he could comprehend beyond his own inadequacy.

Okoa approached him, the warmed and medicated cloth in hand. He gestured to Serapio, asking permission to touch him, and Serapio allowed him his ministrations.

"Do you remember what happened on Sun Rock?" Okoa smoothed the cloth tight to his side.

"Yes." But that was not entirely true. Serapio had been sifting through his memories, trying to distinguish dream from reality, but there were still parts of Sun Rock that felt like he had witnessed them from afar.

"I have never seen such horrors," Okoa admitted.

"You are a warrior. Have you not killed before?"

"I have studied war."

"*Studied* war."

"I am Carrion Crow. We are stained by slaughter." He gripped the collar of his quilted shirt, briefly baring the haahan at his neck. "You cannot shame me for being a man who now lives in peaceful times. They are well earned on the bodies of my ancestors. And I have seen killing before, but . . ." He shook his head. "Nothing like that."

There was something in Okoa's voice, something that made Serapio ask, "Do you fear me?"

"Fear?" He sat back on his heels, studying Serapio's face. "No. But I am wary of a man who walks so comfortably with death."

"But I am not only a man." That hollow feeling, the cupped hand now empty, mocked him, called him a liar, but he did his best to ignore it.

"Some of the bodies were ash and others of the priests laid out in patterns. Why? Was it sorcery? God magic?"

"The shadow of the crow god consumes," was all he said, because in truth, he did not know. He could not remember laying out the bodies. He flexed his hands, the feeling that he had been so fully possessed both exhilarating and terrifying.

Okoa returned to his side of the fire, but it was clear he wanted Serapio to say more.

Serapio sighed. "I know you wish for answers, Okoa Carrion Crow, but the ways of gods are unknowable." *Even to me.*

"And you wonder why I worry."

They sat by the fire, silent in their own concerns, until Serapio asked, "Do you know how I received this?" He touched the wound on his side.

"I think you were stabbed. But more than that I cannot guess. I don't think it was a Knife. I've been on the sharp edge of their wrath before, and my wound festered and would have killed me within the hour. Yours did not. You had deep lacerations around your eyes, too, and those seem to have healed."

Serapio had forgotten he had cut his sewn eyes open. He raised a tentative hand to his face and felt lashes flutter against his fingertips. Strange that it already seemed so natural after so many years of lack. The crow at his shoulder cawed, and he understood. The healing of his eyes and his other wounds were part of the small crows' gift. But if they could not mend the wound in his side, then it must be something of magic, too great for crows alone.

He rubbed his hands through his hair, suddenly tired of this place, this conversation. He did not like any of it, especially his ignorance and patchwork memory. He had always been a man of purpose and destiny, disinterested in what others thought of him, bound to a higher calling. But now he found himself bothered by the way Okoa cast half glances at him and held his words soft on his tongue to avoid offense. Even worse, he was frustrated by his own hesitancy, his own lack of confidence, the missing part of him where his god should be.

He stood. "I need to go back to Tova. I have unfinished business there with the Sun Priest."

He was sure that if he returned, his purpose would return, too, and his god as well. And perhaps, perhaps, if he still lived when it was all over, he could find Xiala and continue what they had begun. The last was too much to hope, but he found himself hoping it anyway.

"How soon can we return? We have lost too much time here while I slept."

Okoa's look was pensive, and Serapio could feel the man's unvoiced thoughts like an itch between his shoulders.

When Okoa finally did speak, his words came slowly, heavy

with portent. "While there are those in Odo who have long awaited your coming and will rejoice that the Odo Sedoh has returned, they are not everyone. You were raised far away. Cuecola? Obregi, you said before?"

"I am Carrion Crow." A thin line of anger threaded his voice. For Okoa to label him an outsider even after all he had done cut through him more painfully than any Knife. Now it was Serapio's turn to show his haahan and bare his red teeth. "Do you not see?"

Okoa's eyes stayed on him. "Even so, there are things about Tova you do not understand. Please." He smiled, a small tilt of his lips. "Cousin."

The familiar address warmed Serapio in a way he had not expected. *Is this what it feels like to have kin?* he wondered.

Okoa's words were careful, measured. "The Watchers were well loved among the Sky Made. Many were scions of the clans. There are even those in Odo who did not hate them as the Odohaa did."

"There are Carrion Crow who loved the priests?" Nothing his mother or his tutors had said had hinted at such a thing. "But they were your enemies."

"There were likely Carrion Crow among the dedicants you killed. Our history with the Watchers is complicated."

The thought rocked Serapio back. Perhaps Okoa was right that he did not understand, perhaps his impatience was short-sighted. He had always seen the world starkly: Crow against Sun Priest, himself against the world. Nothing in his life, except perhaps the brief time he had spent with Xiala, had suggested reality was otherwise.

"You said that the Odohaa would welcome the Odo Sedoh, but what you have not said is that all of Carrion Crow would do the same."

"There is something they taught us at the war college: When you upset the balance of power, there will be those who resent you, no matter if your cause is righteous."

"There is something I learned, too, from one who trained at the war college. 'Make them fear you.'"

"Spearmaiden bravado." Okoa smiled knowingly. "I was told you trained with a spearmaiden. The Sky Made will fear you," he acknowledged, "but not forever. Fear turns to anger, and Carrion Crow clan will surely be the target of that anger. If the clans turn against us, if they seek Crow blood, what then? Will you fight for Carrion Crow now as fiercely as you did on Sun Rock?"

"I thought you said I was a man too easy with killing, yet now you ask me to be that killer for you."

"I am not unaware of the irony, but I see no other way."

A weapon, always. Whether his god asked or this son of Carrion Crow, his purpose was the same. There was a peace in it, the kind a man feels when he excels at his calling. But there was something else there that chafed, made him feel unseen and disposable.

"Are you not the Odo Sedoh?" Okoa demanded, his measured patience replaced by outrage, and Serapio realized he had taken his silence for refusal. "Are there not people crying out not only for vengeance but for protection? Will you not be both a weapon and a bulwark?"

Okoa vaulted to his feet, and Serapio braced for an attack. But the man only began to pace, fresh anger radiating from every powerful stride.

"I helped you," Okoa said. "I watched over you. Took you far away to where your enemies could not find you. I do not think it is too much to ask you to return and fight for Carrion Crow."

"Are you saying I owe you this?"

"Yes! But . . ." Okoa faltered, his expression contrite. "I do not ask it for myself. I ask it for my people."

"Your people and my people are the same. Cousin."

"Then you will do it?"

He cupped his hands, resting them in his lap. They were so empty they ached. He wondered how he could promise anything when he had lost hold of his god. And if he did not hold his god, what did he hold? The stars, Xiala would say, and the thought made him smile. But he was not sure he believed it.

"I will come to Tova," he agreed. "And then we will see."

CHAPTER 4

CITY OF TOVA (COYOTE'S MAW)
YEAR 1 OF THE CROW

> And Coyote said, I have no desire to live among the Sky
> Made. Let me build my home here in the cool cliffsides under
> the light of the moon and call the revel to me. And on the last
> day when the ancestors are accounted, we will see who has
> lived the better life.

> —From *Songs of the Coyote*

Who are you?

A hand stroked Naranpa's hair, soft breath tickled her ear.
And she was a girl of ten again, snuggled tight against her
mother in the room in which her family of five slept. Father and
mother on one side, then Nara in the middle, and Denaochi
and Akel on the other side, all stretched out on reed mats on
the floor, shared blankets between them. Body heat kept them
warm through the cold Tovan nights when the wind rattled
through the Maw strong enough to smooth stone, and in the
sweltering summers, she and her brothers would sleep outside
on rounded rooftops. But it was winter now, wasn't it? Just
after the solstice. Nara's thoughts hitched. There was something
about the solstice. Something she needed to remember.

Nara? Is that your name? Why do you shine here, Nara?

Because she was special. Mama had said so. Smart and kind and special, and that was why she was picked to serve in the tower.

The tower? The voice sharpened with interest. *Do you mean the celestial tower? Tell me what they taught you in the celestial tower.*

So many things, Nara wanted to say. How to map the courses of planets, how to mold the earth to better mirror the heavens, how to understand celestial patterns and predict the future.

You were a dedicant. But who are you now?

She shied away from the question. There was pain there, something she didn't want to think about.

She thought of Mama instead, and the last time she had seen her. It had been the day she left to serve in the tower. A spring morning, and her brothers, Akel and Denaochi, were there, but her father had not come. Mama said it was too hard for him to say goodbye.

These childish memories. The voice sounded annoyed, exasperated by her retreat. *Forget them. Focus. Who are you now?*

A hand trailed across her scalp and then down her neck, the rake of fingernails against her skin raising goose bumps as they passed. She shivered. There was something she was forgetting. About winter and the solstice. And something Denaochi had told her about her mother, something important.

Who are you now? The voice sounded angry, impatient. Fingers that had caressed her moments ago now closed around her throat. She opened her mouth to scream, but only a dry choking cough came out. The hand tightened.

Who??

Nara clawed at her attacker, desperate to break the hold. She couldn't breathe. Desperation welled up, hard and sudden. She was going to die if she didn't break free. If she didn't answer.

I am the Sun Priest!

Silence, like the echo after a bell. And then a swirl of outrage and disbelief.

Why aren't you dead?

Naranpa froze. That wasn't Mama.

A feeling, like someone digging through her mind and picking through memories the way she rifled through papers in the tower library. Someone looking for something. Something inside her head.

How did you do it, Sun Priest? Did you read the stars to thwart your fate? Why were you not on Sun Rock when the crow god came?

Fury flooded her mind. Not her own but from someone enraged at her defiance.

The grip around her throat tightened. She tried to scream again, and this time blood poured from her mouth. It dripped down her chin, across her chest. It spread like a living thing, covering her body in a sticky rust-colored blanket. Her resistance crumbled at the horror of it.

Another voice bubbled up. *Sorcery? How?*

The voice was different. Older, masculine. She recognized it immediately. It was Kiutue, her old mentor. She knew it couldn't be him, that whatever was digging through her mind was not real. But she felt his presence nonetheless, his shock and disappointment at her heresy. She bent under the burden. The blood oozed down her naked torso, past her thighs, over knees and calves and feet.

Yet another voice slithered into her ear. *Oh, Nara. You should have died that day.*

Iktan? Her mouth worked around the name, her lips remembering its sweetness, even now. Iktan's voice was so real it made her weak with want. She knew xe was as seductive as the serpent whose clan xe had been born to, and as treacherous. And yet she desired.

But do not worry. There is a remedy to every problem.
Look! You're bleeding already.

She looked down. The blood now covered her entire body as if someone had painted it on.

Painted it on.

Her mind shuddered.

A dream. This was all a dream. Her mother had never asked her about what she had learned as a dedicant in the tower, Kiutue had never scolded her for heresy, and Iktan . . . oh, the ache in her heart at xir betrayal felt the most real of it all, but even that was wrong. Iktan had torn the tower apart to try to save her in the end. Heat flared in her chest, a mini-sun ablaze. It was enough to illuminate the cracks in her tangled nightmare. She grasped the edges of the dream and heaved. Reality rushed in, filling her all at once. She remembered the apprentices painting her body in the witch's blood, the salt burning her mouth. The bridge, her wild leap, being dragged from the river by—

"Zataya!" she cried.

"Who?" a man in a white jaguar skin asked.

The dream broke.

She reared up from the place where she lay. Her head slammed into a ceiling inches above her. Fabric bound her arms to her side, covered her face, and she sucked it in, choking. Thick clots of earth broke free and cascaded down from the roof. She rolled instinctively, flailing as she tried to free herself from the blanket and avoid the small avalanche she had loosed.

And then she was falling. A short drop, but she could not brace herself, and the ground was hard. It knocked the little air she had from her lungs with the force of a fist. She lay for a moment, stunned. Pain radiated across her back, and she labored to breathe through the cloth. She frantically worked her arms free, finally tearing the blanket from her face. She gulped air as her eyes adjusted to the anemic light in the room. It shone from the dwindling remnants of a small resin candle in a lantern just past her feet. She could see she was underground . . . in a tomb.

Adrenaline shot through her body, her mind bubbling in panic. *Think, Nara!* She chided herself. *There is air here, and light. And no matter where this is, you are very much alive.* That small sliver of logic calmed her panic. She blinked dirt from her eyes and forced herself to think through what had happened and where she could possibly be.

She could see she was, in fact, in a tomb, but she did not allow the terror of it to swallow her mind. She rolled to her hands and knees and crawled to the lantern. Next to it was a clay bowl full of water and a modest meal—corn, a handful of piñons, and roasted cacao laid out on an oversized leaf.

She recognized the food. It was a spirit meal, something Dry Earth relatives left for the deceased to feed them on their journey to the ancestors, for while the Sky Made burned their dead with star maps in their hands, the Dry Earth buried theirs in the endless catacombs deep below the Maw. She laughed, and the sound that came from her mouth was a dry cackle that echoed deranged in her ears.

She ate the spirit meal, even the dry, rubbery leaf. Perhaps it was sacrilegious, but she was the one it was meant for, after all, and she was starving. She wasn't sure how long she had been in this place, but the gnawing pit in her stomach told her that her last meal had been long ago. After she was sated, or at least had

had enough to clear her mind and soothe her parched throat, she sat back to assess her situation.

"Where are you, Nara?" she said aloud. There was an exit to her right, a gaping mouth of a hole that she would have to crawl through to leave. The thought of dragging herself into the dark sent a shudder down her spine, but what choice did she have? Did it matter that she could not see the path forward when her only other option was to stay and perish? She could wait for someone to come back and find her, but how long would that be? Hours? Weeks? Never? Once before, she had put her faith in rescue, and no one had come. She would not make that mistake again.

She looked around the room for anything else she might use. There was the ever-diminishing light of the lantern, the blanket she had been wrapped in, and the now-empty water bowl. Very little to free her from this hell. But there was nothing to be done about it, and nothing else to do, so she gathered her meager items and crawled on her hands and knees into the darkness.

Her journey was awkward. She wore the blanket as a dress, tucked under one arm and knotted on the opposite shoulder. She slipped the bowl into a makeshift pouch at her shoulder, and she used one hand to hold the lantern. Her progress was slow but always forward. Once she passed a deep black hole of darkness on her left, the sudden lack of a wall enough to make her yelp in fear. She shone her lantern into the gaping mouth of earth. Light bounced off bare dirt walls, illuminating nothing but more dirt. She kept going.

She stopped once and fell into an exhausted sleep. She woke, forgetting where she was, her resin light extinguished. The dark was heavy around her, palpable.

"Help me!" she cried, to whom or what she had no idea. But to her surprise, something answered her.

Her chest burned, and a strange glow emanated from her palms. Her eyes brightened with their own light. At first, she did not believe it. It was, after all, impossible. But she was alive, and that was impossible, too. Bewildered but too grateful to question this blessing, she lifted a hand. The glow illuminated the path in front of her for a dozen paces. It was not much, but it was good enough.

She crawled.

Time stretched beneath the earth, long and endless, fifteen minutes indistinguishable from fifteen hours. Once she hit a dead end, and terror clutched at her throat, but a hand against the blockage proved the wall to be soft, and she used the old water bowl as a shovel and dug it out enough to squeeze through.

Her knees were rubbed raw, her palms scraped and began to bleed. The food she had eaten had long ago passed through her body, and her belly was taut with hunger yet again. She was exhausted, and hopelessness threatened to bury her, as sure as the earth around her. But she kept going, warmed by the unnatural heat in her chest and hands. She would not die here and prove right that voice in her dream. She would not.

She wasn't sure how long she crawled through the darkness, holding back her fear, trying not to think of how stale the air felt or how far she might have to continue with only the thinnest filament of hope, when she heard it. Rushing water. The sound of a river through deep canyons. The Tovasheh.

A low, keening wail escaped her lips, a noise that she would not have recognized as her own voice had she not been the only living thing in this never-ending night. Relief threatened to break her open.

She had already determined that she must be deep in the Maw, in the catacombs that dotted the bottomless crevices far from the city proper. How she had gotten here, and why, was still a mystery, but it was enough now to know she could hear the river. All Maw children were taught that if they ever got lost, they were to listen for the river. She knew that if she followed the sound of the water, she would eventually find a way out. She was bleeding and filthy, and her bones begged for rest, but she forced herself on, toward the source of the water, and of life.

• • • • •

Another hour passed. Or a day, or a week. She could not tell in the darkness. All she knew was forward, toward the river.

Finally, she turned a corner, and fresh air greeted her, the rush of water thundering in her ears. And in her eyes, light. She scrambled forward. The opening fell off into space, so she dropped flat on her belly and nudged closer to look. She found herself peering out of a cave situated in the middle of a sheer cliffside. The drop was straight down but not impossibly high. Perhaps the length of half a dozen men. But the waters were swift, and she couldn't tell if they were deep enough to cushion her or hid rocks that might shatter her skull. Of course, such concerns hadn't stopped her from leaping into the Tovasheh before, but now she was not sure she would survive the fall, let alone be able to swim the currents of frigid waters below.

She laid her head down on crossed forearms and fought off despair. What choice did she have but to fling herself into the unknown and hope fate took pity on her, again? She laughed silently, her shoulders shaking. Skies, was this pity? If waking up in one's tomb was fate's mercy, she would hate to know its savagery.

No. This wasn't fate. Fate hadn't left her in that grave-in-waiting to see if she'd wake up or not. Zataya had. Or Denaochi himself. She supposed she should be grateful, but she was not. Rage boiled low in her gut. Rage at that witch, and at her brother for listening to her, and at herself for believing in either of them.

She rolled onto her back, the top of her head dangerously close to the cliff, and stared up at the sheer wall stretching above her . . . and smiled.

A knotted climbing rope, the end only an arm's length away, hung down the side of the cliff.

"Fuck you, Ochi," she whispered. Because she was right. It was not fate that did this but her brother, and he was a man of games and tests, and Naranpa understood now that this had been a test. This test was cruel and unnecessary, and she hated him for it, but at least she knew she could pass it.

She allowed herself a few moments' rest before scooting her body over the edge, shoulders dangling over the canyon drop, to reach the rope. She hauled herself up, span by span, out of the hole. Once she was free of the tunnel and hanging parallel to the cliffside, her old climbing senses came to her, and hand- and footholes revealed themselves in what had looked sheer and unclimbable before. Using toes wedged in rock and knees for balance, she looped the knotted rope around her waist and began to climb. She was weak, and her progress was frustratingly slow, but she was rising.

The sound of the river began to fade, and the light, albeit only the thick gloom of twilight, grew brighter as she ascended out of the deepest parts of the Maw. At last, she reached a ledge, and she hauled herself up on trembling arms to find that she was in the back room of a building. Wooden boxes and tall clay containers lined the walls and crowded the floor, leaving a narrow path to follow. It led to another room similarly crowded with goods and, finally, a front room separated from the others by a blanket hung in the doorway. There were no containers here. Instead, empty stools huddled against round tables, and on the shelves were jars of tea leaves and dried fruits and flowers. She was in a tearoom with a secret exit that led to the catacombs. If she had needed any more confirmation that Ochi was the architect of her situation, this was enough.

She found herself at the nearest shelf, her hand reaching for a clay jar marked with a drawing of a yellow blossom, each floret a profusion of lacy delicate blooms. She could almost taste the pleasingly astringent tea they made, feel the warmth of the steep clouding her face. It had been a favorite of hers in the tower.

The tower. To hell with the tower. That life was no longer hers.

She let the jar fall from her hands and shatter. She crushed the tea underfoot as she pulled another clay jar from the shelf, this one marked with a leaf she knew to be a stimulant. It would be better to brew it, but the thought of finding water and heating it and waiting for the tea to steep was too much. She pulled a pinch from the jar and chewed the leaves well before swallowing, hoping their properties would hold back her exhaustion long enough to see this night through.

Winter winds cut at her bare legs and face as she stepped onto the street, the blanket dress not enough to keep her warm. The strange twilight that hung over the Maw suggested evening, but the streets were empty. Even in winter, Maw streets were rarely empty. An uneasiness pressed down on her. Something was wrong. She laughed, silent and mocking. *What isn't wrong, Nara?*

She walked past abandoned storefronts and shuttered homes. Still no people in the streets, but she caught a little boy watching her from a doorway. His mother came and swept him away, her hand slapping a drawing on the outside wall and fingers throwing the sign against evil. Naranpa studied the drawing. It took her a moment to place it, it was so unexpected. But once she realized what it was, she saw it on another doorway farther down, and there, on a wall beside a shuttered food stand. It was crowsign, the skull that marked the homes of Carrion Crow in Odo. What was it doing here? And why show her? What had happened to make them all fear?

• • • • •

Naranpa saw no one else, not even a curious child, until she reached the Lupine. Denaochi's gambling den was as she remembered it—a windowless round building built into a cliff wall, only the front half of the circle exposed. Its whitewashed walls glowed in the ever-present twilight, a twilight that had not deepened to night but stayed steadily in shadow. It was strange, unsettling, but she had other things on her mind. The most important being her brother and his witch.

She climbed the ladder to the entrance, a trapdoor in the roof. Last time she had been here, a giant with a cudgel had awaited her, and she had been dressed as a man and carried a purse bursting with cacao. Now she came only as herself, a blanket across her body and dried blood and dirt flaking from her skin. She had no idea what kind of welcome she would receive, or whether her brother had hoped she would survive her tomb and his tests, or whether he had hoped the opposite. She wasn't even sure what she would say to him. Was she grateful for his help or resentful of the way he chose to dole it out? All she knew was that her need to prove she was not the spoiled, useless elite he thought her to be was enough to drive her this far, and her own will to be something more, someone worthy, would carry her through the next.

She eased open the door and descended into the hushed space. The gambling tables below were empty, but the square firepits still smoldered, enough to warm the large room. The rich scent of tobacco lingered, too, sweetening the air. She felt a flutter of despair. What if Denaochi wasn't here? What if she had been wrong?

She found him on the interior balcony. He was sitting on a bench, his back against the wall, hands gripping a long-handled club that lay across his lap. He looked as he had before: thin, to the point of gaunt, black hair razored to skin above his ears and greased back above the temples. An old knife scar ran from ear to nose across one cheek, and thick chunks of jade pierced his ears and below his bottom lip. Bands of coral and turquoise encircled his neck, and his porcupine mantle was slung across the bench beside him. Dark eyes stared at her, and she hesitated.

But she had come so far, and he had put her through so much. She did not hesitate for long.

"I passed your test, you damned monster," she growled.

His eyes focused, and she realized he had been asleep. Asleep with his eyes open. He yawned, and then his mouth tipped in a genuine grin.

"Nara," he said, his voice rough. "I never doubted."

She did not strike him as she wanted to, but when she spoke, her voice shook with rage. "You left me there for dead, and then you made me crawl through all seven hells to reach you."

He gestured dismissively. "I needed to make sure you wanted it."

"Wanted *what*?"

Now she moved toward him, hand balled into a fist. She swung. He caught her intended blow before she could connect.

His voice was a resentful hiss. "Life! If I did it, I knew you could, too."

It took her a moment to understand what he meant, and when she did, it stopped her anger cold. "Why? Who?"

"It doesn't matter now. It was long ago." His laugh was low and haunted. "You made the crawl in half the time it took me. You have always been ambitious."

The way he said it did not sound like a compliment, and she let it sit between them.

He dragged himself to standing and limped over to a nearby table. He seemed tired, the energy that had animated him on her previous visit reduced to dregs. He poured water from a clay vessel and proffered a cup. She drained the mug. He poured her another, keen eyes watching, but this one she sipped, feeling greedy under his judgmental gaze.

"Where is Zataya?" She looked down at her arm. Zataya's blood still clung to her skin in flaking patches. "You would think she would be here to celebrate how well her witchcraft fared."

"Not witchcraft," he corrected. "Blood magic, she told me. Southern sorcery."

Revulsion slithered up her spine, and for a moment she heard that voice again, the one that belonged to the man in the jaguar skin who had interrogated her in her dreams. Not a dream but a spell. Magic. Naranpa was so stunned at the insight that she could only gape.

"Your eyes. They've changed."

"What?" She instinctively held a hand to her face, as if she could somehow feel what he meant.

"The brown is flecked with yellow. They weren't like that before."

"A trick of the light." She sounded glib, but the place in her chest burned, and fear clawed at her belly. Was it magic that caused the burning feeling beneath her heart? Magic that made her palms glow and her eyes shine in the dark?

"Perhaps a trick of the light . . . or perhaps the aftereffects of the sorcery."

She grimaced at how casually he articulated her fears.

"Tell me what's happened in the world while I was buried in that tomb," she said, desperate to talk about anything else. She did not want to consider the possibility that magic had transformed her. It scared her in a way she could not quite vocalize. "Was Eche invested as Sun Priest? Does Golden Eagle outright rule the celestial tower now? What of the other Sky Made? Have any asked about my absence?"

He looked at her a long moment, black eyes unreadable. "The Watchers are dead, Naranpa. The pretender and his allies were all slaughtered by an agent of Carrion Crow. Their betrayal of you is the only thing that kept you from the same fate. Your precious tower is no more."

She stared, uncomprehending. She set her cup down, as if it were to blame for the miscommunication.

"Dead, Nara," he repeated. "Your whole damn priesthood is dead."

She swayed on her feet. "Impossible . . ."

"Not impossible if someone did it."

"You misunderstand, Brother. How dead if I planned to kill them myself?" She meant it as a joke, but it was bitter and dark in her mouth, a poor substitute for the irrational grief that was building like a tidal wave inside her. The exhaustion that the stimulant had been holding back flooded over her all at once, and she hunched over, head in hands.

"Who?" she asked.

"It wasn't the Odohaa. Oh, the other clans say it was. They blame the cultists, and the matron for not controlling them.

They even blame the Shield captain, her brother. But there were witnesses who saw what happened on Sun Rock."

"Who?" she asked again, more urgent.

He shrugged, a sharp jerk of one shoulder, and Naranpa realized he was scared. Here was the reason he slept with a club in his hands and his eyes open.

"They say it was a single man, but the details differ, as such stories always do. They say he was twice as tall as a normal man, and great black wings rose from his back. That he bore the haahan, and they crawled with shadow. Shadow that he commanded like you or I might command a pet or a child. That he wept blood and darkness, and he killed many with only a word."

"Shadow magic?"

"Some flavor of magic. They say god magic."

"I always thought of magic as a form of trickery," she admitted. "An herb that paralyzes or confuses, some sleight of hand done with lights and mirrors. Oh, I know the theories well enough. Magic comes from the remnants of the gods left behind. It emanates from their very bones and fossilized flesh. But this? A living, breathing god, not the remains of ones gone a thousand years. Do you believe it?"

He nodded, his face grim.

"It sounds like a fool's tale."

Some emotion passed over his face that she couldn't read. "Then call me a fool, Sister, for I believe the crow god has been reborn."

Things were moving very quickly. She wasn't sure how long she had been in that tomb, or how many hours it had taken to crawl her way out, but she knew she had been rebirthed into a world very different from the one she had left. She still had not quite processed Denaochi's ill tidings, but she understood enough to realize the Tova she knew was no more. And she did not know what to make of the Crow God Reborn, if that truly was what he was. If he lingered in the city, was he still a threat? Would he come for her, too? And if he did, what defenses did she have? She needed allies. It would not do to alienate her only one, no matter how she felt about him at the moment. And yet . . .

Her voice held all the weariness and grief that weighed upon her. "I am not so sure, Ochi. Perhaps I am not ready to be called a fool."

His eyes widened, and she knew exactly what he was thinking. He already considered her foolish. She could not stop the laugh that escaped her lips, sharp and slightly hysterical, because he was right. She was a fool. An exasperatingly naive, overly trusting, and entirely lucky fool. The memory of her naivete in believing she could convince the other priests to do better, to *be* better by virtue alone, was almost comical now but no worse than what had truly happened. She would never have characterized her betrayal as luck, but what else could it be? She had survived, and they had not. A fool's blessing disguised as a curse.

Denaochi was staring at her as if she were mad.

Very possibly, Brother. Very possibly.

He shrugged. "Time will tell which of us is right. In the meanwhile, there are beds here, and water to wash yourself. Why don't you rest? Afterward, I'll take you to Zataya. We will devise a way to survive the storm. We have already beaten the odds."

She did not argue. All she wanted was to clean the grave dirt and witch's blood from her body and sleep. She rubbed at the warm place over her chest. She wanted an answer to that, too.

He stood and held out his hand, the one missing three fingers. She took it and held on tight. No longer angry, only grateful she was not alone.

CHAPTER 5

City of Tova (District of Titidi)
Year 1 of the Crow

There are no tides more treacherous than those of the heart.

—Teek saying

"Xiala, come back to bed," Aishe said, her voice still thick with sleep. "There's nothing to see out there."

"A moment," Xiala said from her perch at the window.

It was a pleasant view across the canyons of Tova at sunrise, or so Aishe had informed her. In the time she had stayed in this room with the Water Strider girl, the sun had not risen, so Xiala could not confirm it for herself. Instead, the sun had hovered on the horizon like a bloated mango, casting only enough light to shadow the city in an eerie perpetual twilight. She knew who was responsible for this impossible sun, if not how he had done it, and despite the fear the unnatural sky roused in her, all she could think about was seeing him again.

"You're not going to find him staring out the window," Aishe said, her voice soft with sympathy.

"I know." And yet she could not stop her eyes from searching the streets below her.

People scuttled quickly between buildings, huddled against

the winter and the darkness. The bridge that led to Sun Rock stood empty, swaying in the violent winds that had rocked the city since solstice. And there was Sun Rock itself, visible in the far distance, the last place she knew with a certainty he had been.

Aishe came to her, wearing only a long sleeping shirt. She wrapped her arms around Xiala and kissed the place behind her ear that she knew Xiala liked. Xiala smiled half-heartedly as the woman continued to lay a track of kisses down her neck. One arm held her close as if she were a rabbit who might bolt, while her free hand wandered. She traced fingernails down Xiala's upper arm, before cupping her breast and running a thumb across her nipple. It was a question, and Xiala tried her best to answer. She closed her eyes and forced herself to relax into Aishe's embrace, but it was useless. Her gaze was drawn back outside to the perpetual twilight and to Sun Rock, seeking the impossible.

Aishe halted her seduction with a resigned sigh, defeated. Xiala hadn't always been so apathetic to Aishe's touch. In the hours after the solstice Convergence, they had found each other on the streets of Titidi. Desperate to put Serapio's death behind her, Xiala had fucked the girl against an alley wall as the world fell to chaos around them. They had done it again in Aishe's rooms in the early hours before dawn, with an urgency that Xiala had to admit was driven more by desperation than by lust. And when the sun had failed to rise, they found themselves entwined again, this time more in fear than anything else.

By afternoon, the clamor that had filled the streets the night before had fallen into stunned silence, as if the whole city held its breath and waited for the end of the world. But the world did not end, and they eventually roused themselves to find food. Aishe had taken her to the house terrace, where they

41

found Tyode and Zash. The brothers told them the accounts of what had happened on Sun Rock under the shadowed sun.

"More than two-thirds of the priesthood dead," Zash whispered, as the four of them huddled over bowls of cold beans. "Every Society head dead. Oracle, Healing, Historical, even Knives. Laid out in a row like some sort of sacrifice."

"It had to be him." Tyode's voice was filled with an awe that bordered on admiration. "Who else could do it? Defeat the Knives and half a dozen Golden Eagle Shields before the clans scattered."

"Don't sound so happy about it," Aishe hissed at her brother. "We brought him here, didn't we? Eyes will turn back to us when people find out." She shuddered and made a sign to ward off evil.

"They won't find out," Tyode protested, but his tone was subdued. "And if they did, we're innocent. We didn't know what he had planned."

Xiala had known, but she had kept her mouth shut, and she kept her mouth shut now again.

"Do you really think they'll care about the details?" Zash's gaze cut to Xiala and then away, as if embarrassed. "We knew he was an Odohaa assassin. He practically told us he was going to kill the priests."

"Maybe he told you." Tyode sounded defensive now. "But I figured he was just a braggart."

None of them bothered to respond, the revision such an obvious lie. Maybe Xiala was the only one who had known for a fact, but the siblings had certainly suspected.

"It just didn't seem possible," Tyode finally said. "No matter what Uncle claimed he was."

Xiala did not argue with the Water Strider siblings. They were good people and had taken her in. They had only known

Serapio for a few days, only seen him on the barge as a novelty. But she had seen him in his power, had been there when he had slaughtered her crew, and she had said nothing, warned no one what he was capable of. Perhaps she couldn't quite believe it, either. It was hard to reconcile the killer with the gentle, solicitous man she knew. The one who had saved her life, the one who had not judged her but cared for her. Who whispered sweet nothings to crows as he stroked their feathers. The one she had grown to love.

"What will he do now?" Tyode asked. "Do you think he will come for us?"

They had all turned to Xiala. At that time, she had thought him dead and said so. Only later would the rumors come to their ears of the great crow that had left the Rock with two figures on its back, and that he had survived, and that Carrion Crow sheltered him even now, had been in on it all along. She knew better, knew Serapio had not known anyone in the clan and certainly hadn't conspired with them. But again, she said nothing. What was there to say? To her new friends, or to anyone?

The four of them had sworn not to speak of it again, and they had held to that promise, as far as Xiala knew. But her instincts told her it was only a matter of time. Four was too many to keep a secret, and eventually one of the brothers, or even Aishe herself, would let slip that they had brought the Odo Sedoh to Tova.

Probably Zash, she thought. She could feel it, in the way he watched her at mealtime but turned away when she tried to meet his gaze. He had never asked about her unusual eyes, never inquired about where she was from, but it would come eventually. And as his suspicions grew and fear gave way to anger, he would be the first to accuse her. It was only a feeling, but it was one she knew well. Soon people like Zash would be looking to blame someone for what had befallen Tova, and experience told her she made an excellent target. She wondered what they did to Teek here. Did they collect their fingers and throat bones? Wear their eyes on rings, as she had once been told? Or would the mob just rip her apart, no time for a delicate filleting when their priests were dead and the sun had somehow ceased to rise and set.

"You can't stay, you know."

Aishe's voice broke her from her reverie, bringing her back to the seat in the window and the hole in her heart. Aishe rested her chin on Xiala's shoulder, and for a moment, Xiala thought the girl had read her mind. But one glance at Aishe's morose expression told her the reason she was kicking her out was more mundane than blaming her for the darkness that had enveloped the city.

"I know I said you could, but . . ."

"You don't need to explain." Xiala understood. They had crossed the line from friends to lovers, but Xiala's heart belonged to someone else, and Aishe was sensible enough to end things before either of them became too entangled to get hurt. In Xiala's defense, when they did what they did, she had thought Serapio was dead.

"I'll be out by—" Xiala was going to say nightfall, but there was no day and night in Tova, just this terrifying in between.

"There's no rush," Aishe assured her, but Xiala could hear the lie in it. "I know you don't have anywhere to go, and things are complicated."

Xiala barked a laugh at that. "Complicated is one way to put it."

"Look, I want to help you. We're friends, right? Even if this"— she gestured toward the bed— "didn't work out."

"And I appreciate it."

"Why don't you go look for him? He's probably at the Great House in Odo with the rest of his clan."

"I've thought of that." Since she had heard rumors that Serapio was seen alive, it had been all she could think about. Her brain had turned the impossibility over and over again, looking for the fault in it. She had not dared to hope, but if anyone could survive, she believed it was him. Not because he wanted to; he had seemed at peace with his mission. But because *she* wanted him to. She had to believe.

She said, "Tyode said Odo's closed its borders. Shields and armed guards everywhere. Bridges closed, and the only way in is through Kun. And that clan . . ."

"Winged Serpent."

"Yes, Winged Serpent. They won't let anyone through unless they're Carrion Crow. It's impossible."

"Couldn't you . . . ?" Aishe touched fingers to her throat and opened her mouth to mime singing.

Xiala shuddered. "No."

Serapio was not the only one with blood on his hands. Xiala had killed innocents, too. *Not deliberately*, she told herself, *but you never do anything deliberately, do you, Xiala? And good intentions make no difference to the dead.*

She caught her breath at that, turning away from Aishe so the girl could not see the hot tears of shame that gathered in her eyes.

Images from the Convergence flashed through her memory— a woman in blue silently tumbling from the bridge, lost to the river below. A green-eyed man in new year finery trampled by the crowd, gentled to inaction like an animal led to the slaughter. Gentled by her Song. If she had not used her magic, that man would still be alive. Of that she had no doubt. And he was not the only one. How many people had she robbed of their lives that night because she used her power so recklessly?

Everything you do is reckless. The trip to Tova that ended in the deaths of your crew, giving your heart to a man intent on his own demise, and look where you are now, in the bed of a woman who no longer wants you. Is it really a surprise that you used your Song to kill again? Wasn't it only a matter of time?

"Xiala?"

"I'm fine." She swiped a hand across her eyes.

Aishe would not understand, thinking she mourned for Serapio. But the truth was that she wept for herself, or, more specifically, for the charade of a life she'd chosen to live, refusing to face the things that had driven her from Teek long ago. The Convergence was proof that she could not outrun her past. So what would she do about it?

"I don't suppose you have anything to drink?"

Aishe hesitated. "We can find some balché, if you like. I'm sure Zash has something." She did not quite sound judgmental, but she did sound disappointed.

"No." Xiala dug a fingernail into her palm and let the pain steady her voice. "Forget I asked."

"Perhaps Uncle Kuy could help you get to Odo," Aishe said softly. "He's Carrion Crow and allowed free pass into the district—at least, he was before they closed their doors. It can't hurt to ask, and if he says yes, then maybe you can go find some answers. Find Serapio . . . if you think he's safe."

"He won't hurt me." Xiala said it with conviction. "No matter who you think he is or what he did or didn't do, he wouldn't hurt me."

"I know you believe that, Xiala, but if he is a god like they say, who knows what he is capable of? And if he's just a man, then he's a man wading in holy blood up to his hips."

Then perhaps we belong together, she thought. But she only said, "I know."

She extricated herself from Aishe's embrace and paced across the room, putting space between them. Aishe folded her arms, her expression resigned.

"I think I know where my uncle is. If all goes well, maybe you can be in Odo before the end of the day."

And then I'll no longer be your problem, Xiala thought, *and you can be done with me. If only it were so easy for me to be done with myself.*

But she didn't speak any of those thoughts aloud, only nodded her agreement and reached for borrowed clothes.

• • • • •

The two women made their way through the streets of Titidi. The cold was biting, something Xiala was unused to, and it chilled her so deeply she thought her flesh might freeze. She huddled in the thick cloak she had procured in the port city of Tovasheh, but anywhere the cloak gaped—at her neck, around her wrists—it felt like her skin would surely crack and bleed frost.

They went to the barge first, down the long, winding path that led to the docks. The boat was much as Xiala remembered it, but it felt like years since she had arrived in the city instead of only a handful of days.

"Wait here." Aishe hopped across the narrow space between land and barge. "Uncle?" she called as she walked the deck. Xiala watched her open the door to the room where she had once shared a narrow bed with Serapio, where she had sat as he confessed that his mission was one meant to end in his death. Xiala looked away, blinking back useless tears.

Aishe closed the door and moved on. After a few moments, she came back, empty-handed. "No one here, and it looks like he's put in for the winter. Cupboards bare, beds stripped."

Xiala's heart sank.

"But there's one other place he could be. He sometimes keeps a room in a house not far from here. One he shares with a lady friend, Omataya."

Xiala looked up at the sun. A habit, to check the time of day, but there was only the eclipse. "Should we pay her a visit?"

"I don't see we have much choice."

They climbed back up the stairs. By the time they reached the top, Xiala's legs were warm and aching. She had been freezing before, so she tried to see the bright side of climbing hundreds of steps but had a hard time convincing herself. Aishe noticed her distress and gave her a wan smile.

"Not much farther."

"I'm meant for the sea," Xiala confessed. "I don't think Teek has a single staircase."

They took a path off the main road that led them deeper into the district. The area around the docks was marked by wide avenues and expansive squares, but here the streets grew narrower, and the houses looked old, mud brick stacked close and high. They finally reached a D-shaped building and entered the courtyard through an unlocked gate. The interior garden was surprisingly pleasant. There was packed dirt underfoot, and vegetable rows lay fallow behind a short wooden fence. In the middle of the courtyard was a bubbling spring, steam rising in the winter air.

"Are there spring waters here?" Xiala asked, surprised.

"There are hot springs all through the district. It heats the ground, keeps the roads from icing. Didn't you see the gutters?"

She had. Narrow gutters running the length of the main roads and even down into these smaller neighborhoods. "I assumed those were for rainwater or waste."

"They do run off the rainwater, but the district architects can redirect the springs for thawing or for irrigation. You should really see Titidi in the spring and summer. It's a living garden."

"I'd like that," Xiala lied. She knew that once she left Tova, she never wanted to come back.

They came to a door marked with a hastily scrawled crowsign over the lintel. Aishe frowned. "What's this doing here?" She reached out a hand and scratched a nail over the red paint. It flaked off under her touch.

The door opened suddenly, leaving Aishe's hand outstretched. A man stood framed in the space before them. Uncle Kuy.

"Niece," he greeted Aishe stiffly. His eyes took Xiala in, but he didn't acknowledge her. "What brings you to my door?"

"What's this, Uncle?" Aishe gestured at the crowsign. "Did you draw this?"

"Leave it. Better safe than sorry." He turned abruptly and disappeared back inside. It was clear the man didn't want to talk to them, but what choice did they have? Aishe wanted to be rid of Xiala, and Xiala wanted to be gone. They exchanged a look that acknowledged the truth between them, and then Aishe stepped across the threshold, Xiala following.

The room was indeed only a room, perhaps fifteen paces long and another fifteen across. She saw a bed, two clothes trunks, shelves holding cups and plates, but no kitchen and no privy. Both were likely communal and somewhere else in the complex, which meant rooms were only for sleeping and personal time. Xiala noticed that a traveling pack sat by the door, but she wasn't sure if someone was coming or going.

A loom took pride of place in the room, and skeins of dyed cotton yarn were piled in baskets around a sitting cushion. And on the sitting cushion, hands busy on batten and shuttle, was the woman Xiala guessed to be Omataya.

"Auntie." Aishe greeted the woman politely, but the woman only grunted, hands still busy. The sharp knock of the batten made them both jump, and Uncle Kuy sighed loudly.

"Talk sense to your uncle, Aishe," Omataya snapped, her command as sharp as the tips of the bone comb she ran across her weaving.

"About what?" Aishe asked carefully.

Uncle Kuy planted his feet and crossed his arms as if he sailed choppy waters. "I'm going to join the Odohaa, and my mind is settled. I won't hear otherwise."

Omataya clicked her teeth, her disapproval thick and un-spoken.

"It's interesting you should bring that up, Uncle . . ." Aishe started.

Xiala stepped forward. "I'm coming with you."

They all turned.

"Who's this?" Omataya asked.

"It's why we came," Aishe explained. "Rumor says borders are closed and they're not letting anyone but Carrion Crow in. Xiala wants—"

"You know something." Xiala had been watching Uncle Kuy, and she had seen his eyes light up when she spoke, a flash of something that reminded her of his demeanor upon learning Serapio was the Odo Sedoh. "That's why you're going now."

Kuy's head bobbed once. "I saw the great crows return, and the young warrior on his back."

"You saw Serapio?"

Omataya scoffed. "Serapio? What kind of name is that?"

The way she said it sounded like an argument previously voiced to Uncle Kuy, most likely, but Xiala hadn't heard it and now wanted to.

"What do you mean?" she asked.

"A foreign name." The woman wagged a finger at Kuy. "A false god who has weak men addled, that's all he is."

"His mother was Carrion Crow," Uncle Kuy supplied quickly, eyes darting to Xiala as if to warn her away from the debate, "and he bore the haahan and the blood teeth. He is Carrion Crow."

Omataya huffed, unimpressed. "What does he know of Carrion Crow?"

The muscle in Xiala's jaw tightened, anger at this woman, at all these people, crashing over her like a wave. "He killed your enemies for you."

"A killer, then! You say so yourself. They say he did it for the Crows, but who knows his motives? And yet this one"— she gestured to Kuy—"is willing to follow him like a once-fed dog."

"Do you know what he suffered for you?" Xiala asked, incredulous. The small room felt hot and stifling despite the winter that reigned outside. "He sacrificed everything to help you, but where were you when he needed you? When he was a boy alone in Obregi? When his mother *blinded* him? And now you wish to judge him because his blood is not pure enough and he bears a foreign name?"

Aishe's hand was on her arm. "Steady, Xiala. No one's saying that."

"You have a responsibility to him," she said, "not the other way around." Her voice trembled with anger, and for a moment, Xiala wasn't sure if she was talking about Serapio or herself.

Omataya picked a nut from a bowl at her elbow and

dropped it into her mouth. She chewed silently, her only answer to Xiala's outburst.

Uncle Kuy turned tired eyes to Xiala. "You wish to go to Odo?"

"Yes."

"I go by way of the bridge across Sun Rock. We'll have to pass Sky Made guards who hold vigil there. They may ask questions, be suspicious. There are stories of a foreign woman with plum-colored hair seen with the Odo Sedoh on the day before the solstice. It is not without danger for you."

So there was already gossip about her. Yes, she did not doubt that soon enough they would come for her, more reason to leave this thrice-damned city.

Xiala straightened. "I'm not afraid."

"But maybe you should be." He hefted a bag and slung it over his shoulder. "Come now, or don't come at all." And then he was leaving.

A burst of icy wind breached the open door as he departed. Xiala shivered, at the sudden cold or at Uncle Kuy's warning words, she wasn't sure which. But she was chilled all the same.

"Old fool," Omataya muttered, but Xiala heard the sadness in her voice. The older woman slammed the batten down. "And don't come back," she muttered.

Xiala shook her head. What was she doing arguing with this stranger? She had been too long already in Tova, she could feel it in her bones. The sea called to her, a yearning that did not quiet. She would find Serapio, and they would go. To where she didn't know. Just away from here.

She followed Uncle Kuy out the door. She was halfway across the courtyard when she heard, "Xiala! Wait!"

Aishe was there, hurrying to catch her.

"I'm sorry about that," Aishe said, her breath huffing white in the twilight. "Omataya was terrible."

"But was she wrong?" Xiala asked, sounding bitter. "You Tovans are obsessed with bloodlines."

"And the Teek aren't?"

"No. The Teek are all bastards. No fathers, shared mothers, every one of us half something else. Kinship is what matters, not . . ." She waved her hand to take in the whole of the city. "Not this blood nonsense."

"Now who's being cruel?" Aishe sounded hurt.

Xiala's sigh was heavy and heartfelt. "I'm sorry. I don't mean to insult you. It's just . . ." She shuddered as a gust wormed through the edges of her cowl.

"Are you coming?" Uncle Kuy's voice carried on the wind. He'd stopped to wait by the gate, but Xiala thought he wouldn't wait long.

"One thing," Aishe said hurriedly. "Here." She dragged her blue fur-lined cloak from her shoulders. "Trade with me. A foreigner may draw eyes, and Uncle could be right that people have heard of you. Wear this, and keep the hood raised and your hair hidden."

Xiala dropped her bag, removed her own cloak, the one she's traded for in Tovasheh, and replaced it with Aishe's deep blue. She ran a hand over the rich fabric, felt the luxurious touch of fur against her neck. "This is expensive."

"It can be replaced."

"Thank you," she said, and meant it. "Not just for the cloak but for everything. I'm sorry I brought my troubles to your door . . . and your bed. I should have never—"

"We."

"What?"

"It wasn't just you. It was we. I'm a grown woman, and if you recall, I seduced you." Her smile was small and knowing. "You think I don't see you, but I see you better than you see

53

yourself. One day, you'll stop trying to drown who you are—and whoever's there to catch you? Well, they'll be lucky to have you. But it won't be me."

"Am I that bad?"

Aishe's smile stretched into a grin. "Like a tidal wave."

Xiala laughed. She wasn't sure if her words were meant as compliment or complaint, but either way, they felt like a truth. And despite her moment of self-pity before, she'd never been shy about laughing at herself. It was not the first time she had been called a disaster.

Aishe shivered, hands rubbing against her arms. "It feels bad here, doesn't it, Xiala?" She was serious now, her face clouded with concern. "I mean, the sun, yes. But the people, too. I'm frightened."

It was the same feeling Xiala had had earlier. The city was holding its breath, waiting for the next terrible thing to happen. Perhaps the sun would plummet from the sky, or the sky itself would crack and shatter. Perhaps a million crows would descend on them and pluck their eyes and tongues out as they had done to her crew. She didn't know. All she did know was that something would break, and when it did, it was going to be bloody.

She grasped Aishe's upper arm. "Stay safe."

Aishe reached out to pull the hood up over Xiala's head. Once it was in place, she straightened the edges. A moment's hesitation, and then she leaned in and kissed Xiala on the mouth. Before Xiala could protest, she pulled away. She pressed a finger to Xiala's lips.

"Go," she said. "Go find him. Just be careful. They say the storm has come, but to me, it feels like it's only beginning."

CHAPTER 6

> Understand your enemy not by the face that they show you
> but by the face they do not.
>
> —*On the Philosophy of War,*
> taught at the Hokaia War College

Okoa had planned to delay their homecoming until the Odo Sedoh's wound was stabilized, but it had been another full day, and the wound was not getting any better. It continued to seep a watery reddish-gold ichor, and although the man hid it well, Okoa could tell he was in pain. It was clear that the sooner they returned, the better.

They had debated how to return. Okoa had favored stealth, but the Odo Sedoh made a convincing argument for spectacle, reiterating his earlier advice that they utilize fear to their advantage. Okoa did not love the idea, but his masters at the war college had often spoken of the importance of theatrics and the benefits of an overwhelming display of power in the face of conflict. He could not deny the Odo Sedoh's reasoning, so in the end, Okoa agreed. They would not hide their return but announce it.

Then came the problem of how they would ride. They had arrived together on Benundah's back, but now that many of the great corvids had joined them, there was no reason to make Benundah carry them both.

"I can ride Kutssah," Okoa offered, as they stood outside the monastery facing the flock. Part of him still felt a childish desire not to share Benundah with anyone, even if it did make sense. "We will have to fashion you some kind of makeshift bridle, although I don't know . . . why do you laugh?"

"I have no need for reins, or a saddle, for that matter."

"How will you direct—?"

"I won't." The Odo Sedoh approached Benundah. The great corvid trilled a happy welcome. He ran his hands across her beak and leaned close to whisper in her ear. "Benundah will serve as my eyes. She has done so before and knows the way better than I."

"And your seat?"

"She will not let me fall." He touched his forehead to hers. "Will you?"

"It is not so easy to ride a giant crow. The scions train all their lives for the honor."

"Then it is good I am not a scion." As if he had done it a hundred times, the Odo Sedoh climbed astride Benundah. He moved confidently, easily. Not as Okoa expected a blind man to move. *Do not underestimate him with your prejudices*, he warned himself. *Remember Sun Rock.*

He had given the Odo Sedoh his feathered cloak, and he wore it still. It was the only protection the man had from the cold, and Okoa did not begrudge it. But the fact that it looked right on him, made him appear regal even in bloodstained and tattered pants, his hair unkempt and his eyes pools of shadow, that did bother him. For a reason he could not quite name—

envy, admiration, curiosity—he found himself staring, a knot in his stomach.

"Are you still worrying, Okoa?" His voice was light, teasing. They had formed a kind of wary friendship over the past day, and the jest was not unwelcome.

"No," he lied, matching his tone. "I trust Benundah to save your reckless hide should you fall."

That earned him a grin, and Okoa found himself pleased by their small moment of camaraderie.

Serapio cocked his head, as if listening. "Benundah said you are worse than a hen with a newly hatched chick. I won't break."

Okoa thought to remind him of the wound in his side and the fact that he seemed quite capable of breaking, particularly if he fell from the back of a crow in flight. "I would not be so sure."

Serapio twisted in his seat, as if trying to find something. "Where is the sun?" he asked. "I cannot feel it against my skin."

"It sits low on the horizon, still swallowed by shadow."

"Good."

There was something sinister in his tone that made Okoa shiver, the small warmth of a shared joke not enough to reassure. He wondered, again, if he were doing the right thing. He had meant the words he said earlier as they sat by the fire, about the Odo Sedoh having an obligation to help Carrion Crow, about how if he claimed to be their god, then he must not only be a warrior but a protector as well. But there was something untamed about the man, something unsettling that he could not quite trust, and now that the moment of return was upon them, Okoa worried about who, or what, he was bringing back to Tova.

The Odo Sedoh grasped the feathers at Benundah's neck, wrapping his hands deep in her ruff. "How long do you think the journey will take?"

The mountains around them were snowcapped, jutting pillars of dark stone with little foliage or growth. Their beauty was stark and deadly. It would be impossible for a person to climb to the rookery, but to fly back to Tova?

"Not long. A few hours."

Okoa threw a leg over Kutssah's back and climbed on, settling on the rug saddle and taking up the reins. Kutssah had arrived shortly after the Convergence, as if she had known the Odo Sedoh were here. It occurred to Okoa that the crows likely all knew. Skies, the Odo Sedoh probably spoke to them all. That thought made the knot in his stomach tighten. What he wouldn't give to speak to crows, even once. *But would you pay the price he has paid for it?* He flexed his fingers inside his gloves. *Would you want that blood on your hands?*

He pressed a hand to the nondescript sack he had attached to the saddle. It held the Sun Priest's mask. He had taken it from Sun Rock in secret, and kept it secret now. He had meant to throw it away, toss it off a high cliff to be forever lost in this empty place, but here he was, ready to return to Tova, and it was still in his possession. *I'll keep it just a little longer*, he told himself. *Once I know more. Once I understand.* And he almost believed it.

"Remember to fly as low as is safe," he said, last-minute instructions. "The air is thin and freezes skin too far up."

"The cold doesn't bother me."

"Must be your Obregi blood." The Obregi Mountains were known for the long winters and impassable peaks, and he had discerned that Obregi must be the other half of his heritage.

Serapio's expression darkened.

Okoa had only meant to tease, but he could tell it had landed poorly. He cleared his throat. "I would ask a favor, Odo Sedoh."

"Ask it," he said stiffly.

"Speak to the flock. Tell them to come back with us. All of them, or at least the great ones. I need us to make an impression."

He relaxed, whatever offense Okoa had committed seemingly forgiven. "So you decided to take my advice after all. Then let us make it a sight that Tova will not soon forget." He leaned in and whispered words to Benundah.

The great corvid cried out, and the mass of crows answered.

She launched herself upward. The entire flock rose behind them, Kutssah included. They left the rookery as one great body of beating black wings, ascending skyward.

• • • • •

Okoa's estimation proved correct, and they arrived in the air over Tova in a matter of hours. They flew in low, coming in from the northwest, crossing over Tsay. He scanned the sky for eagles, knowing that Golden Eagle could have put patrols out, but he saw no riders, only people below in the streets gaping up as the mass of crows passed overhead. He smiled grimly. Word would travel quickly to the Golden Eagle matron that they had returned.

He motioned for the Odo Sedoh to take the flock and continue across the canyon and to the aviary at Odo. He knew Benundah would deliver the Odo Sedoh there safely. He planned to follow but wanted to get a glimpse at Titidi and Kun before he landed.

He banked to his left, and to his satisfaction, Benundah did not follow. He straightened on Kutssah's back to watch them go. Once he was sure they were safely away, he turned his attention to the districts below him. Titidi was quiet, a handful of people on the streets, pointing up at him as he passed. *Another matron warned*, he thought, and then he was over the Maw, skimming the Eastern districts, and approaching Kun.

Keen eyes swept the air, looking for any sign of winged serpents, but the sky there was clear, too.

"Home, then, Kutssah." He patted the great crow on her neck.

Something streaked past him, rising from below. He caught a glimpse of jade and turquoise scales, undulating feathers. He cursed and pulled Kutssah up hard. She cried out as another serpent darted past them, this one so close the breeze from its passing rippling his hair. And then he was face to face with two Winged Serpent riders. They wore armor, thick sheets of green scales that covered chests and arms, and their matching helmets sported twin horns to match their beasts. One of the serpents flared a feathered mane of ruby and citrine and hissed, its forked tongue ululating in warning.

"Peace!" he cried, but he did not know if they could hear him. Of all the clans, Winged Serpent and Carrion Crow were closest. They shared a border, had traded freely with each other for generations, and Carrion Crow had been the first clan to answer Winged Serpent's plea for aid in the War of the Spear. Such bonds were not forgotten.

The riders did not attack, and Okoa's heart rate calmed. Kutssah squawked loudly. She was impatient, eager for battle. He held her steady, legs braced, body hunched low at her neck, ready to act. A minute passed. Two.

Okoa understood. They were only there to send a message. He nodded an acknowledgment of the warning and turned Kutssah away from Kun. They let him go and did not follow, and the tension drained from his limbs as the crow brought him home.

The Odo Sedoh was there in the aviary, waiting.

"The crows heard Kutssah's cries and were disturbed," he said by way of greeting.

"I ran into Winged Serpent." Okoa slid the saddle off Kutssah's back.

"What did they want?"

"To warn us to stay away from Kun." He glanced around the aviary. The flock was all here, making themselves at home. But he had expected stable hands to meet them, the troughs to be full. "Has anyone come? They had to have noted our arrival. And yet no one is here to greet us, to care for the crows."

"Perhaps we are not welcome."

"Or something is wrong."

"Would the crows not alert us? Are you not safe in your own house?"

It was a question that cut to the quick. All the distrust and uncertainty he had felt in the days after his mother's funeral came rushing back. The unexpected bubble of peace he had found at the monastery evaporated, and once again the Great House pulsed with foreboding. "You don't understand."

The Odo Sedoh tilted his head in that way he had, as if waiting for Okoa to explain. And he wanted to. Skies, he wanted to.

He fought the impulse to tell Serapio everything, to let out the secrets he'd been holding under his tongue, desperate for there to be someone with whom to share his burden of ruinous knowledge.

He had worried about bringing Serapio back, aware that he was dangerous, but now he felt a desire to warn him of what waited for him in Carrion Crow's halls. But how could he? His suspicions of murder would make no sense. The letter with the single broken glyph, Esa's lies about their mother's death. Lies upon lies that were allowed to fester. How could he trust anyone with this secret that he held like ruin in his heart? He

61

wanted to shout it from the rooftop of the Great House, muster every Shield to investigate and find his mother's killer, and bring them to justice. But the truth was he had only a cryptic letter penned twenty years ago to support his suspicions, and if he accused people now, it would only destabilize what was already a precarious situation. The Watchers were no more; he would not find justice there, and things had become too complicated to risk his reputation by accusing the Sky Made with baseless claims. He needed proof, and then he would not hesitate.

And there was the reality Okoa feared most, that he dared not whisper, even to the Odo Sedoh. Someone inside Carrion Crow had murdered his mother. And his worst fear of all was that his sister had a hand in it. And if that was true, then what? Accuse her outright with no evidence? Rip his family apart? Damn Carrion Crow to infighting over who would take the matron's throne if Esa was deposed? And if he failed in his accusation, he would no doubt be declared anathema and banished, and as much as he had stayed away from the politics of Tova and his family, this was his home, and he would not abandon it. Part of him wished he had never read that letter that Chaiya had brought him at the war college, and another part called himself a coward for his inaction. Again, it came back to proof. His sister deserved that much. He did, too.

Okoa sighed. "It is a story for another day. Today we need to focus on what lies ahead of us in the Great House, a fate we can delay no longer."

· · · · ·

He hurried them down the winding stairs and through the halls. Okoa saw nothing out of place. He heard no wailing, sensed nothing amiss. Perhaps he was jumping at shadows, seeing conspiracy where there was none. The house was usually quiet, but that could be attributed to the time of day. Still, the Great House was usually filled with servants, lesser families, visiting scions. Had they all fled the seat of Odo for their own homes, worried about what came after the slaughter? There was an eerie mood that gripped the city under the eclipsed sun; it could be the cause. Or it could be his imagination. He chided himself for his paranoia, but he was enough of a warrior to stay alert nonetheless.

They arrived at the entrance to the great room. Raised voices filtered out through closed wooden doors. Okoa raised his hand to push them open.

"Wait." The Odo Sedoh touched his arm.

"Why would I—"

"I heard your name. They speak of you inside. Aren't you curious to know what they are saying?"

Okoa snapped his mouth shut.

The Odo Sedoh rightly took that as an invitation to continue. "They know we have returned and urge each other to speak quickly. Someone insists that the clans must be appeased. That you, Okoa, are at fault, and so it should be you who bears the burden."

"At fault for what?"

"An older voice speaks now. He sounds worried. He says that the clans will not be content with cacao."

"That must be my cousin Chaiya, and the first speaker my sister. Surely Chaiya will speak sense to her."

"Your sister says Carrion Crow will give the Sky Made blood if that is what is required."

Okoa cursed. "Enough sneaking around like children. Let her speak these words to my face."

He threw the great doors open, the boom thundering through

the chamber. All eyes turned to him, the argument—because surely it was an argument—stopped mid-sentence as he strode into the room.

His quick eyes took in the six Shields stationed along the walls of the circular space and the four people standing at the center. Whereas the walls of the Great House had been left the natural ash-gray of the volcanic stone used in its building, this room at its heart was washed white. It made the place feel expansive, welcoming. Windows too narrow and high for even a child to pass through cast bands of light across ornately painted floors. A built-in bench curved around the entirety of the space, enough to fit most of his immediate family when they gathered here. Now the room was empty, except for the guards and the people clustered in the center.

Esa wore a long, fitted dress, the collar, hem, and wrists adorned with the sleek shimmer of corvid feathers. Her hair was pulled tightly back from her narrow face, emphasizing her large dark eyes. Chaiya stood beside her in the uniform of the Shield, his broad shoulders and muscular build a mirror of Okoa's own, aged a decade. Over his shoulders fell a thick blanket of grays and reds. It was held in place by an obsidian clasp, but, to Okoa's relief, he did not wear the single red feather that marked him as captain of the Shield. Okoa was only a handful of days gone, but he had half expected it.

Along with Esa and Chaiya were two of his aunts—women chosen as advisers because they were considered wise. Mataya was the one with the white beginning to thread her long hair, Juuna the one with the square jaw. All caught in acrimonious quarreling. About him.

Esa had frozen when he first entered, but she had already recovered her cool indifference by the time he stormed his way across the hall.

Two Shields detached from the wall to meet him. They locked spears and stood between brother and sister.

Okoa's jaw clenched. "Move!"

"They will not move," Esa said, annoyingly haughty, "until you calm your temper."

"I am your captain," he spat at the two men, "and you will stand down, or you will see the blade of my knife."

"They're only doing what I told them to do. Don't threaten them with violence." She turned to their aunt Juuna, voice mild. "Perhaps he has become a beast, as you said."

"Esa," his other aunt, Mataya, chided. "It is our Okoa. We do not malign family." She pushed her way around the guards to hug her nephew.

Esa gave her a withering look and waved at the guards to stand down.

"How are you, Nephew?" Mataya asked. "We have been so worried. When you disappeared, we feared the worst."

"I am good, Auntie." He gently broke from her embrace. "But it seems I returned just before my sister bargained Carrion Crow blood for Watcher blood."

"Your timing is remarkable, Brother." She proffered a paper to him. "We were just discussing the Sky Made clans' demands."

He closed the distance between them and took the letter from her hand. He skimmed the handful of glyphs. A demand for explanation and restitution for the lives lost. A reminder of the old ways, which meant blood. Signed by all three of the other Sky Made clans. It all confirmed what the Odo Sedoh had overheard.

"And your plan was to turn me over to the other clans as answer? Sacrifice your own flesh and blood to placate our enemies?"

"I would have never allowed it," Mataya protested.

"Respectfully, Auntie." Esa's voice was tight with exasperation. "You are here because I asked for your advice. It is my decision as matron, and mine alone, in the end."

"You are not a queen unchecked, Esa." Mataya's words were bold, but she took a step back from Okoa, a clear acknowledgment of Esa's authority.

Esa did not respond, only lifted her head a bit higher. "As I was saying, the Sky Made clans are not our enemies. Or at least, they weren't until you slaughtered the priesthood."

"I . . . ?" Okoa gaped, the anger draining from him like someone had opened a sieve. Only then did he register what Esa had said to his aunt Juuna, about him being a beast. "You think I'm responsible for Sun Rock?"

"You fled after the Convergence. What else were we to think?"

"Not that I am capable of slaughter!"

"You've been in Hokaia for years at the war college. Who really knows you anymore, or what they taught you there?"

"All Shield captains attend the war college." He gestured to his cousin. "Chaiya attended the war college."

"What we do know," Esa continued, ignoring his logic in favor of her escalation, "is that you met with the Odohaa after Mother's funeral, and we know they attacked the tower the morning of the Convergence—"

"What?" This was news.

"A failed few," Chaiya explained. "They didn't even make it across the bridge into Otsa. A handful of the younger members had gathered at dawn with plans to attack the celestial tower. But there were Watchers on the bridge, and they retreated as soon as they were spotted. No one was harmed, and their own leader confessed it the next day, afraid they would be blamed for Sun Rock. But we know they didn't kill the priests."

"Which leaves you, Okoa," Esa accused. "The only one seen arriving, and leaving, on—"

"I killed the Watchers." The Odo Sedoh's voice came from behind him. "I am responsible for their slaughter."

Silence fell. The lanterns in the room flickered. The light from the windows, which had been weak before, now seemed to retreat entirely, casting them all into shadow. Esa, always so quick with a biting word, stared, mouth open. The guards who had rushed to block Okoa shifted at their posts but did not come close. One fell to his knees, spear clattering loudly as it hit the floor. Muttered prayers flowed breathlessly from his lips.

Okoa felt the Odo Sedoh at his back, his approach like the roll of a dark tide. He suddenly remembered the warnings of the Odohaa, that the Odo Sedoh was a storm, a force of nature, and Okoa shivered, the hairs on his neck rising.

One moment human and joking, the next this darkness, Okoa thought. *How am I supposed to understand this man, this god?*

The Odo Sedoh's warning that the gods were unknowable came back to him.

Cool fingers against his shoulder made him flinch, but he only wanted to pass. Okoa stepped aside.

He watched Esa take the man in. The bloodstained pants, the wild waves of hair and liquid eyes, the brutal haahan that covered his bare chest and arms, and the fact that he wore Okoa's beloved feathered cloak.

She met his gaze, undaunted, but her voice trembled. "Who are you?"

He heard Mataya murmur a prayer, and Juuna suck in a wet sob.

"You know who this is, Sister." The lanterns had steadied,

and the shadows had withdrawn, but he could not suppress the chills that rattled through his core.

Juuna dropped into a low bow, and Mataya followed.

"The Odo Sedoh." It was Chaiya who whispered the name, his face drained of color, as if he witnessed a ghost made flesh.

Close enough, Okoa thought. *For he is something unnatural.*

The Odo Sedoh spread his arms wide. "Okoa's only transgression is that he took me from Sun Rock and allowed me to recover from my injuries among the crows. If your Sky Made clans seek to place the blame on someone, let it be me."

Esa swallowed and seemed to rally. "You are responsible for the fall of the priesthood? You alone?"

"The priesthood is responsible for their own fate. I was only the instrument of our god's vengeance."

"Our god . . ." Esa murmured.

"The crow god," Juuna whispered helpfully.

Esa closed her eyes, and Okoa saw the muscle in her jaw tic. "How—"

Commotion from the hall cut her off.

Esa's laugh was high and shrill. "What now?"

Okoa gestured for the guards to investigate the disturbance, and they hustled to the noise, slipping out the doors and barring them after they passed. There was shouting. It sounded like a dozen people, at least.

Okoa leaned close. "Can you understand anything?"

"There are many voices. Unclear who . . . someone named Maaka. He is requesting an audience."

"Skies," Esa muttered. "The Odohaa are bold. They have been clamoring at my door, yelling to see me, demanding that I do something. But I told them—"

"Not an audience with you," the Odo Sedoh corrected. "An audience with me."

The matron's eyes widened.

Okoa could almost see his sister's mind working. Her sudden realization of how easily the Odo Sedoh could seize power, her power, should she not get control of the situation quickly. A man who had slaughtered the Watchers. A villain to the clans but a folk hero to the Odohaa.

Their eyes met, and she quickly turned, as if to hide her thoughts. But he had already seen something that made him uneasy.

"Esa, what are you—"

"Brother." Her voice was brisk with authority, her eyes bright. "As captain of the Shield, I command you to go and talk to Maaka and the Odohaa. You know each other, after all, and he will listen to you. Appease him. Tell him . . ." Her gaze lingered on the Odo Sedoh, even as she spoke to Okoa. "Tell Maaka and the others the Odo Sedoh and I will meet with them tomorrow. Tell them that tonight he is tired from his trials and his defeat of the Watchers and wishes to rest."

"But what of the other clans?" Juuna fretted behind her. "What of their demands?"

"What of them?" Esa asked sharply. "Let them wait. This is Crow business now."

She stepped forward and slipped her arm around the Odo Sedoh's. Okoa saw the tremor in her hand when she did it but that she did it anyway. "Let us go out the back way," she said, her voice a compelling purr, "away from the crowds. I'll show you the Great House, find a private place we might speak."

Okoa thought to say something, to warn the Odo Sedoh to be careful, that there were dangers in the world more subtle than priests and Knives. But he was a god, was he not? Surely, his warning should be for his sister.

He watched helplessly as Esa led him away.

Chaiya came to stand next to him. "She is not the girl you grew up with anymore."

"I don't know who she is," he confessed.

"She is your matron." Chaiya's voice was flint. "That is enough."

Okoa's face burned. Chaiya was right. What would his mother think to see him doubt his sister?

Chaiya's hand came down on his shoulder. "Duty, Okoa. That is all you need know. The rest will only confuse you. Do what duty requires, and you will always be in the right."

"Of course." He gave Chaiya a sharp nod.

Duty, yes, but to whom? Esa? Carrion Crow? The Odo Sedoh? That last thought came unbidden and unwanted, but he found that he meant it.

"Duty," he murmured to himself, as he marched to the great doors and swung them open. But he was not convinced.

CHAPTER 7

> And they say to me
> You are not one of us.
> Your blood is impure, your birth an abomination.
> You are vile and unwanted, always a stranger.
>
> —From *Collected Lamentations*
> *from the Night of Knives*

Serapio felt obligated to let the Carrion Crow matron lead him through the turning hallways of the Great House, but as they walked, he quickly realized they were not following the same route as the one Okoa had taken from the aviary. He tried his best to mark the differences so he could find his way back: the sound of the matron's hem as it dragged along stone floors, not reverberating the way her brother's quick steps had on the spiraling stairs; the warm air that grew warmer, suggesting they were farther from the outside; the dry smell of stone and human, a sign they must be deep in the interior of the Great House. He did not like it, being so far from the crows and in such an unfamiliar place.

"I'd like to return to the aviary," he said, interrupting the matron as she explained some detail in the architecture.

"What?" she asked, surprised. "Now?"

"Yes."

He felt he owed some sort of respect to the woman who ruled Carrion Crow, but etiquette had never been his strength. He had learned basic manners under his father's roof while his mother still lived, and his tutors, particularly Paadeh, had demanded deference. He knew how to hold his tongue and nod along to useless words, but it rubbed at him like a pebble underfoot, and he did not enjoy it.

"I thought you would be interested in learning more about your ancestral home."

"I am not."

Before Sun Rock, he would have been. He would have reveled in the idea of learning the history of this place and his people. But something had changed in him, something profound, and all he wanted to do was retire somewhere quiet where he could be alone to unravel what that was.

"I find architecture fascinating," she continued. "The kind of stone from which a building is made, particularly. Old stone, local stone, it is by far the best. Foreign stone cannot be trusted."

"Is there much foreign stone in the Great House?"

"None."

"I would think it would not matter where the stone originated from as long as it was strong and fit to the purpose."

"Oh, no. Foreign stone may look the same as local, but the differences begin to show immediately." She led him on. "I remember a story of a man who thought to build his home from foreign stone, eschewing the provincial because he found the foreign new and attractive, a novelty, really. But no sooner had he laid the foundation than he discovered it was much too porous, and it began to crack."

He understood her meaning now, and countered, "Perhaps the man mishandled the stone. Does not the fault then lie with the builder? It is easy to blame the material, but it is only performing the way it was meant to perform."

"The stone was bad from the beginning. No amount of work could have saved it."

"A strange thing to think."

"The fault may have been in the forging. Improper firing and testing, a defect in the native materials. It's difficult to account for all the faults possible if one is not intimately familiar with the process."

He stopped, turning to face her. "There is no fault in my forging."

"We all have faults we cannot recognize in ourselves. It is human nature."

"You forget that I am not only human."

"So you say."

He could feel her eyes weighing and judging him. Deciding if he was worthy material on which to build the future of Carrion Crow, or if he was defective.

"You are not so different from your brother," he said.

"Oh?"

"He seeks to use me as a weapon against your enemies. You test me, seeking to use me, too. Although I am not sure for what."

"It would be naive of you to think we did not want to mold you to our needs. After what you have done. You are . . . explosive."

He smiled. "Do you have a knife?"

"What?" Her voice was wary, and she released his arm and stepped back.

"Do you fear me? Think that I would hurt you?"

"In my own house? You would not dare."

"No, I would not."

He held out his hand, and after a moment, he felt the weight of a blade against his palm. "What is it that a master builder must look for in his stone?"

"Strength, first."

He ran the blade across his forearm. Felt when his flesh parted under the obsidian and the blood welled. She sucked in a breath, more curious than repulsed.

"What else?"

"Porosity," she answered, understanding.

He knew he could not call the shadow from his god, but he thought he still might be able to do so through his blood. He had not thought of it at the monastery; his panic had been too acute. But now he remembered his old tutor's words, and he was sure of it.

"Porosity is essential to sorcery as well, after a fashion." He wiped the knife against his pants and tucked it into his waistband. With his other hand now free, he ran his fingers through the flow of his own blood. "The barrier between our world and the shadow world is porous and breeched by sacrifice." He held up his bloodied hand. "Once it is crossed, magic is the sorcerer's to control." What had once been as natural as breathing now took concentration that brought wrinkles to his brow, but he felt the shadow come to him, wrap around his fingers, and caress his palm as it fed from his blood. "I am no ordinary stone."

"Such magic has not been seen in Tova in an age." Her voice was soft with awe.

"I bring a new age."

He twisted his hand, willing the shadow to mold itself as he wished, and after a moment, he held a crow made of smoke in his palm. She laughed in delight, and he released the bird. It hovered momentarily above his hand before dissolving into the air.

"And the blood is gone."

"The shadow must feed," he said simply. He did not explain the cost of such magic, as he had never truly had to pay it. With the crow god as his unending source of pure shadow, it had always simply been a part of him. But now he felt drained, as if the magic had fed on his very essence, which he supposed it had.

"I admit you interest me." She slipped her arm back around his as they continued down the hall. "But I am not sure how you benefit Carrion Crow, despite what the Odohaa think. Or my brother. If I were to find use in you, it would be for the benefit of my people. All of them. Not just the ones who think you are a god."

"You do not?" he asked, amused.

"I believe you are a killer and an adept sorcerer. But a god? I have never been much for gods."

"You are more like your brother than you know."

They reached a stairwell and ascended. As they rose, the air chilled perceptibly.

"I have been groomed to be matron my whole life, in ways that you cannot understand. I love my people intimately, completely. I serve them, they do not serve me. It is a calling, and with my mother's death, I fully embraced it."

"Do you think I do not know what it is to be raised for a single purpose?"

They came to a stop.

"Then you must understand that I will not let anything or anyone who does not have the best interest of Carrion Crow settle in this Great House. You are impressive, and my brother seems willing to accept that you are what you say you are, enough to bring you into our halls. And the Odohaa certainly believe you are the savior they have prayed for come in the flesh. But I have seen no sign of godhead that cannot be accounted for with magic and skill, and I am not so sure your slaughter of the Watchers benefits Carrion Crow or if it paints a target on our backs. You may think you saved us, but the truth is you may have only endangered us further."

She opened a door.

"Here is your room."

"I asked to return to the aviary."

"It is not far. Here there is a bed and a place to wash, and I'll have food and clothes sent to you. I ask that you stay here for now, although I have a feeling that should you wish to leave, you could manage it. But if you truly do not want us to be at odds, you might prove that to me now."

He inclined his head, willing to give her that which did not require much of him. He stepped through the door.

"There is another element for which stone must be tested before it can be used to build a Great House."

"And what is that?"

"Cost. Often even worthy stone is not worth the price it would require to obtain it. In that case, it is best to rid yourself of the burden early, lest the endeavor ask more of you than you are willing to give."

She shut the door between them. He waited, listening to her steps retreat down the hall. Once she was gone, he tested the latch. It did not move. She had locked him in. He tried the door once more to confirm his imprisonment, with the same result. Amused to find himself yet again confined, he explored his new jail. It was as she had said. A bed, a washbasin, and nothing else. Yes, very much a prison cell.

At the far end of the room, he found another door. It was solid wood, and heavy. He felt for a lock, and, finding only a latch, he pulled it open. Winter wind rushed in, knocking him back a step. The eclipsed sun flared light and shadow in his vision. Somewhere nearby, crows cried out.

"A door that leads to nowhere," he murmured, although he was sure that was not entirely true. He suspected that if he listened closely, he would hear the rush of the Tovasheh River a dozen stories below. "I believe she wants me to consider flying."

He started to close the door and paused, thinking. Instead, he threw his mind out, searching. She had said he was not far from the aviary, and he hoped she had not lied. Crows answered immediately. He called to one. A moment later, the bird was at his hand. He ran a finger across the crow's head, the touch of his friend a comfort in this unfamiliar place.

"Go find Okoa," he told the corvid. "Bring him here." He was about to release the crow when he had another thought. "Find this Maaka, the leader of the Odohaa. Bring him, too. Let us make this interesting."

The corvid took flight.

Serapio closed the sky door. He made his way to the bed and stretched out, tucking his newly acquired knife under the reed-filled mattress. The wound in his side pulled as he stretched out, but he ignored it. Pain was something he could endure, and tolerance for discomfort he possessed in rare amounts. So he settled in to wait for what came next.

Patient as stone.

CHAPTER 8

City of Tova (Coyote's Maw)
Year 1 of the Crow

Magic is chaos. Seek it out at your peril.

—*Exhortations for a Happy Life*

Naranpa walked the network of underground tunnels below the Lupine, looking for Zataya. Denaochi had assigned her a servant who helped her bathe and find clean clothes, so now she wore a simple white dress and a red and yellow string belt instead of a bloody, dirt-stained blanket. It was progress, albeit small progress. The servant, whose name was Baaya, had even managed to find her a cloak and a pair of warm, fur-lined boots. Thus attired, she set out, without her brother, to find the witch.

Naranpa had tried to sleep, but it was impossible, despite her exhaustion. Her mind churned between horrors. First, the faces of her fellow priests in various poses of death—throats slit, heads bashed in, some details so gruesome she wondered at her own macabre imagination. And when she wasn't imagining the violence of her former colleagues' deaths, she dreamed of men in jaguar skins interrogating her, berating her for her failures, and then choking her until she couldn't breathe. Feeling wrung out and unsafe even in her own head, she asked Baaya, who was dozing outside her door, to point her to Zataya's room. She was hoping Zataya might be able to explain the dreams or, better yet, have a way to stop them. And maybe she could ask the witch more about what magic she had worked on the Convergence and if it could be the source of the continual burning in her chest or the strange glow that suffused her hands. Of course, now out of immediate danger and free of the suffocating earth, she doubted whether her hands had glowed at all. Perhaps they had only been a figment of her overactive imagination. She tried to remember if her lantern had truly been extinguished or if perhaps some small illumination had remained, but she couldn't. Her travails in the tunnels were a blur. If only she had learned more about magic when she had access to the celestial tower's library. A better grounding in history and southern sorcery would be welcome now.

"A head always in the stars," Kiutue had scolded her when she was a dedicant newly promised to the oracles, but he had said it with such affection that she had not taken it poorly, even when he went on to chide her. "Look for the pleasure around you, too, Naranpa. You need not always focus on what lies in the heavens. There is beauty on earth, too."

She had thought then of her childhood in the Maw and severely doubted Kiutue's declaration, but love for her old mentor had quieted her tongue. The day-to-day world continued to disappoint, again and again, no matter what others believed.

She found Zataya's room, knocked once, and immediately pushed open the door. She worried that if she waited, Zataya might not let her in.

A powerful perfume greeted her, filling her nose with rosemary, lavender, and mint. She swooned in pleasure. The scent emanated from the steam of small pots bubbling over a hearth fire in one corner of the room. Smoke rose up a long chimney to exit far above them, no doubt bathing the neighborhood above in fragrance.

"What are you making?" Naranpa exclaimed. "It smells wonderful!"

Zataya was hunched over a table in front of the hearth, her long back bent over a mortar and pestle and a mound of wild mint before her. Around her were clay jars of various sizes and piles of herbs and plants, many Naranpa didn't recognize.

"Shouldn't you knock?" the witch complained, throwing Naranpa an annoyed glare.

"I did knock."

"A knock is usually followed by the person inside deciding whether to open the door or not."

"I was afraid you wouldn't let me in."

Zataya grunted, confirmation enough that Naranpa had guessed correctly.

"Although I thought you might want to see me, if only out of curiosity as to how well your working on the Convergence fared."

The muscles in Zataya's shoulders shifted, and Naranpa thought she saw something there. Shame? Denial? How strange. She had been sure the witch would want to gloat.

Again, she did not wait for an invitation but took a seat on the stool at the table. She ran a hand over a pile of green pods that looked like they were covered in silvery fur.

"Don't touch anything!"

Naranpa withdrew her hand. "Is it poisonous?" She had a sudden memory of her mother scolding her for eating mushrooms she had found in a cave once.

Zataya set her pestle down. "What do you want?"

"Only to talk."

The witch looked as exhausted as Naranpa felt. Her cheeks were hollows, and deep rivers carved routes below her eyes. She wore the same silt-colored robes as always, only a shade lighter than her skin, but her hair was longer than it had been only days ago and floated around her face in a soft black halo.

"Your hair grew quickly," Naranpa remarked, rubbing absently at the place on her chest that bothered her.

"You came to ask me about my hair?"

"No, of course not."

Zataya folded her arms across her chest and narrowed her eyes, studying Naranpa. After a moment, she made a noise in her throat. She turned to her clay pots, plucked a black-and-white vial shaped like a long finger, and placed it in front of Naranpa.

"Drink this. Just a drop in your tea at night. More than that, and you may not wake up again. But a drop. It will calm your dreams."

"Dreams?" She had said nothing about dreams.

"You're having bad dreams, aren't you?"

Naranpa was too surprised to answer.

Zataya nodded. "There are stories. Of people who cross over to the world of the dead and come back. They often bring back a miasma with them, something that clings to their soul and troubles their dreams."

"I don't think that's it." She didn't know how to explain that the dreams felt active, more like a visitation. More like magic. "And I didn't die. You saved me."

Another noncommittal grunt.

"I could hear you and feel your touch, but my tongue couldn't move to tell you so," Naranpa explained, rubbing absently at her chest.

"Is that why you've come? To ask about magic? And that burning in your chest?"

Naranpa stared, shocked. "How do you know about that?"

"You keep touching it and making a face. Clearly, it pains you."

Had she been touching it? Perhaps she had. "Is it magic? Sorcery?" The word felt clumsy on her tongue. "A . . . residue of what you did to me?"

Zataya's mouth turned down, and Naranpa rushed to add, "That is what Denaochi thought."

"You told your brother?" She sounded surprised.

"He noticed, too. Not my chest," she corrected. "My eyes."

Zataya scooted her stool closer. "Let me see you."

Naranpa shrank back involuntarily. "What do you mean?"

"Pull down your collar. Let me see."

"It's not on my skin," she said quickly.

"Why are you hiding from me?"

Why was she hiding? She had come to Zataya specifically for answers, and now she found herself hesitant to receive them. She thought Zataya had wisdom to share, but now she was having second thoughts, distrust squatting between them like an unwanted guest.

"Or go." Zataya sounded disgusted. "It makes no difference to me."

Resigned, Naranpa pulled the collar of her dress down enough so that the witch could examine her. Surprisingly gentle fingers probed the place over her heart before Zataya motioned for her to straighten her clothing. She grasped Naranpa's jaw to examine her eyes. She was uncomfortably close, her mint-scented breath hot against Naranpa's skin, but she held still and let her look. After a moment, Zataya let her go.

"Well?"

"Your skin is warm there, over your heart. Maybe there's

an infection inside. Maybe someone more skilled in healing than I could understand it."

"I don't think it's an infection."

Zataya raised an eyebrow.

Naranpa let the words come quickly, before she could change her mind. "It started when I was in the tunnel, and the lantern had gone out. I could see nothing, not even my hands before my face. But then I raised my palm, and it began to glow." She scanned Zataya's face for a response but could read nothing there. "And I . . . I think my eyes glowed, too. And it was hot. I was hot. The tunnels were cold, but I was hot." She flushed, embarrassed. "I know I sound mad—"

"No." Zataya cut her off. "Not mad."

A flicker of hope intertwined with dread. "Then what?"

Zataya chewed at her bottom lip.

"What is it?" Naranpa asked.

"There's a way the grandmothers have to test for such things."

"What things?"

"Those who are god-touched."

"Is that what you think has happened?" Naranpa knew the term in passing, a name the ancients had for people who possessed unusual powers that were attributed to a brush with divinity. But that was before the formation of the Watchers, before they had done what they could to rid the world of such superstitions.

"It's possible. The sorcery was a powerful working. It may have left its mark."

"But god-touched?" She could not keep the skepticism out of her voice. "From your blood?"

"Not just my blood," she corrected. "Salt and smoke, too."

She remembered the salt the witch had placed under her tongue and the acrid white smoke that had enveloped her.

Zataya said, "Those were rare things, precious things, but your brother said do all I could, so I did. The salt comes from the far northern shores of a lake in a place they call the Graveyard of the Gods. They say it is the sweat of a god."

"I know the place. Where the sun god bled the gold that made the Sun Priest's mask. We are taught as much as dedicants." Taught that they were just stories, legends passed down for generations that explained away the natural phenomena of their world, but a shiver trickled down her spine nonetheless. "And the smoke?"

"God bones, ground to white dust."

"From the Graveyard?" She rubbed her hand over the back of her head, where it suddenly tingled. "And you think using these . . . god parts has given me some lasting . . . ?" Lasting what, exactly? *Powers* sounded fanciful. But what else would one call what she did?

"There is one way to find out." Zataya reached across the table and pulled forth a mirror that had been half buried under a bouquet of dried wild onion. Naranpa recognized the scrying mirror, the one Zataya had used to see the Crow God Reborn's return and predict the Sun Priest's death.

"The mirror can tell you if I'm god-touched?"

"It is a gateway into the shadow world, and within the shadows, you can see many things. Past, present, future. It is said that the greatest sorcerers may even travel small distances through the shadow world."

She had never heard that. "How does it work?" But she already knew. She had seen Zataya use it before.

Blood and desire. Well, she had a body full of blood, and her desire was strong. Faith was her struggle, and more than that, a reluctance to cross the line into the taboo. Everything she had learned over the last twenty years had schooled her against the practice of magic, but what choice did she have if she wanted to understand what was happening to her?

Zataya produced a small obsidian knife.

"No stingray spine this time?" Naranpa asked dryly, her tongue throbbing in remembered sympathy.

Zataya grasped Naranpa's arm and pressed the blade into the flesh just below her inner elbow. Naranpa hissed at the pain, but it passed quickly, and Zataya pinched at the wound to draw blood to the surface. When there was enough, she turned Naranpa's arm over and let the warm liquid drip onto the mirror's milky surface.

Skies! Naranpa thought. *Am I really doing this?* Apparently, she believed in it enough to give her blood to the endeavor. If it was folly, what had she to lose but self-respect? And if it was real, the gain might be unimaginable. *If Iktan could see me now. How have you come to this, Sun Priest?*

Former Sun Priest—and that came to her in Iktan's droll voice, accurate enough to make her swallow back a flood of conflicting emotions.

"Go ahead," Zataya said, after she had spread Naranpa's blood across the opaque surface and given her a rag to staunch the bleeding. "Ask it what you want to see."

Naranpa looked into the mirror, her silhouette now more smears of red than shadow. She thought to ask a dozen different things. How had she survived? Who was the Crow God Reborn, and did he hunt her even now, or was his thirst for vengeance slaked? Could she trust her brother? Was magic even real? But what came from her mouth was a surprise, even to her: "Who am I?"

The effect was immediate. It felt as if something or someone had grasped her head with two hands and was dragging her down. She shouted out, alarmed, but the grip only tightened, and down into the shadow world she tumbled.

• • • • •

The screams of leviathans reverberate through the air, the vibrations shaking Naranpa's bones. Talons reach for her eyes, and she pivots, snaking her long tail around to strike the great black bird that threatens her. It falls back, injured, but another creature comes for her, this one a feline with slavering jaws and razored teeth. It leaps skyward, trying to catch her. Its claws rip golden scales from her throat, and . . .

. . . she wakes from an unplanned sleep, head snapping up. She stifles a panicked cry. She has dozed off. Oh, great gods, what has she done? She is supposed to stand watch. Her eyes shoot to the bags. There they sit, still fat with gold, and here are Ano's arms around her still. They huddled together for warmth in this forbidden place, the last two left. Her breath puffs before her, white mist. But Ano's does not. Dread fills her belly. She turns. Ano is tucked against her, skin frosted white, lifeless eyes staring. She screams into . . .

. . . the heat of a smelting forge, flames licking tufa molds as her steady hands pour liquid gold into long, thin strips. Hammers ring around her as others work the four masks of the Watchers. What they do here is good and will ensure peace among the cities of the Meridian for centuries, if not millennia. Someone calls her name, and she turns. Not enough time to scream as a knife slits her throat. She falls, her blood mixing with the gold . . .

Through a dozen faces, a hundred scenarios. She is the dedicant made Sun Priest again and again. Enemies threaten her, and the Knives take them down. Some succeed, and she is imprisoned, deposed, executed. She catches a glimpse of herself hurling from the sky bridge into the open air, the waters impossibly far below.

A man stands, his back to her. Lightning flashes around him, and wind tears at his hair, his cloak. He stands high atop a mountain. No, not a mountain. A tower, smooth stone under his feet. He holds something in his hands. She knows this thing like she knows her own face, the curve of the cheeks and lips, the gloss of gold. He raises the Sun Priest's mask to his face. She cries out, knowing she has to stop him. Knowing that if he succeeds, all is lost. Her heart thumps in her ears. The storm casts her words of warning away. She reaches for him, but he is too far, his figure a blur in the sheeting rain. She tries to run, but her legs, her body, will not move. She cannot see his face, does not recognize the set of his shoulders or his long black hair. He cocks his head, as if he hears her, and begins to turn. Another moment, and she will see his face, another second.

A mouth twists into a smile, speaks her name, and—

Naranpa screamed herself awake.

Into a room gone dark and cold, the fire in the hearth burned to nothing, the air still perfumed with rosemary and mint. She was on the floor, splayed out on her back, and she grasped the stool she had been perched on and pulled herself to sitting again. Her shoulder ached where she must have fallen and struck stone, and her head spun, her heart still pounding in her chest, her body still flooded with adrenaline.

The visions still tumbled in her mind, more emotion than memory. What had she seen, where had she been? Past or future, she wasn't sure. Symbol or reality? The feelings were real enough: of attack, of betrayal and loss. She stifled a sob.

"Zataya?" she whispered, her voice trembling. But the witch was not there.

"Ochi?" she called instead, knowing there would be no answer. The scrying mirror was now clean of the blood she had poured on it. No, the blood she had fed it. Her blood.

She shuddered and heaved it across the room as if it were a live snake. She listened for the shatter as it hit the floor, but none came.

While the mirror might have been clean, her arm was thick with blood. She stared, confused, until she realized the makeshift bandage had fallen off and her wound had bled freely for however long she had been . . . wherever she had been. Wincing and fighting nausea, she retied the bandage around her arm. *I need a healer*, she thought, darkly amused. *But the only one I know appears to have abandoned me.*

Her next thought was to find Denaochi, but she was having trouble thinking at all, still half caught in the wild visions she had seen and suffering from a loss of blood.

A minute to rest. That was all she needed. Just a moment to close her eyes and rid herself of the lingering images—the face of the man she could not quite remember, the driving rain, the terror of seeing the Sun Priest's mask in his hands. She laid her head down on the floor, curled up her shivering body, and fell into a deep unconsciousness.

• • • • •

"Nara!" Rough hands shook her. Denaochi's voice rang urgent in her ear. "Wake up! Nara!"

Her head lolled on her shoulders, and she blinked rainwater from her eyes. That face, the cruel smile, the mask.

"No!" she cried out, shoving her brother away. He fell back, tripping over the stool. His quick hands caught the edge of the table and halted his fall. Zataya stood, mouth opened in surprise, in front of the rekindled hearth.

"Where did you go?" Naranpa asked her accusingly.

"I could not wake you, so I went for help."

"What's wrong with you?" Denaochi asked, somewhere between concern and suspicion.

"Nothing. I just . . ." What to tell him? How much to tell either of them? "I must have hit my head. I'm fine now." She held out her hands.

Denaochi heaved her to her feet, and she swayed. He grasped her arms, careful of the bandage, and helped her sit.

"Zataya said you came to her complaining of nightmares, and she gave you a tonic, but before you could take it, you collapsed."

She looked to the witch, but her expression told her nothing. Why would she not want Denaochi to know about the mirror? Naranpa had said she had not told Denaochi about the details of her glowing palms or the other symptoms of possibly being god-touched, so was Zataya simply respecting her confidences? Or did she think it was dangerous for Denaochi to know? Her instincts told her it was wise to keep this from him, at least for now. At least until she understood it better. But the same instinct made her want to keep the details of her vision from Zataya, too.

What she really wanted was an afternoon in the celestial tower's library and unfettered access to the knowledge there. Surely she could find something about the god-touched, and if not that specifically, something about the visions she had seen. The sun god in her radiant form with a fiery tail and deadly talons, fighting the crow and the jaguar, seemed plain enough. A vision plucked from her own worries. But the rest. The frozen companion named Ano, the murder in the forge. The memories were both intimate and entirely foreign.

"I don't know what happened," she said aloud. "Perhaps I'm still exhausted."

Denaochi made a noise in his throat, part blame and part skepticism. "I told you to wait for me."

"I know. I . . . I couldn't sleep, and I thought Zataya could help. But I'm better now." She rallied and gave him a wan smile. The black-and-white bottle still sat on the table, and she held it up for Denaochi to see.

The suspicion in his eyes softened.

"Well, it is good Zataya brought me to you. There is something else we must discuss." He laid a folded sheet of paper on the table between them, marked with three sinuous plant leaves. "I sent a message to a friend after we parted last. Another boss, the owner of the Agave House. She sent a reply."

"A reply to what?"

"We need them, Nara, if we mean to go up against Carrion Crow."

She had thought to prepare herself should the Crow God Reborn seek her out, but she had not thought to attack Carrion Crow. She had no quarrel with the clan itself, especially that young Shield captain. This was Denaochi scheming, and she did not fully trust it.

Was that why Zataya thought to keep Naranpa's potential powers a secret from her brother for now? Did Zataya know Denaochi would hope to use them, to use her, to dangerous ends?

"It's civil war, whether you wish to see it or not," he said, no doubt noting her skepticism. "Carrion Crow is massing an army in Odo, and there is talk that the Sky Made will be made to follow or else. We will give them another option."

"The other Sky Made might want to distance themselves from Carrion Crow after what has happened, but that does not explain why the bosses of the Maw would wish to rally to me. There is no love lost between the Watchers and—" She almost said *your people* before she caught herself.

"The Watchers are dead, and you are a survivor. The Maw loves nothing more than a survivor. And you are a daughter of the Coyote, lest you forget." His smile was only a baring of teeth, enough to let her know he had heard her unspoken thought. "You are both coyote and sun. You will be a powerful symbol, especially after you kill the Crow God Reborn."

"As if it will be that simple."

Denaochi's voice took on a dangerous edge. "It must be that simple, because that is what I have promised the other bosses."

So that was it. He wanted to use her to solidify his own power in the Maw. His hated sister returned home and dependent on him. Enough like a Sky Made to bestow the respect and authority of her former position upon her chosen allies, but Maw-born enough to be accepted as one of them.

"If you mean for me to be merely a symbol, who would lead the Maw?" Her voice was cool, the answer already obvious.

Denaochi leaned back, his grin bright but his eyes as cold as her own. "Ah, Nara, don't be like that. If you survive your encounter with the Crow God Reborn, we will share leadership."

And if I don't? she thought. *Then all that consolidated power will still be yours, and the Crow God Reborn even more feared.*

"I know I make an unconventional matron," he continued, grin widening, "but fuck tradition, right, Sister? The Sky Made will accept us because it's our side or that murderous crow god, and we know they'll never bow to that. But let's not get ahead of ourselves. First we must prove ourselves to the other bosses."

"And how will we do that? Another trial?" She thought of her crawl and how Denaochi had done it before her. She rubbed at the warm place on her chest, the strange power there now an unexpected comfort.

He tapped the folded paper on the table and then held it up between them.

"We shall find out soon enough."

CHAPTER 9

Only a fool builds her home on a turtle's back and complains
when it swims away.

—Teek saying

Xiala passed through Titidi in silence, Aishe's uncle a step
ahead of her. She was bundled in her new cloak. It was warmer
than her previous cloak had been, and ingenious ties at the
wrist and neck kept the cold out better. She missed her old
harbormaster's cloak for the nostalgia of it but was grateful
for Aishe's parting gift. It was more generous than she felt she
deserved.

"Keep close," Uncle Kuy warned, pulling her attention to
him. "We're nearing the bridge."

The bridge. The bridge where she had Sung and so many
had died.

For a moment, she could not make her feet move. The
woman in blue, the green-eyed man.

"I did my best, didn't I?" she whispered to herself. "The
mob was rioting. I had to try."

A voice came sharp in her memory. *All you ever do is try,*

Xiala. Try and fail, and then run from the consequences. You leave others to clean up your messes. Well, this time, there is no one else. This time, you pay for what you've done.

She shuddered under the weight of the recollection and the truth of it. The deaths on the bridge were now part of her burden, just like that first death on Teek so long ago, and she had to live with that blood on her hands.

"Fuck," she muttered. She should have made Aishe find Zash and his balché. Nothing good came from allowing her mind to wallow in self-recrimination. She wanted, no, *needed* something to turn off the memories and help her forget. But there was nothing here but cold wind and an unfamiliar city.

They passed the wide stone pillars that anchored the bridge to the cliffside and stepped across the landing. The span swayed as they took their first steps, but Xiala had seen it withstand gale winds and did not doubt that it was sturdy. By the time they reached Sun Rock, a fog had bloomed around them, casting an eerie haze over the mesa. A few Tovans trudged along the only path open, heads down and about their business. And scattered along the path, half a dozen guards.

"Members of the Sky Made Shield." Uncle Kuy kept his voice low. "Those there in green are Winged Serpent, not so bad. But watch for them in gold without the horns. That's Golden Eagle. Natural enemies of Carrion Crow. They'll trouble you if they know who you are."

"Why are they here at all?"

"Keep out the curious, mostly. And people looking for souvenirs."

"What kind of souvenirs?"

Uncle Kuy shrugged. "Weapons, knives, body parts. Whatever can be sold."

She rubbed her thumb against her missing pinkie joint.

The back of her neck prickled as she felt eyes on her. She dared a glance to see who was staring and met the eyes of a Golden Eagle Shield. She turned away and looped her arm through Uncle Kuy's.

"Quickly," she urged.

Another few minutes, and they were across Sun Rock and on the bridge to Kun. She glanced back. The guard who had noted her was lost to the fog. Shaken, she kept going.

The fog dissipated as they reached land. The road before them went on a way before forking east farther into Kun or west to Odo. Kun was different from Titidi. The district of Winged Serpent was terraced hills and low-slung houses painted green and blue. She glimpsed the rounded roof of a brightly colored Great House up a winding switchback. Its whitewashed walls were decorated with serpents with feathered manes. In another life, she would have been intrigued, happy to spend a lazy day exploring this place. But now, not only did such an idyll seem out of reach, but the only person she wanted to go wandering with was Serapio. How had he become so much a part of her so quickly? She wasn't sure how to explain it or what she was supposed to do with such unruly emotions. She wasn't even sure she approved. But there it was, and it was useless to deny what she felt.

They had shared something special in their days together. Not the sex, although she yearned for his touch, the taste of his mouth on hers. Even now, she flushed as she remembered how he sucked the honey from her fingers. But it was more than the desire he roused in her. It was the way he cared for her, asked no more from her than she wanted to give, and never judged her. And he had never feared her for her difference, for her magic, when there were times when she even feared herself.

He had simply been her friend and, for one night, her lover.

His presence had felt like the home she never had, the acceptance she craved so desperately, the forgiveness she feared she could never earn. She wanted that feeling back; she wanted him.

I'll take him away from here, she thought to herself. *Now that he has fulfilled his obligations to his crow god, he is free. He can leave this cold place and run away with me. We can find a ship somewhere and sail to the far edges of the Crescent Sea. Find an island of our own, raid merchant ships like proper pirates, live a life unbound from this world and its expectations.*

She wouldn't let herself think of the impracticality of it. How childish the fantasy, how impossible. How, despite their deep connection, there was so much she did not know about him, or he about her. Instead, she stubbornly clung to her dream like the last hope for land in the throes of a shipkiller and prayed that, against all odds, they would reach the nonexistent shore together.

But as she and Uncle Kuy crossed the border into Odo, her hopes sank like an anchor, dashed before the waves even closed above her head.

"Well, fuck me," she remarked quietly.

The district of Odo was shades of shadow, black and gray volcanic rock with red-painted doors like blood-filled gashes in the stone. Charred wood beams made lintels and fences. Even the roads were marked with gray rock. And everywhere, on banners and painted on walls, the crowsign. She didn't let it show, but her heart felt like it was cracking.

"What's that?" Uncle Kuy asked.

"Nothing."

She had hoped to take Serapio from here, but now that she had seen Odo, she could not imagine a place where he belonged more. Would she really take him away from this? If she asked, would he even come?

She was of the sea, born and bred. Could she ever live in a place like this cold and forbidding city? Would Serapio even want her to stay?

Doubt thickened heavy and cold in her gut, but she braced herself.

"Only one way to find out."

• • • • •

As they approached what looked to be a hastily erected gate just across a small bridge that marked the border between Kun and Odo, a guard raised a hand to stop them. She was dressed in black, clearly Carrion Crow, and held a wicked-looking mallet lined with bits of obsidian over her shoulder. She took in their blue cloaks with suspicious eyes, and her mouth drew down in a frown.

"Ho, Water Strider," she said, stopping them. "What is your business here?"

"Not Water Strider," Uncle Kuy said. "Carrion Crow." He unfastened his cloak to pull his shirt aside and expose his chest. Xiala caught a glimpse of haahan. The carving looked new, still irritated on his skin. It was the familiar crowsign, the wings and skull that marked his door and all the doors and walls around them.

The guard peered suspiciously at the marking before reaching out and running a finger across the skin. "Fresh," she accused.

"I come late to my heritage," Uncle Kuy confessed, "but I do come. Talk to Lord Okoa, the captain of the Shield. He knows me. He will vouch for me."

The guard pinched thin lips together. "And her?"

"My niece," Uncle Kuy lied. "I'm the only family she has.

I couldn't leave her behind when the crow god called us. She is true."

Xiala dipped her head, mimicking what she thought an obedient niece might do, and made sure her hair and eyes were well covered.

"And your business?" the guard asked.

"We answer the call of the Odo Sedoh." Uncle Kuy swept an arm around, encompassing the camp just beyond the makeshift wall and the club-wielding guard. His eyes shone, and Xiala thought perhaps some was theater but suspected most was genuine. "We join with our brethren to pledge our lives to—"

"Move on," the guard said, cutting him off. She stepped to the side to usher them through. "Find a fire, a place to rest," she intoned, as if speaking from rote. "Food will come around, latrines are on the northern edge of the camp, no weapons, no fighting, or you're out. No exceptions."

"Praise to Odo Sedoh," Uncle Kuy said, head bobbing.

Xiala was sure she saw the guard roll her eyes skyward. If she had to guess, the woman had heard the same speech and the same fervent farewell a dozen times, and it had ceased to impress. She made note that not every Crow was quite so devout as the ones she'd met before now.

The camp was busy but not so crowded that they couldn't make their way through. She guessed at most two hundred people were gathered in a yard that likely accommodated a thousand if they stood shoulder to shoulder. Most of the people near the gate were families, mothers and fathers with infants and children underfoot. They had already set up small pit fires and looked to be settled in to wait. For what, Xiala was unsure.

As they moved farther into camp, she saw more people who looked to be Odohaa. Many displayed bare arms and backs despite the cold, skin wreathed in haahan. She had only ever seen Serapio's, and while they told a story of who he was, a story she had come to respect and find the beauty in, many of the haahan here were works of art. Delicately carved crows, their wings rendered in loving detail, sigils that she guessed were prayers, and of course, the ubiquitous crow skull. Many were freshly limned in red dye, as were the teeth she glimpsed in prayerful mouths.

"Are they all Odohaa here?" she asked Uncle Kuy.

She had never gotten along with religious types, at least until Serapio, and this many at once made her itch. Experience told her they would not like a Teek, particularly one who might take their precious Odo Sedoh from them. She hadn't shared her plans with Uncle Kuy and decided then and there that silence on the matter was the wiser course. Let him think she simply wanted to see a friend again, not that she wanted to rescue Serapio from this fanatics' den.

"Most are Odohaa," Uncle Kuy acknowledged. "But not all. There are some like me with Carrion Crow blood but no home in Odo. Others who may have homes here but have come to see the Odo Sedoh when he is revealed. And then there are those who read the skies and see the shadowed sun as a sign of what's to come and have chosen sides."

"There are so many."

"And more to come."

"Why?

"They have waited generations for this moment, Xiala. How could they not?"

That sounded too much like something Serapio might say, and it left her uneasy.

"Let's sit there." Uncle Kuy pointed to a nearby fire where three people sat talking. Two women and a third person wrapped in a black cloak, hood up, gender not immediately known. None of the group flaunted haahan or red teeth, and she relaxed at that. She wasn't sure she would know what to say to an Odohaa, and the idea of praying to Serapio was so absurd that it made her laugh. She hoped he would think it was absurd, too, but she suspected he might not.

"May we join you, friends?"

Uncle Kuy's question was directed at the eldest of the group, a woman in a black dress and red cloak with a hem of beads and feathers. Her dark hair was threaded with white and cut into a blunt bang. The woman next to her was dressed much the same and looked enough like her companion that Xiala guessed them to be relations, likely mother and daughter.

"All are welcome," the older woman said genially. Uncle Kuy looked to the other companions, and they both nodded in agreement.

"Our thanks," he replied, and Xiala murmured a thanks as well.

Uncle Kuy sat next to the daughter, and Xiala took the place next to him, the cloaked stranger on her left. She dropped to the ground, grateful to be off her feet. The walk through Titidi earlier and the trek across the sky bridge and through Kun had taken a toll. Before the day she had spent walking with Serapio, she'd been twenty days at sea, and her legs did not adjust to land easily. She was paying the price for it now. The stranger next to her poked at the fire to rouse it, and she nodded, grateful, before leaning forward to catch the warmth against her hands and face.

"Do you come from far?" the older woman asked politely. Her eyes took in their blue cloaks just as the guard's had.

"Not so far," Uncle Kuy said. "My grandfather was Carrion Crow."

"Ah," the woman said, reassured. "And you?" She looked to Xiala.

"His niece," she grumbled, keeping her head down. The woman's smile was not as wide or as friendly for her. So be it.

The person next to her prodded the fire and whispered, voice low and musical, "A niece with an interesting accent. Careful with your words, then, Water Strider."

Xiala tensed, but no one else appeared to have heard. She didn't know if she should ignore the threat, if it was a threat, or respond.

"Peace, friend," the stranger said before she could decide. "It is only an observation. I make it now, or others make it later."

She glanced at Uncle Kuy, but he was caught up in conversation with the Carrion Crow woman and had not noticed their exchange.

"Is there something you want?" Xiala hissed.

"Only to enjoy the fire."

"When did she say there would be food provided, Xiala? Xiala!" Uncle Kuy was staring at her, his face expectant.

"Hmm?" she said, trying her best to mimic Aishe.

Tovan was not a language Xiala knew well, but she had a natural affinity for languages, and time with Aishe and her brothers had helped her vocabulary, but her accent was apparently deficient. She wanted desperately to ask everyone to simply speak Trade, but then her ruse would assuredly be over.

"The guard. She said there would be food."

She shrugged and hunched further down in her cloak, hoping that would be the end of it.

Uncle Kuy sighed his disappointment and turned back to the women. "Anyway, she said there would be food."

"Did she say what?" the older woman asked. "I hope it's stew. A good stew would settle us all."

Xiala tuned out their banter and focused on the stranger. "Are you going to report me to the guards?"

"Why?" The voice sounded amused. "Have you done something worthy of reporting?"

"Xiala!" Uncle Kuy called again.

She swallowed her exasperation. "Yes, Uncle?"

She heard the stranger beside her chuckle softly.

"Did the guard say the Odohaa were meeting with the matron?"

She shook her head and lifted a shoulder in a shrug.

"Maaka and the other Odohaa have gone into the Great House to meet with the matron," the stranger offered to the group. "They plan the future as we speak."

"Who is Maaka?" Uncle Kuy asked.

"The leader of the Odohaa. Friend to Lord Okoa himself," the younger woman answered.

"I know Lord Okoa, too!" Uncle Kuy puffed his chest out a bit.

The stranger leaned in. "How is that, friend?"

Uncle Kuy's face fell as he realized his mistake. "A family acquaintance," he offered hastily. "We met once." His gaze shifted to the women, who looked at him as if he was hiding something, which, of course, he was.

"Is not Lord Okoa the one who took the Odo Sedoh from Sun Rock?" Xiala asked.

"Aye," the older woman said enthusiastically. "The Reckoning!"

"The Reckoning?" the stranger said, voice soft. "Is that what they are calling it?"

"That is what it was! And some say Lord Okoa aided

the Odo Sedoh in his work. That he held the knife that took the Priest of Knives' life as revenge for what happened at his mother's funeral."

The stranger seemed to tense at that, but whatever the emotion, it was gone before Xiala could name it.

"What happened at the funeral?" Uncle Kuy asked, eyes moving between the two parties.

The younger woman launched into her tale eagerly, but Xiala only half listened. She was more interested in studying her neighbors. Xiala had thought at first that the three were together, but it seemed that the person next to her didn't know the mother and daughter and had perhaps only joined them to warm by the fire. She had glimpsed no more than a sharp chin and a bowed lower lip, and the person's hands were sheathed in gloves.

"—a wedding!"

"What's this?" The daughter's exclamation brought Xiala's attention back. "I thought you said a funeral."

"The funeral was before. We were speculating about the matron's wedding."

"They think she will marry the Odo Sedoh," Uncle Kuy said quietly, his voice sympathetic.

Xiala was stunned to silence.

"It's a smart match," the mother said, misreading Xiala's shock for doubt. "Surely, then none would challenge Carrion Crow's supremacy."

Uncle Kuy patted Xiala's knee in reassurance. "It is only speculation. Neither the matron nor the Odo Sedoh has said it is so."

"It's not a marriage of love," the mother said. "It is a marriage of alliances."

"Although it could be love," the daughter protested. "The matron is very beautiful."

"And wealthy," Uncle added.

"And powerful," the stranger said, head tilted toward Xiala.

Xiala stood, annoyed at these strangers speculating on Serapio's fate. She knew it was only gossip, but she did not have to sit and listen to it. "I need to take a piss. Where are the latrines?"

Both women pointed north, the older woman looking slightly horrified at her rough language, but Xiala could not find it within herself to care. Before anyone could reprimand her or, worse, offer to accompany her, she stomped off in the direction they'd indicated.

"Be back for food soon!" Uncle Kuy shouted after her.

She waved over her shoulder to show she'd heard.

The latrines were no more than waist-high fencing arranged as stalls positioned over a trench. She had seen worse, much worse, and she'd never had a shy bladder, so the public display didn't bother her. But her cloak was unmanageable if she was going to squat, so she took it off and draped it over a nearby wall. Her hair spilled down her back in plum-colored waves, but it was dark in the twilight, and people were polite enough to avert their eyes from a woman in a private moment.

She did her business quickly and immediately threw the cloak back on and pulled the hood up. She felt eyes on her. It was the stranger from the fire, the one who had known by her accent that she was lying. They were standing not too far away, watching her. She froze, wondering what they had seen. How much they had seen. Well, there were ways to explain her hair—a fashion from the South or some such—and she thought they were too far away to see her eyes.

What does it even matter? she thought, as a wave of frustration hit her. Who cared who she was or why she was here if Serapio was already halfway to the marriage bed with the matron of Carrion Crow? *It's only speculation*, she reminded herself. *Hear it from his lips, or it's gossip.* And even if it was true, they had promised each other nothing. She had certainly fallen into bed with Aishe fast enough. She would be a hypocrite to begrudge the same for Serapio. *Then call me a hypocrite*, she thought to herself, *because I'll go to all seven hells before I'll let him go so easily again.*

She gave a nod to the stranger. She would have preferred a rude gesture, but a nod would have to convey her thoughts on the matter for now. The stranger nodded back, even touched finger to brow under their hood. She snorted and started back toward the fire.

Someone bumped her shoulder, and she turned, a muttered apology on her lips. It was the guard from earlier, the one who had passed them through the gate.

"Wait!"

The woman turned, annoyed.

"I . . . can you . . . I have something. For the Odo Sedoh. I know him."

The woman glazed over. "You can leave your gifts at the gate. Someone will present them—"

"No! It's not a gift. I mean, it was a gift. To me." She pulled the mermaid carving from her pocket, hesitating a moment before shoving it toward the guard. "The Odo Sedoh. His name is Serapio, and he made this for me. My name is Xiala. I was the captain of his ship. Can you, can you take it to him? Just tell him I'm here. That's all I ask. Tell him I'm here."

The woman turned the figurine over in her hand, her expression interested.

"Please?"

She sighed, put upon, but Xiala could tell she was intrigued. "Fine. Xiala."

"To Serapio," she called after the guard, who had already started to trudge back to the gate.

"Hells." Xiala wasn't sure if she'd done the right thing or if she had just thrown away her most precious possession. But she had to try, didn't she?

By the time she returned, Uncle Kuy and the two women were laughing and sharing stories over bowls of stew. Her stomach growled in sympathy, and Uncle Kuy waved her forward.

"I'll share what I have," he said. It was mostly broth now, the bits of corn and squash eaten already, but she was grateful for anything. She had been suspicious of him on their trip up the Tovasheh before the Convergence, when his interest in Serapio had an uncomfortable fervency, but in the end, he had turned out to be no more and no less than he appeared—a religious man who believed he had glimpsed his god. But that did not mean he was not kind to her.

"Your Uncle Kuy told us that you are a sailor," the older woman said.

Xiala sipped the broth. "Did he?"

"I'm Fress." The daughter pressed her hand to her heart. "And my mother is Haalan."

Xiala looked up as the stranger dropped down next to her, holding a bowl of stew. She peered over to see their bowl still full of vegetables and sighed.

"And who are you?" she asked, feeling put out. Threats she could handle, even being spied on in the privy, but getting a better bowl of stew than she did felt like a backbreaking insult.

"Xe arrived just before you," Fress offered helpfully, "with a group of believers from Winged Serpent."

"Ah," Uncle Kuy said. "Even those born to the serpent can see the wisdom in following the Crow God Reborn."

"Our clans are old allies from the times of the War of the Spear," xe said. "Carrion Crow were the first to answer our call for aid against the spearmaidens. It is only right that we rally to their side now."

"A scholar," Haalan murmured approvingly.

"Well said." Uncle Kuy smiled broadly. "And what is your name, friend?"

Xiala's neighbor paused, as if contemplating choices. When xe spoke again, xir voice held a touch of cynicism, as if this were all some great joke no one else understood.

"The Crow God Reborn remakes us all, but you may call me Iktan."

CHAPTER 10

CITY OF TOVA (DISTRICT OF ODO)
YEAR 1 OF THE CROW

> A conflict between enemies may lose the battle, but a conflict between allies risks losing the war.
>
> —*On the Philosophy of War*,
> taught at the Hokaia War College

Okoa was deep in conversation when he heard the noise. It started low, a sound easily ignored, like the crack of a flag snapping in the breeze. But it was more rhythmic than the wind, more deliberate, and it continued to increase in volume until it was impossible to ignore.

"What is that?" he asked, cutting Maaka off.

The man had been talking about gifts the Odohaa had brought to present to the Odo Sedoh. Weapons, by the sound of it, and something they had found on Sun Rock that they swore must belong to him. Okoa had been surprised that they had gone to the blood-soaked mesa, but Maaka had insisted it was the place of Carrion Crow's greatest victory. Okoa didn't want to argue the point, knowing Maaka's mind was already set, but he could not agree to giving Serapio any weapons. He was formidable enough with only his hands, as

Okoa had discovered. Arming him seemed parlous until they knew more.

Maaka paused with his mouth open to listen. They had stepped into a private corner away from the great room and the crowded receiving area where Feyou, Maaka's wife, and a handful of other Odohaa waited under Shield guard.

There it was again. More of a muffled thump now, like the sound of something hitting a distant wall.

The two men looked around. Okoa could see nothing amiss.

Maaka climbed the handful of steps up the wide, winding staircase and leaned forward to look out the narrow window. The sound again, and Maaka reared back with a curse on his lips.

"What is it?" Okoa asked, concerned.

"Crows, Lord." His voice was breathy, and he stepped to the side to let Okoa see.

Below, a mass of crows circled, a black-bodied whirlwind, hammering against the closed doors of the terrace directly below them.

"They're hurting themselves." Maaka was at his side again, eyes on the strange scene.

"They want in." But why? They had never done anything like this before.

His eyes met Maaka's. "The Odo Sedoh."

The leader of the Odohaa took off at a run.

"Open the doors!" Okoa shouted. There had to be guards down there, although he doubted they could hear him. He was about to follow where Maaka had gone, when he heard the deep, resounding boom of the terrace doors being flung open.

He rushed back to the window.

Maaka stood in the open doorway, arms outstretched, as the mass of crows surged past him. Okoa could not hear him, and his form was soon lost among the corvids, but his last glimpse of the Odohaa had been that of a man in ecstasy. And that frightened him more than anything else.

The next moment, the birds were upon him. Okoa ducked, covering his head, but the flock hurtled past him, leaving him untouched.

Footsteps pounded up the stairs, and Maaka was back, laughing wildly. "They want us to follow them!"

"How do you know?"

But Maaka was already climbing the stairs, pursuing the flock.

"My lord?"

Okoa turned to find one of the Shield, staring wide-eyed.

"Stay here with the rest of the Odohaa," he commanded, and then he was hurrying after Maaka. He caught him on the next landing, and then the two followed the corvids together, up to the second-highest floor in the Great House, just under the aviary. The flock streamed down the hall, and Maaka made to follow.

"Wait." Okoa gripped him by the arm. "This can't be right."

The older man turned. "What is it?"

"This floor is abandoned."

"What was it before?"

"Cells for criminals. With sky doors." He gave Maaka a pointed look. He had almost fallen from Maaka's sky door once.

The birds continued their frenzied flight, more urgent than ever. The noise of it made it hard to think. But Okoa could only imagine one reason the crows would bring them here.

"Check the cells." His voice was terse as he hurried down the hall. "I'll take the far side, you take the other."

Maaka did not argue but strode down the hall, testing the doors that lined the inner wall of the rounded hallway as Okoa inspected the outer. The first door had warped from disuse, and he had to force it. The cell beyond was empty and dark.

The second was the same, and the third. They worked their way around the hall, all the time accompanied by the flock. And then the second-to-last door opened smoothly, and Okoa almost closed it out of habit before he realized it wasn't empty.

"Here!" he shouted, but Maaka was already beside him.

The Odo Sedoh lay supine on a reed mattress, Okoa's feathered mantle covering him like a blanket. His hands were tucked behind his head, and his eyes were closed. He looked to be sleeping, but for a thin line of blood that had dripped from the bed to the floor.

Maaka must have seen it at the same time. "I'll find Feyou!" he shouted, and then he was gone, pounding down the hallway and back the way they had come.

Okoa dropped to his knees beside the bed, hands hovering over the Odo Sedoh. Unsure what he should do and afraid of what he might find when he removed his cloak.

"Okoa." The Odo Sedoh spoke, his eyes still closed.

Okoa startled but quickly recovered. "Are you unwell? Did you . . . did you send the crows to find me?"

The Odo Sedoh opened an inky black eye. "Thank you," he said, and Okoa did not think he was talking to him.

He pushed the cloak aside and rose. Okoa could see now that it was indeed the same wound from before that had bled through his crude bindings. The Odo Sedoh pressed a hand to his side but said nothing about his obvious pain as he made his way over to the sky door and opened it. He was careful to step to the side before he said, "You may go now. I'll come visit once I'm done with the captain."

The crows dutifully took to the wing, filing out as if dismissed. If Okoa had not seen him talk to the crows at the monastery, he would have been in awe, but he realized he was beginning to take the man's strange way with corvids in stride.

"Why are you here?" Okoa blurted.

The Odo Sedoh's lips quirked up, the barest suggestion of a smile. "Why do you think? I did not bring myself here, crow son."

Of course he didn't. It had been Esa. But why? What was she thinking?

Okoa knew exactly what she had been thinking, and his gut told him this cell had originally been prepared for him.

A commotion at the door, and Maaka was back, with Feyou and another Odohaa whose name he did not know. The man carried a large bundle in his arms, something wrapped in a woven blanket. Behind them trailed two Shields.

"He's hurt!" Maaka pointed to the Odo Sedoh, and Feyou pushed her way forward. She stopped short, gaze bouncing between Maaka and the Odo Sedoh, as if unsure what to do.

"We've brought a healer," Okoa explained. "A true healer. She would like to examine your wound, if you will allow it."

"Ah." He removed his hand from his side. It was wet with the same reddish-gold ichor as before. "I would be grateful."

That seemed to release Feyou, and she took the Odo Sedoh in hand. Once he was seated back on the bed, she examined his wound, her earlier hesitation gone as she got about her business.

"What happened?" she asked, voice direct.

"It is a wound from before. It troubles me."

"Before?"

"Sun Rock," Okoa supplied. "I could not heal it."

He heard the other Odohaa, the one still holding the bundle, gasp. He looked back to see that the man had closed his eyes and begun to mutter a prayer.

"Sun Rock." Feyou sounded awed. "From a Watcher?"

Serapio winced as her fingers probed. "I cannot remember."

"So it is days old and still festers. And you did not think to mention it as soon as you arrived, Okoa?"

He flushed. How was it that Feyou made him feel the recalcitrant child? "I mention it now."

"It was carelessly done."

"I meant no harm. The bleeding had stopped before, and I had forgotten about it for the moment. I would have brought him to a healer eventually."

"Eventually." Feyou was unimpressed, and Okoa realized he was making his case worse with every attempt at explanation. "Maaka, hand me my medicine kit, and then leave me to work, all of you. This room is too small for all these bodies and all this useless conversation."

Maaka did as his wife commanded and then stepped outside, dragging the other Odohaa with him.

Okoa hesitated. "He is important, Feyou. It is not that I do not trust you— "

"With respect, my lord, I do not think you are in a position to decide who to trust and not to trust with the best interests of the Odo Sedoh."

Her reprimand hit its mark, and he said no more. *Damn you, Esa*, he thought again. *You make us look duplicitous.*

"Watch them," he told the Shield as he passed. "And aid her in any way she needs. We want the Odo Sedoh hale." He said that last loudly enough for all to hear.

He touched Maaka's shoulder, motioning for the man to follow him, and he led Maaka down the hall away from the others. Once they were well alone, he said, "I would ask that you not tell anyone what you've seen here."

"And what have I seen, Lord?" His deep voice rose, indignant. "The Odo Sedoh locked in a cell like a criminal? Stabbed and left to die?"

"He was not stabbed."

"You saw the wound on his side."

"He wasn't stabbed today, I mean. Esa did not do that."

Maaka folded his arms over his barrel chest. "What did she do?"

Irritation and exhaustion flared, and he leaned in, his voice a harsh whisper. "Do not be so familiar with me. I am still your lord, and she is still your matron." The rebuke felt sour on his tongue, but he had to make the man understand.

Maaka stiffened. He bowed, low and mocking. "My apologies, my Lord Okoa Carrion Crow." When he looked up again, his face was closed, expression flat and unreadable.

Okoa clenched his jaw. Skies, he was stubborn and quick to offense. *Just like you*, he thought, but pushed that away.

"Give me time, Maaka. Before you tell the Odohaa. Before you . . ." What would he do? Go to the Carrion Crow council of aunties and demand Esa explain herself? Maaka had enough respect among the aunties that they would listen to him. But it would be a disaster. He could see the clan fracturing into factions before his eyes.

Maaka was unyielding. "You must understand that while I respect you for your father's sake, the Odohaa answer to a higher cause, and that cause is the restoration of Carrion Crow."

Okoa caught his breath. His father? No one spoke of his father. It was verboten. He wanted to say more, but Maaka was still talking.

"We are a people with hope once again, and the Odo Sedoh has brought us that." He thrust his chin back toward the cell. "Not you. Not your matron."

"And if you had to choose?" He knew he shouldn't ask it, but it was the same question with which he struggled and had no answer.

Maaka's eyes softened, but his arms stayed crossed, his face cold. "Do not ask a question whose answer you will not like, Okoa." He said his name with compassion, as if he knew him better than he did, and Okoa found it unsettling.

"It is treason," he warned.

"Careful, Lord, that you do not confuse fealty to the Odo Sedoh with faithlessness to your family. Your father would not make the same mistake."

Okoa opened his mouth, shocked. Twice he had mentioned his father. "How do you know—?"

"Maaka?"

Both men turned. It was Feyou.

"Now."

Maaka grunted and strode back to join his wife, leaving Okoa staggered. He had a sudden memory of riding a great crow for the first time. He had been twelve, still at odds with his adolescent body, awkward and gangling. Chaiya had taken him out to a blue lake beyond the city where the riders trained. The earth was vast and flat, the horizon stretching forever, blue water against a summer blue sky. When he had urged Benundah into the sky for the first time, the world had fallen away all at once. He had spun, unable to tell the heavens from the earth. His stomach had heaved as he tried to find something steady to focus on, but it had been too much, and he had fallen into the water below.

It was the same feeling he had now, unable to get his bearings, to tell up from down, destined to fall into the cold waters below.

He heard Maaka and Feyou talking and made his way back to the door. He did not enter the room but stood next to the Shield by the entrance. The other Odohaa had unwrapped his bundle. The gifts, Okoa remembered now. The first was a white staff, ornately carved with the wings of crows. He recognized its like from his time at the war college; it was a spearmaiden's traditional weapon.

"We looked for your knives, Odo Sedoh." Feyou pressed the staff into his hands. "But could not find them."

The Odo Sedoh was sitting on the bed, his torso bandaged, his hand folded around the staff, his expression reverent. "The knives were likely shattered. This is gift enough, and irreplaceable."

"When word came back of your victory, some of us dared to go to Sun Rock to see for ourselves. We retrieved this, knowing it must be yours, before Golden Eagle or any of the clans could claim it or try to destroy it."

"I thought it lost."

Maaka spoke. "Then it is all the more our honor."

"And what did you think of what you saw? There on the Rock?" He addressed the Odohaa kneeling before him, but his head was cocked slightly toward Okoa.

"Justice." Feyou spoke first. "Our ancestors' honor paid back in blood."

"Freedom," Maaka intoned, voice like the clarion affirmation of a bell. "Never again will Carrion Crow bow to anyone."

"If you have started a war, as some in the clans say you have," the Odohaa who had brough the staff said, voice eager, "then know that we are ready to fight."

Feyou pressed her face to Serapio's feet, and when she raised her head, Okoa saw tears streaking her cheeks. He shifted, uneasy at the display.

"We are ready to die for you, Odo Sedoh," Maaka said. "You need only ask, and we will answer with our blood."

Okoa watched helplessly, unable to stop the feeling of free-fall.

CHAPTER 11

City of Cuecola
Year 1 of the Crow

> Some have called me a fool for seeking to master the wild
> magics. But they have called me a fool only once, and the
> plaints of the dead matter not.
>
> —From *The Manual of the Dreamwalkers*,
> by Seuq, a spearmaiden

"We have a problem," Balam said as Powageh entered the office he kept on the lower floor of his estate. He would have preferred to receive his cousin in his private rooms, if only to spare himself the labor of dragging his body downstairs. He was a man in his prime, physically fit and without injury, but his muscles ached from sitting still too long, and his head felt like it had been stuffed with the honey of dreams, sticky and thick. The *Manual* warned that dreamwalking taxed the body, but he hadn't quite understood how. It was, after all, a practice that only required one to sit. But Balam felt like he had been beaten by a very large man with rocks for fists, and he stifled a groan as his lower back spasmed.

Despite the tolls on both body and mind, he would gladly still be traveling the dreamworld if his servant had not interrupted him with an urgent missive from his man in Tova. At first, he had railed, as he had left explicit orders not to be disturbed. But once he had read the letter, he was glad his servant had the sense to disobey his commands when the occasion demanded it. It was news that could not wait.

"Hello, Cousin," Powageh greeted him. "You look like something the dog shit out today."

Balam's look was baleful. He ran a hand self-consciously through his hair, now loose instead of properly tied up. The movement pulled at his shoulder, and he winced. "Is this your small talk?"

"No. Small talk is full of pleasantries. This is my anger. I have been trying to see you for days, but your damnable servants won't so much as let me past the door. I've even left written messages."

"Have you." Balam tried not to let his eyes drift to the small pile of unread missives on the corner of his desk.

Powageh noticed, of course, and grimaced. "And then you summon me here in the middle of the night, as if I have nothing better to do than come at your call."

Balam studied his cousin. The freshly laundered clothes, the thick gray hair neatly coiffed. "Did you? Have something better to do?" If Balam had to guess, Powageh had been waiting, breath bated, for his summons.

"Of course not," his cousin said, "but that's not the point. The point is—"

Balam waved Powageh's protests away. "I have news from Tova, come from my man in Golden Eagle. Do you want it or not?"

Powageh's eyes flickered, annoyed, but xe could not hide xir eagerness. "You know I do. Did our boy succeed? Have the Watchers fallen?"

It was not the first time Powageh had referred to Saaya's son as "our boy." Balam certainly did not think of Serapio with such affection, but he had not spent years with him as Powageh had. And thank the jaguar god for that. Because what he must ask of his cousin would be difficult.

"He did. The Watchers are dead but for a handful of the young or feeble, and they have scattered back from whence they came."

Powageh nodded, but xe did not look entirely happy. "Ah, he was a fine young man in the end. I hate that this is the fate we laid for him."

The same lament as before.

"Well, I have some spectacular news for you," Balam said. "He's not dead."

Powageh's face clouded. "Your humor leaves much to be desired."

"Then it is good that I am serious."

Powageh sat forward, rubbing at xir throat as if trying to dislodge whatever emotion was stuck there. "Tell me."

"While he succeeded in killing the Sun Priest, unbeknownst to myself, Golden Eagle had already staged a coup of the Watchers and installed their own Sun Priest." He glanced at his cousin, letting his contempt show. "A priest who was not invested."

Balam watched the news sink in.

"Seven hells," Powageh breathed. "Now I hope you do jest."

"If only, Cousin. If only."

Powageh's laugh was half amusement and half sob. "Twenty-two years of planning, only to be foiled by Golden Eagle's scheming."

"More than twenty-two," Balam observed dryly, "if you count our years of research. The star charts you mapped, the hundreds of glyph books deciphered, me translating those obscure workings Paadeh dug up from the gods know where."

"And Saaya." Powageh's voice was soft.

Balam would not have mentioned her sacrifice, but he was glad for Powageh to say it. Balam was not sure he had loved Saaya, but if he had ever loved anyone, it was her. She had been his equal in all ways, and their time together had been a rare and precious thing. But in the end, Saaya had loved revenge more than either of the people sitting now at this table.

He cleared his throat, and with it those bittersweet memories.

Powageh's eyes were bright with unshed tears. "How is it possible he lives?"

Balam shrugged. "I am but a lowly merchant lord."

"Humility has never suited you."

"And yet." Balam sighed dramatically.

"Your best theory, then, Cousin."

"That the true Sun Priest, the one invested with the sun god's power, is alive somewhere in the city. As long as she lives, a part of the sun god lives in Tova. Likewise, my guess is that Saaya's son must have survived because the crow god is not done with him. He still needs a body to spill Sun Priest blood."

"If she lives, will she rally the remaining Watchers? Attempt to recreate the priesthood?"

"Who can say? I imagine her days are few, and the Odo Sedoh will not rest until he has hunted her down."

"But the more time passes, the more the sun's power returns. The crow god may have missed his window of opportunity."

"Interesting that you should mention that. It appears the eclipse still hangs over Tova, the sun caught behind the moon, both neither rising nor setting."

"Impossible!"

"Apparently not."

"The gods locked in battle?" xe ventured.

"Until one of their earthly champions is victorious. It does seem that way. But I am doing what I can to aid our cause."

Powageh's gaze narrowed in suspicion. "Is that why you look like shit? What sorcery are you working, Balam? Are you spending time in the shadow world?"

"No. Something better." He had brought the thief's sack down to his office with him, and he pulled the book out and set it on the table. Powageh rotated it around and read the cover, eyes growing wide.

"Seven hells," xe murmured. "Where did you get this?"

"I had dinner a month ago with Lord Tuun, who mentioned hearing that it was in the royal library here. All this time, I'd thought it was locked away in the celestial tower."

"They confiscated everything related to dreamwalking after the Treaty was signed." Powageh ran a hand reverently over the cover. "I thought this burned three hundred years ago."

"I don't know how it came to be in Cuecola. I imagine there is a story there. But for my needs, Lord Tuun's gossip and an enterprising thief were enough." His mind flashed back to the spill of warm blood against his chest as he sank his knife into the thief's belly, the light leaving the man's eyes. The image stretched in his mind, the dead man's mouth moved, called his name. He shook off the vision. "It is considered only a relic these days. No one takes dreamwalking seriously in this modern era."

Powageh sat back, fingers steepled beneath chin. "Except you." They held each other's gaze for a long moment, until Powageh broke first, barking a laugh. "Hells, Balam, what is it like?"

"Terrifying," he admitted. Even now, the world around him seemed insubstantial, colors too bright and time elastic. It took all his concentration to remember to speak aloud, to remind himself that another human sat across from him. "Addictive."

"They say it brings madness."

Balam rubbed hands across his face. "I believe it. But I also believe it is the power that started a war and came close to ruling a continent. Tell me it was not worth the risk."

"I cannot."

Of course not. Powageh had the same wild ambition. There was a reason they had once conspired with Saaya to make a god.

"What have you seen there?" Powageh asked. "In the world of dreams."

"Many wonders." He shuddered. "Many horrors. I am not quite ready to share the details"—he held up his hand to delay Powageh's protests—"but I will in time. There is something else I need from you now."

"Name it."

"Golden Eagle travels to Hokaia as we speak. They will officially declare the Watchers fallen and Tova in need of leadership. Their goal will be twofold. To dissolve Tova's Speakers Council in favor of Golden Eagle rule and to rally the powers of the Meridian to support them against the menace of Carrion Crow and their embrace of the old gods. We will support them, of course. Both before the Sovran of Hokaia in their petition and with military force should they need it."

"Have the Seven Lords agreed to this? How much do they know?"

"Leave the Seven Lords to me. They will fall in line quickly enough once they realize Golden Eagle will not enforce the Watchers' taxation program."

"Greed first." Powageh sounded disgusted.

"Commerce. Be thankful they are so practical and can't see farther than their own treasuries."

"And the Teek? To truly dissolve the Treaty, you will need them to agree."

"The Teek have not been seen in any numbers in two hundred years, but a message will be sent informing them of the fall of the Watchers and of our gathering in Hokaia. I do not expect them to come, but protocol will be followed so that what we do cannot be challenged later."

"I will write the missives."

"And arrange the ship, if you would. I will convince the Seven Lords that only two of their number need accompany us. That should be enough to see to Cuecola's interests."

"If I may, Cousin . . ."

Balam gestured for Powageh to continue.

"It will take many days to reach Hokaia. To convince the Seven Lords, to arrange households, to secure the ship, perhaps more than one. Let us meet at the equinox upon the first day of spring."

Balam frowned. "A balancing of powers. I do not like it. Better for us to meet in Hokaia under the smoking star." Balam was not the former Watcher that his cousin was, but he knew the return of the smoking star was only a month away.

"The comet that marks the death of a ruler . . ."

"And the rise of a new order." He smiled. "I quite like it, and the meaning will not be lost on the others."

Powageh stood. "Then let me leave you and get to work. There is much to do if we plan to arrive in a month."

"There is one more thing."

Powageh paused, waited.

"How is your health?"

His cousin frowned. "It is fine. A return to wetter climes has much improved my lungs."

"Good." He folded his hands together. "Saaya's boy. He is a problem."

The former priest's face shuttered as Balam thought it might. But it had to be said.

"There is not room for him in our schemes," Balam said, not unkindly. "He was supposed to die."

"I don't see the harm—"

"But you do. You do. It may be that the chaos in Tova takes care of our problem and he is killed in battle with the Sun Priest, but if he somehow lives on . . ."

Powageh's shoulders slumped, chin dropping to chest.

"He is powerful," Balam said. "We saw to that. And now he is in the hands of Carrion Crow. If they figure out how best to use him, their opposition to Golden Eagle becomes a true problem. It is one thing to occupy a city already broken by the loss of their leadership. It is something else to wage a war against a city possibly united behind a god reborn."

Powageh was quiet for a long time. When xe looked up, a sad smile twisted xir lips. "He killed them, you know. Paadeh and Eedi."

Balam blinked. "You failed to mention it."

"I wasn't quite sure until I saw he possessed Eedi's staff. She would not have given that up."

"No." There was a touch of fondness in his tone. "She was quite serious about her weapons."

His cousin sighed. "It would be a lie for me to say part of me is not glad that he still lives. He became precious to me, a son I never had. But he is dangerous, I admit it. He has always been dangerous. Paadeh made him disciplined, Eedi and I made him a fighter and a sorcerer, and Saaya gave him a confidence in his purpose."

"And now he has a taste of slaughter."

"Let us hope he has not taken to it."

"The man I met also possessed a certain charming innocence, as religious fanatics often do, and some of the beauty and charisma of his mother. If he prevails over the Sun Priest, he may indeed be able to raise an army."

"And the draw of family, of Carrion Crow, will be strong. We kept all that from him. It seemed the right course of action then, but now . . ."

"Carrion Crow will use him to defend their city. We do have one recourse. I've been searching for him in the dream-world, but with no luck. If he exists on the human plane, he does not dream, or the crow god shields him. It shouldn't be possible, but then again, I am not a master of the magic yet."

"What will you do if you find him?"

"For now, only observe. Plant the idea of failure, perhaps. I only wanted you to know that whether it be through dreams or other means, he must go. And if I fail, you may be the only one able to get close enough to him to . . ." He trailed off delicately.

Now Powageh looked xir years. "What you ask of me . . ."

"I would not unless there are no other options left to us. But you should prepare yourself, prepare your gentle heart, Cousin."

"Don't mock me, Balam. I was once a Knife of the tower."

"I do not mock you. I only know what losing Saaya did to you."

"Losing her twice," xe corrected softly. "First to you and then to death. And yet you would ask this of me, to kill her only child?"

Balam was tired, and already the dream work beckoned him back. "Perhaps it will not come to that." He waved a hand. "Go. Send messages to Hokaia and Teek. I meet with the Seven Lords in the morning. We set our feet upon this path long ago, and we will see it through. No matter the cost."

CHAPTER 12

Don't sink your ship just to prove you can swim.

—Teek saying

Xiala listened as the Carrion Crow and Winged Serpent talked, idle words that were mostly gossip or worry about the weather and the price of corn to come in the wake of the never-ending twilight. Every so often, the mother and daughter, Haalan and Fress, would theorize on the nature of the Odo Sedoh and what the matron and her captain and the rest of the residents of the Great House must be doing just inside the walls in the distance. Xiala found their chatter more stressful than enlightening. Uncle Kuy would give her occasional looks of sympathy, but neither of them offered up any personal information about Serapio. They understood implicitly that what they knew was both valuable and dangerous, as secret information often was. And it was secret, wasn't it? Because the things Haalan and Fress said could have been said about anyone; there was nothing there of the Serapio she knew.

Iktan seemed mostly content to listen, only occasionally offering up commentary, and often xir words were sharp, the edge

125

of a well-honed knife, or amusing enough to send the group into fits of laughter. She was still wary of Iktan but decided xir earlier behavior was motivated by curiosity, not malice, and she couldn't blame xir for wondering about the woman who claimed to be Water Strider but clearly was not. She would be suspicious of herself, too, had their positions been reversed. The times made for strange confederates.

The hours wore on, and the natural course of their conversation diminished. With no word on the return of the leaders of the Odohaa or the matron and the Great House, the camp settled into sleep.

"I'll find more wood for the fire," Uncle Kuy offered over a yawn. He stood, scratching at his back, and then wandered off toward the center of camp.

"Should someone sit watch?" Iktan asked softly.

"What for?" Haalan sounded alarmed. "There's Shield nearby, and no one dare attack us here. I say we're in the safest place there is in the whole city."

"I think xe means for thieves and such, Mother," Fress said. "Although I think we are all among friends here."

"Common cause does not keep people honest, much as we'd like to believe so." Iktan did not look at Xiala, but she felt xir words were meant for her.

"I'll take first watch," Xiala offered, and not simply out of spite. There were many strangers here, and while the fear that seemed to coil around the rest of the city felt muted in Odo, it was replaced by another kind of energy. That of anticipation, of blood already spilled and a desire for more. She wasn't sure which she preferred.

"I'll take first watch, Xiala," Iktan said. "I prefer it. And I'll wake you for second. Agreed?"

She yawned, suddenly aware that she had not slept well

since before the Convergence, and conceded first watch to Iktan. Relieved of the need to stay awake, she huddled down in her cloak, hoping sleep might come. She was out immediately.

· · · · ·

Xiala dreamed of the bridge, but now, instead of the woman in the blue dress and the green-eyed man dying, it was Callo, her old first mate. He stared at her, mouth open. His eyes were hollow sockets, plucked clean by crows. *You should have used your Song to save us*, Callo cried, his voice the sound of crashing waves, *but instead you Sang us to our deaths!*

Her protest was lost in a gale wind. She stood hip-deep in blood, as rain whipped around her face and dead men floated past.

Callo morphed and became a Teek woman. Powerful. Regal. And even in her dream, Xiala felt the weight of her judgment. *Stupid girl!* the woman hissed. *You're not supposed to fall in love with them!*

She woke, shaken. The nightmare clung to her like seaweed around her ankles, threatening to drag her underwater. But it was only a nightmare, and she eventually shook it off. Soon the only voice in her head was the soft sound of Uncle Kuy's snores.

She sat up, bleary-eyed, and looked around. Kuy and the two women slept, but the place beside her where Iktan should have been was empty. Xe had promised to wake her for second watch, but now xe was gone.

It did occur to her that perhaps Iktan was the very thief xe had warned them about. What better way to steal from your new companions than to convince them to let you take first watch? She reminded herself she had nothing worth stealing except the cloak on her back and a small purse of cacao; she had given away her only real treasure to the guard. Which seemed to have been a mistake. It had been hours, and nothing had come of it.

The camp had grown since she had gone to sleep. What had been two hundred people when they arrived had easily doubled. For the first time, the yard was beginning to feel crowded. There were small camps of families and the faithful stretched across the entire yard from checkpoint to cliffside to Great House gates. If the crowd continued to grow, they would have to start turning people away. And then what? People denied access to their god might riot, especially considering the strange tension that already blanketed the city. When that happened, Xiala wanted to be very far away from this place. Teek did not fare well among angry hordes.

But that was a concern for the future. For now, most of the camp still slumbered peacefully in the perpetual blue-hued twilight, all but a handful of fires banked to a glowing orange. A few people sat talking quietly or playing patol.

Done with sleeping and feeling restless, she decided to seek out the guard again. If she had misread the woman, she could at least ask her to return her mermaid.

She picked her way through the camp, cowl up and head down. The path they had taken when they had first arrived was now crowded with sleeping bodies, and it took her twice as long to make her way back to the gate. Despite the fact that it was ostensibly the middle of the night, people were still arriving. She approached the nearest guard, an older man slumped sleepily on a bench, his back against the wall and his feet up.

"Pardon." Xiala rallied her best Tovan accent. "I'm looking for a particular guard. A woman, about my height. Black hair tied back, thick eyebrows, a scar on her chin. She was working the gate earlier."

"You mean Uuna. She went off duty about an hour ago. Why?"

"We're old friends," she lied.

"Sorry. I'll tell her you came looking. What's your name?"

"I'll just try again later." She backed away with a bow.

"You can look for her over near the Great House gates. You might still catch her."

Xiala mouthed words of gratitude and slipped away. She had expected some animosity, suspicion at the least, but the man had been surprisingly helpful. Maybe once you made it past the checkpoint, you weren't considered a threat. Maybe everyone here really was united in common cause. She hadn't truly considered that Serapio's coming could have a wider impact, could be something positive for these people. She'd only thought of it in terms of what she wanted and how it affected her. She had that same feeling that she'd had when she first saw Odo and knew in her heart that this was where Serapio belonged: doubt.

She was within sight of the Great House gates before she knew it. She could see the massive doors of charred wood carved with the crowsign, where a handful of guards stood, looking ominous and much more intimidating than their checkpoint fellows. But farther down the curving wall, she spied a small door the same ash-gray as the wall itself. She wouldn't have noticed it at all if a familiar figure hadn't been slipping out the door and immediately caught her eye.

It was Iktan, and this was the last place she'd expected to see xir. She caught a glimpse of a guard's face before the door closed, and then Iktan was moving back through the camp, as if xe had not just been inside the Great House doing who knew what.

Iktan had given no sign that xe knew anyone in the inner

circles of the Great House, and certainly not that xe could ask favors of a guard. If she had known, she could have gone directly to xir.

"Hey!" she called.

She thought she saw Iktan look in her direction, but instead of acknowledging her, xe ducked xir head, sped up, and disappeared into the crowd.

"United in common cause," she growled, "I think not." She laughed at herself. She had been so concerned that Iktan might think she was a spy that she did not see the true spy right under her nose. But what kind of spy conspired with someone inside the Great House and then had to be sneaked out? She had a nose for deceit, and she sensed it now. She needed to know what Iktan was hiding.

She hurried after xir, her chase leading her to the north end of camp, past Uncle Kuy and the sleeping mother and daughter and toward the latrines. Interesting. Clearly, Iktan wasn't returning to play pilgrim at their common fire. So where was xe going?

"Ho! You, there. In the blue!" She turned to see two Carrion Crow guards coming her way in a hurry. Had Iktan told them she was a fake? Had xe reported her as a foreigner, despite earlier assurances that xe would not?

Xiala had a well-earned distrust of authority and a strong desire not to spend any more time in a jail cell. It was enough to keep her moving in the direction she thought Iktan had gone and avoid the guards who had called out for her. She tried to lose herself in the crowd once she came to the latrines, weaving between stalls and out the back, skirting the edge of the cliff. She came around the far end of the ditch just in time to catch a glimpse of Iktan heading down a staircase.

Stairs? Where could they lead but over the side to the river below? Did she dare follow there? Maybe it would be better to face the guards. She had no proof they wished her ill. She laughed at herself. When had things ever gone well when someone was shouting for her and trying to run her down? Following Iktan was the only option that felt like freedom.

The staircase did run down the side of the cliff face to the river. The steps were wood and looked none too sturdy. Wind buffeted her, blowing her hood back, and she could see below her the small caps of the Tovasheh peak and fall. She took a deep breath, said a prayer to her Mother, and stepped out onto the first landing. The wood creaked beneath her weight, but she didn't let herself stop to think about it. Twelve steps down to the next landing, and then down the switchback, and again.

She caught a glimpse of Iktan's cloak and sped her descent. She called her Song to her throat, just a hum. But what used to be a comfort now made her anxious. What if she killed someone again? Someone innocent, as she had at the Convergence, because she couldn't control it? She let her power recede and pushed herself to catch up, but she was slow, her legs still aching from being on land too long, and Iktan was very fast.

She took the next flight, and the next, pausing once to look up and see if anyone followed. No one above, but there was someone below in the river. A boat. One of the smaller river crafts Aishe had called a skimmer, meant for traveling back and forth across the Tovasheh between districts. Two figures manned the boat, pulling it up next to no more than a pile of planks lashed together to form a makeshift floating pier at the bottom of the staircase.

That boat was for Iktan, she knew it. She also knew that if she didn't catch xir now, she would never see xir again. She willed her legs to move, less concerned with stealth than with speed. She took the corner, fingers only grazing the rail, and was practically airborne when arms grabbed her and slammed her against the rocky cliffside.

Rock scraped the back of her head, and she gasped for air. The sharp point of a knife pricked her chin, and a familiar songlike voice whispered, "Careful, Xiala of the Teek. Your next words determine if you live or die."

She froze, eyes wide and breath stuttering.

"Following me was incredibly foolish," Iktan whispered, mouth against her ear. "Tell me why you did it."

"I saw you with the Shield." She panted, eyes on the knife at her neck. "I need to know what you told them."

"Why?"

It was a simple question, and she could have said half a dozen things that might satisfy Iktan and save her life, but all she could think of in the moment was one: "Because I can't lose him again."

Seconds ticked by, the knife so close the edge of the blade kissed the hollow of her thoat. Her knees ached, and she couldn't get enough breath into her lungs. It was too much like what had happened to her on the ship when Baat had almost killed her, that wound barely healed a fraction lower on her neck. Panic was creeping up her gut, lodging in her gullet. She couldn't stay like this much longer.

"You mean the Odo Sedoh."

"I mean Serapio!" she hissed, near tears.

A shout above them, and Iktan growled out a curse. "It seems you led the Shield to us."

The Shield? But weren't they Iktan's friends?

"I imagine I have approximately twenty seconds before the people in that boat leave, with or without me. You can either stay here and explain to the Shield why you, clearly a lying foreigner, were down here with me, who is very much a spy and, honestly, worse. Or you can climb onto that boat with me and escape. On the condition that you tell me who you are and what you know about the Odo Sedoh."

"Fuck off," she spat through gritted teeth as the first tear leaked down her cheek.

Iktan's smile was a murderous thing. "I will share a secret with you, Xiala, because I find you intriguing, if a little stupid. Carrion Crow are not your friends. They likely aren't *his* friends, either. Whatever plans they have for him, they do not include you. So pick, Teek. Come with me and have a chance, or stay and face whatever mercy Carrion Crow might give you."

Iktan released her and stepped away. She collapsed, hands on her knees and back bent, and when she looked up, xe was gone.

Mother waters, how had she ended up on the wrong side of this? Reason told her Iktan was right and that whatever words she might speak in her defense to Carrion Crow would fall on ears already decided. If fact, she had probably sealed her fate when she naively told the guard Uuna of her identity. She had no doubt she would end up in a dank cell somewhere deep in their Great House to rot until they got around to remembering she was there. Serapio would likely be married and crowned the king of crows or whatever he was by then. If she went with Iktan, it would be a setback but nothing as dire as jail. She could not, *would* not, go to jail again. The thought made her insides seize with dread.

But to walk away from Serapio when he was alone with those vipers, when he might need her most? She'd walked away before. Could she do it again and still look at herself without shame?

"I won't leave you, Ser," she whispered. "I promise it. I'll come back. Just hold on." *And seven hells, don't marry anyone.*

A shout to halt from above. She'd been spotted. She had to decide now.

She followed Iktan, taking the steps two at a time. She hit the landing and ran, not looking back. Iktan was already aboard, the boat pulling away. She jumped the distance, not needing any aid to board a ship.

"There." One of the sailors pointed her toward a small seat next to Iktan, well out of the way of the short rectangular sails they worked to cross the waters. She dropped to the seat, heart pounding. Odo faded behind them, the guards who had chased her left behind.

"Wise choice. Not so stupid after all."

"Now tell me—"

Xe pressed a finger to her mouth and rolled eyes toward the two sailors meaningfully. "Quiet, now, until we're in friendlier waters. We'll have plenty of time to chat on the way to Hokaia."

CHAPTER 13

City of Tova (District of Odo)

Year 1 of the Crow

A man divided against himself is profound only in his misery.

—*Exhortations for a Happy Life*

Okoa stood on the Great House terrace that overlooked the district of Odo and watched the masses come. The yard had been empty when he and the Odo Sedoh had flown back to Tova earlier in the day, but people had begun to trickle in soon afterward, no doubt on the word of their return spreading across the city. More followed with the Odohaa when they came to see for themselves. But it had been hours since Maaka, Feyou, and the others had departed, and still the masses grew. Now they stretched from the walls to the far cliffs that overlooked the Tovasheh, their campfires glowing in the unnatural twilight, their prayers a soft murmuring on the winds that buffeted the Great House.

Are they our salvation? Okoa wondered. *Or our ruin?*

Soft footsteps behind him had him glancing over his shoulder. Esa had changed out of her formal dress and was wearing a simple black robe that covered her sandaled feet and tied at the waist. Her dark hair fell loose down her back, and her face was scrubbed clean. He turned away.

"You look like Mother," he said, gaze focused across the masses below them.

"How many do you think they are?" she asked softly, coming to stand beside him.

"Five hundred. Maybe more."

"Not all Carrion Crow."

"No. Other clans, too. The Shield have reported Winged Serpent and Water Strider among them. And some of the clanless from the smaller towns downriver and even some foreigners who were here for the solstice. Most have fled the unnatural sun, but enough remain."

Esa shivered, the wind catching her hair and tangling it around her face. "What do they want?"

"To see a god?" he ventured. "To witness a miracle?"

She nodded and pulled her robe tighter. "Where's your feathered cloak?"

"I let him keep it. He offered to return it, but . . ."

He could not read the look on his sister's face, but he guessed it to be dismay. Irritation tightened his mouth. Who was she to judge him after what she had done?

"What were you thinking?" he finally asked, voice harsh with frustration. "A cell, Esa?"

"He is going to destroy us," she said softly.

"You don't know that." But he felt it, too. Perhaps he had felt it from the moment they had fought in the monastery. And after what had happened with Maaka, the inevitability of it felt like snow high on the mountain, waiting to become the avalanche.

"Where is he now?" she asked.

"He wanted to stay in that damned cell with the sky door. I left a Shield at his door should he need anything. It was hard enough to convince Maaka not to whisk him away to Odohaa headquarters after your stunt, so I let him stay. Why he chose to I have no idea."

"To make a point."

"Of our poor hospitality?"

"Worse than that. He's planning something."

"Can you blame him? We didn't exactly welcome him with open arms."

"We can't lose him to the Odohaa. That would be a disaster."

"Perhaps you should have thought of that before locking him in a cell."

"Do you think Maaka will go to the aunties? You saw how they reacted today. He could bend their ear. And if word gets out to the common population and spreads through the district, it could be fatal to our cause."

"And what is our cause, Sister? I thought it was saving Carrion Crow, but I feel I've lost the thread of our purpose somewhere along the way, perhaps when you threw the Odo Sedoh in jail."

She at least had the sense to look chagrined. "I thought perhaps if he understood that he is not wanted here, then he would leave. It was . . ." She exhaled. "It was a game, Okoa. He could have escaped that cell whenever he wanted. He knew it. I knew it."

"The Odohaa did not see it that way."

"I had not meant for them to see it at all."

"Why did you think you could play games with him?"

"The Sky Made scions would understand—"

"He is not a scion!"

She crossed her arms and turned her back to him. "Do not scold me like a child. I am still your matron."

Duty, he reminded himself. *You are on the same side.* "My apologies," he said, and meant it.

Her shoulders softened. "He understands better than you think." Her voice was subdued. "Tell me, whose idea was it to bring the Odohaa to his cell?"

"It was a coincidence. We were standing together when his crows came to fetch us."

"A coincidence?" she scoffed. "You really believe that?"

"It doesn't matter." He didn't see the point of arguing about what had already passed. "We will find our way through."

There was a stone railing that ran the length of the terrace, and she sat against it, hands tucked in the sleeves of her robe. "I wish Mother were here. Don't you miss her?"

Her words pricked at his heart. He realized he wished for her, too. Things would have gone differently if she were still alive. She would have known how to greet the Odo Sedoh, how to manage Maaka. But she was gone, taken from them, and now they were left to muddle through on their own.

"Did she ever write you letters?"

Her brow furrowed. "Letters?"

"Yes, something personal. Perhaps something before she died."

"Why would she write me a letter when she saw me every day? If she wanted to say something to me, she could simply say it."

"But what if it was a secret?"

"Did she write you a letter, Okoa? Is that why you've been acting strange since you returned?"

Esa might have been shallow, but she was not a fool. He nodded once, wary, watching her for a reaction. She pushed the hair from her face and took a step toward him.

"What did she say?" Her voice was breathy, unsteady.

"How, again, did you tell me she died?"

She pressed a hand to her mouth. "Skies, Okoa, did she tell you why she jumped?"

"I . . ." He faltered. He had expected her to say something different. Evade his question or feign ignorance, but tears had gathered in her eyes, and she looked at him expectantly. Had he misjudged her? Shame stuck like a pebble in his throat. "It was not a suicide note," he admitted.

She inhaled sharply, fluttering her hand before her face as if to rid herself of some emotion. "I miss her." Tears wetted her cheeks. "But it would have been worse if she was here."

Okoa frowned. "What do you mean?"

"She was too gentle with the Odohaa." She gestured to the hundreds below. "The proof is there. And Maaka at our door demanding, *demanding*, to see the Odo Sedoh." Some of her grief shifted to outrage.

"You just said you wished she was here."

"I do, in a selfish way. As her daughter. But she had a soft spot for Maaka and his cultists, and now they have become overbold."

"I think you do not give her enough credit."

"You weren't here. You don't know." That cut him to the core, but she continued, as if unaware. "She was too sympathetic to their cause, and it put us at odds with the Sky Made and the Watchers. And now that the Odo Sedoh is here and has fulfilled our worst nightmare, her leniency has left him with an army of believers to command, more faithful to him than to the matron, or the Shield, or any other power in Tova. Don't deny it."

How could he, after what Maaka had said? But he did not tell her that.

"We could join them," he said quietly.

She drew back as if he had hit her.

"An alliance," he said quickly. "You are too smart not to see the benefit in it, Esa."

She shivered, and he stood to offer her his cloak, but she waved it away. It was not the cold that made her tremble.

He said, "If we bind him to us, Carrion Crow never need bow to the other clans again, We've been a long time under their boot and at their mercy. We've had little to be proud of, little to celebrate, the Night of Knives always heavy on our backs. We've allowed the weight of it to bend us. I know that better than anyone."

Her look was piercing. "You are no more of a believer than I am."

Was he not? He was no longer so sure. He did know he was desperately trying to find a way to bring his sister, his people, and his god together, but he felt like he was searching for handholds on the side of a cliff, knowing one wrong move would send him plummeting to the earth below.

"What did you think when he approached you in the great room today?" he asked.

Her laugh was short and sharp. "That I must survive him."

"He is not so terrible. There is a side to him . . ."

"He cut down the Watchers like stalks in the field. Do you think he would hesitate to do the same to you, to us, if he thought he must? It is the curse of the fanatics who only answer to their god. We are simply a means to an end to him."

"That's not true. At the rookery, he—"

"Did you know that I spent this evening in the library looking for every text I could find on the old gods who had manifested as humans or had human vessels?"

Tread carefully, he thought. "I thought you didn't believe."

"A precaution."

"And what did you find?"

"There was a story of a woman in Cuecola who claimed to possess the appetites of the jaguar god and had eaten her husband before she was killed by the neighbors in a house fire. And another account of a dreamwalker during the War of the

Spear who claimed to have killed a god in her dreams, but the encounter had left her brain scrambled, and she was locked away, screaming about visions and shadows."

"Horror stories."

"Yes," she acknowledged, "but it does suggest that a god in human form can be killed and that they do possess weaknesses."

He thought of Serapio's confusion when he had awoken in the cave at the rookery. He had been vulnerable then. "And there is his wound that won't heal." He felt traitorous for mentioning it, but it was nothing she likely had not already learned on her own.

"That is a start." She gave him an encouraging look. "I also have people looking into his past. He had to come from somewhere, and I want to know who his people are. If he has attachments."

"I believe he was raised in Obregi." He told himself these were simple facts, not confidences betrayed.

"Then I will send agents to Obregi. Discreetly," she added, to stave off his look of disapproval.

"I don't know what that accomplishes."

"Yes, you do, Captain. Surely the war college taught you to learn everything about your enemy before you go to battle."

"I didn't realize he was our enemy."

She snorted. "Don't be naive, Brother."

Everyone is my enemy. Serapio's words at the monastery came back to him. Okoa had objected fiercely at the time, but here he was, proving him right.

"All I am saying is let us try to tame him first through alliance, and if that fails, we can consider pursuing your more . . . aggressive tactics. But betrayal and murder cannot be our first route, Esa."

"You seek to cage the uncageable. To subdue the storm."

"Where you seek to take up your knife against the lightning."

"What choice do we have? It is that or be consumed." Her laugh was short. "He told me that shadow consumes, and what is he but living shadow? God or not, I can tell it is his nature to consume, and Carrion Crow will not survive him. I say you kill him now while we have the chance, or one day, you will look up, Okoa, and find it is too late."

Voices rose up to them from the camp below. A song, low and mournful. Okoa recognized it as one of the lamentations from the Night of Knives. A prayer of loss, a cry to their god for justice. Okoa tried to convince himself that the Odo Sedoh had indeed brought Carrion Crow their longed-for justice, but surely justice did not look like what he had seen on Sun Rock. He remembered Maaka's words from earlier: *We are a people with hope once again, and the Odo Sedoh has brought us that. Not you. Not your matron.*

And Okoa doubted.

Everything.

"Lord Okoa?"

They both looked up as one of the Shield, a man named Ituya, stood in the doorway. Ituya was one of Chaiya's recruits, only a few years older than Okoa and eager to serve. He had been one of the guards in the room when he had returned with the Odo Sedoh who had not fallen to his knees.

"What is it?"

"There is a woman in the camp asking to see the Odo Sedoh."

Okoa laughed dryly. "Gods, man. There are five hundred people out there who want to see the Odo Sedoh."

"Her name is Xiala, and she called him by the name Serapio. She said she was the captain of the boat that brought him here. She said he would know her. That she knows him, and he would know it was her." He opened his hand, holding his palm out. On it sat a delicate wood carving of a mermaid. "She said to show him this."

The siblings exchanged a look, words said between them without speaking.

Okoa took the carving and slipped it into his pocket. "Find this Xiala. Immediately. Use whatever Shield you need. I'm right behind you. Go!"

"I'm coming, too," Esa said.

"You can't." He crossed the terrace in a dozen long strides. "You're the matron, and I need to know you are safe."

"Okoa!" She followed him into the hall, warning in her voice. "Do not grow soft," she hissed. "She is a gift fallen into our laps. You know why we need her. Let me help."

"I have the Shield," he tossed over his shoulder, halfway to the stairs.

"And you have me." A figure materialized from the shadowy staircase just above him.

Okoa's heart thumped. Where had he come from? Skies, how long had he been there, and more important, what had he heard?

Serapio was dressed in black. Someone had replaced his tattered pants with a long black skirt that billowed around him as he walked, and he wore the padded armor of the Shield over a long-sleeved shirt. The crow-feather cloak graced his shoulders, and he clutched his bone staff in his hand. Okoa suspected one of the aunts had chosen his regalia, and she had chosen it for impact, as it made a formidable impression.

"If Xiala is here, I must find her."

Okoa swallowed down his spike of fear. "Come with me." He pointed at Esa. "Watch from the terrace. It's not safe for you in the crowd."

He didn't wait to see if she would comply, just hurried down the stairs, the dark god at his side.

They went down four flights at a run. The Odo Sedoh kept pace, his hand lightly dragging along the wall as a guide. Okoa pushed through the door into the inner courtyard. It was self-contained, a killing ground for those who breached the outer gate before they could penetrate the Great House itself. It ran like a river between the inner wall of the house and the outer wall, encircling the entire structure. Ituya had already gathered a handful of Shield.

"They lost sight of her, my lord," Ituya said. "She was last seen on the far northern side of the camp wearing Water Strider blue. They called for her, but she ran. They didn't see her face well, so she might be hard to identify."

"Hair the color of plums." They all turned to Serapio. "And Teek eyes, like a rainbow after a spring storm."

Okoa's breath hitched in surprise, but he recovered quickly. "You heard him." He nodded to the Shield. "The woman we search for is Teek, with plum-colored hair and Teek eyes. Find her, but don't hurt her. Tell her . . ." He hesitated. "Tell her the Odo Sedoh is looking for her, too."

A few men glanced furtively at the Odo Sedoh, but thankfully no one seemed overcome by religious fervor at the sight of him. Okoa went to clap a hand against Serapio's shoulder but stopped himself. He had just been entertaining the possibility of killing the man if he had to. He could not stomach being that much of a hypocrite. He bit his lip, his self-doubt a jagged blade in his heart.

If the man next to him sensed his internal struggle, he did not let it show. He slid by Okoa, pushed open the outer doors, and stepped into the camp beyond.

It wasn't until they were both through the gates, the sea of people before them, that Okoa saw the problem. From the terrace, he had guessed there were five hundred people gathered in a yard, but he hadn't accounted for how difficult it would be to identify any single individual in the twilight. In addition, many in the camp were sleeping, bodies wrapped in blankets around low fires. The ones who were awake were drawn to the commotion of armed men coming through the gate, and now the Shield were moving among them, peering into startled faces and rousing slumbering figures. He cursed under his breath. He should have given a different order, told the Shield to be more subtle. Soon the whole camp would be awake.

"Perhaps you should stay near me," Okoa whispered to the Odo Sedoh. "They do not know who you are yet, but it is evident that you are not the Shield." He looked at Serapio, the crow mantle on his shoulder, his tousled hair and regal bearing and that sense of something otherworldly about him that could not be disguised. No, the crowd would know exactly who he was. How could they not?

He put his body between the Odo Sedoh and the crowd.

"I don't think it's a good idea for you to come. It may cause chaos, and if it does, there are simply not enough Shield to contain it."

He knew the man was blind, but his eyes locked on Okoa all the same.

"This is Xiala," he said plainly, as if the woman's name was all Okoa need know to understand. "You cannot stop me, Captain. No matter what you try."

Serapio pressed past him, moving purposefully into the darkness. Okoa watched him go, watched the heads that turned to mark his passing, and heard the muffled excitement that rose in his wake. And then he was jogging to catch up.

CHAPTER 14

No truth can stay hidden forever.

—*Exhortations for a Happy Life*

Common sense should have kept Naranpa in her room waiting for Denaochi to come for her, but Naranpa had never been much for doing what was common. *Or sensible*, she told herself. Because what she had in mind certainly wasn't. She knew she should be preparing to meet the bosses of the Maw, but Denaochi had not shared the details of their upcoming gathering, nor had he told her anything more about what would be expected of her. Only that he needed her to win their support, which would be his support, so that when they moved to persuade the Sky Made to side with them, they would already have the resources and loyalty of the Maw at their backs.

She had considered simply going to Ieyoue, the matron of Water Strider who had helped her after the riot on Sun Rock, and explaining the treachery of Golden Eagle and their collusion with certain priests in the tower to remove her, but what good would it do now? Perhaps Water Strider's backing would make a difference if she had a tower to reclaim, but she was building support from nothing but a mandate, and a tarnished one at that. Faith in the teachings of the Watchers and an adherence to a three-hundred-year-old treaty seemed fragile against the return of a god. She needed more. She needed power of her own, both before the bosses of the Maw and when she finally called upon the Sky Made clans. And the only possibility that came close to that was what she had seen in Zataya's mirror.

She also thought about returning to Zataya and confessing her strange visions, but the witch's knowledge seemed limited to Dry Earth magic—potions and herbs—and she herself admitted to only dabbling in southern sorcery. Naranpa was starting to think that bringing her back from the brink of death had less to do with blood and god bones and more to do with whatever power resided inside her and revealed itself as a golden glowing heat. And that made her think it must have to do with the sun god herself. The firebird in her vision, the history of the Sun Priests. They all lived within her somehow. If she could discover how and what it meant, she was sure she would have the power she needed to convince the bosses and the clans to follow her, and ultimately, to confront the Crow God Reborn. And the only place to find that knowledge was the celestial tower.

She was afraid to go back. Part of her feared what she would find there, but most of her feared what she would not. No chattering dedicants, no priests arguing about how best to interpret the stars, no Iktan. No life. She cursed herself for a fool to care at all about these people who had betrayed her, but it had been her every day for twenty years, the family she had known best. She did not doubt it would be haunted by ghosts, and truths she did not want to face would lurk in its twisting staircases and hallowed halls. But as much as the past might hurt, it would not kill her, not like the future.

Leaving the Lupine was simple. Perhaps Denaochi had not anticipated that she might want to leave, for where was there for her to go? Or perhaps it was another test of her ambition. But the guard at the door allowed her to pass without as much as an inquiry. She did not question it, just nodded her thanks, pulled up the hood of the cloak Baaya had given her, and hurried out the rooftop door and into the street.

She retraced the path that had brought her back to the Maw and her brother only weeks ago, but this time, the roads were mostly deserted. The sun still burned black on the horizon, and few were willing to venture out. A few more lights shone muffled from windows than they had two days ago, but the revelry for which the Maw was famous was nowhere to be found. No music, no laughter, no cooking fires and drunken revelry. No colorful clothes, no dancing, no joy. Before she had felt a mixture of outrage and jealousy upon returning to her childhood district, but now she only felt sorrow and a sense of urgency. She did not linger as she made her way through the streets and was glad to reach the gondola for the crossing to Titidi.

The district of Water Strider was much the same, shuttered and hushed, as if holding its breath in anticipation of what might befall the city next. She made quick work of crossing and found herself at the border to Tsay within the hour. She had worried about whether she would be able to enter the home of Golden Eagle, but the dozen guards at the border took one look at her Maw robes and waved her through. Servants moved more easily than priests, she reminded herself, and anyone from the Maw was presumed to be a servant or a thief, and what self-respecting thief looked like her? For once, she was glad for her unassuming appearance and the prejudices of the elite.

She reached the bridge to Otsa and found herself entirely alone. The foot traffic that had been sparse through the districts evaporated altogether here, as if the citizenry did not want to get too close to the place where death had come for so many. She could see the celestial tower now. Normally, a signal fire burned upon its ramparts, but now there was nothing. It looked not only empty but as if it had been abandoned for centuries. It had not begun to crumble yet, but the living heart of it had been extinguished. It had been a place of great power once, but, more important to Naranpa, it had been a beacon of enlightenment, a house of learning. The residents had been bound in common and higher purpose . . . until they had not. And for that she found herself already weeping before her feet even touched the Otsa earth.

· · · · ·

The heavy wooden doors of the tower had been flung open and left that way. She pressed a hand to the carving at the entrance, the symbol of the Tovan sun that greeted all who entered. Would it ever shine here again, or would the city wither in darkness? *That question is for you to answer, Naranpa*, she thought to herself. *Is that not the very reason you are here?*

She passed through and paused. Everything looked in place. The benches just inside the entrance, the wide stone stairs that circled the perimeter and led to the half dozen levels above. Nothing was overturned, nothing broken or looted. Just empty, as if everyone had left in an orderly fashion and all at once.

There were still thick globs of resin in the lantern basins, and she lit one and brought it with her. Her steps echoed through the hall like the solemn toll of a bell announcing her approach. But there was no one here to hear it or to welcome her, and she was not sure if that made it better or a hundred times more difficult.

She reached the library level. Always there had been a ta dissa dedicant at the desk to greet those seeking knowledge in the great archives of the tower. The collection here, the scrolls and bound books and tablets, had no equal in all the Meridian. The other great cities, Cuecola and Hokaia, had libraries, but most of the books in Hokaia had been claimed by the Watchers and taken from the palace, their knowledge considered too dangerous for the spearmaidens to possess. The royal library in Cuecola had suffered a fire a century earlier, many precious works in their collection lost. That left Tova and the celestial tower as the seat of ancient knowledge in the world. What would become of it now?

I'll save it, she vowed. *I will save this library, if not for the Watchers, then for future generations, for scholars to come, in whatever form they might arrive.* It was a bold promise and entirely beyond what one woman could do. *But I am not just a woman*, she reminded herself. *I am the last Sun Priest.*

She moved deeper into the library, past the more commonly consulted volumes and the sky charts rolled into scrolls. She wove her way through curving stacks until she found Haisan's old desk. He was dead, killed by the Crow God Reborn, as were all the Watchers who had gone to Sun Rock that day, but for a moment, she expected the old man to come padding around the corner, grumbling about some new policy she wished to institute. She wondered how much he had known about Abah and Eche's conspiracy with Golden Eagle and if he had approved. Or if the old scholar had just gotten caught up in the net, blithely unaware of the hook through her throat. She supposed it didn't matter now, but she liked to think he had not known. It eased the ache in her heart.

She dug through the top drawer of the dead priest's desk until she found a key. She took it and walked down another hallway. This one ended in a door marked with the same Tovan sun that had decorated the entrance of the tower. The key slid into the lock, and she turned it. Her heart sped up in anticipation. In all her years at the tower, she had never been allowed in this room. This space was sacred to the Order of the Historical Society, so much so that even the Sun Priest, or at least Naranpa in her diminished status as Sun Priest, was forbidden.

The room was round. Along its walls ran bookshelves populated with ancient texts. In the center stood a waist-high wooden table. On the table was a single document, written on bark paper and bound in book form. It was the original Treaty of Hokaia, the most sacred document on the continent. Naranpa approached it with reverence, her hands suddenly trembling. She knew what was in it; it was one of the first things all dedicants had to learn before they were divided into their respective orders. But she had never seen it, had only heard secondhand what it contained, and for a moment, she doubted. What if she had been lied to? What if they all had been lied to? What if the Order of the Historical Society had kept things from the other orders, concocted stories that favored themselves or distorted their sacred mandate? What if it was all a fabrication?

She flushed, feeling foolish. She sounded like Denaochi, paranoid and seeing trickery at every turn. The Watchers were not built upon a falsehood. And yet, as she looked upon the leather cover of the book embossed with the four seals of the great powers that fought in the war—the sun of Tova, the jaguar prince of Cuecola, the mermaid tail of the Teek, and the spear fortress of Hokaia—dread made her stomach clench.

She opened the book. It was divided into four sections, each section's edges stained with a different dye. The first part of the manuscript was a series of recitations laying out the terms of the Treaty. It was dry and rote, and Naranpa recognized the words that established borders and responsibilities and proscriptions against a formal military and the like. The second part of the book was short but devastating and called for the execution of dreamwalkers, the banishment of all spearmaidens who had supported the insurrection, and the prohibition of magic and worship of the old gods in all the realms of the Meridian. There was also a sentence barring travel to the Graveyard of the Gods and a penalty of death for any who broke the edict. She thought of Zataya and her strange powders and wondered, again, if they were fakes.

The next section of the book set out the parameters for the establishment of the war college at Hokaia, as no longer a school to train the elite spearmaidens but a place open to all within the Meridian, so one culture could not master war the way the spearmaidens had and use their knowledge against the others. And it demanded that ways of peace be taught, too. Alternatives to slaughter and violence with an emphasis on diplomacy and compromise. She skimmed through these pages, too.

But she slowed to read the last section, titled "On the Establishment of the Watchers." It was further divided into four sections that explained the overall responsibilities of the Watchers, the individual responsibilities of each order, and the methods of replenishing their number. But the part she was most interested in was the section on the rites of investiture.

She had been thinking about it ever since she'd had the vision of the firebird losing her scales in battle, and on the heels of that, the woman who had brought back the sacks of golden scales to be forged into something worth dying for, and the spill of human blood mixed into the mask mold. The rest of the visions fit the pattern, too, right up to the one of the man on top of a tower in the rain, mask in hand.

She wasn't sure of the mechanics of it all, but she was convinced there was something more than theater in the wearing of the Sun Priest's mask. She had always loved the mask, felt a strange connection to it, even though it had not been in her possession long. She had thought herself simply attached to a symbol of her station, but now she wondered. If the vision had been true, and the mask was not forged gold but instead was wrought from the very essence of the god, what did that mean? And if the teeth and sweat of a god were used in southern sorcery to attempt to resurrect the dead, what might be done with a god's golden scales? And what did it mean to wear it? Might wearing the mask infuse the wearer with power? She wasn't sure, but she hoped to find the answers in the book.

She read it through carefully, and while it confirmed her suspicions about the origin of the mask, it said nothing about it granting the wearer any powers. She turned to the pages describing the other priests' masks, hoping to find something there, but there was even less written for those, only that the priests were meant to be anonymous to guard against any one individual rising in popularity. The priesthood was meant to be a selfless vocation and not one that allowed any single priest to develop leadership based on the strength of personality. It was something that had become less important in her time, but the signers of the Treaty had railed against individual charismatic leaders at length, no doubt a reaction to the spearmaiden who had started the war.

Tired, and disappointed that she had come so far and found so little, she read through the final page. She skimmed it so quickly and the ritual seemed so mundane that she almost missed it.

She had experienced the ritual herself, and yet she had not recognized it for what it was. The blood-marred scales that made the mask, the invocation of the sun god, the will of the raised dedicant, and the declaration of desire. It was all there, plainly written.

Anyone who knew what to look for would have seen it immediately. In fact, she had no doubt that those who established the Watchers three hundred years ago knew exactly what they were doing. But she had never thought to see it, because she had been told a thousand times that the Watchers did not practice magic. That they did not worship the old gods. That there was nothing mystical in their rites, only reason and order.

And they had been sorcerers all along.

• • • • •

She hurried from the ta dissa's sacred room to a more familiar section of the library. On these shelves were the day-to-day references of the Sun Priest, the oft-consulted *Manual*, and other documents. She flipped through them, an unnamed urgency pushing her forward, but there was nothing about the Sun Priest's powers. Nothing about magic. Skies, to even say "Sun Priest" and "magic" in the same sentence felt blasphemous enough to rot her tongue.

Exhilaration buoyed her on to the next document, and she flipped through the pages looking for any information that would help her understand the heat in her chest and the change in her eyes. Her eyes! With a sudden jolt, she remembered Kiutue's eyes. They had been flecked with gold as well. Almost a deep amber by the time he reached his end. Why hadn't she thought of it? How had she not put the puzzle pieces together?

All the elements right in front of her, but she had been taught not to see them.

She slammed the last book closed. Nothing. There was one more place to look.

She ran up the stairs to her old rooms. She was at the door and pushing it open, caught up in the giddy joy of discovery, before it truly hit her. There was her old bed, and there her desk, and there her washbasin . . . and there the stand where the Sun Priest's mask should have been. It was gone. Someone had taken it. It took her brain a moment to realize that Eche must have been wearing it when he was killed on Sun Rock. Had it been lost, or had her vision of the man in black holding it been the past and not the future after all, a vision of the Crow God Reborn claiming it for himself? She didn't know, and she could not answer the question now. She had other mysteries to solve.

She had always kept a small library here of her personal books, things like Kiutue's journal and her own. She hoped perhaps there was insight there in her old mentor's words, something she had overlooked in her previous ignorance. But as she opened the drawer in the bottom of her desk to retrieve the journal, she realized her mistake. These were not her old rooms—they were Eche's old rooms. And in the one day he had been Sun Priest, he had managed to dispose of anything here that might have been hers.

She dropped heavily to the bed, defeated. If there was nothing here to tell her of her potential powers, and there was no one alive of the Watchers to consult, then she was on her own. She might have powers within her, gifts from the sun god passed to her through investiture, but if she didn't know how to use them, what use were they? And what chance did she have against the Crow God Reborn if she couldn't wield anything more formidable than a glowing hand?

Somewhere a voice cried out. She lifted her head, listening, unsure if she had imagined the sound. No, there it was again, faint but real. Her pulsed ticked up. Someone else was here.

She made her way to the door, listening. It was coming from above, but the only thing above her was the open-air observatory where the Conclave met. Another sound, this time a thump, like a heartbeat awoken, and she took the stairs, one by one.

CHAPTER 15

CITY OF TOVA (DISTRICT OF ODO)
YEAR 1 OF THE CROW

No miracle is beyond the Odo Sedoh!
He shall heal all wounds
And bind all that is broken.
He shall cast down our enemies
And lead us out of despair.

—Prayer to the Odo Sedoh,
recorded at a meeting of the Odohaa

Serapio swept through the crowd, leaving Okoa behind. He whistled for his crows, asking one to come and help him see, but he dared not wait for a reply. Every moment he waited was a moment away from Xiala.

He could see enough to make out the barest of shapes and shadows, enough to realize there were people everywhere. Where had they all come from? There were hundreds. It gave him pause. The only time he had been in a comparable crowd was during the Convergence festivities with Xiala, and she had led him through it, making the unfamiliar more adventure than threat. But there was no Xiala to hold his hand now, and peril surrounded him.

Find her so that you need not fear being alone ever again, he told himself, and set his purpose. He pressed forward, using his staff to guide him. As he passed, he heard the crowd react to his presence. Songs died on reverent lips, the sleeping woke to bear witness to his coming.

He hated it.

Once, when he was no more than fifteen, his tutor Paadeh had locked him in a box. It was long and flat, and to this day he remembered the feel of wood pressing down on him. He had panicked at first, screamed and beat his fists against the unyielding lid. Only when he had exhausted himself and lay tearful and hyperventilating in his own piss had Paadeh let him out.

"You must learn to control your emotions," his tutor had warned, "or you will always be their slave. If you can't survive being locked in a box for fifteen minutes without wetting yourself, how will you ever become who you are meant to be?"

Fifteen minutes? Serapio would have sworn he had spent hours in those narrow confines.

The next time Paadeh put him in the box, he lasted twice as long. And by the season's change, he found himself seeking out the box. Lying there, bereft of the noise and riot of the world around him, he felt at peace. Confinement became second nature.

But now his senses were overloaded. A controlled space he could manage. Paadeh had never thought to acclimate him to a mob.

Here in the yard, he was exposed, vulnerable. He clenched his empty fist and prayed for his god to fortify him, but his god did not answer. He reminded himself that he had the shadow magic he could call from his blood if he needed it, but it came at a cost. And the shadow consumed what it touched; he did not want to hurt these people, but he would if he had to.

He only wanted to find Xiala.

To hear Okoa speak her name, to know she was looking for him and had not abandoned him—he could not explain the emotion it roused in him. The desire to take to the sky and fly to her was so strong he had to force his breath to steady. It was as if he were made only of need, a thousand shards of desire in the shape of a man, and he would give whatever he must to reach her.

The ground was uneven, the dirt made mud by the recent snows and then churned by hundreds of feet and refrozen into dangerous peaks and valleys that snatched at his feet. His staff helped, but he could not move as quickly as he wished, and frustration blackened his already anxious mood. He heard the people around him, unfamiliar voices speaking mostly in whispers that he could not quite decipher, but what he could hear was their rising awe as he swept past them, the hum of their excitement, their gasps of disbelief. Their only words now "Odo Sedoh."

They knew him. Of course they did. He cursed himself that in his haste, he had not considered the implications of Okoa's warning fully. Surely there were those with ill intent within the camp, and he must be on alert for any attack. He listened for Okoa's distinctive footsteps, but either he had lost the Shield captain somewhere in the milieu or his gait was impossible to distinguish from any other on the treacherously uneven earth.

"Xiala!" he called, knowing even as he did it was unlikely she could hear him. "Xiala!" he called again, stopping to turn where he stood.

Murmurs around him, voices soft but growing bolder. "Odo Sedoh?"

He could feel them coming closer, encircling him. Someone touched his skirt, the brush of fingers against his leg making his skin crawl with violation. A stranger's hand pressed briefly against his back, an unfamiliar heat. He pulled away, shifting to hold his staff two-handed. He spun in a slow circle, his weapon extended, a warning to the crowd to give him space. He heard people scramble away, muttering words of surprise as those too close had to duck to avoid being struck.

"Xiala!" he shouted, again, and this time he heard a faint voice answer.

"Serapio?" His pulse quickened, and for a moment he thought he could smell her, that scent of ocean magic in her hair, the warmth of southern sands on her skin.

"Serapio!" someone cried again, and he realized he recognized the voice. It was the uncle, the bargeman who had brought them to Tova. But it was not Xiala. Despair buckled his knees, and the sense of shattering he had been fighting threatened to overwhelm him again.

Hands reached for him to hold him up, but all he felt was the panic of being touched by people he could not see. Someone pulled at his staff. He tightened his own grip and knocked them away with a shout.

"I don't want to hurt you!"

They were not the Watchers, their legacy staining their souls. They were the opposite, the very people the Watchers had sought to destroy. They were *his* people, Carrion Crow, and he would do his best not to bring them to harm. But he needed them to leave him alone.

"Bless me, Odo Sedoh," someone cried, and the call was picked up. "Bless me! Bless me!"

He stumbled away from the pleas, confused. He was no priest to bestow a blessing, and he did not have the mandate of his god to grant such a petition, even if he was not the emptied hand. *I am a weapon*, he thought. *The only blessing I can grant comes at the edge of a knife, the only boon your death.*

"Leave me be." He swept his staff wide again.

"Heal me, Odo Sedoh!" another voice cried.

A woman shouted, "My neighbor struck me. Can you help me seek my vengeance?"

"My child is ill! It is a wasting disease!"

"I know you can work miracles!"

People crowded at his back, their closeness making his breath come too fast. The hair on his neck rose in warning. This time, when he swung his staff, he meant to wound. He connected, a heavy blow against flesh, and heard a body fall. He thought it would be enough to deter the crowd, but it seemed only to encourage their boldness.

"Look at me, Odo Sedoh!"

"No, look at me, Crow God!"

I'm blind! he wanted to shout. *Can't you see that I'm blind?* And where were his crows? He tried to throw his mind out, but there was too much noise around him, too many people. He thought he heard the uncle again and the shouts of Okoa to clear the way.

Desperate, he slid the knife from his belt, the one he had stolen from Esa. He tucked it in his palm, ready to use it. Not on the crowd but to draw his own blood. He would call the shadow to clear his way if he needed to. If he saw no other way out.

But first, he tried again to reach his crows. A mournful cry at the edges of his hearing was the only reply, and he knew something barred their passage, and they could not come. He was surrounded and alone.

"Fifteen minutes," he whispered, thinking of the box. If only he could withstand the crowd for fifteen minutes, surely he would find Xiala by then.

Hands touched him again, some soft and pleading, some more aggressive. All stifling in their need. He pushed back with his staff, kicked away another who clung to his skirt. Someone, caught in religious fervor, wailed a high, keening petition to the crow god. More and more seemed to press on him, although he could not be sure of their number, only that he could not breathe.

And then it happened. His heel caught on a runnel of frozen mud, and he lost his balance. He flung himself forward to overcompensate and found himself falling hard on one knee. The blade flew from his hand, his ability to call the shadow gone with it. He groped the ground around him, but it was impossible. It was gone.

Somewhere above him, the crows screamed, a mirror of his distress. His body vibrated in response.

More hands on him. On his arms, his back, trying to drag him to his feet. He shouted for them to go away, to give him space, but they didn't understand.

He was being overwhelmed, suffocating in the crush.

He collapsed to his knees, hands over his head, body shaking like a tuning fork to the calls of the circling crows. His limbs trembled, and the crows screamed, and the hands and the voices and the box, and all at once . . . he shattered.

He felt himself break apart, burst into a half-hundred crows.

He could see through a hundred eyes. He struggled skyward on a hundred wings.

People shouted and scattered as his talons ripped at hands and faces, as beaks plucked at exposed flesh.

Do not hurt them! he reminded his half-hundred selves, and the crows only did what was necessary to be free. And then he was a flock rising up, up, silhouetted against the blackened sun. And then he was whirling high around the Great House. He looked for a woman in blue but could not find her. He looked for Okoa, and there he was, surrounded by his Shield, who were surrounded by bloodied bodies made that way by his hand. They all had their heads raised skyward. He saw the matron on the terrace, watching. He saw the great crows in the aviary, heads turned upward to him. And then he was wheeling westward, looking for somewhere away from humans to land.

He spied a tower, not so far. He recognized the tower but could not quite remember why, his human memory and crow mind out of sync. It looked abandoned now, and he only needed to rest. It would serve his purposes.

He flew in a half-hundred bodies to the top of the celestial tower, and there he landed, trying desperately to knit himself back together into a man. He lay gasping as the world shifted and spun around him, the dark sun vibrating like a living beast. He watched his arms pulse black and feathered, and then solidify into flesh, only to burst into birds again. He screamed, a roar of terror, as he willed himself back together.

Slowly, reluctantly, his flesh solidified. Brown arm encased in black fabric. He flexed his fingers, opened and closed his fists, and almost wept when they did not break apart.

He collapsed back against the wall behind him, hair stuck to his head, body bathed in a cold sweat. He had never felt anything like this, not even with the crow god at his apex. He had flown as a flock, seen through a hundred pairs of eyes, sliced through the wind on a hundred pairs of wings. It was exhilarating. It was terrifying. And now he was drained, as if the transformation had used up some essential part of him.

Out of habit, he reached for the place where his god dwelled to refortify himself. He caught his mistake too late, as the image of an empty hand flashed through his mind. He tried to withdraw his desire, to stave off the inevitable disappointment, but to his wonder, he was not empty. Divinity flowed, cool and soothing as a dark river, as the sun above him flared brighter. He glanced up to see that the eclipse had shifted, that the shadow had moved to expose more of the sun.

His heart soared, and tears dripped black down his cheeks. The crow god had chosen to come to him, even if it allowed the sun her advantage. But why?

He turned his head, his crow eyes searching.

He was not alone.

A figure hunched low along the stone wall across from him. A woman, her expression caught between terror and awe. She glowed, the light that poured from her body mirrored by the growing sun above them. Shadow and light flicked and danced between them, and his divine powers crashed around him like an angry tide.

He knew who this woman was.

"Sun Priest," he growled, in his voice of a thousand wings. He pushed himself to standing, and his hand against the wall was a talon that cracked through stone like soft wood.

She backed away.

He moved to pursue but found himself on his knees, gasping, the wound on his side ripped open. He looked down, and light burst white and cold through the bandage Feyou had so carefully wrapped around his middle. He knew what the wound was now, or at least who had given it to him.

"Sun Priest," he hissed, the pain so dense his crow vision began to fail.

He could not catch her, not like this, but there were other ways to follow.

"Go!" he cried, thrusting his arm out. "Find her!" And this time, he willed himself to break, and his arm shattered into a half dozen crows.

She ran, hurtling down the stairs and out of sight, and the crows pursued with one purpose.

To kill.

CHAPTER 16

THE TOVASHEH RIVER
YEAR 1 OF THE CROW

Even a shark must sleep.

—Teek saying

Xiala and Iktan's boat sailed down one of the Tovasheh's tributaries in silence. Iktan hadn't shared their immediate destination, and Xiala didn't know what was safe to say in front of the two Golden Eagle sailors. They had passed the familiar Titidi port earlier. Xiala was even sure she had seen Uncle Kuy's barge, docked and empty. Which made her remember Uncle Kuy and what he must be thinking of her disappearance. She hoped she hadn't gotten him in trouble, that her escape, if that was what it was, could not be traced back to him. She had asked Iktan, but xe had shrugged as if Uncle Kuy's fate was of little importance and they had larger concerns ahead. Which she supposed they did. But she couldn't help but worry.

Past the port, they had tacked north through a deep canyon Iktan told her was called Coyote's Maw. The limited light fell to almost nothing here, and they traveled through a place where they were unable to see their hands before their faces. The sailing here was fraught, and the two crewmen labored

165

to keep them away from jutting rocks and riotous currents. The first time they grazed a hidden shelf that almost sent Xiala tumbling over the side, she cursed them for their amateur efforts, explained that she had excellent night vision, and insisted on taking lookout point. Perhaps it was her ferocity that convinced them not to argue, or perhaps even in the darkness of the Maw, they could see that her eyes were not entirely human. Either way, they quickly conceded, and she led them through the treacherous waters with no more scrapes.

Hours passed in the darkness, and Tova slid to nothing behind them. The progress down the tributary was slow as they worked against crosswinds and currents, and she understood again why the Water Strider's beasts gave them such an advantage in river waters. The walls of the canyon began to diminish until they found themselves sailing past high grasslands on a steady breeze. They finally approached what looked to be a small encampment just as the sun breached the horizon.

The sun.

"Mother waters," Xiala whispered, overcome. She pushed back her hood and let the light warm her face. It was still winter, still cold enough for pockets of snow and morning frost to paint the prairie, but the presence of the sun made everything more tolerable. She was an island girl from an island people, had grown up with palms and sand. Even the jungle of Cuecola felt more natural than Tova cliffs and bone-breaking cold.

"I lived my whole life with the sun and took it for granted," Iktan said, tone pensive. "I will not make that mistake again."

She opened her eyes to find Iktan beside her, hood still up but facing the dawn.

"The loss disturbed me more than I realized it would," xe said.

She suspected Iktan was talking about more than just the sun, but before she could ask, a shout of greeting rang out from shore. She braced herself against the rails as the sailors brought the skimmer to ground on the riverbank. Several people came ambling down the gentle slope. The tawny-skinned young woman in the lead looked to be in charge. Her clothes were the finest and freshly washed, her white shirt and trousers made of woven fabric and embellished with gold beadwork along the seams. A white deerskin cloak was fastened over one shoulder by what looked to be a spray of feathers made of hammered gold, and a white fur collar encircled her neck. She wore a braid of gold on her brow like a signet, and gold nuggets pierced her earlobes. She glowed under the morning sun, light catching in her brown hair and sparkling in her hazel eyes. *Pretty*, Xiala thought, *but there's something cold about her, imperious in the way she looks down her nose at us, as if she knows already we are her inferiors. And she's dressed for a parade, not for living rough on a half-frozen prairie.*

"Did you see him?" the woman asked, before they had even exited the boat.

"No," Iktan said, as xe leaped lightly to shore. "But I've brought a friend."

The woman's eyes cut to Xiala. "Who's this?"

"Xiala of the Teek, meet Ziha Golden Eagle, second daughter of the matron and commander of our expedition to Hokaia." Iktan headed up the incline, forcing everyone to follow.

Ziha flashed Xiala an irritated frown before pushing forward to walk beside Iktan. "Your mission was to get close enough to evaluate the truth of Carrion Crow's claims. You said you had a man in the Shield—"

"To whom I spoke," xe cut in smoothly, "and who reassured me that it's true."

"What part is true?" Ziha asked.

Iktan waved a hand. "All of it, Ziha. The arrival of the Odo Sedoh, the subsequent slaughter, which the Odohaa are now calling the Reckoning, by the way. We should have seen that coming. Honestly, between my resources and yours, we should have foreseen all of this. I'm not sure where the failure lies, but a failure it was. Of truly epic proportions."

"One man," Ziha scoffed. "One man killed everyone? It's not possible."

Iktan stopped. Pivoted back to Xiala, who was trying to make herself inconspicuous. "Is it possible?" xe asked.

They both stared at her expectantly.

"Is it possible your friend killed all those people on Sun Rock?" Iktan repeated. Xe counted off on xir fingers. "My fellow priests, including Ziha's cousin, Abah; a cadre of Knives; and a handful of Golden Eagle Shield."

Xiala stood dumbfounded. Did they really expect her to answer? Hells, did they blame her? Was that why she was there?

"One word will do," Iktan said. "Yes or no."

She pressed her lips together.

Iktan sighed. "The answer is yes. She won't speak it because she just realized who we are." Xe started walking again.

Ziha's eyes lingered on Xiala. "Who is she, again?"

"Come, Ziha. Is there a meal to be had in this place? I'm tired and hungry, and I stink. The last meal I ate was some kind of gruel. Utterly tasteless. I could use a decent plate."

"Should we shackle her?" Ziha asked, eyes still on Xiala.

Iktan had reached the top of the hill. "What for? Tova is a hundred miles south from here. She has no food and no water, and it's cold enough to freeze. She's not going anywhere."

"Am I a prisoner, then?" Xiala asked, trying to keep the trembling out of her voice. Iktan was right. The reality of her situation was crashing down on her with the terrifying undeni-ability of a rogue wave.

Iktan's dark eyes softened. "We are all prisoners here, Xiala. You, Ziha, even myself. Prisoners to fate, that unreasonable bitch. But I prefer to think of us as people who can help each other, yes? After all, we're all on the same side, now."

Xiala watched Iktan disappear over the crest, and after a moment, Ziha hurried after, the guards who had accompa-nied her trailing. Finally, the sailors from the skimmer passed, talking quietly to themselves and ignoring her.

"On the same side," she murmured. "I do not think so."

But she was hungry, and Iktan was right that she had no-where to go. *You've survived worse, Xiala*, she told herself. *Survive this and get back to Serapio. It sounds like he's in need of rescue.* And maybe she could learn something here among Serapio's enemies. Something she might bring back so that when she did see him again, she would have something useful to offer him besides tears.

·····

The camp was not as large as Xiala had first thought. There were three dozen tents made from tanned and treated hide stretched around flexible poles. The hump-shaped structures looked quick to assemble and disassemble and light enough for a person to carry in a pack on their back. A small refuse pile on the outskirts of the encampment suggested they had only been here a few days, and the lack of more permanent structures like a well or a ditch to the nearby river suggested they didn't mean to stay for long.

Ziha escorted them to a tent six times as large as the others and able to fit a dozen people at once.

"You may refresh yourselves here," she instructed. "There's water and clean clothes. I'll see about a meal, and then we'll talk. You'll tell me everything you learned, Iktan."

"Of course."

Her brow crinkled. "It would be proper for you to call me Commander."

"You don't have an army yet, Ziha. When that day comes, I'll consider it." Xe lifted the tent flap, motioned Xiala inside, and then followed.

Xiala heard the woman growl a curse before storming off. Shadows at the door meant Ziha had left guards to watch over them.

"You like to irritate her," Xiala observed, eyes on Iktan as xe pulled the cloak from xir shoulders and let it drop to the floor.

Xiala had not gotten a good look at the priest before now. Xe was tall and sinewy, with a prominent nose in an angular face. Xir black hair had recently been shorn but since had grown in as a soft fuzz. Xe rubbed a hand over it now, as if annoyed at its length.

"She irritates easily," xe said.

"But why poke her at all?"

Xe walked to a water basin and dipped both hands in. "Could she not bother to heat the water?" xe complained, before leaning over to wash xir face. "Ziha is young and spoiled and has had a tremendous amount of power given to her purely because of who her mother is. If things go as planned, she will soon have even more."

"Then I understand your motivation even less."

Iktan searched for a towel and, finding none, used xir gray shirt to wipe xir face. Xe looked back at her with large intelligent eyes. "Perhaps you're right, and it is simply my nature to provoke. But be glad her temper is focused on me right now and not you. The Odo Sedoh killed her cousin and spoiled her clan's long-planned coup of the Watchers. She wants him dead. You would make a fine proxy."

Iktan pulled off xir shirt, knotted it up, and dipped it in the water. Xe continued xir ablutions, wiping across xir underarms. Xiala turned to give the priest privacy when xe began to unself-consciously strip off xir pants. She heard the splash of water and the soft rub of cloth against skin. The scent of yucca and lavender soap filled her nose. She caught sight of Iktan's backside as xe padded over to a trunk in the corner and threw it open. It was piled with fabrics, and xe plucked various articles of clothing from inside, holding them up for size. Once satisfied, xe dragged on a pair of white pants and a plain white shirt that looked very much like the lesser cousin to Ziha's finer ensemble.

"But here's the thing, Xiala." Xe sank down on the thick furs covering the floor of the tent. "Her cousin killed my friend first, and I won't forgive that." Xe stretched, a yawn catching the corner of xir mouth. "You should get comfortable. Ziha will be back soon, and then it's all business. It's going to be a long day, and tomorrow? Even longer."

She stared. "Why are you telling me all this?"

"I like you. And I'm lonely. Do I make you uncomfortable?"

"No . . ."

The truth was she liked Iktan. There was something about xir that made her want to trust. Her instincts were usually good about people, and she thought xe might be a friend, despite their strange circumstances. After all, xe had spared her life when xe could have simply gutted her and dumped her into the Tovasheh.

Moisture trickled down her face, and she realized she was sweating. After being outside for so long, the heat in the tent was stifling. Thick furs covered the ground inside, and a pit fire burned in the middle, smoke drifting up through the center hole.

She unfastened her cloak and let her hair spill down her back in plum-colored coils. Following Iktan's example, she washed in the basin and picked clean clothes from the trunk.

"I have never seen a woman who looks like you before. Do all Teek look like you?"

Xiala turned to find Iktan lying down, hands propped behind xir neck and eyes closed.

"No," she said. "We are as varied as the people of the Meridian, except . . ." She hesitated. To talk about being Teek felt like she was sharing secrets, but she wasn't sure why. She had never been good at hiding who she was, what she was, so it really shouldn't have been a surprise that pretending to be Water Strider was such a disaster. The fact that Iktan had so quickly and easily unmasked her convinced her that she should stop trying. *Live as a Teek, die as a Teek*, the saying went, and it had never felt more appropriate to her than now.

"Except for the eyes," she finished. "We all have Teek eyes."

"And hair?"

"The hair is all mine. A gift from my unknown father, perhaps."

She came to sit across from Iktan, unsure what else to do. At least, she felt decently refreshed. She wondered what food Ziha would bring them. After her experience in the Crow camp, her expectations were modest. But from the looks of this tent and Ziha's clothes, Golden Eagle had wealth to flaunt. She hope that indulgence carried over to their cooking.

"Do you have bayeki in Teek?" Iktan asked idly, eyes still closed.

"We have only women."

"I'm no woman," xe said, "but I'm no man, either. It is a gender most common to my clan, but I have heard there are others."

She shrugged. "I have not met all the people in the world. It is a very large place."

"So it is," Iktan said, grinning. "So it is."

"How did you know I was Teek? I met some in Tova who had never heard of us."

"It is the nature of my profession to know people," xe confessed. "I would not take it personally."

"You called yourself 'priest' before, on the shore," she said, "but I've never met a priest who looked like you. Or moved like you. Or kept a sharp knife up their sleeve and a sharper tongue in their mouth."

Iktan chuckled. "I do like to think myself singular, but in truth, we were half a hundred tsiyo. The Order of Knives."

She shook her head, still not following.

"Assassins for the Sun Priest," xe said when she was silent.

"Shit."

Iktan laughed, genuinely amused. "I did say you were fucked."

The flap opened, and Ziha and three others ducked inside. Iktan sat up as the Golden Eagle commander joined them on the furs. Two of the people who had accompanied her began to set a breakfast before them. Xiala spied both corn and knotweed breads. Jellied persimmons and wild plums, small blue-tinted fowl eggs, and a mix of greens and roots that looked to have been gathered from the shores of the river.

"This is generous," Xiala remarked.

"She only wants to fatten you up before the slaughter," Iktan said. "Golden Eagle hospitality is always double-edged."

Ziha's tone was as icy and jagged as the cliffs of Tova in winter. "I have chosen to ignore your insults, Priest, and assign them to your lack of couth. I would have nothing to do with you if given the choice, but Mother has made it very clear to me that you are valued, and I am to treat you as an ally and trusted adviser, so I will do so. But there is no need to insult me or my clan."

Iktan dipped bread into the fruit mélange and popped it into xir mouth.

"You say nothing now?" Ziha challenged.

"Is this what you came to discuss?" xe asked. "My manners?"

Ziha frowned. "No." She straightened her shoulders as if resetting herself with great effort.

It was clear Iktan had won the skirmish, but Ziha was determined to soldier on.

"We are six days out from the Convergence," she said, "and by now word has traveled on eagleback to Cuecola and Hokaia recounting the fate that befell the Watchers. Layat says his lord in Cuecola is a sorcerer who reads the shadow mirror and would—"

"Layat is the matron's adviser from Cuecola," Iktan interjected for Xiala's sake. "They financed a great deal of what you see before you, your meal included, in exchange for Golden Eagle's loyalty."

Ziha glared at the priest. "As I was saying. If Layat's lord did his job, the Seven will have set sail for Hokaia by now. Word has been sent to Hokaia and to Teek—"

"Teek?" Xiala's adrenaline surged, and her breath lodged in her throat. A memory of her mother, hand outstretched as a messenger handed her a summons, flashed before her. She could almost smell the caustic scent of her mother's disdain, feel the heat of her impending fury at being summoned anywhere.

"Just perfunctory," Ziha said dismissively. "It is a condition of the treaty. We don't expect Teek to answer. Why would they when they've not bothered to answer a correspondence in a hundred years? In fact . . ." She tilted her head, hazel eyes curious. "I'd assumed the Teek were all dead until today."

"How far from here to Hokaia?" Iktan asked, a deft refocusing away from Xiala's heritage and Ziha's astonishingly rude observation. Xiala wasn't sure why xe did it, but she was grateful nonetheless.

"Twenty days or more," Ziha said, letting the matter of Teek drop. "We'll break camp in the morning and head for the headwaters of the Puumun River. It would have been faster had we waited until spring thaws, but we dared not with Tova under that unnatural sun. We don't know what Carrion Crow will do in our absence, but we have to bear the risk if we want the combined might of the Meridian at our backs when we act."

"When you act?" Xiala asked. "What is it you plan to do?"

"We plan to take Tova back from Carrion Crow."

"The Carrion Crow do not hold Tova. We were just there. They rally only to Odo to see the Odo Sedoh." It still felt strange to call Serapio by that name, but that was how they knew him, and instincts told her it was better not to share his true name with his enemies. "They're not hurting anyone."

"Not hurting anyone?" Ziha leaned in, face flushed and nostrils flaring. "My cousin Abah was only nineteen. She was a beautiful woman, a healer. She brought good into the world. The Shield found her on Sun Rock with her throat slashed and her head bashed in. And for what? What had she ever done to hurt anyone?" She ended in a shout, rage cording her neck.

"She bit a boy's tongue off once," Iktan offered.

Both women turned to stare.

"She was twelve, I think, a new dedicant, and the boy the same. They sent the boy to the healers but brought her to me. They thought perhaps her show of violence meant she had a propensity for becoming a tsiyo. People think it takes a certain kind of moral flexibility to be an assassin, but it's really quite the opposite. Our values must be absolute. So I questioned the girl. Asked her why she had done it. Said that if she liked the boy, there were better ways to show her affection. She solemnly informed me that no, she did not like the boy. She had only wanted to taste his blood. She was curious, she told me, to see if it was salty or sweet."

"Seven hells," Xiala whispered, fighting the urge to touch a finger to her own tongue to make sure it was intact.

"They were not able to heal his tongue, so he never fully recovered his ability to speak. I don't know what happened to him, if he left the priesthood or stayed on as a dedicant. But your cousin was a viper, Ziha. Let us not pretend otherwise."

"A child's misunderstanding. You would damn her for that?"

"I would damn her for many a thing, but one thing in particular."

Ziha shifted, uncomfortable. "Naranpa should have never—"

"No," Iktan said, voice suddenly lethal.

Xiala's instincts made her still like a rabbit sensing the presence of a wolf. Ziha's eyes shifted toward the door and the guards just outside. But she must have realized that Iktan was much too close, and much too fast, and if xe wished it, she would be dead before help could find her.

"Keep her name from your mouth, Golden Eagle," xe whispered. "Your clan made promises to me and then broke them. You do not get to blame the dead with your excuses now."

Ziha swallowed. "There are complications to what happened," she said, voice as careful as footfalls on a frozen lake, "and I should not speak of them. Perhaps we have strayed too far from why we are here together, traveling treacherous roads with our careless thoughts. Golden Eagle is not your enemy, tsiyo. Or yours," she said to Xiala.

Iktan's eyes were hooded, glazed with a deceptive calmness. Xiala remembered xir earlier quip about them all being prisoners. She had thought the comment mocking, but now she wondered if Iktan had in mind a particular bitch when xe had spoken of fate.

Ziha stood. Xiala could see the sweat on the back of her neck, the slight tremor in her hands. "I'll let you finish your meal. I have things to see to in camp. We will talk again tonight and plan to be moving toward the Puumun River before dawn. Xiala of the Teek, I would very much like to hear what you know of the Odo Sedoh when I return this evening. And perhaps then Iktan can share what xe learned from xir man in Carrion Crow Shield. But for now . . ."

She bowed slightly at the neck and was out, the tent flap blowing behind her. Words were exchanged with the guards, and they stayed where they were instead of following their commander.

"Looks like we're under guard now," Xiala said.

"It's theater," Iktan said confidently. "If I wanted them dead, they'd be dead in seconds. Assassin, remember?" Xe had risen and was searching through the trunks and pots in the back of the tent. Xiala heard the clatter of things being pushed aside.

"What are you looking for?"

"I'll know it when I find . . . ah." Xe came back bearing a bottle of xtabentún. "I knew she had to be keeping a bottle somewhere."

Xiala had not touched drink since the Convergence and was not sure now that she should. But she did not protest when Iktan uncorked the bottle, took the two clay cups left from their meal, and filled them with alcohol. And she said nothing when xe set one in front of her and took the other.

Iktan drank, long and deep, before topping the cup off and settling back in the furs, back propped against a pile of cushions.

"Tell me about the Odo Sedoh."

She folded her hands in her lap, trying to ignore the cup that seemed to beckon. "Tell me of the Watchers first," she countered.

"What do you want to know?"

"You're a priest?"

"Was a priest," xe corrected, tapping xir cup. "Drink is forbidden in the priesthood. I was a priest until Ziha's mother and her murderous cousin killed a friend I cared very much about. And then *your* friend killed all but a few children and graybeards left in the tower, which means there's not much of the Watchers left." Xe drank more. "Clearly, people having murderers for friends is the problem here."

"If there are some Watchers left, couldn't you rebuild?"

She couldn't believe she was even asking. Serapio had explained how corrupt they were, the transgressions they had committed. But this person before her seemed lost, and she knew what being lost felt like, so her instinct was to offer some comfort.

"There is nothing to rebuild," Iktan said with a note of finality. "The Watchers served for more than three hundred years. They did what they could to keep the Meridian at peace, and now war comes, and they are done." Xe glanced at her. "I think you mistake 'priest' for 'martyr.'"

"So if you are no longer a priest, what are you?"

"Now I am a person with an enviable skill set and an exciting amount of indifference."

"I don't believe that," she said quietly.

"No? You will."

She watched Iktan's face, looking for signs of that cool rage that she was beginning to understand was when xe was most dangerous, and seeing none of it, she ventured, "Can I ask you something?"

"Please do."

"How is it that you were not on Sun Rock with the rest of the Watchers?"

"Ah, Xiala of the Teek," xe said, pressing a hand over xir heart. "Again, we must look to fickle fate. I was in a rage when Nara went missing. I blamed myself. Eche tried to claim that Nara had killed the tsiyo at her door and run, and while I am a fool, I am not an idiot. I tore the tower apart, sent dedicants out to search for her, and nothing. I couldn't prove it, but I knew what they had done. When the time came for the Convergence ceremony, I sent one of my tsiyos in my stead. It was a thing I did often when I didn't have the patience for their pomp and bloviating, and I was in no mood to stand shoulder to shoulder with those who had killed my friend."

"If you believe they killed your friend and you hate them for it, what are you doing here?"

"I considered staying in Tova," xe admitted. "But once I realized Golden Eagle was already shifting the game to Hokaia, I knew I needed to see the larger battlefield. Nara is gone, and I cannot bring her back. The Watchers, likewise, are no more. Whatever happens in Tova will happen. Carrion Crow may well take leadership of the Sky Made and hold dominion over the city. Or perhaps they will remain a peculiar little religious sect content with worshipping their dark god, as you seem to think. But either way, the Meridian is in revolt. With the fall of the Watchers, the Treaty of Hokaia has been broken. The signatories are free to do what they wish, and what they wish is war."

"But why? What does Tova have that makes them so powerful? Why did the four cities bow to them to begin with?"

"Do you not know the history of the War of the Spear?"

"The Teek do not teach it to their children. We do not talk much of the outside world except to warn against it."

"Hmmm. I can tell you, if you like. It is taught to us when we are dedicants. It is the reason for our existence." Xe took a moment to refill xir cup and settle back before beginning.

"It began with a spearmaiden named Seuq. She was said to be the greatest of her people. The smartest, the bravest, the strongest. Always looking for adventure, afraid of nothing. She was the leader of her class at the war college. So when a group of young maidens decided to venture to the Graveyard of the Gods, no doubt on some drunken dare, she was the first to volunteer. It was forbidden, of course. The Graveyard of the Gods lies far to the north. It is said to be the place where many gods from the God Wars fell, and great magics run wild there. It is said that those who enter do not return. But it is also said that if anyone is brave enough to breech the Graveyard and eat from the fruit at its heart, the one they call godflesh, then they will have power unimaginable. The power of not just one god but all the gods.

"Seuq could not resist this challenge. What daring spearmaiden could? She led four companions north that summer. Herself, Gwee, Odae, and Asnod. It took months to reach the Graveyard. They battled giant bears and frost giants, flesh eaters and revenants. But at last they made it to the Graveyard. It is said to be a place of both horror and beauty, a living forest of calcified white stone hoodoos, the bones of gods, cut through with swaths of earth the color of blood. They followed the path, careful not to stray, for they knew the enemies beyond the path were the spirits themselves. They passed the lake where the sun god shed her scales in battle, and the deep crater where the coyote god fell and bent the earth, leaving his salty sweat upon the shore. And finally, they reached the center, where the rare godflesh grows. And one by one, they ate.

"Asnod died immediately, tearing her own flesh from her face, screaming of creatures burrowed under her skin. Odae died on the journey back after she attacked the other two in a rage of madness. But Seuq and Gwee returned and found they had a prodigious new power. They had the power to walk in a person's dreams."

Iktan paused to take a deep drink, eyes on Xiala. "It may not seem like it now, but it was a power to break worlds. Imagine it. They could enter anyone's dreams and make them into nightmares. Suggest horrors to enact during the day. Plant suspicions enough to ruin alliances and invite murder. No one was safe, for we all must sleep. The only thing that slowed their ambition was that the power carried the possibility of madness with it. They remembered Asnod's and Odae's fates well enough. The result of their hubris might have remained a deadly secret adventure, but they shared their knowledge and the godflesh they brought back with others, and soon the dreamwalkers became a dozen, and then a dozen more.

"The winter they were gone had been hard on Hokaia, and the harvest the season before had been thin. They eyed their neighbor across the river, the city of Barach, and coveted. So they took what they wanted. And then they took the whole river valley. With the military might of the spearmaidens and the spirit magic of the dreamwalkers, they were unstoppable. Soon the river valley was not enough, so they looked to the south. It is said that back then, the Teek did not travel on their floating islands but lived in one place and traded freely with the world. Until the spearmaidens and the dreamwalkers came and ravaged their home. Your people do not speak of it?"

Xiala shook her head, enthralled by the story.

"Once Teek was subdued and stripped of wealth, they ventured farther south to Cuecola and the southern coastal cities. But the Cuecolans had sorcery of their own—shadow, stone, and blood magic—and were prepared. Their battles were fierce, and many strange things were seen. The elders speak of it only in hushed voices and call it the Frenzy. But in the end, the Jaguar Prince and his army of sorcerers fell. In desperation, the seven remaining families, themselves ravaged, reached out to their brethren to the west. My people, the Winged Serpent, had long ties to the southern cities and shared ancestors, so it was said. So when they cried out for help, we answered. We brought the winged serpents who are also our kin to war, for the great beasts were immune to the dreamwalkers' powers. They were made of the same kind of magic, and it proved remedy enough. But we were few in number, so we called to our neighbors, the clans you know as Sky Made. Carrion Crow were the first to answer, bringing their great corvids to bear. Then Golden Eagle and Water Strider. The only clan that did not answer was Coyote. They had long ago lost the last of their great beasts and feared the dreamwalkers, so they stayed in their caves and hovels and let the clans go to war.

"The last battle was fought on the plains outside of Hokaia. The spearmaidens had been driven back to their homeland, and all the dreamwalkers were killed save a small coven that had barricaded themselves in their newly built palace. But eventually, even they fell. Only the spearmaidens who had not joined the conquest were spared. The rest were put to death. Not a single dreamwalker escaped execution. And on that very day, the Treaty of Hokaia was signed. The four great peoples of the Meridian agreed to outlaw all magic and to forbid the worship of gods. They created a body called the Watchers, a collection of priests who were to guard against gods and magic and uphold order, reason, and peace across the continent. They set the Sun Priest over them all, for the priest was to be a light in dark times, a symbol always present in the sky to remind the peoples of their agreement not to war and of the Watchers' duties.

"And so it was, for three hundred years. But the gods cannot be silenced altogether, it seems, and Carrion Crow were the first to reject the edict against their worship. And so the Watchers did what they thought was best, what they thought they were meant to do."

"The Night of Knives," Xiala said.

Iktan nodded. "It is our unforgivable transgression, the stain on our mission. After that, we were lost, for even we could not justify the slaughter of so many innocents. I understand it now, even as I did not understand it a month ago. Nara understood it all along. She saw what we had become, what we had lost, but the rest of us . . ." Iktan shrugged, but the weight of history, of xir role in it all, bowed xir head. "I should have listened to her. Should have acted. Not sided with Golden Eagle and plotted with the corruptible in the Crow's Great House."

"Your man in the Shield."

"Aye. All is not what it seems in that place."

She shivered. She wondered if Serapio knew there was a traitor in their midst and whether he was safe. Another reason to stay here and learn his enemy's secrets, so if war came, when it came, he would know how to fight back.

"I thought perhaps I, the Priest of Knives, owed them the most." Iktan finished xir cup and tossed it to the furs. "But I fear that all I did was pour salt on a festering wound in hopes of covering it up. And then the event even I had not anticipated . . ." Xe pointed to her. "The Odo Sedoh came and tore our plans to nothing, less than drops of blood on a windswept mesa. So what am I doing here, Xiala? I'm seeing this through until the damnable end."

Xe turned on xir side, pulled a fur around xir shoulders, and closed xir eyes. Moments later, xe was asleep.

She sighed. It was much to take in, even more to understand. She wondered why the Teek were not taught these histories, why she had not known about what went on in the world around her. Small things came back to her now. The way Serapio had thought her Song was the power of a goddess, but she had laughed, said no Teek would think that. Even how she had never been taught that the Sky Made had any connection to the Teek, although they had much in common in their reading of the stars. There were layers here, kinship and obligation and promises made and broken, that she could not fully comprehend. But one thing she did know. She was caught in the maelstrom, standing in the center of it all, the tide coming in and the waves growing higher.

She reached for her as-yet-untouched cup. "I don't think I am the only one fucked here, Iktan," she whispered, raising a toast to the sleeping figure. She drained the cup dry and reached for the bottle.

CHAPTER 17

CITY OF TOVA

YEAR 1 OF THE CROW

> Do not talk when you can walk,
> Do not walk when you can run.
>
> —Coyote wisdom

Naranpa ran. She flew down the winding stairs, driven by a burst of energy birthed from fear, her feet barely touching the steps. She could feel the crows at her back, beaks only a hand's width from her scalp, talons grazing her neck. She swept past her old rooms and the library, and when she hit the terrace landing, she swerved tightly.

She barreled through the kitchens, ducking as she passed low ceilings. It had occurred to her panicked mind that she would never outrun these birds. Once she left the tower, the grounds around were wide open. The little cover there was now winter-bare trees and nothing else all the way to the bridge. Inside the tower, there were at least halls to navigate and tight spaces in the dark. And doors.

She took the back kitchen stairs at a run, momentarily airborne. Her knees buckled with the force of landing, and she cried out. She turned and slammed closed the door through which she had just passed. The heavy impact of bird bodies against the other side made her hold her breath. Despite the sturdy wood, she half expected the creatures to break through. But after a moment, the awful thumping faded. She bent, hands to knees, breathing hard.

Her heart was still racing wildly, her mind reeling from what she had seen.

She had been drawn to the rooftop observatory by what she had taken for a voice, and a compulsion she could not name. Around her, the wind had howled and the blackened sun hissed and crackled. A corvid the size of her lower arm was perched on the ledge before her. Naranpa had watched as the bird cocked its head and seemed to look at her, as if it was expecting her.

"Who . . . ?" she had whispered, but before she could finish her thought, a shadow passed over her head. She had looked up as more shadows flew above her, and she realized the darkness was the flock. Their eerie cries filled the air, and the wind gusted with the beating of their wings as dozens and dozens, no, half a hundred, gathered on the tower. The light in her lantern danced and then was snuffed out. Some deep instinct had told her not to relight it and even more urgently screamed at her to run.

She had walked backward, eyes on the growing mass of birds that swarmed before her. The swarm had begun to take shape, and she had not known what it would reveal, but she'd been certain she did not want to be anywhere near when it did. She had dropped the useless lantern and run.

She had made it only as far as the stairs when light flared around her. Instincts had made her duck and throw herself against the wall, hands over her head. She had waited for something to strike her, but all she felt was heat . . . and the warmth of the sun.

The sun!

The shadow of the eclipse had diminished, and the sun had brightened, illuminating the top of the tower. Her power awoke, the heat in her chest flaring alive. Her palms burned. She had stared at her hands in wonder, the heat of the sun against her face like the kiss of a long-missed lover. Until she heard a voice where there were only corvids before. It did not sound human. It was the voice of a thousand wings, the voice of the killing field, the voice of a god.

"Sun Priest," it had said.

And she knew who it was, who had called her to the rooftop. Trembling, she had turned to face her enemy.

Her memory shuddered, trying to make sense of what she had seen.

A man, young, sheathed in black, ebony hair wild. A face with eyes of midnight that wept black tears. He had called to her in a voice that shook the air like thunder. And then, impossibly, his arm had shattered into half a dozen crows, and the birds had come for her. And she had run.

But now she was safe, at least for the moment.

She leaned against the kitchen door, listening, but all was silence.

Were the crows gone? Was the Crow God Reborn even now stalking down the stairs in search of her? She was certain that if he found her, she would not survive their meeting. She looked around the kitchen, a place she had spent many hours as a servant before her promotion to dedicant. There was a back entrance here, one that led into the once neatly tended rows of corn, beans, and squash that fed the tower. It was her way out.

She dragged herself to her feet and quietly made her way to the back door. Tentatively, she opened it. She half expected to find a flock of crows waiting for her, ready to rend her limb from limb, but there was nothing. She looked up at an empty sky. She caught the edge of a black murmuration retreating east, and she let herself breathe again. He had not pursued her after all, and she could only be grateful that her fool's luck had held.

She gathered her courage and ran toward the bridge to Tsay.

• • • • •

Naranpa opened the door of the Lupine a full nine hours after she had left. The guard who had so easily let her leave now took off running, shouting of her return.

She collapsed on the nearest bench, exhausted, and waited for her brother.

He arrived before she could kick the boots from her aching feet, his porcupine mantle flaring around him and his wooden cane beating a rhythm of displeasure that matched his stride. He was dressed for travel, boots laced to knees and hands gloved. His hair was freshly shaven on the sides, the rest slicked back in a knot. He trembled with the effort to suppress his rage.

"I thought you were dead," he shouted, inches from her face.

Another time, she might have been shaken by his anger, but now, the memories of the Crow God Reborn fresh, she could only laugh. "Very close."

Denaochi reared back, as if he had not expected such a glib dismissal of his hostility, but he recovered quickly, his tone shifting to sarcasm. "A brush with death is the only acceptable excuse for your behavior." He sniffed, still annoyed, but his curiosity was clearly getting the best of him. "Where did you go?"

"The tower."

"The *celestial* tower?"

"I know." She ran a trembling hand across her face. "Perhaps not my best idea. But there was something there I needed."

His eyes narrowed. "And did you find it?"

"And more." Her smile was small and fraught. "I saw the Crow God Reborn."

"And yet you live," he murmured, intrigued.

"As I said, it was a close thing. If he had not been injured already, I do not think I would be standing here."

"You hurt him? You were able to fight him?"

How could she explain what she had seen? How the birds seemed a part of him, his arm pulsing human one moment and corvid the next?

"A weakness," Denaochi said eagerly. "The first weakness we have seen."

She shook her head. "Not one we can count on should our paths cross again." All her looking for some hidden power felt suddenly futile. Even if she did possess some remnant of the sun god within her, what she had seen was something beyond her. She could not fight the Crow God Reborn and win. She understood her folly acutely.

"I cannot," she confessed.

"Cannot what?" His question held an edge of his earlier anger.

"He is a god, Ochi. I am not. I cannot win against him."

"You must!" He thumped his cane emphatically. "I have already promised his defeat to the bosses."

"Tell them we know better now." She slumped, the adrenaline that had sustained her flight from the tower ebbed, leaving her exhausted. "Tell them it might be best to cede Tova to Carrion Crow."

His hands on her shoulders surprised her, and he shook her hard enough that her teeth rattled. "You are not giving up! We are not giving up! Even now, the bosses await us, and we must answer to them, Nara. They are not your Sky Made matrons you can reason with. They follow the old ways, the ways of blood, and once a promise is made, there is no recision."

189

"Then perhaps you should not have bound me to action without my consultation!" Her own anger was roused now, and she pushed his hands aside.

Thin cracks formed around his eyes. "You crawled back to life! You said you were with me! Why, if you are only a coward in the end?"

"I . . ."

She lowered her head. Was she simply craven, afraid of death at the hands of what she had seen on top of the tower? She had faced death before and jumped into its embrace. And Denaochi was right that she had refused to accept that tomb as her final place of rest. But this was different.

"We should run while we can," she said finally. "Tova is a lost cause."

He stepped back, his dark eyes raking over her, and his judgment flayed her like no other could.

"I have an appointment to keep," he said stiffly. "Gather yourself and join me at the Agave as soon as you can." He hesitated, and Naranpa saw the unspoken *please* in the shape of his lips, but it remained there, unsaid. And then he was up the stairs and out the door.

Naranpa bent over, head in her hands, and let the tears come.

"He goes to his death," Zataya said.

She looked up to find the witch standing before her. She held a weathered scroll in her hand and tapped it lightly against her thigh, her eyes on Naranpa.

"You do not understand the bosses," Zataya said, "but I do. And once a boss gives his word, it must be done. He risked everything on you."

"A foolish gamble," Naranpa countered, wiping her eyes. "One he made without even consulting me."

"What consultation was needed when his way is faith?" She

shoved the scroll toward Naranpa, and she reflexively grasped it in her hands. "He had faith in you. I told him he should not, that you were fickle and spoiled by that tower, but he insisted you were still his sister."

Naranpa gaped. Denaochi had faith in her? "What are you talking about? He barely tolerates me. He is always testing me to see if I am worthy."

"Is that what you think? Is that the wisdom of a Watcher? Foolish woman. He is not testing you to see if you are worthy, he's testing you to see if he is worthy of you staying."

Skies, was that why he pushed her so hard? To see what it would take to finally drive her away? And had she not proven him right again and again? Shame curdled her insides.

"I will go," Naranpa said, subdued, "but if the bosses are as ruthless as you say, why would they listen to me?"

Zataya tapped her chest. Naranpa understood but found herself wanting to protest anyway. Her power was nothing compared to what dwelled within the Crow God Reborn.

Zataya gestured toward the scroll. "Your answers are there. You are more powerful than you think."

Naranpa unspooled it. The paper was old and frail, weathered at the ends as if it had not been well cared for. It was a painting of a spoked wheel, its outer ring divided into eight sections, and each section detailed a different magic. Shadow, she knew, and blood. But these others—spirit, sun, fire, sky, water, and stone—were unfamiliar. And under each magic were origin, instructions, and invocations.

"A manual of magics. Where did you get this?"

"From the same one who gave me the god bones and god sweat. It came at a cost, and I did not do it for you."

She saw the tears edging Zataya's eyes and understood. "For him."

The witch gave a sharp nod. "He had faith in me, too, once, and it saved my life. I would not see him come to such an end. And if he cares about you, then I must care about you also."

"Then why encourage me to hide my powers from him?" It was the question that had plagued her for days.

"I thought I could change his fate. If he did not know what you were, what you had become, he would not risk himself so." Zataya slumped, defeated. "But the mirror does not lie, and his death is beyond my control."

"What do you mean?"

She met Naranpa's eyes. "Your powers and his death are connected. I do not know how, only that they are, and that it cannot be denied. It was foolish of me to think I could change that."

And now Zataya's attitude toward her since she had arrived made sense. The dark circles under her eyes. The bend in her back. She was afraid.

"How do I stop it?"

"You cannot—"

"I was once an oracle. I do not fear fate. Tell me how."

"Read the manual, master your powers, and hope that is answer enough."

CHAPTER 18

THE MERIDIAN GRASSLANDS
YEAR 1 OF THE CROW

True friendship is given in grace.

—*The Obregi Book of Flowers*

Xiala woke to the noise and bustle of breaking camp. Her head ached, and her memories of the night before were fuzzy at best. She clearly remembered Iktan's history lesson and her decision to drink, but the rest refused to come back to her in any detail. She had a recollection of Ziha returning to interrogate her about the Odo Sedoh and then leaving in disgust when Xiala couldn't focus enough to tell her what she wanted to know. Well, perhaps that was for the best. She had not wanted to tell the woman about Serapio anyway. Oh, she knew one day she would have to, but a day delayed was a day delayed, and she took the small victories where she could.

She also recalled waking in the night to hear someone retching into the water basin. A figure in white, black hair shorn short. Iktan. She had groaned and gone back to sleep.

And then it was morning, and Ziha had stuck her head in through the flap and called their names. "We leave in twenty minutes, but this tent is coming down in ten. Do what you need to do, and get out." She sounded disgusted, but Xiala found herself slow to sympathy. Iktan's cynicism seemed to be rubbing off on her, at least when it came to the Golden Eagle commander. Of course, Ziha had done nothing to counter Xiala's unfavorable opinion. She was not an approachable woman.

"Skies, my head," Iktan muttered from the other side of the tent. "Tell me, why do people drink?"

Xiala sat up, yawning. "Because the pain you feel now isn't as bad as the pain you felt when you decided to drink."

Xe glared at her. "I don't think I like this philosopher side of you. No wonder xtabentún is forbidden among the priests."

"Well, it's certainly not forbidden among sailors. In fact, I'd say it's encouraged." She tentatively made her way to the basin, wary of what she might find there, and was relieved to see someone had emptied it of sick and left a pitcher of fresh water on the adjoining table. She drank, letting the water revive her, and then filled the basin to wash. Once she was finished with her toilet, she dug through the cushions for her blue cloak. She threw it around her shoulders, appreciative of the fur lining all over again. She didn't see the clothes she had arrived in, but the ones she wore now were sufficient, and she thought perhaps someone had taken the others to be laundered. *Or burned*, she thought, *for not being up to Ziha's sartorial standards.*

"Why *do* sailors drink?" Iktan asked as xe went through xir own morning ablutions. "I've heard as much, but I've always wanted to know. It would seem you need your wits about you even more when facing the terrors of the sea."

"The terrors of the sea are why we drink," she said, laughing. "Living at the whim of the waters? No sane woman would do it."

"But you do it."

"Aye," she agreed sagely.

"It would seem to me," Iktan said as xe pulled xir cloak back on and raised the cowl, "that a Teek would not fear the waters."

"There is a saying they teach us in the cradle. 'The sea has no mercy, even for a Teek.' You learn it then, and you remember it the first time a drag tide catches you and throws you up miles out to sea. A healthy fear is nothing to be ashamed of."

"A healthy fear." Xir smile was the cat's smile. "I'm going to look for breakfast before Ziha comes back to scold us, again."

Iktan left, but she idled behind, xir words nagging at her. Why did she drink? Was it as simple as what she had blithely quipped, some philosophy about drowning sorrows and fears, or was it because that was what sailors did, and it had become a habit? Or was it something else? She felt that pressure again, the feeling that told her she was digging too deep at her own insides and was not ready to face what she would excavate there. Her mother's house, a pool of blood not hers, a body at her feet. She slammed shut the door to that memory, threw the lock, and barred the chain. If she let herself face what lurked there, she was sure it would eat her alive. She was not ready for it, perhaps never would be.

The camp was a shadow of what it had been when she had arrived the day before. Most of the tents save a couple here and there had been struck and packed away, and now the company was making final preparations before the march began. Someone was breaking down the cookfire, and she could hear Iktan's voice over the din, complaining about the lack of breakfast. Others shoveled over a latrine. And yet others were down at the river filling their drinking skins. She saw Ziha moving through it all, keeping things orderly and progressing. She watched her for a while, admiring her way with her people. It was like running a ship, Xiala figured, and, like any good captain, she was efficient and seemed well liked by her people. She decided Iktan's assessment of her was too harsh.

"Here." Iktan was there, handing her a warm cup. It was filled with an unfamiliar gruel.

"What is this?"

"Your breakfast. Drink it, and be glad I got that much out of the cook. Oh . . ." Xe pulled a small package from xir pocket and sprinkled a bit of salt on her meal.

She drank the creamlike mixture from the cup. It was grain and ash, not unlike the street breakfasts popular in Cuecola. "It's good," she remarked.

Iktan made a sound as if her opinion was offensive. She wondered if all ex-priests were such snobs.

"She's good, too," she said, gesturing toward Ziha with her cup.

Iktan watched the Golden Eagle commander at work. "Yes, Ziha makes a lovely despot."

She laughed, unimpressed by Iktan's negativity.

"You laugh now," xe said, "but wait until we've been traveling under her thumb for a week. Then tell me what you think."

Ziha shouted to them, as if she had known they were talking about her. She warned them they were marching out, and they each needed to pick up a pack from the ones yet to be claimed, and once they had a pack, they were to join her in the front. Iktan sighed and lifted a hand to Ziha in a half-hearted salute. Xiala drank the last of her breakfast and grabbed a pack. She threaded the straps through her arms so it rested comfortably on her back, and fell in with the rest of the company.

Together, they walked north across the empty prairie toward the river called Puumun.

• • • • •

The first days of the journey were the monotony of endless walking, setting camp, and then breaking camp, only to do it all again the next day. And again the next day. Xiala found that traveling on land was much like traveling by ship. There was a sameness to the work of taking one step after another that was similar to that of working a paddle, and the Golden Eagle company passed time the same way Cuecolan sailors did; they gossiped, sang bawdy songs, and told stories.

At first, Xiala had tried to stay close to the front. Ziha and Iktan were the only people who spoke to her, and they both led the company. She would catch the others staring, most looks simply curious and none truly hostile, but she was wary of the fact that she was still among Serapio's enemies, which made them her enemies, and she did not desire to make friends. She did, however, enjoy the stories, in particular those of the folk heroes called cliff runners and a queen who wore a pair of wings made of hammered gold and took many lovers, so she lingered close to listen. Golden Eagle's Tovan was slightly different from both Carrion Crow's and Water Strider's, with crisper vowels and swallowed word endings. It took her a while to pick it up, but once she did, she enjoyed the shared tales. She imagined telling them to Serapio, his delighted looks and tentative smiles, the rare occasion when she could coax a laugh from him. And oh, her heart ached at the memories. Perhaps they had not known each other that long, but the time they had spent together had meant more to her than any other. It was the first time since she had left home that someone had cared about her, had been genuinely interested in her—not for what she could do for them but simply for her company. She treasured it, and she missed him more with every mile she walked.

By the third day of the journey, she had begun to drift toward the rear of the company. She still started the morning with Iktan, often gathering gossip over a breakfast of gruel, but by midday, Iktan and Ziha would usually be bickering in fast-paced Tovan, and she had trouble following it. Not that she wanted to. She suspected Iktan picked fights with the commander the same way others cultivated hobbies; it started as something to break the boredom and had grown to genuine enjoyment. Their fighting exacerbated her headaches, too. At first, she had thought them a symptom of her exhaustion, but by the second day, she had begun to suspect that they were caused by something the Teek called land sickness. Stories warned against Teek living too far inland, said there was something about the Teek temperament that made them ill suited for such places, and it was true she had never been this far from the sea for this long.

Whatever it was, it found her at the end of each day falling into her blankets, exhausted. She thought the walking would have made her legs stronger, but they only seemed to be growing weaker. In addition to the headaches and the aching legs, her stomach often wouldn't settle. It felt as if something had started to suck her dry.

And then there were the dreams. All versions of the same one from the camp in Odo. The woman in blue, the man with the green eyes, both dying because of her reckless Song. Sometimes they would speak to her, accusations and recriminations. Other times, they would simply stare. They left her unrested and haunted, worsening her already deteriorating health.

The fourth evening, when they stopped to make camp, she

found herself struggling to set up her tent. The first night, when she and Iktan had raided Ziha's xtabentún and fallen asleep in what she later found out was Ziha's private tent, was an anomaly. After that, she had been given her own small tent that she carried on her back and was responsible for pitching and breaking down on her own. The next two nights, she had managed fine, but now, as the sun fell closer to the ragged, snowcapped mountains in the distance, her hands shook, the poles blurred in her vision, and she promptly passed out.

She woke briefly to Ziha's face above hers, and then someone strong picking her up, and then nothing for a while.

When she did wake again, she was back on the furs that served as rugs in Ziha's tent, the Golden Eagle woman sitting across from her, hazel eyes watching her intently.

"Water," Xiala croaked.

"Beside you," Ziha said, and Xiala looked to her right to see a pitcher and cup.

She drank, and it soothed her somewhat, but she needed something else.

"Iktan is here?" she asked.

"Somewhere in the camp."

"Xe had salt before."

The girl frowned. "I have salt."

"Good. I'll take yours. And I need pumpkin seeds, crushed. Wild spinach. And fish bones, or bone marrow if you don't have fish."

Ziha stood. "I'll have the cook make a broth."

Xiala whispered a thank you and fell back into the blankets. She awoke to Ziha proffering her a steaming bowl.

"What is it?" Ziha asked, as Xiala drank.

"I cannot go to the sea, but perhaps I can bring a little of the sea to me. It is seawater, or as close as I could approximate this far inland. My hope is that it will stave off some of the land sickness."

Even as she drank, her headache began to lessen, and after she had finished the bowl, a measure of vitality had returned to her limbs.

"Is that what made you ill? I found you collapsed beside your tent." She picked at the skin of her thumb with her teeth, a nervous habit Xiala had not noticed before.

Tonight Ziha looked very young. She had seemed somewhat formidable before, but now Xiala saw the things of which Iktan had accused her—privilege, inexperience, bravado.

"I'm fine now. Thank you." She shook her head at how easily the lie came. "I just need to get back to the sea."

"I'm glad you're better. There are things we need to discuss."

Xiala's grip on the bowl tightened. "Perhaps not that much better."

Ziha bit at her finger, looking undecided. "I've sent Iktan on a mission," she blurted. "Xe won't be occupied for long, but I knew it was the only way to talk to you without the tsiyo interfering."

"What is it you need to say to me that Iktan cannot hear?" she asked, wary.

"You cannot trust Iktan, you know. Xe is not your friend."

Xiala set the empty bowl down carefully, then poured herself and the girl each a cup of water. She offered one to Ziha. She stared at it a moment, as if it might contain poison, before seizing it and swallowing a mouthful. The girl paused, as if waiting for any ill effects to commence, but when they didn't, she dropped to the place across from Xiala with a tentative smile.

"And we are friends, Ziha?" Xiala asked. "Is that what you came to say?"

"I think we could be friends," she said, her face sincere.

Xiala did not believe for a moment that they could be friends, but she had no doubt that Ziha believed it. Iktan had warned her that Ziha would be looking for a proxy to punish for her cousin's death, and her relationship to Serapio made her a prime choice. But Xiala wondered if Iktan had the wrong of it and it was that Ziha was looking for a replacement for her cousin herself.

"I wish to tell you something, as a friend. About Iktan. You heard xir speak of having a man in the Carrion Crow Shield, but it is more than that. Xe conspired with this man to kill their matron."

Xiala remembered Aishe telling her the Carrion Crow matron had died and that there were rumors that it was not an accident, but she hadn't thought of it again since then.

Ziha continued excitedly. "The way I hear it, there was an attempt on the Sun Priest's life. Some foolish attempt by an outspoken contingent in the Odohaa that failed before it was begun, but it alarmed Iktan's Crow conspirator—"

"Do you know his name?" Xiala interrupted.

"I do not. Only that he took it to his matron, who refused to act. Said the Odohaa were harmless and did not see the danger such actions posed for her clan. This Crow was so distraught that he reached out to Iktan as the Priest of Knives to beseech leniency, worried at what the tsiyo would rain down on them should the Watchers decide to retaliate. I do not know what transpired between them, but the decision was made that the matron must go. She was known to indulge the Odohaa, but her daughter, the one who would inherit her place, was less tolerant. She is known to have a pragmatic nature."

"And so Iktan killed her."

"Not before xe brought it to some of the other priests, my cousin included. I think that is where the idea came from for the second attempt on the Sun Priest's life."

"The Odohaa tried again?"

"No, the second attempt was not the Odohaa." She worried her thumb. "It was my mother."

"The Golden Eagle matron?"

"It was an opportunity she could not pass up. The pressure from Cuecola has been increasing, willing us to action against the Watchers. But the merchant lords are far away on the other side of the sea. They do not understand the delicate balance between the Sky Made. They would have us act outright, not understanding how Winged Serpent and Water Strider would turn against us. No, it was best to frame Carrion Crow. But then that failed, too. Mother had kept the second assassin secret, thinking the less people knew, the better."

Mother waters, these people! Xiala thought. She had always considered Teek politics an entanglement, but Tova and her Sky Made clans were raveled in their own nets.

"It was after the second attempt that Iktan killed the matron and the Watchers began to plan their retaliation after all. Which also gave Golden Eagle the perfect excuse to take over leadership. We were so close, Xiala, so close!" Ziha had sat forward, face flushed with excitement and eyes shining. She leaned back abruptly, as if remembering to whom she was speaking.

"Why do you think I need to know all this?" Xiala asked carefully. It felt like dangerous knowledge to her, something that made her a liability should someone not want this information made public. Ziha had to know Xiala would pass it on to Serapio. Unless she didn't think Xiala would ever see Serapio again. A thought that made her shiver even in the fire's heat.

"To prove to you that we are friends," the girl said, voice plaintive. "To show you that Iktan is a schemer and will lie to your face. As xe lied to xir precious Naranpa. I know xe is charming and funny and—"

"Attractive." A voice came from outside the tent flap. "Don't forget shockingly attractive."

Ziha scrambled to her feet as Iktan slid through the entrance, steps as light as cat's paws. Ziha fumbled at her belt, pulled forth a knife, and brandished it in front of her. "Guards!" she called, at first just a frantic whisper and then louder. "Guards!"

"I gave them the night off," Iktan said. "Also started a game of patol and lost enough cacao to keep everyone interested and betting for a few hours. No one's coming to save you, Ziha."

The girl was sweating, eyes wide with fright, but Iktan hadn't drawn the blade from xir sleeve, and xe didn't have that uncanny calm about xir as xe had when Xiala thought things might come to violence before.

"Care to join us, Iktan?" Xiala asked smoothly. "We were just talking about you."

Xe tilted xir head toward her, a smile leaking sideways across xir face . . . and then burst into laughter. It was a high, wheezing laugh that bent the ex-priest over, hands on knees. Ziha gaped, dumbfounded. Xiala gave her a reassuring smile.

"Stars and skies, Ziha!" Iktan said, rubbing at xir eyes. Xe dropped down to the furs next to Xiala. "You do not cease to amuse, I will credit you that."

The Golden Eagle commander still held the knife in front of her, but she was starting to look foolish. Xiala guessed she had no idea what to do. It reminded her of when her own sailors had crossed someone and had to make peace while still saving a bit of dignity.

"Come sit with us, Ziha," she offered. "Iktan won't harm

you." She lifted her chin and cut her eyes to the assassin, who was now leaning back on one elbow, looking completely at ease. "I won't let xir."

A flicker in Iktan's eyes, there and gone, sent a cold trickle down Xiala's spine, telling her she walked a fine line, and she would be sorry if she crossed it.

"Yes, come sit with us," Iktan coaxed the girl, "and bring some of that tea you have hidden away. The kind they import from Obregi."

Xiala nodded hopefully, and Ziha rallied. She sheathed her knife, collected the tea, and joined them. Her hands shook as she poured the water into the pot, but Xiala and Iktan said nothing. Ziha placed the pot over the fire to boil, the familiar sounds of preparation too loud. When she drew back her arm, she knocked against a cup, sending it rattling against its neighbor. She let out a small scream, which Xiala pointedly ignored.

They waited in silence for the water to heat, perhaps the most awkward minutes of Xiala's life. She had been in many uncomfortable situations before. Faced down belligerent drunks, vengeful crewmen, and pompous merchant lords. But she had never played counselor to a seasoned killer and a girl commander, and she did not intend to start now.

"I should leave you both to work this out on your own," Xiala said, as she took the pot from the fire and prepared the tea. "I'm not one of you, and frankly, I don't care to know your secrets." She shot a meaningful glare at Ziha, who still looked like she might piss herself if Iktan so much as sneezed. "I don't want to get involved in your politics, I certainly don't want to be your friend"— she thought she saw Iktan's shoulders fall at that—"but as I was told upon my arrival into this thrice-damned company, it seems we are people who are in a position to help each other." She handed a cup of tea to Iktan, and then to Ziha. "So, might I suggest we do that?"

"I know how you can help me, Ziha." Iktan leaned forward. "You can run."

Ziha paused with the cup raised midway to her mouth, her expression puzzled.

Iktan nodded. "That's right, you heard me. Run away." Xe gestured, a wave of fingers. "Go on. Run. Run!"

Ziha dropped the cup and bolted for the door. Tea splattered across the furs, struck Xiala's knee, and hissed in the fire where it hit the hot coals.

"Really?" Xiala asked, annoyed.

Iktan laughed, an amused chuckle, and sipped from xir cup. Xe glanced at Xiala.

"Do not give me that look, Xiala. She's lucky I don't have her spanked and sent back to her mother. A careless tongue is one thing when you are a scion in the Great House idle with gossip, but Ziha is here to command. And when we get to Hokaia and the stakes are that much higher, she will damn us all if she thinks she can share secrets to make friends and somehow that will serve the interests of Golden Eagle."

She could see the logic in Iktan's thinking, but she thought the lesson could have been done better.

"Why was she sent? She is very young."

"Twenty. Not so young. Old enough for the responsibility that she asked for, I may add. Nuuma wished to come herself, but that would compromise any subterfuge. The other clans do not know that Golden Eagle plots with Cuecola for now, and they want to secure allegiances before taking action. Nuuma thought it best to stay in Tova. She does have another daughter, Terzha, who might have come, but Ziha wanted a chance to prove herself. Well, I will make her prove herself."

Xiala pursed her lips, thinking. "You're here to look after her," she said, with sudden clarity. "All this bickering and threatening, it's all for show."

"Not for show. For a purpose. But one she cannot see, yet. I am better as a thorn in her side than as a nursemaid."

"Skies, Iktan. Your games are too much for me."

Xe smiled. "Cursing like a Tovan? You'll be one of us soon enough."

"Mother save me," she said, and they both laughed.

She rubbed at the wet spot on her knee and then poured herself a bit more tea.

"I heard you were ill." Iktan's voice did not give away xir concern, but Xiala felt it and was surprised.

"I'm fine."

"Xiala . . ."

"I said I am fine." She didn't want the ex-priest prying.

"No. What she said about me was true."

She exhaled, setting her cup down to give herself time. "I know."

"I betrayed not just a friend but the woman I once loved. I killed the Carrion Crow matron. I conspired with Golden Eagle and conspire still."

"I know."

"What will you do?"

She knew what Iktan was asking. Would she think less of xir, as Ziha had hoped? Had the girl's words driven a wedge between them in their budding friendship? But she also knew Iktan wanted to know if she would tell Carrion Crow who had killed their matron. She could only assume there would be punishment for such a crime should the clan be given a chance at justice. It was a secret that carried a death sentence, and she held it in her hands, unwillingly.

"I think," she said, "I will go back to my tent and go to bed. It has been a long day, and tomorrow we reach the river. I want to be ready for whatever is next."

She briefly touched a hand against Iktan's cheek before standing and slowly, deliberately, walking out the door. She pretended she did not see the glint of light off the blade cupped in Iktan's palm, but her legs shook on the long walk back to her tent.

CHAPTER 19

What strange creatures humans are, to dream so much and achieve so little.

—From *The Manual of the Dreamwalkers*,
by Seuq, a spearmaiden

Balam stood at the bow of the great ship and watched as it cut neatly through the Crescent Sea. The waters were calm on their first morning out of Cuecola and parted like flesh under a sharpened blade. An image popped into his mind: his fingers wrapped around the hilt of an obsidian knife, the chest of a blue-painted man sliced open under his hand, blood welling like the froth of the tide.

He closed his eyes, willing the vision to pass. It was a memory, but not his. Since he had started dreamwalking, such images came more and more frequently, often when he was wide awake. Walking nightmares, he had thought at first. But he had quickly begun to suspect they were something more.

He saw himself as a priest of old most often, but sometimes he was the blue-painted victim, the terror thick in his throat as the blade sliced open his own chest. And there were worse

208

things. He stood atop a mountain and watched a city burn. He waved his hand, and the sea boiled crimson as dead fish floated in the maelstrom. He spoke a word, and a line of men walked calmly to the edge of a great pyramid and stepped off to splatter on the ground below.

These were memories from the War of the Spear more than three hundred years ago, he had no doubt. But he did not know why they haunted him. Were they some strange remnant of spirit magic from the time of the dreamwalkers? Was he seeing their deeds play out as if they were his own? Or did the visions serve as a warning for what was to come should he pursue the path he had set for himself?

If it was the latter, he was unswayed. There was no cost he was not willing to pay to achieve his goal, even if cities burned and oceans boiled. And people died every day. What were a hundred more in service to a greater cause?

Raised voices behind him turned his head, and he saw the captain of the ship, a short, bow-legged man in a wide-brimmed hat by the name of Keol. He had a map of the western waters of the Crescent Sea splayed out across an unused bench. Three of the seven merchant lords of Cuecola gathered around him, peppering the man with questions. Balam shook off the dark visions of war and death and wandered over to see what the fuss was about, his presence making the lord count four.

"A few days extra is all that is required, my lords," the captain was explaining. "We have to go the long way around. Through the shallow parts."

"Shallow parts?" a lord named Sinik asked. "It looks all one depth to me." He was a small man with an industrious demeanor, a pinched face, and a ridiculous braided forelock that he insisted was in fashion. Balam had no great quarrel with him, and he often found his comments in the gatherings of the Seven Lords quite astute when it came to finances, but it was difficult to take him seriously with that absurd hairstyle. *Perhaps that's why he wears it*, Balam thought. *To distract one from the keen mind beneath.* Or perhaps Balam was giving him too much credit.

"The sea is deeper here." The captain poked a gnarled finger at the middle of the map between Cuecola at the bottom and the mouth of the river that led to Hokaia at the top. "We go around the longer way near the islands, where it's not so deep and the weather is kinder."

"Deep enough to drown, still." That was Lord Pech, who had insisted on coming despite Balam's pointed assurances that his presence was not needed and the equally direct reminder that Pech could not swim.

He was sure Pech had insisted on making the journey to spite him. The man had not forgiven Balam for stealing his captain away, although *stealing* was a rich word when Pech had insisted he was done with the Teek woman before Balam had sought to employ her. *One never wants something more than when it is denied them*, he thought.

"Aye, you can drown." The captain grinned. "But you can drown in pond water, too. Don't you worry, Lord. Skies are clear this time of year on the western side, and we're close enough to break for island lands if storms threaten. I won't let you drown."

"Pity," Balam murmured, and Pech glared over his shoulder. Balam smiled blandly at the petty little man.

Lord Tuun pointed a black-stained finger at the map. "Those are Teek islands. They are notoriously unwelcoming." She was the only lord of the seven merchant lords Balam actually wanted on the voyage. They were kindred spirits, after a fashion. Both with powerful fathers, deceased. Hers recently, and with no male heirs, which was how she seized the title and privileges of lord, and his long gone but with the same benefits. But most important, she practiced the old magics. A stone sorceress, just as he was blood, and, more recently, spirit. Together, along with his cousin Powageh's mastery of shadow, they made a formidable force.

"Mistress Tuun." The captain had an annoying insistence on calling her "Mistress" even though her proper address was "Lord," and every time he did it, Balam thought he saw the corner of Tuun's slate-colored eye twitch. "As long as we stay to the shore, the Teek won't bother us. If you trespass inland or, worse, try for the interior islands, the ones that don't show on no map. That's when . . ." The captain made a cutting motion across his neck.

Lord Tuun straightened. "I see."

"Don't you worry, neither," Keol said, making a settling gesture the way you might to a worried child. "I'll get you all there safely. And the others." He pointed with his chin to take in the other two ships that ran beside them, one port and the other starboard. They were far enough away to avoid getting caught in their trailing wake but close enough to hail with a collection of symbol-marked pennants Balam had spotted near the stern. One ship ran heavy, weighed down with enough gold and jade and quetzal feathers to impress even the most spoiled Sovran. Each merchant lord's house had contributed to the bounty, even the ones who had chosen to remain in Cuecola. This diplomatic mission was, after all, a joint effort supported by all the ruling houses. The other ship held his cousin Powageh and a contingent of personal guards and household servants for each lord. Powageh had wanted to travel with Balam and the other lords, but Pech had argued that one more might overturn the ship, and Sinik had said something about protocol, and

Balam had not even had to discuss it with Powageh before his cousin simply muttered, "You owe me for this," and retired with the servants. Balam almost envied xir. At least, Powageh did not have to hear Pech drone on about water safety.

"There's shade and refreshments under the awning, and strong men to paddle us on," the captain was saying. "I know this route well, and there's land by sunset. Until then . . ." A beleaguered smile creased his sun-wrinkled face, and the lords shuffled toward the awning, as instructed.

Perhaps we are like children to him, Balam thought, and the idea so amused him that he chuckled quietly to himself.

Tuun bumped against his shoulder. She motioned him back toward the bow out of earshot. She was tall, a match to his height, with a long, sloping forehead and pale eyebrows against rich, soil-dark skin. Jade clinked softly at her wrists and ankles, and she wore a deep green dress that cut low at the neck and belted below her breasts. Not exactly seafaring attire, but who was he to argue? He wore his formal jaguar whites.

"Does Pech ever shut up?" Tuun complained, as he joined her on a bench at the bow of the ship. "How you failed to convince him to stay behind . . ."

"He came to spite me, I'm sure of it."

"What did you do that would make that fool risk it all on the Crescent Sea?"

"He thinks I'm plotting."

"Well, he's right about that."

He laughed. How could he not?

She pressed a tattooed hand adorned with rings to her stomach, her mouth twisting in discomfort.

"Seasickness?"

"Nothing I cannot manage, but I admit I am not wont to take up sea voyaging as a pastime anytime soon."

"A shame. You would make a splendid pirate."

She laughed, showing a top row of teeth implanted with tiny, rounded pieces of jade, turquoise, and pink coral. "Why, Balam, are you flirting with me?"

"Would it help my cause if I did?"

She studied him, her slate eyes tilted in speculation. "You're a handsome man," she admitted. "And wealthy."

"Exceedingly wealthy."

"Alas, so am I. And I've never felt the need for a husband before. I don't expect that to change now."

"Ah," he said. "I assure you I am not in need of a wife. I was hoping you would consider a much more promising proposal."

"House Balam and House Tuun as allies?" She shrugged. "Perhaps. Although I have yet to understand why I should support you in this war you seek. The last time Cuecola warred, the Sorcerer Prince himself fell. You think you can avoid the same fate if you rule the city alone?"

His face showed surprise.

"Did you not think I knew of your aspirations?"

"I have tried to be discreet."

"And you have been. I doubt Pech or Sinik or any of the other lords suspect your warmongering is for anything less mundane than lower taxes and more power over the Meridian trade routes. But I am a sorceress by birthright, and I know these things."

"Because they are your aspirations, too?"

She lifted a shoulder noncommittally. She turned her head, the bright sunlight catching the subtle sheen of gold powder rubbed into the smooth skin at her neck. "We'll be sleeping on Teek soil tonight," she observed, her eyes fixed on distant islands that they could not yet see. "I can feel it as we grow closer."

"The Teek?"

"Their land. It is ancient, their islands the refuse of old volcanoes."

Balam followed her gaze but saw nothing but endless sea. "I thought the isles of the Crescent Sea were formed by coral reefs."

"Some of the outliers, but these . . ." Her expressive shoulders shivered. "I feel them in my bones. Still alive, always growing."

"The land is made from the remnants of your ancestral gods," he said, understanding.

"Angry gods that belch fire and sulfur."

"The stone gods of your house namesake."

She turned to face him, her eyes glittering under pale brows. "I want them, Balam. Legend says they were once my family's territory, made from the spine of the great stone serpent god. I want them back."

"But these islands are already populated," he observed dryly, "by a people who are quite fond of them, as I understand it."

"That is my price for your alliance. We both know the Teek fell to the spearmaidens before, and what is left of them can fall again. I simply want them to fall to me." She smiled, all viper. "To us."

He held his tongue and kept his face entirely blank.

"You have ten days until we reach Hokaia to decide," she said. "It is likely that the Teek will not answer the summons of the Treaty, and you only need to convince Hokaia and Golden Eagle to hand the islands over to me."

He raised a doubting eyebrow. "You would still need an army at your back to enforce such a declaration."

"Perhaps. Although a cadre of sorcerers may serve just as

well if the Teek are as few in number as I suspect. Who knows? They may welcome a new queen."

He laughed, thinking of the Teek captain he had hired. "I would not count on that. They are stubborn creatures."

"Then I will bend them until they break, and if you want House Tuun beside you, you will help me do it."

She pressed a long-nailed hand into his shoulder before she excused herself to go back to the awning where the other Cuecolan lords waited.

Balam stayed a bit longer, letting the sun beat down on his head and warm his skin to a richer brown. He searched the horizon for the islands Tuun could feel in her bones, wondering if a civilization of women with sorcery in their Song awaited them just out of sight. Her demand had taken him by surprise, although he had hidden it well. He thought he knew all about House Tuun and their stone gods, but he had failed to associate them with the volcanoes that dotted the eastern side of the Crescent Sea. He was unfamiliar with the legends Lord Tuun had referred to that gave them to her in birthright, and he suspected the Teek had conflicting tales, but he had no interest in sorting out such history. He simply berated himself for not anticipating her. He had known she was as ambitious as he, and he had thought she might demand a district of Cuecola as payment once he ruled the city, or even a neighboring city of her own. Huecha or some such down the coast. But the lands of the Teek? It was a foolish thing to ask.

Then let her die for it, he thought. *Once she has used her magic to topple your enemies' cities. After she serves her purpose, her fate is no concern of yours.*

He rubbed at the back of his overwarm neck, which he suspected was beginning to sunburn. He really should go join the other lords under the awning before he overheated. He could see they were eating small plates of seafood and drinking cold cups of thick papaya juice.

He exhaled a long sigh. He would promise Tuun her islands if it would make her amenable to his cause. She was likely correct, and the Teek were so diminished they would not be much of a challenge. And if they were? He had reconciled himself to a hundred deaths. Why not a thousand? Ten thousand?

He stood, pasted a neutral smile on his face, and went to join his peers.

CHAPTER 20

City of Tova (Coyote's Maw)
Year 1 of the Crow

And Coyote cried, I have been cast down! Here does the thorn pierce me! There does the rock break my back! And yet I live!

—From *Songs of the Coyote*

Naranpa called Baaya to her rooms. Denaochi had left her an ensemble worthy of the Sun Priest's first conference with the bosses. Her skirt was a deep yellow, patterned with narrow lines that seemed to shine like beams of sunlight when she moved, and blue and white ribbon ran along the hem like the horizon at dawn. Her shawl-like blouse was the same shade of yellow, and small string tassels hung from the sleeves, threaded through with blue and white. Her cloak was deer hide lined with dark-dyed fur, dots of white, like stars, placed within, and she wore heavy bands of gold at her wrists and even more as cuffs on her ears and ankles. Baaya also fixed her hair, pulling it back from her face with golden combs while letting the heavy bulk of it fall loose down her back. Her ensemble was regal and meant to impress, and Naranpa donned it like armor.

She read over the scroll while Baaya worked, trying to absorb as much as she could about the eight magics outlined in the document. Each had an opposing magic along the wheel: spirit in contrast to blood, fire to water, stone to sky, and the one that most interested her, sun to shadow. The map linked the sun's power to the firebird and to life. In opposition, the shadow was represented by the crow and death. But it didn't tell her how to invoke the power or what it could be used for. Or how she might call on it to aid Denaochi. But if Zataya was right and even now her brother was facing the wrath of the other bosses, she didn't have time to decipher the mysteries of the manual. She hoped that the power would come with her need, as it had before. And if it didn't, she would have to find another way.

Zataya met her at the door of the Lupine. "I can take you as far as the entrance of the Agave."

Naranpa remembered the letter Denaochi had showed her marked with three agave leaves. "Is that where he is? What is it?"

"A pleasure house run by a woman name Sedaysa. She is an ally, an old friend of Denaochi's from days past, and she does not wish him ill. But she will be unable to delay those who do for long."

Zataya hurried them out onto the streets. Naranpa found herself scanning the rooftops, looking for crows, but saw none. She could only hope the Crow God Reborn had given up on finding her, but to even think it felt like a lie. This was only a reprieve, and she knew it.

"What must I do when I arrive?" They walked quickly down the near-empty street, cowls up and heads together.

"Show them your power. Assure them you will fight for the Maw, that you can bring the Sky Made clans to bend to your authority as Sun Priest, and that the Crow God Reborn can be defeated by your sorcery."

"I cannot promise all that."

"Then Denaochi is dead."

She pulled Naranpa down a side street, and then another, until they came to a building that resembled the Lupine, its half-circle facade facing out. But where the Lupine was white-washed except for the painting of the flower that was its name-sake, this building was a pale blue, and its door was set at street level. Next to the door, itself the deep purple of a bruise, was the painting of an agave plant. The succulent sprouted three fat blue-green leaves that curled sensually upward, their tips crowned with dark maroon thorns.

"I can go no farther." Zataya smoothed shaking hands over her lap. "I will pray for you to the small gods, and to the Coy-ote, too." She hesitated. "And to the sun."

Naranpa had never wanted anyone's prayers, much less to gods whose worship the Watchers forbade, but all she said was, "Thank you."

Zataya squeezed her arm, the most affection she had ever shown Naranpa, and then she was hurrying back down the street.

Naranpa squared her shoulders, took a deep breath, and pushed open the door.

She had expected the Agave to be much like the Lupine, a gambling den redolent with tobacco smoke and fermented drink, but she found herself in a courtyard filled with uncom-mon greenery and unnatural heat.

"A hothouse," she murmured, as she noticed the braziers burning every few paces and the clay diffusers that warmed the space. A white stone path wound through the courtyard, and she followed it, already sweating under her fur cloak. Around her, vines sagged with orange and pink blossoms, and small ponds burst with teal and yellow flowers. She passed a young boy sitting cross-legged on a rug, sweet notes rising from his flute. The air was heavy with spice and citrus, and lanterns in painted paper boxes flickered gently under a ceiling adorned with the stars of the night sky. Just outside was winter, as cold and mean as Tova had ever seen, but inside its walls, the Agave offered a summer night in the southern lands of the Meridian.

She did not linger, as much as it tempted, but pushed through another set of doors, these deep red, into the inner chamber.

If the garden hothouse had been a paradise, this room was something out of a story. A very particular kind of story. There were plants here, too, growing in glorious and colorful profusion, and the air was perfumed with the same decadent scents, but among the vines and pots full of blossoms were thin woven screens that hung from ceiling to floor, and behind those screens were beds. And on those beds were people in various stages of undress, their low moans intermingling with the flute and drum.

A pleasure house, she reminded herself. *What did you expect to find here, Nara?*

She had thought to find Denaochi in pain, being tortured in some cold, awful place by equally cold and awful men, not this sensual idyll. She averted her eyes, keeping her gaze on the tiled path that led through the room, but she couldn't block out the sounds around her, and her face flushed in embarrassment. She was not particularly worldly when it came to matters of the flesh. While the priesthood did not frown on sex among its order, it did not encourage it, either, and marriage was forbidden. Iktan had been her only lover, and it had never bothered her, but she was suddenly and acutely aware of her lack of experience.

Head down, eyes averted, and mind distracted, she did not see the woman standing in her path until it was almost too late. She came to a halt, startled.

"You must be the sister."

The woman's eyes appraised her. Her skin was a deep brown and oiled to a shine. Her hair was pure silver. She wore a skirt the shade of moonlight, and a shawl of silver netting covered her otherwise nude chest. A collar of iridescent feathers floated around her delicate neck. She smiled, parting generous red lips.

Naranpa could not hide her sharp inhale. This was the most beautiful woman she had ever seen, and for a moment she forgot her words.

The woman's smile spread, no doubt knowing the effect she had, and that was enough for Naranpa to rally. "And you must be Sedaysa," she replied, remembering the name Zataya had given her.

"He said you were not coming."

Naranpa lifted her chin. "He was mistaken."

Something flashed across Sedaysa's features that looked like relief. "He agreed to give blood sacrifice in payment for his failure. In fact, he gives it still."

Which meant he still lived, but in what condition? "I know of blood sacrifice. I have given my own blood before."

"As Sun Priest?" Sedaysa was doubtful.

"No." She didn't explain further, but she thought of Zataya's stingray spine and her obsidian knives and braced herself for what she might find ahead.

"Now that you are here, he no longer needs to suffer." Sedaysa stepped to the side. "Go free your brother."

Naranpa stepped forward tentatively. At first, she only saw the people, small groups of men and women in fine clothes drinking from long, delicate cups, and she knew these must be the bosses of the Maw. She spied a tall woman in a wrap dress of deepest blue, heavy jade beads around her neck, leaning close to talk to a man in a billowing red cloak, a crown of speckled feathers on his head. There was a feast laid out on a low table, and another handful of people lingered there, eating with their hands and laughing. They stopped to watch as Naranpa passed, their eyes like pinpricks against her skin.

And then she saw him.

Denaochi knelt naked upon a dais strapped to a wooden rack. His head lolled on his neck, and his hair which had been so neatly coiffed hung loose and tangled around his face. His arms were splayed wide and tied at the wrists and shoulders with heavy rope, and familiar white stingray spines pierced his body. One through his tongue, more through each ear, and one through his genitals. Where there were not spines, there were knives. At his shoulders and elbows and hands, through his hips and thighs, inner and outer, but none through his torso. He was meant to bleed to death, very slowly.

Naranpa shuddered.

She was dimly aware that around her the sound had stilled, and she knew they watched—the woman in blue, the man in red, and all the rest. She felt someone beside her, but she could not tear her eyes away from her brother.

"It is the old way," Sedaysa said beside her, her voice so calm Naranpa wanted nothing more than to scream.

"The Watchers ended this practice," she said through gritted teeth. "It is forbidden."

"Do not judge us, Sun Priest," the woman said. "Denaochi consented, and it is his atonement."

"Release him," Naranpa growled, the sound of her voice so filled with anger that she did not recognize it.

"No," the woman said simply. "*That* is your atonement."

Naranpa wanted to shout that she owed these people nothing, but it was too late for argument. And the longer she delayed, the more he suffered.

She forced herself forward, the hem of her fine dress dragging through blood. Once she stood directly before him, she paused, hands raised, not knowing what to do first. Untie him? Remove the spines?

"The spines first." It was Sedaysa again, behind her, voice gentle.

Naranpa pulled the one from his tongue first, and then the others, her hands steady for Denaochi's sake. And then, one by one, she removed the knives, counting a dozen as they clattered to the floor. The ropes were last, and once released, he tumbled into her arms. She caught him and pulled him into her lap. Blood soaked through her dress, but she did not care.

"I'm so sorry," she whispered, pushing his hair from his face. He had not opened his eyes, and she didn't know if he heard her.

If he was still alive to hear her.

Grief bubbled up, dense and drowning. Her tears wetted his hair as she held him close.

"Which one of you did this?"

They had assembled before her. Sedaysa, the man in red, the woman in blue, and nine others who made up the company of the Maw known as the bosses.

"We all did." It was the red-robed man who spoke. "I am Pasko of the Blackfire, and my blade is there." He stepped forward to retrieve one of the discarded knives.

"I am Amalq of the Wildrose," the woman in blue said, stepping forward, "and my blade is there." She took another knife.

And so on they went, until Sedaysa took the last blade and they stood before her, waiting. For what she didn't know. It all stank of ritual, not malice, but she had no use for any of it.

"And who pierced him through with those?" Her eyes touched on the stingray spines, the desire to catalog her enemies strong.

"Those he did to himself," Pasko said. "He was not craven."

She had not expected that, and it tore at her heart. She imagined him there, kneeling, knowing their knives would come next, as he drove the needles through his flesh.

What if I was too late? She pressed her hand to his chest. She felt a heartbeat and the slow rise and fall of his breath. He still lived, but barely. "He needs a healer."

"No." Sedaysa's denial was flat and did not brook argument. "If the gods will it, he survives. If they do not . . ."

I must save him. But how? She thought of Zataya's manual and its decree that the power of the sun was life itself. But what use was that here when death loomed so near?

"Life," she whispered. "I have the power of life. I am a survivor." She pressed her lips to her brother's head. "And so are you."

She closed her eyes and concentrated. She thought of the shock of hitting the icy river from a great height, the terror of waking up in her own tomb, the exhilaration of escaping the Crow God Reborn's attack. She drew from those moments, those memories, and let them build within her. She fed them to the place in her heart, the place where the sun god dwelled within, and she willed it to spark. She knew when her hand began to glow from the low gasps of the watching crowd, and she pressed her palm to Denaochi's chest, willing his breath to strengthen, his heart to answer the beat of her own.

And it did.

Slowly, he came back to her.

She felt a mirroring strength leave her body for his. She let it happen, let her vitality flow to him. Her head began to pound, and the room around her swayed, the heady perfume of flowers making her dizzy. Only when Denaochi coughed and began to stir did she cut the connection between them.

They gasped at the same time, and then they were both laughing, and the bosses were murmuring in shock and approval, but in this moment, she cared nothing for what they thought, only that Denaochi was alive. She turned his arms, then his hands. The wounds were pale and raised, halfway to healed.

"Ah, Sister." His voice was weak and strained, but it was enough. "I knew you'd come. You were always so ambitious."

She hiccupped around her tears, smiling. "Another test, Ochi?"

"The last one, I swear it." His eyes flicked to their audience. "Are they with us?"

She looked up.

At her attention, Pasko went down to one knee, murmuring, "Sun Priest."

Amalq followed. "Sun Priest."

And the others likewise.

Sedaysa was the last, "Sun Priest" triumphant on her lips, and Naranpa caught the shadow of a smile.

She brushed his hair from Denaochi's face and whispered, "They are with us."

A deep calm settled over her, a purpose she had not known before. Even when she had sung the stories and performed the rituals of the Sun Priest, she had never felt as much at her purpose as this. Was this what the signers of the Treaty had wanted when they established the Watchers? A Sun Priest not only to lead the Meridian but to heal a war-ravaged land? A Sun Priest to find order in the chaos, to know the future so that the past was not repeated?

She did not quite understand what she was meant to do with healing powers or if they offered her anything that she might use to fight against the darkness that the Crow God Reborn brought, but she was closer than she had been only hours ago to finding an answer. Her brother was alive, and as she looked out over the lowered heads and bent knees of the bosses before her, she knew they would face what came next together.

CHAPTER 21

CITY OF TOVA (DISTRICT OF ODO)
YEAR I OF THE CROW

Beware the faithless for whom duty is but an inconvenience. Better a single zealot than a thousand pragmatists who believe in nothing.

—*On the Philosophy of War*,
taught at the Hokaia War College

"Wake up, Okoa." Persistent hands shook his shoulder, and he came to all at once.

His cousin Chaiya stood over him, his broad face serious. "Asleep on duty, I see," he chided, but his tone was light and teasing.

Okoa rubbed sleep from his eyes. He was in the barracks on the lower floor of the Great House, the members of the Shield busy around him. His back ached from sleeping on the hard bench, and he must have done something strange to his neck, because it pinched when he turned his head.

"I was . . ."

"Up all hours, waiting for the Odo Sedoh. I know."

"Is there news?"

"No." The frustration was clear on Chaiya's face. It was a

frustration they all felt. Two days had passed since the incident in the yard, and still no sign of the Odo Sedoh.

"I should send out another aerial patrol." Okoa stretched his neck to loosen the muscles.

"Let Ituya handle it. We need to talk."

"No, I—"

"Okoa." Chaiya's tone brooked no argument. "Now."

"So talk, Cousin."

He glanced around at the Shields coming and going, a man eating in the corner, two women laughing as they went off duty. "Not here."

"We can go to my office. Have the kitchen bring—"

"No, not in the Great House. Let's fly."

Okoa could think of nothing he'd rather do than climb onto Benundah's back and go, even if only for a few hours. But he was the captain now, and the Shield operated at his command.

"I shouldn't leave," he said. "I have people out looking for the Odo Sedoh. In fact, I should go back out there—"

"He's been gone two days, Okoa. You must do other things. Eat, sleep."

"You don't understand. The Odohaa—"

"I was once captain of the Shield, too, and Maaka a thorn in my heel longer than he has been in yours. The search for the Odo Sedoh can continue without you for a handful of hours. You need to get out of this place. And there are things we need to discuss. In private."

"Last time we talked in private, you brought me news of my mother's death," he said bitterly. "What will you say now?"

Chaiya looked taken aback for a moment, but he quickly recovered. "Wash up. I'll meet you in the aviary." And then he was gone.

So it was bad news. Okoa was already drowning in bad

news and did not want any more, but better to hear it from Chaiya first, even if he'd rather not hear it at all.

• • • • •

Chaiya was already waiting for him, Kutssah saddled and ready. Okoa hurried to Benundah, feeding her a handful of grubs as he greeted her. She returned his welcome and allowed him to bridle her and slide a rug saddle on her back. He tightened the saddle straps before he climbed on, gave a curt nod to Chaiya, and then they were away, soaring out across Odo.

The district shrank below them as they ascended, but for a moment, Okoa could see the entirety of Odo stretched out below him.

The camp at the Great House's gates had swelled even more since the Odo Sedoh's disappearance. Okoa remembered what it had been like in the crowd that day. They had rushed in, trying to find the Teek woman who had come to their gate. The crowd had quickly closed in around them, and he'd lost sight of the Odo Sedoh. He'd spied him again at the center of a mob, his white staff swinging, and dread had tightened his chest. Images of the slaughter at Sun Rock had reeled through his memory, and Okoa feared he would see violence unleashed again. And then the sky had filled with crows, sharp beaks and talons, and Okoa had instinctively ducked, and when he had looked up again, the flock was gone. Only later would he learn from witnesses that the Odo Sedoh and the flock were one, that he had transformed into a half-hundred crows and fled. He did not believe it at first, but it was the only explanation that made sense.

He laughed at himself. Sense. It made no sense that a man became a flock of crows, and with that, he was starkly reminded that the Odo Sedoh was no normal man, which troubled him even more.

In the wake of his disappearance, Okoa had gone to the aviary hoping to find Serapio there among the crows, but he had found no sign of the man. The only other place he could think of was the rookery, and he had taken to Benundah's back and urged her into the sky. They had circled around, crossing the district, even passing the celestial tower, but when he had tried to lead her westward, she had balked. The great corvid would not leave Tova.

"He's gone somewhere and asked you not to follow, is that what you're telling me?" Okoa had murmured to his crow.

He could not understand in words her answering cry, but he had discerned her meaning well enough.

"Can you at least tell me if he plans to return?"

Silence from Benundah. The only answer was the wind that tore at his hair and the darkened sun above.

So he had brought her home. Since then, the Shield had searched, sending out patrols around the district and aerial watches across the city. But with the other clans actively keeping the crows out, there was not much he could do.

Esa grew worried that the Odo Sedoh had come only long enough to plant a fanatical force at their door, undermine her authority, and then abandon them.

Okoa had been incredulous. "I thought you wanted him gone."

"Did you not counsel me to consider embracing him and joining common cause with the Odohaa?"

"I am only surprised you listened."

"They still come, you know. A hundred more today and half that yesterday. It is a disaster looming at our gate."

Maaka was not making things easier. He had kept his word

and not told of Esa's foolish stunt, but the leader of the Odohaa had not been idle. He gave daily sermons recounting his
trip to Sun Rock to see the "glorious Reckoning" and details of
his meeting with the Odohaa. Worse yet, an armed militia had
begun to form under his leadership, an expansion of the Odohaa's war council called the tuyon. Okoa knew he had to put
a stop to it before they became big enough to overwhelm the
Shield, but he was afraid he had already missed his opportunity for a peaceful dissolution. His present hope lay in the Odo
Sedoh returning and putting a stop to it himself. He did not
think the man he had befriended those first days in the monastery would condone Maaka's tuyon, but he was not sure.

Now Chaiya led them south across the open mesa. The city
gave way to open vistas: wide, flat, high desert spotted with lingering snow. Clumps of cedar ceded to bare-limbed aspens and
thickening pine forests, and the softened humps of long-dead
volcanoes reclined in the distance. He was not surprised when
the lake where they trained riders came into sight. Usually, it
sparkled a deep, cold blue under the winter sky, but under the
eclipsed sun, it was half frozen, sheets of ice creating a fragile
crust that stretched from shore to shore.

Kutssah dipped landward, and Benundah followed. They
landed on the stretch of cleared waterfront. Okoa spied a small
camp. He remembered there had always been a training ground
here for aspiring young scions, a place where they not only
learned to ride but could practice some of the war arts that
required open space, like archery and hook-spear throwing.

"Are we meeting others?" he asked once they had landed.

Someone had been here earlier and laid out various war-
game paraphernalia. Cane hook spears, obsidian-tipped arrows and the rounded bows used to fire them, even a display
of hand knives on a table.

"No, only us. I wanted privacy."

Chaiya slipped from Kutssah's back, loosened the straps of her saddle, and pulled it off. He rubbed the scruff at her neck and removed her bridle, then whistled a series of commands. The great crow squawked her reply and took to the sky.

Okoa watched, surprised.

"Benundah, too." Chaiya gestured to the other corvid.

"Why?"

"She talks to him, doesn't she?"

His voice was pitched low, but Okoa was sure Benundah heard him. And there was no mistaking what "him" Chaiya meant.

"She would never repeat what we say."

Chaiya looked down for a moment, as if thinking. "She stayed with him on Sun Rock that night, didn't she? During the storm before Convergence."

Okoa didn't have an answer.

"I heard that the crows have a name for him. Suneater."

"How would you know that?"

His cousin cocked his head. "Do you doubt it?"

"I . . ." Why would Chaiya lie? "Even if it is true, I don't see how it matters."

"Send her away, Okoa. I did the same to Kutssah."

Okoa wanted to protest that Chaiya did not have the same relationship with Kutssah that he had with Benundah, but he knew his cousin cared for his mount as much as he did his. And he remembered that Benundah *had* helped the Odo Sedoh at the monastery and told him Okoa's name. And it was true she had sheltered him, not just from the storm but from Okoa when he sought him after the incident in the yard. He had never doubted Benundah's loyalties . . . until now. *Damn you, Chaiya*, he thought. But he unsaddled Benundah and sent her away all the same.

As she took to the wing, he thought she glared at him with one baleful eye, but he couldn't be sure if it was her or his own guilt at not trusting her.

Once she had disappeared out over the forested mountains, Chaiya motioned him over to the display of weaponry.

"Choose."

Okoa tensed. "Why?"

Chaiya laughed and stepped to the hook spears. "Don't look so frightened, Okoa. I thought we'd get in some practice while we talk. You haven't had any proper training since you returned from the war college."

That was true enough, and he relaxed a bit. His cousin wouldn't hurt him. The very idea was ridiculous, a sign of the paranoia that had plagued him since his mother's murder. He vowed to leave that behind, at least for the brief time here at the lakeside.

"Not the throwing spear." He motioned to the arrows.

Chaiya raised his hands in surrender and shifted over to the archery display. The two men busied themselves with choosing and testing bows and then evaluating arrows for warps and cracks. Once they were both satisfied, they moved to stand before the padded targets, each one set out about forty paces.

"Youth first, Cousin," Chaiya said.

Okoa grinned. "Are you sure? If you don't go first, you won't be able to brag that you once had the lead."

"I'll take that chance."

Okoa inclined his head. He stepped forward and found his stance, nocked the bolt, and, straightening, drew the bow. He allowed himself to focus, breathing into his feet, connecting to the earth and the world around him. He noted the slight breeze lifting off the lake, the faint sounds of an animal somewhere in the shrubbery, the in and out of his own breath. He continued to draw until there was an invisible line between his jaw, his nose, and the arrow tip. His arm trembled slightly from maintaining the tension. He focused on the distant target, and then, all at once, he exhaled and released his shot.

The arrow flew true, striking the target dead center.

"Ho!" Chaiya commended him. "A clean hit. I forgot you were good at this."

"Better than the hook spear," he said, pleased at the praise.

It had been weeks since he'd drawn a bow, and the weather here was colder and drier than Hokaia. He was worried the unfamiliar bow wouldn't respond well, but it had behaved exactly as he'd wished.

Chaiya stepped up to take his turn, and Okoa made room. Chaiya's bolt was fletched with brown feathers to distinguish it from Okoa's white. Okoa watched as he found his stance, drew, and loosed. His arrow hit just to the left of Okoa's, off-center.

"Skies." His cousin made a show of stretching out his shoulder. "The old injury acting up."

Okoa smiled, giving him his excuse. He took up his next arrow, and Chaiya stepped aside.

"I bet you can't do it again," he teased as Okoa passed.

"Care to wager?"

"Ah, you Tovans and your wagers!"

"Are you not Tovan?"

"I didn't say I wouldn't take the bet!"

They both laughed at that, and Okoa felt the tension ease. It had been a good idea to get him away from the Great House. He was working too hard, worrying too much. The simple pleasures of bow and arrow, the natural world, and companionship were doing him good.

He took his stance and drew, bolt aligned along his cheek, target in sight.

"Your father was an impressive archer, too." Chaiya's words were quiet, but they had their intended effect.

Okoa froze. His heart accelerated, and he was suddenly light-headed. First Maaka the day in the sky cells, and now Chaiya. It was no coincidence, of that he was sure. But it was treacherous ground he did not wish to explore.

"Chaiya, no."

"I know it was forbidden to speak of Ayawa when Yatliza was alive—"

He turned to face Chaiya, arrow pointed at his head. "I said no."

Chaiya raised his hands, stepping back. "Easy, Okoa. I only want to talk of your father. There's no one around to hear us."

The strain pulled at his shoulder, but he kept the bowstring drawn. He had been gone from Tova since he was twelve, but he knew this much: "My father was a traitor. There is nothing else to talk about."

"There is more, if you will hear it."

His arm trembled. A growl started in his chest, pain manifested as sound. It escaped his lips in a low scream as he loosed the arrow, turning his aim just in time to miss hitting his cousin. The arrow flew harmlessly into the trees. Chaiya turned to watch its flight before facing him again. His eyes were wide.

Okoa did not bother to reply to his look of outrage.

Chaiya said nothing for a long minute. "Cousin . . ."

"I told you no." Anger sat thick in his chest. He grabbed another arrow, nocked it, and drew, this time facing the target. He searched for the calm he had had before, but his concentration had fled. He lowered the bow, frustrated. "Damn you, Chaiya. First you make me doubt Benundah, and now this? What game are you playing?"

"No games. It's just . . . we need to talk about your father. It is important, more so now."

"Why?" The word came out a strangled plea.

Your father is a traitor. He could hear his mother's hissed whisper as if it had happened that day and not a dozen years ago, her fingers gripping his arm, tears thick in her eyes. *He has betrayed us, Okoa. And now the Sky Made will have his life for it.*

"Did your mother ever tell you of his crime?"

"It doesn't matter." Okoa had been eight when his father was taken away. He had worked hard to forget the details, afraid of the memory. Fearful that if he spoke of his father, no, if he even thought of his father, people would remember his deeds and see the same taint on his son.

"He plotted rebellion."

Okoa's hand flexed, tightened around the bow. "Stop."

"Independence for Carrion Crow. That's what he believed in. He said the Sky Made had failed us on the Night of Knives and were as much our enemies as the Watchers. He dragged his best friend and your mother into his schemes, but during his trial, he took the blame upon himself and cleared their names. It is why they were spared, and he was not."

"Why are you telling me this?"

"Because I do not want to see you make the same mistake. I see your face when you speak of the Odo Sedoh, Okoa. He confuses you, gives you false hope of some Carrion Crow future that can never be. You think that if we align with him and Maaka's fanatics, Carrion Crow can be independent and free of the Sky Made."

Had Esa told him what he had said?

"Is that so impossible?" Okoa's voice was a whisper, as if he had confessed something in shame. As if his hope was not meant to be spoken aloud. "He is worth a hundred men, a thousand if he rallies the crows to his side." His voice rose. "And look at what gathers in the yard. An army. And with the Watchers gone, what Shield could stand against us?"

"Think practically, Okoa. We need access to the mines north of Titidi, the farms east of Kun, and the trade routes through the Tovasheh. Tova functions only as a city, not divided into districts."

"Then we use him to bring all of Tova under our wing."

Chaiya's mouth tightened in disapproval, and Okoa flushed, exasperated. It was treason he spoke now, he knew, but he would not take it back. He still held the bow clenched in his fist, and he slammed it down on the table, sending the remaining arrows tumbling to the ground. He strode away, hands gripping his head in frustration.

"Then what would you do, Chaiya?" he yelled. "Tell me, because I do not know!"

"Do your duty."

"Duty to whom?"

His cousin's expression tore at his heart. "If you must ask, Okoa, then I am too late." He started to walk toward the edge of the lake.

"No!" Okoa grabbed his arm, whirling him around to face him. "Don't walk away. Tell me what to do!"

"Convince Esa to answer the Sky Made's missives! Tell her to promise them the Odo Sedoh. And have her arrest Maaka!"

"Arrest Maaka?" The demand set him back. "On what grounds?"

"Have you not seen him preaching in the yard every day? Calling what happened on Sun Rock 'divine justice'?"

"It is his right. Besides, if you jail him, you will make him a martyr."

"If you don't, he will use the Odo Sedoh as an excuse to drive your family out of the Great House. Mark me, there are things you don't know about Maaka. That man has always hated this family since they allowed the Sky Made to take your father."

He thought of Maaka's warning not to confuse fealty to the Odo Sedoh with disloyalty to his family and how Okoa's father would not make that mistake. There was a connection there, but he did not have time to tease it out.

"Well?" Chaiya's look was grim.

"I . . ." he faltered. Chaiya asked too much of him.

His cousin's look was long and weighing, his voice cold with disgust. "You are your mother's son."

The words hurt coming from his cousin, more than he could say, and he lashed out. "First I am my father, now I am my mother. Which is it?"

Chaiya leaned close, finger digging into Okoa's chest. "I said they spared your mother your father's fate, not that she did not deserve the same."

He flinched back. "Are you saying you are glad she is dead?"

Chaiya paled, the color draining from his face.

Okoa saw the opening and pressed. "She did not die by her own hand." He had never voiced his suspicions aloud, but he felt wild and unmoored, as if a door within him had opened and he could not close it.

His cousin's eyes widened before he quickly looked away. "Careful what comes next, Okoa."

"Esa—"

"Esa is innocent."

"I believe that now, but . . ." He frowned. "What do you know?"

"I know that only a fool accuses without proof."

237

"No, you were going to say something else." He had seen the moment of panic in Chaiya's eyes, heard the quick breath that suggested he was nervous. "What do you know?"

"Go home, Okoa. Go back and convince Esa to give the Odo Sedoh to the Sky Made for trial. It is the only way forward." He turned his back to him and walked to the edge of the lake. He put his fingers in his mouth and let out a piercing whistle. A few moments later, Kutssah and Benundah rose from behind the hills and drifted over the water. They came to land beside them.

Okoa watched, his mind turning. "Why are you not angry?"

Chaiya exhaled, sounding weary. "What?"

"I just suggested that my mother, your matron, was murdered on your watch. Why are you not raving? Where is your outrage at such a crime?"

"Your grief confuses you, Cousin. There was no murder. Your mother leaped from her balcony and was found in the river. It was tragic, but considering the shame of your father and the guilt she bore these long years, can you blame her?"

"But you said Esa was innocent. Innocent of what?"

Chaiya paused, and Okoa held his breath. His heart beat so loudly he was sure Chaiya could hear it. He knew something, Okoa was sure. But his cousin only picked up Okoa's tack and began to walk to Benundah.

"I've said my piece."

"Do not touch her!"

Okoa rushed forward and wrenched the tack from his hands. Chaiya did not fight him. He felt his cousin's eyes on him as he saddled his crow and set her bridle.

He was mounted and ready to take flight when Chaiya asked, "Are you going to do the right thing?"

Okoa recoiled. He had told the Odo Sedoh he only wanted

to do what was right, but at the time, he had not realized how difficult it was to know what that was.

He did not answer, only turned Benundah away and took to the sky.

• • • • •

It was late when Okoa returned to the aviary, no Chaiya at his side. It was better his cousin had stayed behind. He did not think he wanted to see his face again for a while. What he had said about his father, that he had spoken of his father at all, was a burr under his skin.

His memories of his father were hazy at best, a smear of images from his early childhood. But they were good memories, until they were not. Hours spent in the library, where his father had taught him to read. Long nights hiding under a bench, listening to his father speak of grand philosophies and debate history with his glamorous friends. He remembered the momentous feel of those times, if not the words or the faces of the people.

It must have happened then, he thought. Sometime when conversation became dangerous and someone his father had considered his friend was in fact his enemy. He had no idea what had truly happened, and he suspected he might never know, but it made his stomach knot to think of it.

He was not proud that he had abandoned his father's legacy so completely, but traitor was a heavy burden for a boy to carry, and his mother had not tolerated any mention of her late husband. She must have feared that people would remember her part in his rebellion and how she had escaped his fate and reconsider. No wonder she was so sad, even to the end. And no wonder she had sent him away to war college as soon as he was old enough.

He sensed someone waiting in the shadows, just down the steps, and half expected it to be the Odo Sedoh. "Who's there?"

Ituya stepped forward, looking sheepish. "Apologies, Lord. I did not want to disturb you. You looked to be in thought."

Okoa's mouth creased with a small smile. "When am I not in thought, Ituya? Is there news?"

"A letter, Lord." The Shield held out a folded paper.

"Any news of the Odo Sedoh?" He took the letter in hand.

"No, Lord. Nothing new."

"No sightings? Nothing?"

"No, Lord."

"What is this?" He held up the letter he had not yet bothered to look at. "Another demand from the clans? Why not take it to Esa?"

"It is addressed to you."

"Who is it from?" He paused, eyes raking over the letter for the first time.

Ituya hesitated. "It is marked with the sigil of the Sun Priest."

Okoa examined the seal. It was indeed the Tovan sun. His brows knit in suspicion. "Who brought this?"

"A runner, Lord. We stopped her at the gate. She was no more than a Maw brat."

"The Maw . . ." He remembered another letter that had come from the Maw and the Sun Priest. But surely even she was not so bold.

"My thanks." He waved Ituya away. "And find me when Chaiya returns, no matter where I am or what I'm doing. It's important."

"Of course, Lord."

Once his man was out of sight, Okoa slipped off his gloves, tucked them in his belt, broke the seal, and read. He recognized the style of the script, the shape of the glyphs. They were written by the same hand that had penned him a letter before the Convergence. That message had read, *Storm, Betrayal, Friendship.*

He looked again at the new message in his hand, so similar, only now it said, *Storm, Friendship, Survival,* and there was a curving line like a rounded roof and, under that roof, the sigils of the Sky Made clans. He understood what it meant— together, the Sky Made as allies survive the storm.

The note ended with the insignia of a place in the Maw, a column of flowers on a single stalk, and a note that the runner would return to fetch him should he wish to come.

He leaned against the wall, bewildered and intrigued.

Was this the same Sun Priest? Had she somehow outlived all her counterparts and was now in the Maw? And even more surprising, did she think he, a son of Carrion Crow, would be her ally against the Odo Sedoh? It was bold. And foolish.

Because now he knew where to find her.

He grimaced, uncomfortable with the idea of hunting her down. He had liked the Sun Priest he met on the day of his mother's funeral, thought her different and promising. That was when he had dreamed of peace between the clans. Only now that the Odo Sedoh had come, his dreams were those of war.

Not war, he told himself, *independence.*

The aviary was quiet, all the patrols in for the evening and the birds roosting.

He grabbed a clay bowl from a nearby shelf and filled it from the water barrel. He dug into the bag he always wore at his belt and retrieved a handful of grubs. He offered them to Benundah.

"I am sorry I ever doubted you."

She cawed once, a reprimand, but took his peace offering. Using his fingers, he dribbled water from his bowl onto her wings and began to groom her. He plucked the loose feathers and set them aside for the new mantle he was making, having gifted his old one to the Odo Sedoh. Once he had removed all the loose quills, he ran fingers across her lustrous plumage, smoothing the water across her feathers. It was more a bonding exercise than necessity, as the crows groomed themselves, but both man and beast found it soothing.

"I do not deserve your trust, but I would ask you this thing."

He looked into her eyes, brimming with intelligence, and wished again he could hear her voice the way the Odo Sedoh could. But for all his desire, he was no god.

"Go find him, and bring him back. I would speak to him before I decide anything."

The great crow clicked softly, tapping her beak to his cheek. He nodded and stepped back, letting her go. She flapped her wings, spraying him gently with water, before she launched skyward. Once she was gone, he took a blanket from a peg along the wall, found a shadowy corner of the aviary where the reeds were fresh, and settled in to wait.

CHAPTER 22

> Take a friend where you find one.
>
> —*Exhortations for a Happy Life*

Even with Naranpa's healing powers, it took a full day and a half for Denaochi to recover. She had wanted to take him back right after the bloodletting ritual that had almost killed him, but Sedaysa had insisted that he stay and that Naranpa stay with him.

"It is too cold, and he cannot walk that far," the boss of the Agave had declared.

"I can send word for the Lupine to send men to carry him."

"Carry a boss through the street like a child?" Her mouth had turned down in disapproval. "What if someone sees?"

"Those who wish him ill have already seen." Naranpa meant the bosses themselves.

"There are enemies everywhere." Sedaysa dismissed Naranpa's unsubtle reprimand. "Best not to show weakness."

It wasn't so much Sedaysa's persuasions that convinced Naranpa, rather that Naranpa was aware that it might be best for her to stay inside and out of sight, too, not knowing if there were crows somewhere in the city looking for her even now. But she did have Sedaysa send a runner back to the Lupine to tell Zataya that Denaochi was alive and on his way to well. And Naranpa drafted letters to the Sky Made matrons and the Carrion Crow captain asking them to come to the Lupine the next evening, and she would send the same runners at the hour to escort them. She had hesitated before deciding to send a letter to Carrion Crow. Asking them to come had certainly not been part of the original plan she had discussed with Denaochi. And part of her worried that the captain might send the Crow God Reborn in his stead, and that would be the end of her. But if she could send one to Golden Eagle and not expect assassins to answer, she could send one to Carrion Crow. It was a risk, but she felt it was one worth taking. She would not unite Tova under the banner of the Sun Priest once again without taking risks.

"I've invited the others to meet you," Sedaysa declared, as Naranpa sat dozing beside her brother's sickbed.

"Pardon?"

"Pasko and Amalq. You remember them."

Pasko she remembered as the man in red with the speckled feather headdress. He had been the first to claim a knife. And Amalq had been the woman in blue beside him.

"Was not our meeting previously sufficient?"

Yes, they had sworn their support to her and Denaochi's cause on the strength of his bravery and her display of sorcery, but Naranpa kept envisioning them stabbing her brother and then sitting around making polite conversation while courtesans fucked in the background and he bled to death in the middle of the room. She had no warmth toward her new allies.

"You need to share a meal."

"You hope to make me like them."

Sedaysa smiled. "On the contrary, I hope to make them like you, Sun Priest. It is an alliance of common cause that Denaochi has brokered. Let us see if we can deepen that."

"Why are you helping us?"

Sedaysa came to sit on Denaochi's bed. She rested a hand on his arm, her face gentling. "We have a history, your brother and I. Has he told you about it?"

Naranpa sat up. Denaochi had told her almost nothing of what his life had been for the past twenty years. She was both eager and apprehensive to learn more.

"My husband owned the Agave before I did, and Denaochi worked for him. Not here but at another house. One that catered to more specific tastes."

"Pain." She raised her chin. "He has told me something of those days."

"Has he?" She sounded surprised. "And that my husband purchased him for his own? That is how we met. He was brought into our household but kept . . . separate." Sedaysa met Naranpa's gaze. "But we still encountered each other. At meals, passing in the hallways. How could I not be intrigued? He was funny and so handsome." Her face softened. "And for the first time since my marriage, I was not alone."

"So he kept you separate, too."

"From the world." She sighed. "Perhaps it is no surprise that Denaochi and I became lovers. I had married a much older man for security, not love. The Maw is not like the Sky Made districts. Might rules here, and that often leaves girls like me and boys like Denaochi with few resources."

"I grew up here. I know what it's like."

"Of course you do. But you're a woman of power now. I thought perhaps you had forgotten. But safety seemed a small concern compared to first love." She brushed a hand across

Denaochi's cheek. "I was willing to risk it all on this handsome courtesan."

"Your husband found out." That was easy enough to see.

Sedaysa looked up. "I suspect he set us up all along so that he could administer his righteous punishment." Her eyes were sad. "Me, he only beat until I passed out. I do not like to think on what he did to your brother, and I have never asked for specifics, but I heard the screams every night for weeks. He made sure of that."

She threaded her fingers through Denaochi's. "Your brother came to me a month later, and he was a changed man. His humor gone, that scar on his face. Together we conspired to kill my husband." She tilted her head. "Does that shock you?"

"I am not here to judge you or him."

"My husband was a cruel man. Not a drop of kindness in him. I did not mourn his death, and I inherited all of this and more." She spread her hands to encompass the Agave. "But it broke something in Denaochi. We were never lovers again. But I owe him much. I owe him my life. So if he comes to me and asks me to help him unite the bosses to his cause, and his cause is you, then I do it. And I continue to do it, until he asks it no more."

• • • • •

Pasko and Amalq arrived shortly after, and Naranpa, bathed and wearing a new dress from Sedaysa's overflowing trunks, found herself around a table in the Agave's decadent courtyard having tea with her new allies, the criminal bosses of Coyote's Maw.

"I must admit that when Denaochi told us his sister was the Sun Priest, I did not at first believe it," Amalq said, once they were settled with their cups.

Naranpa took a sip. The tea was bright and summery, a fit

for the hothouse if not for the weather outside. "I left for the tower when I was a child, to work as a servant."

"That does not explain things." Pasko was a large man with a deep voice that Naranpa imagined was used to menace.

He seemed ill suited for the tea table, and she found herself reluctant to sit with him. She attributed it to her own biases and tried her best to set it aside, but it was there in the back of her mind. Something that told her Pasko was to be watched.

Naranpa set down her cup. "I became Sun Priest almost by accident. I was working in the kitchens, and one of the other girls had fallen sick. Her duty was to bring tea to the Sun Priest every evening, which for that night became my duty. The Sun Priest then was a man named Kiutue. He was striking. Tall, with a beard. Winged Serpent by birth, but he must have had Obregi heritage somewhere. I thought him a great bear when I met him first. But he was kind. Gentle. He became my mentor."

"You seduced him." That was Sedaysa, and Naranpa flushed.

"I did not. It doesn't . . ." She caught the edge of a smile on Sedaysa's perfect lips. Was she teasing her? Naranpa didn't think it amusing and refused to rise to the bait.

"I took his tea up that evening," she continued, "and he was working with one of his dedicants, an unpleasant man the kitchen girls knew to stay away from. Seeing him there made me nervous, and I ended up spilling the tea on one of their star charts."

"And he beat you," Pasko said knowingly.

"No!" Skies, did all these people expect the worst of their fellow humans? "But he did yell at me. The dedicant, not Kiutue. And as I was cleaning up the spill, I noticed an error in his chart. A star in a constellation he had drawn too far to the south. It was a small error, and no doubt that they would have caught the mistake eventually. But I was thirteen and humili-ated, and I blurted it out."

"Ho!" Pasko said, laughing. Too loudly, as if to make a show of it. "Just like a Maw brat to talk back to her betters!"

"But he was not my better. That was the point."

"And what happened?" Amalq asked intently, her cup held in long-fingered hands that Naranpa could see were criss-crossed with white scars.

"He made me a dedicant."

"You were ambitious," Sedaysa murmured over her cup, her gray eyes knowing.

"I did not mean—"

"Don't apologize for it. We are all ambitious." Amalq gestured around the table. "Else we would not be in our positions."

"From kitchen girl to Sun Priest is quite a tale, no matter how it happened."

There was admiration in Pasko's voice. Admiration she was not sure she deserved. She had been smart, yes, and worked hard. But part of her still felt she had been picked because she was not the right kind of ambitious. It had always been her suspicion that Kiutue had chosen her to succeed him precisely because he thought she would be content to bend the order of oracles away from the political and toward the more mystical, and he had mostly been right. But once she had become Sun Priest, something had changed for her. She could not pinpoint what it was, or even when the shift had occurred, but she had begun to care. About the future of Tova, about the legacy of the Watchers. Now it all seemed so pathetic. The fate of the city rested in the hands of a vengeful god, and the Watchers' legacy had died in one fell swoop on a single day.

They were staring at her, waiting for her to speak, and she realized she had gotten lost in her thoughts. She sipped her tea, biding time, and finally asked, "And how did each of you become . . . ?"

She trailed off. She knew Sedaysa's story now, and it had involved murder. She could only imagine they all had similarly bloody ascensions.

"We know what we are," Sedaysa said, her laugh as light as moth wings. "Thugs, criminals, bosses. I certainly have no shame in it. Although I might prefer the term *independent merchants*."

They laughed at that, Pasko the loudest.

Amalq said, "If the families of the Sky Made were to run the workhouses or gambling dens, they would call it simply commerce. But when we do it, it is illicit, forbidden. So we operate here in the Maw or in the Eastern districts and pay a tithe to the Sky Made to turn an eye, and they let us live unbothered. Mostly."

Pasko nodded his agreement. "We were born clanless, and in Tova, there is no greater transgression. No family, no clan, no life unless you make your own. So we made our own, each of us in their own way. Just as you did."

Is that what she had done? She was not so sure, but she let it pass.

"I am a moneylender and the proprietor of the Blackfire." Pasko leaned in. "If I were Sky Made, I would be admired, considered a generous man of the community. But since I am not . . ." He shrugged his large shoulders.

"I run a workhouse and club called the Wildrose," Amalq said. "I was once indentured there for a debt my husband owed. But now I run the house." She lifted a scarred hand. "We make textiles for export."

"How did you come to be a boss?"

"A worker's revolt. I killed the boss and took her place." She tossed her head back, guiltless. "If not me, then another would have."

"And I peddle pleasures of the flesh here at the Agave." That was Sedaysa. "Not just sex, although very much sex. But also flowers, herbs, and other botanicals that relax the mind and body. Some of the very ones that you see here."

Naranpa eyed the blossoms around her. They abruptly took on a more sinister cast. "Do you also sell god magics?"

The woman tilted her head. "Are you in the market?"

"No, I only wondered."

She was thinking of Zataya and her rare items from the Graveyard of the Gods. She wondered if Sedaysa had been the one to sell them to her, but she dared not ask it now while their wary alliance was barely birthed. *My allies are all criminals and murderers,* she thought to herself. *But how is that different from the Sky Made or even the Watchers themselves? Only that the law favors one form of corruption and frowns on the other. The principles are the same.*

"You have earned the right to claim a name and a club," Sedaysa said.

Naranpa flushed. "Me? I have no need for a club."

Amalq's smile was knowing. "Perhaps not now, but the vagaries of the future are uncertain. It is still a right you have earned should you need it."

"It would honor us if you picked a name," Sedaysa said.

"Something meaningful," Amalq agreed.

Naranpa thought of Denaochi's lupines and Sedaysa's agave plant. Even the blackfire and the wildrose. "They're all flowers." It seemed obvious enough once she said it.

Sedaysa motioned a servant forward, and she handed her mistress a book. Sedaysa opened it and turned to a blank page. "Put your mark here, Naranpa, and those who rule the Maw shall know it is yours and can be claimed by no other from this day forward."

It felt surprisingly formal, but Naranpa was a former priest who appreciated ceremony. She took the proffered stylus and drew her insignia. Her drawing was simple, a black-and-white replica and cruder than she would have liked, but it resembled well enough the blue flower with the three bladelike leaves that peeled back from the starburst center that was its inspiration.

Amalq nodded, looking pleased. "A handmaiden."

"And now you have the right to call yourself the proprietor of the Handmaiden." Sedaysa closed the book and handed it to the patiently waiting servant.

"But I don't even have a building."

"In time."

Naranpa had not expected to come out of this evening as an actual Maw boss, and she understood it was only in name, but she found herself smiling anyway.

Pasko cleared his throat. "Denaochi told us you had a way to defeat Carrion Crow."

Naranpa refocused, knowing that Handmaiden or no, she needed to convince these people to align their interests with hers. She chose her words carefully. "I hope to offer an alternative to Carrion Crow. Tova cannot go on in darkness under this weakened sun. Already, we move toward spring, but with no planting season and no flowering plants, save these." She thought to take a nearby blossom in her hand, but after Sedaysa's warning, she thought better of it. "I want to offer the city life. Healing. I want to be the Sun Priest it should have always had."

The three were quiet.

Amalq spoke first. "We have also heard word of plans from our neighbor cities to the east and south. That they eye our wealth and wonder why it is not theirs."

"Denaochi has told me the same," Naranpa said. "That Cuecola and Hokaia see Tova as a prize worth taking and that there are those in the city who would barter us away for their own benefit."

"Golden Eagle," Pasko growled.

"We do not know that," Sedaysa cautioned.

"It is clear enough to me."

"Not to us all. Now, let her speak."

"I suspect Golden Eagle of treason, too," Naranpa said. "We will find the truth tomorrow, when the Sky Made matrons come. But I must ask you first. What is it you want from this? If you give of your coffers and your people in support of me. What is it you want in return?"

"A seat at the table," Sedaysa said promptly. "The Maw should have representation on the Speakers Council, just like the Sky Made clans do."

"It is not right that they make decisions and laws without us."

"They have written back?" Amalq asked.

Naranpa looked to Sedaysa, who shook her head.

"Not yet," Naranpa conceded. "But I know them, and I know they will come, if only out of curiosity."

She had signed their letters with her sigil, the Tovan sun, and named herself Sun Priest. And her script was familiar—they would know it was her. And if they thought her an impostor, they would want to know who had the audacity to claim the title as their own. No, they would come. She was sure of it.

"And what will you say to them?" Pasko leaned in, intrigued.

She did not answer at first. Instead, she lifted her hand, letting it glow. She heard their murmurs and knew her eyes shone golden, too.

"I will show them what I have shown you," she said. "Power."

CHAPTER 23

City of Tova (the Crow Aviary)
Year 1 of the Crow

> Duty is a fine thing for those whose shoulders are stooped to
> the yoke, but it smothers those born to the wing.
>
> —*Exhortations for a Happy Life*

Okoa awoke to the sound of beating wings. He roused himself
from the corner of the aviary as Benundah returned. He looked
to her back, hoping to see the Odo Sedoh, but she was rider-
less. He slumped, disappointed. Had she not found him?

He yawned, stretching his arms over his head, and shook
the sleep from his body. It was the first time he had slept well
in longer than he could remember, but he still longed for more.

He had stepped from the corner when the first small crow
arrived. Then there were ten, then twenty, and then fifty. They
flocked before him, a great whirling wind of black feathers,
and he pressed his back against the wall, arm over his face.
Slowly, the whirlwind began to take form, birds morphing into
man, and then the Odo Sedoh stood before him.

He was as he remembered him, in Carrion Crow black and
wild hair. And to Okoa's surprise, he still wore the feathered
mantle he had gifted him that first day.

It felt like a good omen, and he smiled despite himself. "I thought you might not come."

He turned his head toward Okoa's voice. His movements had always been reminiscent of a bird's, but now they seemed more pronounced. "I almost did not." He flexed his hand, and Okoa thought he saw talons, long and black, instead of fingers.

"I have news that will interest you." He touched the letter in his pocket but did not remove it. "But first I would ask you what happened."

"What happened," Serapio repeated. He felt his way toward the water barrel, dipped his hands in, and brought water to his mouth to drink.

"In the yard, when you attacked the crowd."

Serapio paused, hands in the barrel. "Attacked." He splashed water on his face and through his hair. "I only did what was necessary."

"They were innocent people. No one was armed. You could have found another way."

He pressed his wet hair back from his face. He blinked black eyes, droplets clinging to his lashes. "My way is death. There is no other way."

"Crows are not only creatures of vengeance and the grave. They are loving, caring, nurturing. Is there not that in your making, too?"

"Once, perhaps." He cupped his hand, running a finger over his palm as if tracing invisible lines. "But now?" He clenched his hand into a fist. "What do you want of me, beyond trying to make me something that I am not?"

Okoa hesitated. He had asked him to be a weapon for Carrion Crow, and now he was. He need only point him toward their enemies, and his dreams were in reach. Not only his dreams. His father's dreams.

"I know where you can find the Sun Priest and all the matrons of the Sky Made. They are meeting—"

Benundah squawked loudly, and they both turned. Serapio tilted his head up, eyes on the open sky. "She says they're
coming."

"Who's coming?"

Before he could answer, Okoa felt the wind of giant wings
and looked up to find Kutssah barreling toward them. He
shouted and threw himself to the ground, sure that the giant
meant to skewer them. But at the last moment, she pulled up,
and something came hurtling off her back.

It was Chaiya, and he leaped from his mount to tackle
Serapio.

They went down in a heap.

Chaiya had something in his hands, netting of some kind,
and he threw it over the Odo Sedoh.

Serapio shouted, and the air around him vibrated. His form
shifted, man to black bird and back to man, as he realized his
crow form offered no escape.

His hand morphed into a talon, and he ripped through
the netting. Chaiya reared back, narrowly avoiding the sharp
claw, and then there was a black blade in his hand. He stabbed
toward Serapio's face.

Okoa cried a warning, to whom he wasn't sure.

Serapio turned his head, avoiding the blow, but the blade
sliced a line across his jaw. Blood welled, and Serapio did not
hesitate. He called on the shadow, and it came. Black smoke
laced the veins beneath his skin, crawling the pathways of his
body like dark rivers, until shadow burst from his fingertips.
He grasped Chaiya's wrist, the hand that held the knife, and
shouted words in a language Okoa did not know.

The shadow enveloped his cousin's hand and slithered up

his arm. The bigger man scrambled back, eyes wide in horror. His obsidian blade clattered to the ground, the hand that had been holding it half eaten away, the flesh melting into a pool of black rot halfway up his forearm.

"Seven hells," Okoa breathed, horror shivering up his spine. He had to stop this, but how?

Chaiya weighed twice as much as Serapio, and vision, experience, and the element of surprise had given him the quick advantage. But Serapio had been honed for one purpose only, and he had shadow magic at his command, his very blood a weapon. Okoa feared his cousin would quickly become outmatched.

But not yet.

Serapio stumbled, the netting wrapping around his legs and catching his feet. Chaiya, even with half his arm withered, attacked. He dug a fisted hand into Serapio's wound, the one on his side that had never healed, and Serapio's whole body shuddered in agony. Chaiya staggered to his feet and slammed his boot into Serapio's skull.

Serapio collapsed, insensible.

The crows in the aviary screamed, Kutssah the loudest.

Chaiya froze, foot raised for another blow.

"Kutssah?" Confusion twisted his features.

Okoa did not think, just moved. He tackled Chaiya, throwing him well off the stunned Serapio. "What are you doing?" he shouted.

Chaiya did not fight him but lay panting under his weight. His arm was a black ruin, and Okoa felt nauseated when he caught a glimpse of it. But the hardest things to see were the tears in his cousin's eyes.

"She would choose him over me?" His voice sounded small, heartbroken.

Okoa understood all too well. It was his unspoken fear, that one day Benundah would choose the Odo Sedoh over him. There was no comfort for the irrational feeling of betrayal except to say, "He is her god, too."

His words juddered through Chaiya like an earthquake.

"Do you believe?"

It was a simple question, and until that moment, Okoa had not had an answer. But now he did. "Yes."

"That he can free Carrion Crow?"

He nodded.

Chaiya heaved, his body shaking. It was grief, but it was more than just the sorrow of Kutssah's rejection. The fight had drained from him, and he motioned Okoa to let him up. Okoa stood, wary, putting his body between the two men. He glanced over his shoulder and saw Serapio's chest move. He was stunned, but alive.

Chaiya fell to his knees before him. "There is something you must know."

Okoa's stomach dropped. All his instincts shouted at him that whatever Chaiya meant to confess, he did not want to know it. Tears streamed down his cousin's face, the way they had when he had come to the war college and first brought news of his mother's death.

Panic spiked his adrenaline. "No, Chaiya. I don't need to know. Whatever it is, I forgive you."

"It is about your mother, Yatliza."

Okoa pressed his back against the wall. He had stumbled away from his cousin without even realizing it. He held his hand out, fingers splayed, as if he could hold off his words.

"You have to understand, it was different from how it is now." Chaiya bowed his head. "There had been two assassination attempts on the Sun Priest's life, and the Sky Made were

257

already blaming Carrion Crow. The Odohaa had been quiet since your father's death, but they had been getting louder, more emboldened in their talk of prophecy and vengeance, and Yatliza was allowing it."

There was a buzzing in Okoa's ears, as if a million bees lived inside his head.

"We could not survive another Night of Knives."

"You killed her." It was the barest whisper, a breath of horror.

Chaiya shook his head. "I did not touch her. But when the Priest of Knives climbed the cliffside and stole into her room, I stood on the other side of the door and did not stop xir."

Okoa sank to the ground. He wrapped his arms around his head and pressed his forehead to his knees. There had to be a mistake, some strange misunderstanding. This could not be real.

"Can you forgive me, Okoa? I thought I was doing the right thing, fulfilling my duty to Carrion Crow. How could I know, how could any of us know, that the Crow God Reborn would come and change our world?"

A voice like a thousand black wings spoke. "You should have had faith."

Okoa looked up. Serapio loomed behind Chaiya, who was still on his knees. He lifted a hand, Chaiya's obsidian knife in his grip.

"No!" Okoa screamed.

Chaiya's smile was small and resigned as his eyes fluttered shut, and Serapio drew the black blade across his neck. Blood poured from his throat, and he slumped to the aviary floor.

A clatter on the stairs, and suddenly the room was filled with Shields.

"Ituya, no!" Okoa shouted, but the man had seen Chaiya's

body fall and was already charging toward Serapio, knife raised. It was a reckless attack, doomed from its inception.

The Odo Sedoh turned to the side, catching Ituya by the arm and neck as he slashed wildly. He forced the guard to the ground, crushing his wrist until Okoa heard the bones break. Before Okoa could move, the Odo Sedoh had grabbed Ituya by the head and twisted, snapping his neck. The effect was instantaneous, and Ituya fell dead beside Chaiya.

Another dozen Shields had spread out across the room, and Serapio turned to face them. He cut across his forearm, letting the blood rise and his veins blacken, and shadow dripped from his fingers.

He would kill them all, Okoa realized in horror, and he could only stand by and witness it. *My way is death*, he had said, and Okoa had not understood. He understood now.

He struggled to his feet. He saw Serapio tilt his head at the sound, as if taking note of his position.

"Hold!" he shouted to his Shield. "I am your captain, and I command you to hold!" And to Serapio, "Please. I am not your enemy. The Shield is not your enemy."

Serapio's voice was a soft whisper, no longer that sepulchral horror. "I don't believe you, Okoa Carrion Crow. I think perhaps you lured me here hoping to kill me all along."

"I didn't know, I swear to you."

"What do your promises mean to me, crow son, when they are nothing but lies?"

He could see Serapio was breathing hard, his eyes too wide, his wounds at his jaw and forearm and the old one on his side leaking blood and ichor. *He's hurt and believes himself betrayed.*

He thought of how he would calm an injured crow, what words he would whisper, what soothing he could offer.

"Chaiya conspired to assassinate my mother, his matron." He said it with a steady voice, but his hands shook, and the image of Chaiya on his knees, eyes fluttering closed, played across his vision. He forced himself to breathe. "And Ituya attacked you first. These are explainable deaths. But you cannot hurt the Shield. It will break our trust."

"Our trust?" Serapio laughed, showing red teeth. "You asked me to be your weapon, and when I am a weapon, you complain that my edge is killing sharp?"

"It was a mistake." *I thought I could control the storm, but Esa was right. We must only survive it.*

"Tell me where to find the Sun Priest."

Okoa glanced at the two bodies between them. "No."

Serapio looked to him, incredulous. Okoa understood his danger a moment too late, when the obsidian blade was at his own neck, Serapio's face inches from his own, his breath ragged and hot against his face.

He heard the Shield move. "Hold!" He forced the word through gritted teeth. "He will not hurt me."

Serapio's bloodied cheek pressed, viscous, against his own, intimate with the promise of murder. "And why would you believe that?"

"Because the Sky Made, the Odohaa, even Benundah, would turn against you. You would truly be alone, everyone your enemy, your predictions fulfilled."

The blade pricked his skin, a thin, burning line of pain that made him shudder. Okoa closed his eyes and whispered, "And what use is a god if there is no one alive to worship him?"

Serapio roared and tossed him away. Okoa tumbled to the ground. The Shield rushed forward, the great crows screamed, and Okoa watched as Serapio broke into a flock of crows and scattered.

Hands were on him, helping him to his feet. Fussing over the small wound on his neck. He brushed them off with assurances that he was not seriously injured and went to where his cousin lay.

A lake of red stained the reeds, but Okoa pressed fingers to Chaiya's wrist anyway, hoping for a miracle. But there were no miracles today. He bowed his head. He had thought he wanted revenge for his mother's murder, but now that he had gotten it, he found the cut of it too bitter for his tastes.

"Look to the bodies, and inform the matron of what has happened," he commanded his Shield. "There is something I must do."

The letter sat heavy in his pocket, and his heart was weighted by grief. But he knew it was as he had been taught as a child. When injured, crows may become feral, a danger to their own flock. When that happens, you must choose the collective over the individual. If you cannot save a broken crow, it is a mercy to put him down.

CHAPTER 24

CITY OF TOVA (COYOTE'S MAW)
YEAR 1 OF THE CROW

A moment to love the living, an eternity to mourn the dead.

—*The Obregi Book of Flowers*

"Are you sure about this?" Denaochi asked, eyes on Naranpa's skirt.

"Yes." She smoothed her hands over the yellow stripes. "It's a fine dress."

"That's not what I meant."

He was lounging on her bed back at the Lupine, hale as he had been before the ritual at the Agave. Sedaysa's ministrations had done him well, as had Naranpa's healing powers. She was glad of it. She had acted on instinct, knowing only that she had to save Denaochi before he bled to death on the pleasure house's floor, but she was very aware that healing was yet another area in which she had no training.

"Do you mean the bloodstains?"

"I mean my blood."

She looked down. She had cleaned most of the blood from the garment but left the hem, now stiff and discolored. "I am not the same Sun Priest I was when they knew me. I have survived betrayal by those I cared for, crawled from my own tomb, and waded through my own kin's blood." She turned a palm up and let the light come. She had been practicing calling the glow on command. "And I have accepted the presence of a god I served but did not believe in." She released the glow. "Let them see how it has marked me."

"It is impressive, I do admit. But there's a touch of madness in it, too."

She laughed, relieved. "Is that all? I am the most sane I have been since I left the Maw all those years ago."

"And yet you invited both your enemies here tonight."

"Do you mean Carrion Crow and Golden Eagle?" She motioned Baaya over to finish her hair. The young woman had formed her hair into a bun, spikes radiating out around her head like a starburst. She had coated Naranpa's black hair in a thick yellow-dyed paste to set the spikes and then used the same paste to paint her neck and the edges of her face to evoke the mask of the Sun Priest.

"Unless you have yet more enemies."

"It is possible, but I hope to find allies tonight."

"It's a gamble."

"Yes, it is. I learned that strategy from you."

"Ah, but I play that way because I don't expect to survive."

She didn't like the sound of that. "What do you mean?"

"*We are but fevered stars*," he intoned, like an orator on a stage. "*Here a little while, bright with promise, before we burn away.*"

"Is that a quote?"

"*The Obregi Book of Flowers*. Do you not know it?"

"No, and it sounds depressing."

"It's poetry, Nara."

She grinned. "Oh, and you are a patron of the arts?"

"Skies, no. But I've bedded a poet or two in my day. It's good to know a bit of verse to make a good impression."

She laughed. This was another side of her brother she had never seen, and she found herself charmed. There was so much to learn about each other, so much time together to look forward to.

A knock at the door, and Pasko stuck his head in. "They've arrived. Sedaysa and the others are keeping the matrons busy. And there is a man at the door, Okoa Carrion Crow. Shall I let him enter?"

"Okoa?" She exchanged a look with Denaochi. "He came."

Her brother shrugged. "A good sign for us. We'll use it to our advantage."

"Keep him on the roof for now," she instructed Pasko. "Tell him it will not be long, but I think we can use his arrival to make an impression."

Pasko nodded an acknowledgment. Naranpa waited for the man to leave, but he hesitated, gaze lingering on her.

"Is there something more?" she asked.

The look he gave her was dark as he hastily pulled the door closed, her question unanswered.

"Strange," she murmured.

"Pasko is a hard man, but he's loyal. A Golden Eagle scion killed his brother. He hates the clans more than even I do."

"I didn't know that was possible."

He laughed and pushed himself to his feet. His mantle settled around his shoulders. His eyes glittered with delight, and a half smile carved across his narrow face. He looked dangerous. Not the way the Crow God Reborn had, like a creature of divinity and shadow, but like hunger and violence, like the coyote son that he was. And she found that she did not mind it.

"You're enjoying this." She allowed herself her own smile.

"As are you."

"Not enjoying it. But it does feel right." She could not deny that. She had tried to be someone she was not when she was in the tower, thinking if only she mimicked Sky Made ways, they would be forced to see her worth and that she belonged. But she was not Sky Made and should have never tried to force herself to be who she was not. The events since the Convergence had stripped all that away. All her naivete, all her fool's luck. She had said she was someone else now, and it was true. She was the handmaiden of the sun god, and the coyote stood at her right hand. And together they would remake Tova.

"I am glad that we found each other again." She pressed a kiss to his hollowed cheek.

He looked at her, truly looked at her. "It has been my greatest joy."

He took her hand in his. Her fingers were adorned with gold and jade. He kissed her palm where the sun god's power had danced only moments ago, and together they went to meet the matrons.

· · · · ·

Despite Naranpa's optimism, the meeting proved to be an exercise in futility. She had hoped that the Sky Made might recognize that they shared a common purpose in the preservation of Tova, but the matrons were women used to power and wholly unused to fear. And now they were frightened, unsure of the future, and could feel the dominance that they had once thought bedrock and a birthright shifting beneath their feet. They were in no mood for reason, particularly from Naranpa, and Nuuma Golden Eagle let it be known immediately.

"Well, Naranpa. It seems it is true. You are alive."

"Disappointed?" Naranpa took her seat.

Nuuma had come draped in mourning white, her tawny brown hair loose and tangled, a signifier of her grief. Contempt curled the edges of her mouth, coating her words in venom. "It's not entirely surprising that a Maw dog ran from the censure of her betters and was found here among her kind once again."

The other Sky Made at least played at egalitarianism, and their murmurs of shock at Nuuma's incivility shivered around the room. But Naranpa had expected Nuuma to be vicious and did not rise to the bait.

"I should probably be thanking your niece for trying to murder me. Without her interference, I may have never found kindred spirits among the Coyote clan, and even more so, an awakening of my true gifts."

"Coyote clan?" Ieyoue interrupted. "What's this?" The Water Strider matron had worn her hair down and tangled but had chosen to adorn herself in Water Strider blue, which suggested her mourning had limits. She was also the only one who had smiled in greeting when Naranpa had entered.

Naranpa turned away from Nuuma. "I recently read an interesting thing in the history books of the celestial tower. A book that was held in secret by the ta dissa and not shared with the other orders. It spoke of the Coyote clan, a clan that existed before the War of the Spear and was forcibly dissolved in the aftermath of the war."

"It is true," Ieyoue acknowledged. "Haisan once spoke of it to me."

At Naranpa's surprised look, she added, "He was Water Strider by birth, and a cousin. We often spoke of history and such things, particularly when he was in his cups. It is said the Coyote clan was disavowed because they refused to fight in the war. And from there, their entire history was erased. They became Dry Earth, clanless."

Peyana cleared her throat. She had forgone any signs of mourning at all and wore a dress of shimming green and blue scales, her hair wrapped in dramatic horns atop her head. It was shockingly festive and sent a clear signal as to where Winged Serpent's sympathies lay. "Is that the legacy you wish to claim now, Naranpa? One of criminals and proven cowards?"

"The people of the Maw are loyal to this city, which is more than I can say for some at the table today." Her reprimand was not harsh, but it was firm. "You will show some respect, Peyana."

"I do not object to the Coyote clan having a representative here." Ieyoue spoke before the others could respond. "Would that be you?"

Naranpa nodded. She heard the bosses come to stand behind her. Denaochi's hand came down on her shoulder. "And my brother will stand as my Shield."

They all understood what Naranpa was saying, what rights she was claiming. The title of matron, a seat on the Speakers Council, a voice in the political and economic future of the city as a representative of those who lived in the Maw.

"You will never be Sky Made," Nuuma hissed.

"We don't need to be," Denaochi said. "We are proud to be Dry Earth, children of the Coyote. But you *will* see us as your equal."

"And if we refuse?"

Naranpa's voice was casually lethal. "We'll end your diplomatic mission to Hokaia cold in its tracks." It was a bluff but one she and Denaochi had decided on. Maw spies had seen Golden Eagle's forces leave the city via the river and had followed at a distance until they could discern their purpose. They had not stopped them, only gathered information, and hoped it would be enough now to force Golden Eagle to show their hand. "We know your daughter leads a contingent north and east to the Puumun River in a bid to reach Hokaia by stealth before the spring thaw. We know you planned to take control of the Watchers. The only thing we do not know is what price you asked to sell out your city and from whom."

Nuuma's face was a mask, giving nothing away, but Naranpa was sure they had struck true.

"What's this?" Peyana rose in alarm.

Ieyoue's face had fallen in consternation. "Tell us it is otherwise, Nuuma."

"Baseless lies." The matron of Golden Eagle raised her chin, eyes steady on Naranpa. "The kind of lies one might expect from the self-appointed matron of a false clan."

Denaochi leaned forward with his crooked smile. "Shall we bring your daughter here to tell us herself?"

That had not been part of their plan, and as far as she knew, there was no daughter to bring forward. They had left the Golden Eagle contingent unmolested. But Nuuma didn't know that, and panic widened her eyes before she could control it.

Denaochi lifted a gloved hand and snapped his fingers. The door to the Lupine opened, and Naranpa half expected Nuuma's daughter to walk down the stairs, even though she knew who was waiting outside.

Nuuma must have expected her daughter, too, because she had stood and was moving toward the door before she recognized the young man dressed in black, a single red feather emblazoned over his heart.

"Okoa Carrion Crow," she breathed. Her eyes ricocheted between Naranpa and Okoa, wild. "Is this a trap?"

"No trap. Okoa is Sky Made. Surely you cannot object to his presence."

"He is not the matron."

"I speak for the matron," Okoa said.

Naranpa had forgotten the rich tones of his voice, and how they carried, and what a striking figure he cut. Nuuma's voice equaled his in volume, if not control. "And where is your monster?"

"I came alone."

"That beast that killed my niece is a monster, and you are harboring him in your house. Your sister knows our demands. There is nothing you can say here that will change my mind. So speak all you want, Crow. It means nothing. I will not be satisfied until I have your Odo Sedoh's head rolling at my feet."

Okoa's expression had been mild, his tone civil, but now his face darkened, and Naranpa caught a glimpse of the fire that had animated him when last they had met.

"Then you will have to learn to live with disappointment."

Nuuma's thin lips flattened. "And you will not live long at all." Her command was a dark growl. "Kill them."

The Golden Eagle Shield moved toward Okoa. Naranpa rose, shouting a warning, but it was unneeded. The Carrion Crow scion leaped from the stairs, taking the captain down to the floor. She tried to run to them, but Denaochi was there, holding her back.

"Leave it," he warned. "You'll only distract him. He looks capable enough."

She watched them struggle, and her brother had the right of it. Okoa had the man pinned. But Naranpa caught the flash of obsidian across the man's knuckles, some kind of sharp weapon, and he struck Okoa in the chest. The Crow fell back.

"Naranpa!" She heard the mistress of the Agave, Sedaysa, scream her name. She turned just in time to see Pasko in the midst of a throw, something small and black flying from his hand.

Her mind had barely registered it as a knife before Denao-chi was there, hurling himself between her and the blade. She sensed more than saw the knife find flesh, and Denaochi collapsed to the floor.

She screamed and fell to her knees, hands reaching for her brother. It didn't make sense. Pasko was on their side.

Blood pumped from Denaochi's chest, already coating his shirt, a blade sunk deep into his heart.

He smiled.

"I am your Shield," he whispered through blood-flecked lips.

"No!" She called her healing powers, and warmth came to her palms, but she didn't have time to touch her brother before Pasko came barreling toward her.

Her rage flared, and she scrambled to meet Pasko's charge. She threw her arms open as if she would catch him in an embrace. They collided, and time seemed to slow, eternity stretching before her.

She wasn't sure when it happened. The healing power she had called to aid Denaochi morphed into something else. And in the cauldron of her anger, that something became heat, became fire, and flames roared from her palms.

Her back slammed into the ground but she did not let go. She clamped her hands to the sides of Pasko's face, willing the fire to consume him. At first, his skin only smoldered, tendrils of smoke intertwined with his curling black hair. Then heat built as if from inside, and his skin began to bubble like water on the boil. His cheeks collapsed, then his forehead, and his eyes popped and sank.

She watched, mouth open in a wordless scream, as the proprietor of the Blackfire burned.

Eventually, she became aware of Ieyoue Water Strider kneeling in front of her. Just over her shoulder was Okoa Carrion

Crow, his handsome face bloodied and drawn at what he saw before him. He and Ieyoue's Shield rolled Pasko off her, and Okoa gently peeled her hands from the dead man's face. She stared at her palms. Perfectly normal-looking palms, except for the flakes of burned flesh that stuck to them in patches.

Behind her, someone was weeping.

It was Zataya, and her anguished howls brought Naranpa back to the present.

"Ochi?" she asked, her voice small.

Ieyoue shook her head.

Naranpa stumbled toward her brother.

"Heal him!" Zataya knelt beside Denaochi's body, her face a molted mess of tears and rage. "Use your power to heal him!"

Denaochi's face was empty and his eyes staring. Pasko's blade still protruded from his chest. She absently noticed the hilt on this blade was the same as the one he had driven into Denaochi's flesh at the Agave, but there, a spark of life had lingered, and she had been able to feed it with her own lifeforce and coax her brother back. Here, it did not seem possible.

She met Zataya's gaze, already haunted, and she knew the witch understood.

"Please," Zataya whispered anyway. "Try, anyway."

"Maybe it is not too late. Do you have your god magics? The salt and smoke."

"I only had enough to help you."

Then Naranpa was his sole hope.

She found the healing place within her, the power rising to her palms. She pressed her hands against Denaochi's chest. Warm blood seeped between her fingers.

Silence welled around her, and she sensed the others in the room watching. It was as if the world held its breath and waited.

271

But the wait was for naught.

Tears fell and her body shook as the glow faded from her hands. Zataya wailed beside her. She beat her fists against the floor until someone, Naranpa didn't notice who, pulled her away.

She looked around. The room had been demolished, tables overturned, benches broken, and the unmistakable stench of blood and cooked flesh permeated everything.

Cooked flesh. Skies, she had killed a man. No, not a man. Her brother's murderer.

It was a strange comfort, if a comfort at all. She had never wanted to take a life, even for vengeance. She felt lost, unsure of who she was supposed to be. All her plans of only hours ago were destroyed as if they had never been. Her imagined future lay like ash on her tongue.

"Where is Nuuma?" she asked, suddenly remembering why they were all here.

"Fled." Okoa had come to kneel beside her. His expression was wary but unafraid, as if he had seen worse and expected to see worse again in the future. "Her captain is dead." His voice had a strange hitch to it.

She nodded, because she was not sure what else to do.

She became aware of someone else hovering on her other side. Sedaysa. "What happened?" Naranpa asked. She meant *why*. Why had Pasko betrayed them?

Mercifully, Sedaysa understood. "He asked me earlier if there was any gift great enough to buy my soul. I told him Denaochi had already given that to me, long ago. He nodded, as if he understood. I should have known then that something was amiss. There is only one thing he wanted in all the world, only one thing that would have made him turn traitor, and that was vengeance against the man who killed his brother. Golden

Eagle must have given him that. And in exchange for the scion's life, he agreed to take yours."

He must have known that even if he succeeded in killing her, Denaochi would have hunted him down. Why do it? Why pay such a price?

"His demons are quieted." Amalq joined Sedaysa, her face wet with tears. Tears for Pasko or Denaochi? Maybe both.

"We should leave this place," Ieyoue suggested gently.

"The Agave is not far." Sedaysa stepped forward. "You are welcome to continue your talk there." Her voice was steady, but it had lost its smoky charm and was raw with grief. She had loved Denaochi, too.

See, Brother, Naranpa thought. *Zataya, Sedaysa, your foolish older sister. You were well loved after all.*

"Go," Naranpa said, voice subdued. "I need to take care of Ochi."

Ieyoue exhaled softly. "He's gone, Naranpa. There is nothing to do for him now, and the living of Tova still need you."

Tova. Thrice-damned Tova. She knew now that the city would take and take from her until there was nothing left. How could she hate something and love it all at once? "If you cannot help me, go."

"I will help you." Zataya pushed her way forward to join her. She grasped Naranpa's hand, still coated with Denaochi's blood.

"I will help you, too." That was Sedaysa.

"I will take the others to the Agave," Amalq offered. "Come join us when you are able."

She stepped forward to usher the Sky Made up the stairs. Naranpa watched them go. Once the matrons and Okoa had left, she turned to the Dry Earth women beside her, and together they tended to their newly dead.

CHAPTER 25

THE MERIDIAN GRASSLANDS
YEAR 1 OF THE CROW

> There is not enough water in the Crescent Sea to wash clean
> a guilty conscience.
>
> —Teek saying

Xiala woke to find a bowl of her seawater broth just inside her
door the next morning. There was no indication of who had
left it, but it had to have been Ziha. She wondered how the girl
was faring and if she had recovered from her encounter with
Iktan. She supposed she would find out soon enough once the
march was under way.

She drank the broth and then struck her tent. She had been
meeting Iktan for breakfast, but today she did not. She wasn't sure
xe would be waiting for her, and even if xe was, she wasn't sure she
wanted to speak to xir just yet. Mostly because she wasn't sure
what to say. She didn't know if she should pretend that last night
didn't happen, or if she should acknowledge the secrets shared
and discuss them. Neither sounded particularly desirable.

"Let it wait," she murmured, as she strapped on her pack.
As the company moved forward, she fell back to the rear to
avoid both commander and assassin priest.

They passed through beautiful country, the sameness of the prairie ceding to soaring mountains that pierced a bright blue sky, their slopes dressed in blinding blankets of snow. Her legs noted the steady incline, and her lungs labored to take in the thinner air. She would not live in a place like this, so far from the sea, but she admired the majesty of it and believed, if only briefly, that gods must have formed it with their own being.

Around midday, they reached a lake nestled in a valley buttressed by mountains, and by that lake was a town. They set up camp within sight of the single-story stone buildings and slanting roofs, and Xiala caught sight of Ziha assembling a group to go to the town and purchase supplies. Another group was assigned to procure transportation down the Puumun, which she could see snaking off the body of the lake downslope and to the east. She lounged in her tent for a while, but the town beckoned to her. She missed people who might speak to her, share the news of what was happening in the larger world. She doubted news of Tova would make it this far and precede them, but she wondered if she might send word back to Serapio. Tell him of what she had learned of a traitor in Carrion Crow, and of Golden Eagle's alliance with Cuecola. Her restlessness pushed her to her feet, and she donned her blue cloak and ventured down to the town.

It was not much to see, particularly after the grandeur of Tova, but its roads were well packed and clean of refuse, and the handful of shops and houses were tidy and well tended. She spied a traveler's house, a squat rectangle with an inner courtyard, and wondered what drink she might find there. But the land sickness still lingered, headache never far off, and she decided against imbibing. Instead, she wandered down to the lake's edge, where a kind of harbor had been built out over the water.

She spotted the problem immediately.

It was the lake itself. More to the point, it was the lake in winter. It looked to be still navigable, but there was a thin sheet of ice along the bank that suggested it would not be for long, although surely if they left now and went east, descending, they could outrun the winter freeze. It had not been nearly as cold here as it had been in Tova, although she was unfamiliar with this part of the Meridian and did not know what the coming days would bring. Xiala imagined Ziha was at this moment rehearsing an impassioned speech about the necessity of taking fifty people downriver and how many craft that would take and at what cost. No doubt the local riverman was about to become very rich.

She didn't relish the idea of having to turn around and walk back to Tova, but she doubted it would come to that. Golden Eagle had the funds, and in the end, she was sure a bargain would be struck. It just might take a few extra days and substantially more cacao to do it.

After a while, she grew bored, and her stomach reminded her she had not eaten yet. A headache also threatened, and she worried she had stayed too long. She glanced up at the sky. The sun had begun its descent behind the mountains, but a good half hour of light remained. If she returned to camp now, she might be able to eat and retire to her tent before either Ziha or Iktan came looking for her.

She had made it halfway up the slope and past the town, the camp just over the next rise but still hidden by the tall grass, when she heard someone shout, "Teek!"

She turned to see three people approaching. A woman in the lead and behind her two men. The woman looked a bit like Ziha, brown-skinned and brown-haired but light-eyed. She wore the gold and white of Golden Eagle, and Xiala thought she looked a bit familiar, like she had seen her around camp. The men she did not know. They were paler in complexion and wore patchwork clothes, heavy furs on their shoulders, and rough hide and string for leggings. She tensed, unsure what to think. The woman gave her a friendly wave. Xiala looked back over her shoulder. She could almost see the tops of the camp tents and, below in the twilight, the town. Should she wait? The men looked none too savory, and her keen sense of danger urged her on. She turned her back to the strangers and quickened her pace, but her legs wobbled, and her breath came labored.

They sped up to catch her, and before she could reach the crest of the hill, a hand spun her around.

"Ho, Teek," the woman repeated, and Xiala caught the scent of alcohol on her breath. She must have come from the travelers' inn in the village.

"What do you want?"

"I come in peace!" The woman lifted her hands in innocence. "I was hoping you could help me settle a bet with my new friends."

Xiala's stomach clenched. "What kind of bet?"

"I told them about you, said we've got a Teek traveling with us. They said there's no such thing, so I was bringing them back to see. And to collect on my bet," she added, patting a small purse at her waist. "And there you were, the eagle's luck!"

"The eagle's luck, indeed," said the first man, smiling, but she saw only avarice in his eyes, the way he licked at his lips.

Xiala took a step back. She knew this game, had been here a dozen times in port cities across the Crescent Sea. She rubbed her thumb across her pinkie, the one with the missing joint, and remembered the last time someone had caught her unaware. She could run, but her legs were weak. She could scream and hope to be heard, but that might prompt her harassers to action when all they'd done so far was leer. *Be smart*, she told herself. *Bide your time. You've been in worse situations.*

"Is it true, then, that you're a Teek?" the second man asked. He snaked out a hand and took a curl of Xiala's hair between his fingers. Xiala pulled back. He let the lock slip, laughing. "I hear Teek parts fetch a nice price in southern ports."

"Especially the eyes," the other man said, holding thumb and finger in a circle around his own. "So big and round, like fish eyes."

She reached for her Song, and her headache flared. She sucked in a breath and grabbed her head between her hands. Images assailed her. The woman in blue, the green-eyed man. People screaming, bodies trampled underfoot. She tried to focus, to push past the bad memories, but her mind felt empty as untrod sand, as if the Songs of the ocean did not travel to places so far from her Mother's purview, and Xiala had lost the right to Sing them.

The woman laughed, but it was clear to the men this was no jest, and they were noticeably more sober than the one who had led them here. Someone grabbed her arm, thick fingers digging into her flesh.

She didn't have her Song, but she still had her fists. She threw a punch that connected hard against the man's cheek and sent pain shooting up her arm. She received an ugly curse and a backhanded blow in return that sent her to her knees. She swayed, dazed, as hands reached for her again. She heard the sound of a blade slide free of a sheath and knew she might die, right there in the grass so far from the sea.

"Fuck off!" she screamed, but it came out mumbled and hoarse. Her head throbbed, but if she was going to die, she was going to do it fighting.

"What's this?" the second man said. "The fish talks? Maybe we take her tongue, too."

"The fish does more than talk," came a soft, singsong voice, and Xiala almost wept in relief as Iktan seemed to appear from nowhere, the grass parting to make way. "She Sings. Do you know about a Teek's Song, my friends?"

"Tsiyo!" the woman exclaimed in surprise.

"It is an ancient magic, a gift from the time of the gods woven into their very making," Iktan continued. "It is said that they can kill with a single note. Imagine that. A simple melody"— xe hummed a note, stretched it out until it bent into something strange and unsettling—"and your brain will burst and leak from your ears. Or was it that your heart will shatter and leak from your anus? Well, either way, you're leaking, so . . ."

The hands that held her let go.

"Just a bit of fun, tsiyo," the first man said with a nervous laugh. "We wouldn't have really hurt—"

"Careful, friend," Iktan said, voice as cold as the frost on the riverbanks, "that your next words don't call me a fool."

"Our sincere apologies," the woman offered, voice shaking. "We should have never come." And then they were scrambling away, falling over themselves as they scattered back toward town.

"Pathetic," Iktan murmured as xe watched them go.

Xiala heaved, trying to find air.

"Skies, Xiala!" Iktan swore. "Did they hurt you?"

"Land sickness," she croaked. It had to be. Oh, Mother waters, it had to only be that. She rubbed at her throat, panic heavy on her chest.

"Land sickness? Shall I take you to the river?"

"No," she mumbled. "Rivers feel different. They are not the sea. They don't . . . they are not the Teek Mother."

"No," Iktan said. "They spring from the gods of snow and rain."

Xe dropped down beside her and opened a waterskin. She took it and drank, swallowing as quickly as she could.

"Those things you said about a Teek's Song," she said, once she had drunk enough. "They are forbidden. We don't use our Mother's gift as a weapon." She didn't know why she said it when all she could think about were the times she had used her Song as exactly that, and why she thought Iktan would care. "We soothe the waters, can soothe men, too. Only sometimes . . ."

"Shhh," Iktan whispered. Xe hoisted her arm around xir shoulders and pulled her to her feet. "Please don't ruin it for me, Xiala. Right now, I live with the fantasy of you bursting Ziha's insides until she shits her guts out. It keeps me going. Don't take it away."

She choked, wanting to laugh, wanting to explain her Song was not supposed to work on women, but instead, she only found tears.

• • • • •

Their progress back to camp was slow, and Xiala had to stop and rest even for such a short distance. Ziha was there to greet them, her face a mask of anger that morphed into alarm once she realized Xiala was sick.

"I was about to send scouts out to find you," Ziha said. "I thought you had run."

"Run where?" Iktan asked, exasperated. "Never mind. Just help me get her inside."

"Take her to my tent," Ziha said, and Iktan brought her in and settled her down on the now-familiar furs. Xe covered her with a blanket while Ziha built up the fire.

"Are you comfortable?" xe asked, and Xiala nodded. "Good. Rest. I must speak to our commander."

Xe motioned Ziha to come with xir outside. She could see them talking just beyond the doorway, heads close. She wished she had Serapio's hearing, but even without it, she knew their talk was about her. She tried to stay awake to follow their conversation, read gesture and tone, but her eyes grew too heavy.

She awoke once only long enough to see that both Iktan and Ziha were gone, and then she awoke much later to Ziha coming through the entrance. She was sweating, and her shoulders were high around her ears. A muscle worked along her jawline, and her eyes were hooded. Tension thrummed through the room, enough that Xiala fought through her exhaustion and forced herself to sitting.

"What's wrong?" she asked, wary.

Ziha threw something down on the furs. A white stone with a light brown center, its end trailing ragged, bloody threads. No, that didn't make sense. Stones didn't bleed, and this one looked too round and perfect to be a river stone. With horror, Xiala realized what it was and skittered backward, trying to put distance between herself and the gruesome trophy.

"Iktan told me what happened," Ziha said, voice terse. She wiped at her brow with a shaking hand. "It was unacceptable. There are rules of hospitality, lines that cannot be breached, else they shame us all. I hope this punishment is satisfactory."

Xiala looked up at her, face pale. "You took her eyeball?"

"Only one, same as they wanted from you. Iktan told me that there are some who collect Teek parts for cacao. Or luck. Or sport. I want you to know that will not happen as long as you are under my protection."

Xiala wasn't sure what to do, what to say to such justice, even when it had been committed on her behalf. Ziha was staring at her, hazel eyes turned as hard and unyielding as tourmaline, so Xiala only nodded and whispered, "Thank you."

"All agree that a punishment was necessary, but there may be hard feelings among the company tonight because of Kuya."

"Kuya is her name?"

"She's popular, and her family is well known. They will not be pleased. I'll have your dinner brought to you here, and more of your broth, if you like. And maybe once we're on the river, you can tell me of the Odo Sedoh."

Of course, Ziha had not forgotten, and now Xiala owed her a favor.

"Good." Ziha shifted on her feet, as if there was something else she wanted to say, but before she could speak, Iktan was slipping through the door. Xe took in Xiala's face and smiled, and then xir gaze traveled to the eyeball on the blanket, and xir smile widened.

"Congratulations," Iktan said, patting Ziha on the shoulder. "Your first disciplinary action as commander. A rousing success, I think."

Ziha stood stiff and silent. Iktan could not see the woman's face from where xe stood, but Xiala did. Her expression was part loathing and part resignation, as if she were held together at that moment through will and duty alone, and they were not enough to keep her whole. She nodded curtly to Xiala before pivoting on her heel and striding out of the tent.

"Did you put her up to that?" Xiala asked.

"The eyeball? No. That was her idea."

"It's gruesome."

"Yes, it is. Sometimes things are most effective when they are a bit gruesome. Words are easy to ignore, especially from a commander as untried as Ziha. The scions do not like to take orders, especially from the matron's second daughter. She needed to show her mettle."

"So the woman Kuya is not a soldier?" She had suspected she was not, despite the uniform, but she didn't understand what Iktan meant by *scions*.

"Oh, no." Iktan brought the pitcher to her. "None of them is. These are all volunteers. The children of important families in Golden Eagle, a diplomatic escort for our party in Hokaia. Ziha will represent Golden Eagle in the negotiations, so she is more envoy than general, and this company more entourage than army."

"And the other two? The local men?"

"You need not worry about those men again." Iktan said it with enough finality that she could guess their fates, and who had brought them to their end.

It wasn't that she was ungrateful, but there was so much death around her lately. When had her life become so dark?

"What happened out there, Xiala?" Iktan asked. "My words weren't all bluster, no matter how you protest. Why didn't you use your Song?"

"I . . ." She wished that Ziha had already brought the broth. It seemed to be the only thing that cleared her head, gave her strength. She settled on "I don't know."

Iktan's gaze was uncompromising, but xir tone was sympathetic. "I think you do know."

She rubbed her palms against her thighs, her eyes searching the room for that half bottle of xtabentún she knew had to be somewhere.

"I know you don't trust me," Iktan said, "and you can choose not to tell me. But you must tell someone, sometime. Else whatever happened out there might well keep happening."

Iktan's words had the feel of truth to them, and she hated it. "Do you know where the drink is? From before?"

"Drink will not fix this." Xe stood. "I'll go see about your dinner." Iktan gestured to the gory eyeball that still lay on the furs at her feet. "What do you want to do with that?"

She shuddered. "Throw it away."

Iktan scooped it up and dropped it into the pocket of Xiala's blue cloak. "You might want it later."

"I won't want it." She was sure of that much.

Iktan's voice was sad, xir half smile knowing. "We don't always know what we want, Xiala, until it is taken away."

· · · · ·

Xiala slept fitfully by the too-warm fire, plagued by the fear that she had lost her Song. She had tried again to call it, but it felt distant, just out of reach, like the clear fish that darted in pools on the shores of her home. Iktan was right. She had to face her fear, face her memories. Not just the guilt of what had happened during the Convergence that plagued her dreams but the deeper shame. The one that the Convergence had roused in her and the land sickness had compounded. She had to face the memories of her last day on Teek.

Desperate, scared, but knowing she had no option, she loosened the chain on the door of her mind.

She could almost feel the cold wind that had swept in from the north that fateful night, bringing rain and the bright flash of lightning with it. Could almost see herself, standing on her mother's porch, hair and skin soaked through, the rope of bells by the door clanging angrily as their voices rose to match her ire.

She pressed her hands to her mouth to keep from screaming as the wind tore at her hair, ran phantom hands across her skin. She remembered the touch of other hands, the hands of a man. Sibaan. He had come to their island days after her fifteenth birthday, and her mother had claimed him, as was her right. But his dark eyes had lingered on Xiala, and his lazy, arrogant smile he reserved only for her. He had spoken her name, his voice as rich as late-season blueberries, and her heart had roared like the surf under a full moon. They had stolen away from the feast, and he had kissed her, lips like honeysuckle off the stem. He had coaxed her dress from her hips, dipped roughened fingers between her legs, and she had burned like the sun at the height of summer. He had made promises, too. Give me this, and I will take you away, Xiala. We will live in a fine palace in a great city, and we will marry, and you can have anything you want.

A ship? she had asked, breathless with possibility. I want to sail my own ship.

Women do not sail in the Southern Cities, he had said, annoyed, as he laid her on the sand. But you can bear me many children. And then he had pushed himself inside her.

I love him! she had screamed at her mother, and for her declaration had received a backhand that split her lip.

We do not love them, you stupid girl, her mother had hissed. We beguile, we seduce, and then we rut to bear children. And then we Sing them to the sharks so that they may never tell another how they found us.

I won't let you hurt him. Sibaan loves me, and I love him.

You little fool. The contempt on her mother's face had made her want to run, but she stood her ground, facing down both her mother and the storm that raged around them.

And then her mother had stepped to the side to let her see what lay behind her. There, in her mother's house, on her mother's bed. The man with the long black hair and the sun-bronzed skin, the one with honeysuckle kisses and a voice like wine, lay sleeping and spent, tangled naked in her mother's sheets. If he loves you, then why is he in my bed?

He promised!

Men promise, Xiala. But you are the fool who believed.

The roar in her head was deafening, her fear morphing into rage. Her Song beckoned, begged her to act. She would howl a Song of rage, of betrayal. She would shake the heavens. She would make them both pay.

• • • • •

"Wake up, Xiala." A hand on her shoulder, shaking her loose from the past. Iktan dropped to a crouch in front of the fire and handed her a bowl. "Ziha's gone to town. I brought you your broth."

She exhaled, tried to gather herself. The memory so long suppressed now felt fresh. It shivered through her like she was fifteen again, lost and alone. And guilty of the greatest crime known to her people.

"I killed someone once with my Song," she whispered.

Iktan gave her a half-smile. "Only one?"

"Please." She sighed, tracing a finger around the edge of the bowl. "Do not make fun of it."

Iktan raised xir hands in forbearance. "I am a cynical being, Xiala. It is good that you are not. Do you want to tell me about it?"

"No. Yes." She scraped her hands over her face in frustration. "It is the reason I cannot go home."

"Ah." Iktan dropped to sitting, hands folded, patient. "So someone important to you. Someone you loved."

She nodded, the shame welling up to stick in her throat.

"Who was it?"

She could not meet Iktan's eyes when she said it. "My mother."

She told xir the meat of it. The foolishness of first love, the promises, the betrayal.

"I was so angry to find them together, to know the depth of my naivete. I lashed out. I wanted to hurt them. To hurt her."

"And so you did."

"But it wasn't supposed to be possible. Women are immune to our Song."

"But your mother was not?"

She pulled her knees to her chest and wrapped her arms around them. "There was so much blood. I'm not even sure what happened after that. I just remember the blood, and the screams . . . and the bodies. And my aunt was there, a curse on her lips, and I ran. But where is there to run on an island except into the sea?"

"And one cannot run from such guilt."

"I tried. I became a captain, the thing I had wanted most. I commanded men, I sailed the Crescent Sea. I told myself as long as I used my Song only to soothe, only to defend and not to attack, that it was okay. That I was okay. But then the day of the Convergence, I used it to try to clear my path, and people died."

"You did not mean for them to die."

"Does it matter?" She rested her head on her knees. "They were in my way, and I wanted them gone. I did not think of the consequences. So when those men threatened me today, all I could think about was the people I killed before. What if I accidentally killed them when I only meant to defend myself? What if others in the camp or the town heard my Song and it killed them, too? What if there is no safe way to Sing, and this is why the Teek stay hidden?"

"I do not believe the Teek hide themselves away because they fear the power of their Song. From what you told me, your mother seemed perfectly willing to feed your onetime lover to the sharks. I imagine it is their independence they protect after the War of the Spear, and so they keep themselves separate from all of the Meridian."

"I don't know." She closed her eyes. "I feel so lost so far from the sea. Even away from Teek, I always had her, my true Mother. And now I have nothing."

Shouting from outside the tent broke her reverie, and Ziha came striding through the entrance.

"Good, you are both here." Her voice was clipped and her eyes wild, like an animal caught in a trap. "Xiala, are you well enough to travel to town?"

"What's wrong?" Iktan asked.

Ziha hesitated, just a breath, as if bracing herself. "My mother is here."

Xe whistled low in surprise. "It seems it is the day for maternal reckonings."

"She came in on eagleback. My sister is with her." She bit at her thumb, now raw and red. "Something has happened in Tova."

That was enough to rally Xiala. "Is it the Odo Sedoh?"

"She wants to speak to you."

"How does she even know of me?"

Ziha flushed. "I told her. Hurry. She is not a woman to be kept waiting even when she's in a good mood."

"And I take it she's not. In a good mood." Iktan sounded suspiciously cheerful.

Ziha blew out a breath. "You are not wrong, tsiyo. Let us go, before her mood turns even worse."

CHAPTER 26

CITY OF TOVA
YEAR I OF THE CROW

> How long will I mourn my father
> and weep for my mother?
> Is my brother departed
> And my sister no more?
> Am I nothing but the living
> waiting on the dead?

—From *Collected Lamentations*
from the Night of Knives

Serapio stood on the bridge that spanned the distance between Odo and Otsa and listened for Maaka's approach. He had sent the small crows to fetch the man, unsure after all that had happened if the leader of the Odohaa would come with the information he had requested. But he heard the shuffle of feet and felt the sudden sway of the bridge, smelled the distinctive scent of medicinal plants that clung to Maaka's clothes, and heard the rhythmic tap of something solid against the bridge, that last thing making him smile.

"It seems you keep having to retrieve my staff," he called. "I have been careless with it, but it will not happen again." He had lost it in the yard when he had first transformed, but now he understood that whatever touched his person changed form along with him. He would not lose it again.

"It is my honor, Odo Sedoh," Maaka said, and he heard true pleasure in his words. "I wish to serve."

Serapio took his staff, weighing it in his hands and testing the balance. All was as it should be.

"News from the Great House?" It had been two days since his confrontation with Okoa that had ended in him killing two of the Shield, one of them Okoa's cousin. He had left in a rage, close to killing Okoa himself. He would have hated himself for it, but it had always been his way to eliminate those who threatened him and the things he loved. His first two tutors, the sailors on the ship. Only Powageh had been spared, and even now, he wondered if he had erred, just as he wondered if leaving Okoa alive was a mistake. Okoa had warned him of many dire consequences should Serapio kill him, but that was not what had stayed his hand. In the end, he could not bring himself to kill the man who had nursed him to health and who had once called him cousin. They had been family, if only for a fleeting moment.

"No news of consequence, my lord. It seems there was a training accident at the lake, and two of the Shield were killed."

So Okoa had not told the truth of what had happened and Serapio's part in it to anyone. He did not know what that meant, but he thought subterfuge eased his way with Maaka now, so he was grateful.

"One of them was the former captain, a man named Chaiya." Maaka's voice was wistful.

"You knew him?"

"He was a boy when we first met, a nephew of the Matron Yatliza, Okoa's mother. I was close to both Yatliza and her consort, Ayawa. He was a brilliant man, well read, a philosopher. A good friend."

"Not a warrior?"

"No, but his ideas were revolutionary."

"What happened to him?"

"Ah . . ." He heard Maaka shift, the question making him uncomfortable. "He paid a heavy price for his ambitions, for our ambitions, as I was as much to blame as he." There was something in Maaka's voice that spoke to grief long held, and regrets, but Serapio did not probe.

"He made a sacrifice for his people." That Serapio understood.

"No." Now Maaka's bitterness bloomed fully. "He was only sacrificed." His words seemed to lodge in his throat, and he coughed. "But that was a long time ago, my lord. Let us talk of more important things. The Odohaa grow restless for your return. I speak to those gathered, every day. But I am a poor substitute. They wish for the Odo Sedoh."

"Last time I was among the gathered, it did not go well." He remembered the desperate prayers, the reaching hands, the overwhelming need.

"A misunderstanding. It would not happen again."

"In time," he assured him, knowing he had no intention of walking among the mob again. "But there is something I must do first. Were you able to find it?"

"Yes, I think so. There are local records, and some of the elders remember."

"Take me there," he whispered, his voice hoarse with unexpected emotion.

"There is the problem that you will be recognized. Word of your appearance has spread, and it may not be safe for you to walk the streets of Odo without a Shield."

"Then I will not walk. Go, and I will follow. When you enter, I will know that is the place and meet you there."

A rustling of robes as Maaka bowed. And then he was striding away.

With the merest flicker of thought, Serapio broke into a flock.

• • • • •

He followed from high above as Maaka crossed the bridge and climbed the narrow, well-worn steps that brought him back to the main thoroughfare that cut through Odo. In the distance, he could see the road ended at the Great House, but Maaka did not take him there. Instead, he passed through a copse of cedar, turned north, and came out on a hill overlooking the canyon. There was a long, dark stone wall here, and he walked the length of it before coming to a gate and ducking inside. Serapio transformed in the shade of the cedars and followed on foot, calling a crow to help him see.

They were in a courtyard. In the middle was the roof of a round house, the chamber itself sunk into the ground below them. To the right of the round house was a garden, fallow now but big enough to feed a half dozen families, and beside it benches, tables, and an outdoor oven marked the communal kitchen. Around the edges of the courtyard were two- and three-story adobe homes. They were quiet, their inhabitants sleeping or otherwise occupied. A lone dog came trotting up to them and sniffed Maaka's robes. The Odohaa bent to scratch its ear.

"This was your family compound," Maaka explained. "Your mother's family was of notable means, weavers and artisans and distant cousins to the family who now rule the Great House."

"Who lives here now?"

"Another family, unrelated. After the Night of Knives, entire families were lost, with no one to claim their houses. It is not so unusual to find homes once abandoned now lived in by others."

"Not abandoned," Serapio corrected.

"No," Maaka agreed, voice solemn. "Not abandoned."

"If they were a notable family, why did my mother's people not live in the Great House? She spoke of visiting the aviary there, of having an uncle who was a crow rider."

"Who can say? Maybe a disagreement that led to a falling out? Perhaps even their devotion to the crow god caused the rift."

"They must have been one of the first houses to fall, being so close to the bridge." He stepped farther into the courtyard, his crow vision taking it in. He imagined what it must have been like on the Night of Knives. If they had had any warning or if the knocks on the door had come as a surprise. He could almost hear the screams reverberating off the walls, see the bodies falling, sense the cries for help to a god in whom they had placed their faith but who refused their pleas.

Just as he refused Serapio now. Except, of course, when he needed him to kill the Sun Priest.

"You are right, of course," Maaka agreed. "Most in the Great House survived, but the smaller houses and the outliers like your family, they had no defense for an enemy like the Watchers, who were meant to protect them, not slaughter them."

"No wonder my mother taught me as she did."

"What did she teach you?"

That everyone is my enemy, he thought. *Even you, Maaka.*

When he did not answer, Maaka continued. "I tried to ask discreetly if any of the elders remembered a girl named Saaya, but no one here did. That is why I think these inhabitants are new and your family is scattered."

"Or dead."

They stood a moment, then Maaka said, "This way, Odo Sedoh."

Serapio released his crow and followed. They stopped in front of a door. Maaka knocked. They heard sound within, an infant crying and quickly hushed, and then the door opened. Maaka whispered words of greeting, and a woman answered, her Tovan accent thick.

"Welcome, Odo Sedoh," she said, and Maaka touched his arm to motion him forward. They crossed the threshold into the place where his mother had been a child. It smelled earthy and sweet, the scent of mother's milk. There was the sound of children from another room and then the approach of running feet.

"Is that the crow god?" a small voice asked.

The woman whispered for the child to be quiet, but Serapio said, "Let them come." He remembered what it was like to be a child, even before he had been dedicated to his purpose. His mother always mourning for the life she had lost, his father angry at her melancholy, the long stretches of loneliness he had endured, even in a home full of other people. He knew how difficult it was to be young, so small and so powerless.

He bent down and motioned the child forward. After a word of encouragement from the mother, hesitant feet approached.

He held out a hand. He no longer needed a knife for this trick. He imagined his thumb a crow talon, long and black and sharp, and knew it had changed when he heard the others gasp. He sliced the tip of his finger to draw blood and then called the shadow.

"Don't touch," he warned the child. "Just watch."

He formed the shadow into a crow. The shadow crow flapped its wings and hovered over his hand, and the child exclaimed softly. He broke the crow into two crows, who circled each other before uniting and reforming into a single crow and then into a single feather. The smoke feather drifted down to lie against his palm. He willed it to dissolve, and in its place was a real feather.

"You can touch this one," he told the child. "Go on. Take it." Warm fingers grazed his skin, and then the feather was gone. He quickly closed his hand into a fist, hoping the adults did not notice the thin layer of skin peeled from his palm.

"A gift from the Odo Sedoh." The mother bowed. "We do not deserve this."

Serapio straightened. "Nevertheless."

And then Maaka and the woman were talking again, which left Serapio to wander through the house on his own. He walked carefully, exploring the place that should have been his had the Night of Knives never happened. He tried to imagine his mother here as a child, no older than the one he had gifted with the feather, but it was difficult. His thoughts snagged on the last time he had seen her, the leaden weight of the poison flower milk in his veins, the dull bite of the needle through his eyelids. He shook those memories off and tried to imagine himself in this house instead, but that felt like pain and betrayal. Frustrated, he thrust all his memories aside and tried to let the walls of the house speak on their own. But the murmured conversation between Maaka and the mother blunted whatever the walls might say. More noises that did not belong to him or his memories: the snuffling wails of an infant, the delighted giggles of a child with a feather. He bowed his head. There was nothing of his family left in this place.

He felt dizzy, untethered from the earth and out of control, falling upward as everything he knew shrank below him. His breaths came short, panicked, and he hurried to the door, stumbling past Maaka.

"Are you unwell, Odo Sedoh?" Maaka's concern trailed him as the man made rushed apologies to the mother and caught up with him halfway across the courtyard.

"Is there a bench here?" Serapio gasped, remembering the kitchen. "Somewhere to sit?"

"Over here." He pulled at Serapio's arm.

He shook him off, annoyed. "Just tell me! I don't need your help!"

"Apologies," Maaka said, chastened. "Four paces forward and to your right."

Serapio used his staff to find the bench and collapsed, trembling. Memories poured over him, none of them good, and he hunched into himself. He turned to Maaka abruptly. "Do you know my name?"

"I . . ." The man sounded flustered. Unsure. "You are the Odo Sedoh."

"I mean the name I was given at birth. The one my mother and father chose."

"To me you are the Odo Sedoh. It is the highest honor."

"I have a favorite food I enjoy. Did you know that?"

"I . . ." The Odohaa sounded almost frightened, clearly at a loss.

"I very much like chocolate. I had it once when I was a boy, a present from my tutor on my birthday."

"If the Odo Sedoh wishes chocolate . . ."

"No, I do not wish chocolate."

"Then why . . . ?"

"The kind I had was very spicy. I had something like it on the solstice, too. Here, in Titidi."

"Shall I find the chocolate vendor, Lord?"

"No, Maaka. I only wanted you to know that I like chocolate." He tried again. "Do you know any stories?"

"What kind of stories does the Odo Sedoh wish to hear?"

"Something from your childhood. Something of this place, of Odo."

"My stories are not worthy of the Odo Sedoh."

"Nonsense. I am asking."

"Please!" Maaka choked out a half sob.

Serapio closed his eyes. He understood that to push more would only be a cruelty. He had proven his point. "Forget that I asked."

He had only wanted to be seen for a moment. Recognized as a man, not a god. But he understood he had asked too much of Maaka, perhaps even of Okoa and the rest of Carrion Crow. Sometimes he felt as if he were two people. One was the Odo Sedoh, a man molded into a vengeful god and honed to a single purpose. Blessed with a destiny above all others.

The other was a lonely boy constantly seeking connection, trying desperately to find his footing in a world that had no place for him. He hated the boy and his weakness, his foolish desire to find friends and family. It had been the boy who had contemplated a life with Xiala, the boy who wished to be Okoa's cousin and not the Odo Sedoh, the boy who wanted chocolate and stories like a child.

He understood now that when his mother had warned him that everyone was his enemy, she had meant he was his own enemy, too. He knew he could drive this frailty from his consciousness, embrace only the pain, the purpose. Become fully the weapon that he had told Okoa that he was. It only took courage . . . and a letting go.

He willed his fingers to become talons and drove them into the flesh of his hand.

"My lord!" Maaka cried out.

"I thought I might sense something of my mother in this

place," he said, the pain making the words crawl from between his teeth. "But there is nothing for me here." *Nothing for me anywhere . . . unless I make it.*

"You're bleeding! Skies, your hand!"

"Come. Kneel before me, Maaka."

He heard the man shuffle forward and fall to his knees. "Have I failed you?" His voice shook. "If you only tell me what I can do, what you need."

"You have not failed me," he assured him. "I will call on you soon, Maaka. You and the Odohaa. Can you answer when I do?"

"With our blood."

"Yes, you will answer with blood." He pressed his bloody palm to Odohaa's cheek. "We both will."

He could hear the man weeping. Serapio breathed one last breath in, and when he exhaled, he shattered and took to the sky.

CHAPTER 27

The hubris of divinity is but one more gift that is yours!

—From *The Manual of the Dreamwalkers*,
by Seuq, a spearmaiden

Balam was pleased that Captain Keol had been correct and their voyage across the eastern isles of the Crescent Sea had been a generally uneventful one. The islands were never more than a day's journey between them, which meant they slumbered on land every night. The fresh water was plentiful and the food along the shore abundant, particularly fish and crabs and the other creatures that called the shallow waters their home. Fruit was harder to find, but Keol explained that it was out of season and on their return voyage, the trees would be heavy with their bounty.

They saw no Teek, which was both relief and disappointment. Lord Tuun sat across from the fire each night, her slate eyes fixed on him. He brushed her off with disarming smiles and clever words that made her shoulders rock with laughter. But her humor was always short-lived, and by the end of the evening, he could feel her demand for the very islands around them weighing on him like the thick seaweed that washed up along the island's rocky shore.

They arrived at the mouth of the Kuukuh River on the tenth day and bade their captain farewell, swapping the seafaring canoes for barges. Hokaia was another two days up the mighty river, and they arrived on the third day just as the sun rose, the great city of the spearmaidens stretched out before them, bathed in light.

For six square miles on either side of Kuukuh, great earthen mounds soared skyward. A hundred, if there were ten, and while most were four or five stories high, in the distance Balam could see the mound on which the spearmaidens' palace sat. It dominated the horizon, rising ten stories at least, a behemoth and a wonder to rival any of the stone pyramids of Cuecola. Balam thought of the labor that must have been required to build such a thing, and then of what it took to maintain a mountain made by human hands. He was impressed.

They passed first through smaller districts, each dominated by an earthen mound situated on the north edge of a central plaza. Around the plazas, Balam noted oval thatched houses much like those in the outlying districts of Cuecola and cleared fields that resembled the great ball courts of his own city. Each plaza also featured a circle, wide enough for twenty men to stand inside, constructed of upright logs.

"Is it a cage of some kind?" The poles were too far apart to keep anything but a giant inside, and there was no roof, so he knew *cage* wasn't accurate, but he couldn't place the circle's function.

"Solar calendars," Powageh said at his shoulder. They all traveled together now, lord and servant and soldier. It was an uncomfortable closeness but tolerable for the few days it took to traverse up the river, and Balam did prefer Powageh's company to Pech's. They had taken up a position near the front of the boat, but guards hovered nearby, scanning the shorelines, a reminder that despite the fact that Cuecola and Hokaia were allies, the reception of the Seven Lords was unsure.

"The log circles?" Balam asked. "How do you know?"

"I was at the tower. We studied such things."

"And the fields?" Tuun stood at his other shoulder.

"Ball courts," Balam said. "They play a game called chunkey. I saw an exhibition match once from a traveling troupe when I was younger."

"And there farther on is the war college." Powageh pointed to another plaza barely visible on the western side of the river. Balam thought he spotted the flags of the Tovan clans, or at least crude imitations of them, flying over what looked to be an animal pen.

"Remind me to have any Tovans at the war college eliminated tonight. Golden Eagle can join us, but the rest cannot find out we are here on the chance they would alert their clans." He caught the look on Powageh's face. "It shouldn't be many."

"Slaughtering scions? It's an act of war."

"Is it?"

"And to think we were here as tourists," Tuun observed dryly, and it was enough to make Powageh flush. She waved a bangled wrist. "It is all very impressive. One grows used to having Cuecola as the center of one's world and forgets there are others who think themselves the center."

Balam had to agree. Perhaps it was a matter of perspective. Cuecola was surrounded by dense jungle foliage, and a sea approach hid much of its girth. But from the banks of the Kuukuh, one could see for miles across the flatlands. Flat except for the hundreds of man-made mounds, perfect layered platforms for the temples and palaces on top, graced with wooden stairs and fences and populated by thousands of people.

Because, despite the early hour, everywhere they looked there were people. Balam considered Cuecola a cosmopolitan city, but Hokaia teemed with the people of a continent. Mountains sat at Cuecola's back, cutting it off from the larger landmass to its south, but Hokaia had no natural barriers for hundreds of miles. And an easily accessible river ran through it, never mind the half dozen smaller rivers that met at its headway in the north. It was truly the heart at the center of the Meridian, its vast riverways stretching across the continent like arteries.

He saw people of various shapes, sizes, and shades, and the fashions seemed as diverse as the population. The smells of cooking fires had begun to rise as the day proceeded, and there was such a plethora of scents mingling in the morning air, many new to him, that his nose felt slightly overwhelmed.

"I can see why this place aggressed against its neighbors and began the War of the Spear." Tuum leaned her arms against the railing. "It must seem like the whole world sits at your doorstep, ripe for plucking."

"True, but the very things that served them in offense left them vulnerable in retreat. Wide lands with no natural barriers, accessible waterways."

"They are master mound builders," Powageh said. "Why not dam your rivers? Use your man-made mountains to your advantage?"

Balam looked skyward. "Their downfall came from the air. What defense did they have against the Tovan clans and their flying beasts?"

"They should have planned ahead."

"Three hundred years ago? I'm not sure they even knew of

Tova until the clans brought Hokaia to its knees. Imagine what it must have been like to be faced with a rider on the back of a winged serpent for the first time."

"Better a flying serpent than a crow." Tuun shuddered. "For some reason, it is birds that frighten me more."

"It is well we have Golden Eagle on our side," Powageh observed.

"It is a reminder that we must account for everything," Balam agreed, "even the unknown."

Powageh gestured with xir chin. "And who is that? Are they accounted for?"

Balam followed xir gaze to the approaching lagoon. Docked along the shore were half a dozen longships, their deep V-shaped hulls painted silver and black. Each had a triangular sail, wider at the top and narrow at the bottom, which hung from a stout pole closer to the fore, trailing numerous ropes. The sail was made of a bright blue fabric and hewn from smaller pieces sewn together. It had been collapsed while at port but must harness a powerful wind at sea.

"I believe those are the kind of ships that have not been seen in an age," Balam said. "They are meant for long voyages, not the sort of seafaring we do along the coast of the Crescent Sea."

"Where else would one sail?" Powageh asked.

"And why?" Tuun echoed.

"I suspect we will find out very soon." Their overloaded barges drew alongside the sleek black and silver vessels like lumbering sea turtles approaching a school of barracudas. Balam glanced up at the ten-story palace mound before them. He saw people gathering along the tiers, leaning over the wooden fences to watch them. He suspected the Sovran of Hokaia waited at the top to greet them, and beside him, no doubt, stood the owners of these fine-sailed ships. He smiled despite himself. Another player on the board but one not entirely unexpected. In fact, it solved the problem of a sea attack quite nicely. If they were willing to play.

· · · · ·

Balam watched from land as their entourage assembled on the pier. Even more people had gathered to watch the Cuecolans, and Lord Pech with his loud nasal whine was putting on quite the show. He stood on the pier in his yellow and red box headdress and insisted he required an honor guard of at least twelve men, while Sinik and Tuun argued that too many soldiers would be a threat and four for each lord would be sufficient.

On the other side of the dock, Cuecolan servants were loading great baskets with the riches of the merchant city: gold, jade, feathers, and bolts of fine woven cloth. Balam surmised it would be some time before their assembly was ready. He took the opportunity to meander down the docks. He let his gaze roam over the idling crowd but did not see the familiar face he was looking for. Patient, he wandered a bit farther until he was walking along the dock where the mysterious black and silver ships were anchored. They were even more impressive up close, their hulls shaped to cut through the waters at high speed. He suspected they could not hold many people or goods, but they were not meant to. He bent and ran his hand along the rail on the nearest vessel, enchanted by the possibilities of such technology.

"Hands off," drawled a feminine voice. "Don't you know it's impolite to touch a lady's ship without permission?"

He looked up to find a woman, no more than thirty, lounging at the far end of the ship. Her hair curled thick and dark around a heart-shaped face, and big blue eyes the color of island waters sparkled over wide cheeks. Her skin was the color of her ship, as black as night, and her smile flashed in challenge. He hadn't noticed her there, hidden behind the sail spar, but now that he had, he wondered how he had missed her.

He smiled his most disarming smile. "I am only admiring beauty where I see it."

She grinned, eyes alight. "Aye, you're quite a beauty yourself. A bit old for my usual, but I'm willing to take you for a ride . . . on my ship." She winked exaggeratedly. "What do you say?"

He took the opportunity to step down into the vessel and sit on one of the small, narrow benches. "My name is Lord Balam."

"I don't usually keep my passengers around long enough to learn their names," she said, leaning back, arms and legs wide in loose-cut pants, "but I never had a lord on board before. Sounds promising. Tell me, Lord Balam, is there a difference between a lord and a regular man?"

"There are many differences."

"I mean in the boom and thrust. Where it counts."

He laughed.

"Nice hat, too."

He touched a hand to his headdress, long white feathers on a golden crown.

"How does a man like you, all in white, stay so clean?"

He tilted his head, catching the shift in her tone, the slight mockery. "Who says I do?"

She laughed at that, and the moment of tension faded as if he had misheard. But he had not, and he marked it as a warning.

Someone called his name, and Balam turned to see Powageh waving furiously. Pech was already leading the group toward the palace mound, trailing guards and gift-bearing servants.

Balam straightened, brushing his hands off. "It seems my friends are calling me."

"A pity," she said, sighing heavily. "I was hoping *we* could be friends."

"Do you have a name?"

"Alani."

"I'm afraid I don't have time for a tour of your ship, Alani, but I appreciate the offer." He let his eyes linger on her form and was rewarded with a grin.

"But you'll come back, eh? I mean, if you survive." Again there was that hint of portent in her tone.

"I can make no promises."

"Your kind never can." Her mouth made a moue in false disappointment.

He touched his hand to his brow in respect and climbed out of the ship. It rocked only slightly under his weight.

Powageh was waiting for him, the rest of the contingent already well ahead.

"Who were you talking to?" his cousin growled, annoyed. "Pech would like nothing more than to leave you behind."

"What Pech does doesn't concern me."

Powageh huffed, sounding like xe wanted to say something more but declined. "And who was that?"

Balam looked back over his shoulder. Alani blew him a kiss, her laughter echoing on the wind.

"I believe, Cousin, that was a Teek."

• • • • •

They climbed the steps, picking up gawkers as they went. Some were merely interested; others shouted welcomes or taunts, Balam was not sure. He, of course, spoke Hoka, just as he spoke all the known languages of the Meridian, but there were subtleties of the common language that eluded him, his studies being limited to the more formal form. There were noisemakers and drums and flutes, and the din grew louder as they rose. Hands reached out and touched his white jaguar cloak, until one of the guards made his presence known with the shaft of his spear. After that, the jeers increased, but no one tried to handle him again.

"Who are you looking for?" Powageh asked.

"Hmm?"

"Don't play coy with me. I see you searching the crowd."

"I do not like to walk into these situations uninformed."

"You have a spy here," Powageh said. "In the palace."

"Of course I do. But he was to meet me when we boarded the barge at the mouth of the Kuukuh and did not come. And now I don't even see him here, and it worries me."

"A dangerous game, Cousin. What if he was discovered?"

The prospect worried Balam, but he kept his expression smooth and untroubled. "And what if he was? We are friendly, Hokaia and Cuecola, are we not?"

Powageh snorted, unimpressed.

They reached the top of the mound, and Balam took a moment to look back over his shoulder. The whole of Hokaia was visible from here, riverland and city as far as the eye could see. No mountains or forests to break the sightlines, which meant enemies could not hide their approach. What Hokaia had not foreseen was an army approaching from the air. It was the combined armies of Tova and Cuecola that had taken Hokaia, warriors on wingback and water striders moving swiftly upriver with Cuecolan foot soldiers and sorcerers. Balam was sure that if he allowed himself to sink into that place in his mind that he now associated with dreamwalking, he would see it all before him, a memory that would look and feel as real as the events that had created it.

"And who is it that rules Hokaia these days?" Powageh asked.

"A man named Daakun. His title is Sovran. I know he is relatively young but, by all accounts, a reasonable man and practical."

"You mean malleable."

Before the War of the Spear, Hokaia was ruled by spearmaidens, women married only to war and trained at the war college when it was still exclusively for the scions of Hokaia. They had no lovers and therefore no blood heirs, and often succession was decided by combat. It made for a warlike people, but their skirmishes had never strayed beyond the river valley, so the rest of the continent had not taken notice of their provincial practices. Until a spearmaiden named Seuq became not only a warrior but a warrior-sorcerer, the first dreamwalker, and used her knowledge and power to lead her people to conquest. After she was defeated, the spearmaidens were forbidden to rule Hokaia, and leadership had gone to a politico, one of the men who had helped broker the peace that saved what was left of Hokaia from ruination. Combat had been replaced with debate, and now the city was ruled by the person most skilled in rhetoric rather than warfare.

"Do we need to worry about him?" Powageh asked.

"Daakun? No. But rumors are there is a faction of spearmaidens who oppose his rule, led by a woman named Naasut, and she is a concern. How much of a concern . . . ?" He lifted one shoulder in an elegant shrug. "I was hoping to find that out beforehand, but here we are."

A shell horn blared, and Balam took it as the signal to join the others at the front of the entourage. They stood together left to right, the four merchant lords of Cuecola—Balam in his pristine white, Tuun in her green, Pech in his yellow and red, and Sinik in conservative brown—and waited for the leader of Hokaia to greet them.

She did not keep them long.

She stood upon the top step of the palace, keen eyes sweeping over them. On her head was a crown of elk antlers, and across her shoulders the elk's tanned hide. Gathered around her were spearmaidens, each in armor of leather and fur, faces painted black below the eyes, hair divided along a central part and braided close to the head. They held bone spears in hand, as did the woman in the crown.

"Welcome to Hokaia," the woman said, her voice booming across the mound, "Bright Star of the Riverlands, Heart of the Meridian, Forger of the Great Treaty." She tilted her chin up. "I hear you have come to help us make war."

The four lords exchanged looks, and Balam, for the first time, felt a slight twinge of concern. Clearly, this was not Daakun. He ran his overlong pinkie nail across his palm, thoughtfully. Even if he spilled blood and called shadow magic now, there were more than a hundred and fifty steps between him and their boat. And a long river on a slow barge to the Crescent Sea. And he was certain that those black and silver ships would make quick work of anyone trying to escape on water.

He could see Lord Tuun thinking along similar lines, her slate eyes narrowed, and he wondered if perhaps she could turn them all to stone long enough for them to run.

"And who are you?" Lord Pech asked, stepping forward. "Why has not Sovran Daakun come to greet us?"

"Daakun is indisposed," the woman said, and the spear-maidens around her rippled in amusement. "But you may call me Sovran."

"And why would we call a woman Sovran of Hokaia? Were not your kind found unfit to rule this city three centuries ago?"

The woman's eyes flashed, and she raised her spear. Two dozen maidens followed suit. "Careful, little man, lest I remind you how Cuecola fell to spearmaidens before she was rescued."

Pech stepped back, affronted. Cuecolan guards moved

between them, their own spears ready. The promise of violence filled the air.

"His low opinion of women will get us all killed," Lord Tuun whispered to Balam.

Balam had often wondered how he would die. A traitor cousin within his house, a disgruntled trader who felt cheated, wild magic that turned against him. All possibilities for a man like him. However, dying because piddling Lord Pech could not set aside his prejudices and his ego was intolerable.

"Sovran Naasut." He pressed a hand on a guard's shoulder to let him through. "It is our honor to be welcomed to your fine city. And although we hope that we will not have to call upon the people of the Meridian to take up arms once again, I am afraid you are correct, and these are dark times we must discuss. But I assure you, we are not your enemy."

Naasut's sharp eyes seemed to flay him, skin first, then flesh, and finally bone. He stood there and let her look. Whatever she saw of him made her grin. She thumped the white spear in her hand against the ground three times. The maidens around her echoed her call with answering thumps and howled in delight.

Lord Tuun's eyes tightened. Lord Sinik made a small whimpering sound. Lord Pech covered his ears.

"And who are you?" Naasut asked.

"I am Lord Balam of the House of Seven, Merchant Lord of Cuecola, Patron of the Crescent Sea, White Jaguar by Birthright."

"All those titles, and yet you know *my* name."

"As do all across the four corners of the Meridian," he lied.

Her smiled widened, and Balam took it as a sign that she was a woman amenable to flattery. Perhaps this would not come to bloodshed and magic after all.

"And the rest of you sulking behind your soldiers. All of you are Cuecolan lords?" she asked.

The other three had the sense to step even with the line of guards and introduce themselves. Lord Tuun first, then Sinik, and Pech last. He did not look pleased, but at least he did not insult Naasut again.

"And to which lord does this man belong?" Naasut snapped her fingers, and two spearmaidens came forward dragging Balam's spy between them. His hands were tied, and he had been beaten badly. They tossed him down the wooden steps, and he crumpled to a heap at their feet, whimpering.

Balam shifted his expression to mild concern, but he hid well the acute chill of terror that slipped down his spine. He watched the others for reactions. Tuun's face was a mask. If she suspected the man belonged to Balam, she did not let it show. Sinik gasped, his hand over his mouth, and Pech's expression darkened, but to his credit, he did not speak.

Naasut sauntered down the steps, two maidens breaking off to follow her. She propped a sandaled foot on the man's back.

"Well? Does no one claim him?"

She bent over and hauled him up by his hair. Balam could see that his fingers were crushed and his face swollen from blows. And there was something distinctly wrong with his mouth.

"He's swallowed his tongue," Tuun whispered, part awe and part revulsion.

Naasut's eyes fixed on the stone sorcerer. "Yes. It seems he was able to break his own fingers and swallow his tongue before we could beat a confession from him."

"How do you know he is one of ours?" Sinik said, and Balam could see his horror slowly turning to outrage. "He could belong to anyone. Golden Eagle or another of the Tovan clans, your own rivals here in Hokaia, even the Teek!"

"He is no instrument of the Teek," a voice said from the top of the stairs.

Another woman had joined them while they had been focused on the poor spy at their feet. She was a good head and a half shorter than Naasut, but she commanded the space much the same. She wore a netted blouse and wide pants like the sailor on the ship, Alani, and her waist-length hair cascaded around her in waves, her overlarge eyes the angry gray of a hurricane.

"The Teek do not truck with men." She said that last with a sneer, and Balam thought she and Pech made a fine pair.

"Queen Mahina has proven herself to the spearmaidens. Her loyalty is not in question."

Balam's expression was a flawless mask of cool indifference, but his mind was racing. The Teek had come, and not only had they come, they had brought a queen. And, if he guessed correctly, a fleet of elegant racing ships. He should be afraid—the true Sovran of Hokaia clearly deposed, his spy unveiled, an alliance between the Teek and the spearmaidens brewing—but all he could think of was the possibility in it. The potential in the chaos.

"The fact that I do not know who this man belongs to is the only reason you are still alive," Naasut said.

"You would dare to threaten a lord of Cuecola?" Pech said, finally finding his voice.

"I dare many things," she replied.

"It would be unwise to injure a lord of one of the Houses of Seven," Tuun said unexpectedly, "particularly under the laws of hospitality that rule us all."

"The rules of the Treaty no longer bind us," Naasut countered. "If the Watchers of Tova have fallen, as your own messengers say they have, then the Meridian is remade."

"The laws I refer to are older than the Treaty." Tuun lifted a hand, freshly bloodied. She whispered words, and the air filled with a deep rumble.

Balam planted his feet, as everyone but he searched, eyes wild, for the source of the reverberations. Someone cried out as the earth around them shifted. Naasut's eyes went wide, and Mahina on the stairs above them cursed. Tuun snapped her hand shut, and the earthquake immediately ceased.

"Sorceress," Naasut breathed. "Such magic is forbidden!"

"Forbidden by the Treaty. Which you reminded us is no more. It seems we are indeed in a new age. So be careful whom you threaten, Spearmaiden." The two women stared at each other, hungry dogs circling before the first bite.

"Perhaps now would be the time for hospitality," Balam said. "I certainly would not mind a drink."

Naasut's gaze flicked to him, annoyed at first but then, to his relief, amused. "I was told all the lords of Cuecola were men with shriveled balls, but I see I was wrong." She looked back at Tuun admiringly. "And no one told me of the women."

The Sovran snapped her fingers, and the spearmaidens dragged Balam's spy to his feet and back up the steps.

"To the tables, then," she declared. "Hospitality calls. We will settle this breach of etiquette when Golden Eagle arrive. There's plenty of time to root out our enemies and slit their throats."

She turned on her heel and strode back up the stairs, the rest of her spearmaidens folding in behind her, following in precise lines.

Sinik exhaled a shaky breath and turned to Balam, accusing. "Seven hells, Balam. What have you led us into?"

"A coup, it appears," he murmured.

"Should we follow?" Tuun asked.

"I don't think we have a choice. And I was quite serious about wanting a drink."

The three of them headed up the stairs. Their own guards and servants and secretaries trailed behind, Powageh among them. Pech shook himself free of whatever had bemused him and hurried after. Before them stood the Grand Palace, and just beyond the doors, Balam spied a long table laden with food and drink.

It had all been a test. Oh, Sovran Daakun's situation seemed suitably dire, assuming the man was still alive, but Naasut had been testing them, playing at barbarian. Perhaps to expose the spymaster, but clearly, she had been expecting them to join her in a meal all along.

Balam's confidence surged, his mind already spinning with the possibilities.

"You know," Tuun said, "I think she was flirting with me at the end."

"You think everyone is flirting with you," Balam observed dryly.

"Aren't they?"

"Spearmaidens are married to war, and war only. I do not think they flirt."

"Nonsense. All beings flirt. Except you, apparently."

"You offend me, Lord Tuun. Although I suggest you keep your eye on Queen Mahina."

She huffed a laugh. "Self-styled queens do not concern me."

"Whose spy is he?" Pech shouted loudly enough that they all stopped to stare. He looked sweaty, his eyes too wide.

Shock, Balam thought. *And he's not handling it well.*

"Balam," he cried, "is he yours? Tuun? Whatever game you are playing, you are to stop it now, before you get us killed!"

Balam's smile was all concern. "None of ours, I assure you. No doubt, Golden Eagle seek to gain advantage. Or perhaps he belongs to Carrion Crow. All the more reason we must ally."

Pech made a sound like a strangled dog, and Balam almost felt sorry for him. Almost.

"Do not concern yourself, Pech," he said over his shoulder, as they entered the palace. "I have this entirely under control."

CHAPTER 28

Beware the woman who would drown her own daughters.

—Teek saying

Xiala followed Ziha and Iktan through the doors of the tavern to find Nuuma Golden Eagle sitting at the far end of a long table, eating soup. The room itself was unusually dark, and Xiala felt her eyes change to accommodate the low light. The ceiling, soot-stained and heavy, felt uncomfortably low, and she was sure that if she simply lifted her hands over her head, her fingertips would scrape the roof. The walls were similarly tight, and Xiala felt the itch of close quarters tickle the skin between her shoulders.

There were two lanterns, one on each side of the room, but Nuuma seemed to suck all the light toward her. She wore a uniform so white it glowed. Xiala recognized it as identical to her daughter's, down to the fur-collared deerskin cloak and the golden spray of feathers at the shoulder, and she did not have to wonder who was copying whom. Nuuma's tawny hair was tangled and wild, but her eyes as she glanced up at her second daughter and her companions were hard stone,

315

as bleak and uncompromising as the tall mountains around them.

Ziha hurried forward to prostrate herself at her mother's feet, arms outstretched. Nuuma looked down at her, expression unreadable, until her lip curled slightly in what was clearly distaste. She had paused with her bowl halfway to her mouth when they came in, but now she began to eat again. The room was silent save the sound of slow slurping.

The moment stretched.

The girl commander on the floor. The matron noisily draining her soup bowl.

Xiala tried to catch Iktan's attention, but xir face was lost in the folds of xir cowl, only the tip of xir narrow nose visible.

More seconds passed, and still Ziha didn't rise.

And still Nuuma ate.

Xiala's nerves were starting to itch, worse even than the claustrophobic tickle at her back. Cruel mother, humiliated daughter, no one intervening. It was all a bit too familiar.

She exhaled, telling herself she would likely regret what came next, but it couldn't be any worse than standing there watching Ziha debase herself for someone who clearly enjoyed seeing her suffer. She channeled some of the bravado she employed as a sea captain, squared her shoulders, and sauntered over to the table. She pulled out the side bench. It groaned and scraped across the floor. She swung a leg over and dropped her weight, equally loud.

Xiala banged a hand against the table. Heads swiveled, and the Shield shifted their attention to her. Nuuma lowered her bowl, stone eyes glowing like hot ash.

Nervous sweat dampened Xiala's collar, but her righteous outrage overwhelmed any fear. She reached for her Song, a precaution, but as before, it felt as if someone had built a fence between her and her power. Seven hells, what was she doing provoking this woman? She caught a glimpse of the back of Ziha's head, face still kissing the ground, and that was all the reminder she needed.

"Soup!" Xiala shouted. "Where can I get some damned soup?"

One of the Shield looked like he would speak, but Nuuma lifted a hand to stop him, her expression curious.

Iktan slid onto the bench beside Xiala, and she caught the edge of xir smile. "I think I'd like some soup, too," xe said, voice mild.

Xiala grinned.

"Get up, Ziha." Xiala kept her voice casual. "We're ordering soup for you, too."

Nuuma glanced to her side, and Xiala spotted a door there. Someone must have been waiting just outside, watching for the matron's signal, because a server came forward immediately, bearing a pot that leaked a fragrant steam. Another followed with bowls and yet another with flatbread. Xiala helped herself, and Iktan after her, and finally, *Mother waters!* Ziha pushed herself up and came to sit across from them. She was as shaky as a kitten, but at least she was off the damned floor.

Nuuma clapped. A long, slow strike of palm against palm that echoed through the room. Three times, four, five, until she had all eyes on her. Ziha was trembling. *Skies*, Xiala thought. *What has the woman done to make her daughter fear her so?*

"Charming," the matron said, voice thick with scorn. "Is that what you've been doing in my absence, Ziha? Imagining silly little ways to defy your mother?"

Xiala cleared her throat loudly. She grabbed her bowl and drank, the sound of her slurping loud and rude. She slammed the empty bowl down and forced herself to belch before grinning at the matron.

"And who are you?" the woman asked.

"Someone who hates a bully."

Nuuma stared a moment longer. "Get her out."

"A moment, Nuuma." Iktan rose to hold off the Shield who were already moving. "She is of value. A friend of the Odo Sedoh."

"I don't care who she is. She's disrespectful to her betters. I should have her beaten. Perhaps that would teach her manners."

"Doubtful." Iktan cleared xir throat. "The fact remains she is beneficial to our plans. I suggest you hear me out before you make any rash decisions. If you still find her of no use, you can have her beaten afterward."

"Iktan," Xiala growled under her breath.

"No, you've made your point, Xiala. Unsubtly, I might add, but I understand. Your heart means well. But that's enough." Xe looked toward Nuuma. "Tell us why you've come and what you know."

Nuuma motioned for the Shield to stand down and then for the servants to remove the soup and bowls. Once everything was cleared, the matron commanded her Shield to guard the doors from the outside. Satisfied that they were safe from prying ears, she spoke.

"Something's happened in Tova. Something that forces us to accelerate our plans and makes the city unsafe for Golden Eagle."

"They know of your treachery?" Iktan asked.

Irritation pulsed across her face. "The other matrons know that Golden Eagle sought to influence the Watchers, but to what extent I cannot say. And whether it matters with the Watchers dead is unclear, too. What is clear is that they side with Carrion Crow to decide the fate of the city."

"So it is war." Iktan's voice was soft with emotion. Regret? Excitement? Xiala could not be sure what.

"War, yes, and quickly, before they can raise an army to control the Eastern districts."

"The Eastern districts?"

"Coyote's Maw have declared themselves a clan again."

Ziha raised her head. "Again?"

"They were a clan before the War of the Spear, but when the Watchers were established in Tova, they were stripped of their status and named clanless as punishment for their cowardice."

Xe tapped a finger against the table. "Does that mean . . . ?"

"They've named a matron," Nuuma confirmed.

"Who?"

Nuuma hesitated, only a hiccup, but Xiala noticed, and she was sure Iktan noticed, too.

"Does it matter who she is?" Nuuma glanced down at the table. "What concerns me is that the other clans appear willing to acknowledge her, and a Coyote clan adds thousands more to any fighting force meant to defend the city. If they have any brains, they will start building a perimeter at the far eastern edge of the city and raze the farmland between. It's what I would do. If our army breaks through, there will be no stores to feed them, and the damnable Maw will stand between the Sky Made and the rest of the world."

"Six months for the clans to fortify and store food," Iktan murmured. "Destroy the bridges, and the cliff districts could last for months, perhaps years. And with giant crows and winged serpents in the air, any eagle assault against the city would be costly."

"Not to mention Tova is practically unassailable by riverway if we have no answer for Water Strider's creatures."

"The southern sorcerers are working on it."

Xiala tried not to react, but Iktan's words startled her. It was the first xe had spoken of being in league with Cuecolan sorcerers, and it chilled her like no other war plans had. She had to get the information back to Serapio, but how?

"Land is still our best option if we move before summer," Nuuma continued.

"You are forgetting. You have yet to convince Hokaia that war against Tova is necessary. It was a cleaner argument when Water Strider and Winged Serpent were with us. The enemy was clearly the Crows, murderers and breakers of the Treaty. Practitioners of dangerous magics. But if the city has united around Carrion Crow . . ." Iktan spread xir hands.

Nuuma's jaw tightened. "They slaughtered my niece and a dozen others of my clan. They killed my Shield captain. I will convince Hokaia, no matter the cost."

There was a commotion at the door. Raised voices, a woman in protest, and the rumble of a Shield soldier denying her entrance.

"Stars and skies!" Nuuma cursed. "Let her in. Let her in!"

The voices quieted, and a woman pushed through the doors, looking exasperated. "Why are they always so fucking literal?" she complained, before flopping onto the bench next to Ziha. She leaned over and embraced the girl. Ziha hugged her back.

"Because I command them to be literal," Nuuma said. "Where have you been?"

"Where you commanded me to be, Mother. Securing passage down the river for Ziha's army." She turned to Ziha now. "Seems the rumors of your eyeball taking shook a few stubborn heads loose. We should have no trouble with the barges tomorrow." She sniffed the air. "Was there soup?" She looked around the table, face expectant. "I'm starved."

"They've run out," Nuuma said flatly. "What's this about eyeballs?"

"A disciplinary problem." Ziha straightened. She glanced

quickly at Xiala and then at the new woman, whose presence seem to fortify her against her mother. "I handled it."

"Save me from the tyranny of daughters." Nuuma rolled her own eyes heavenward. "I don't want to know."

"I'm Terzha," the new woman offered to Xiala.

She had a smattering of freckles against her brown skin and dark brown eyes that danced in the light. She was tall, as tall as the matron and twice as broad, solid muscle underneath her white uniform. Her smile was wide and genuine.

"Xiala."

Iktan leaned forward. "Terzha is Nuuma's firstborn daughter, the next in line for matron."

And now it made sense. The confident firstborn, the striving secondborn who could never quite please. They were a standard kind of family, after all.

"And the weather?" Nuuma asked.

"We scouted west before we lost all daylight, and I asked the boatmen. They're always good at reading for storms."

"And?"

"Clear skies tomorrow and the next day, but a storm follows next week. Rain likely on the grasslands, snow in the mountains, but we'll be in Hokaia by then."

"What's this?" Iktan asked.

"I told you we must accelerate our plans. The river route will take too long. We fly to Hokaia tomorrow at first light."

"We?" Ziha sounded wary.

"Myself, Terzha and Iktan, the Shield. You will stay and complete your mission of bringing your people down by river. Layat is a week behind us. He is escorting select Golden Eagle families from the Great House who did not wish to stay behind in an unstable Tova. Not all will make the passage to Hokaia. Those you will accommodate here. The rest will come with you."

Ziha's face was a mixture of disappointment and relief, as if the distance from her mother was to her liking but she understood the inherent demotion in being left behind.

"Xiala will come with us, too," Iktan said.

Nuuma's brow furrowed. "We have a dozen eagles and already thirteen riders. You will double with Terzha, but I would not ask one of my Shield to share their mount."

"She comes with us, or I do not."

The matron's mouth tightened, but she did not gainsay Iktan. "Who is she, again?"

"A bargaining chip," xe said, voice smooth and detached as she'd ever heard it. It was that killer voice, the one that shivered like claws dragged along her spine. "She is precious to the Odo Sedoh, which means she should be precious to you, Nuuma. If the opportunity comes to strike against him, she will be our weapon."

For the first time, Nuuma smiled. "Not just a tool of my daughter's, after all." She stood. "Very well. She comes, too. Be on the far prairie before dawn."

And then matron and Shield swept from the room, flickering the lanterns with their passing. Ziha stood to follow, but her older sister grabbed her wrist, holding her back.

Once their mother was gone, Terzha exhaled a hard breath. "Stars and skies, she's in a mood." She banged a gloved fist against the table. "I really am hungry," she confessed to no one in particular, "but I'll take balché over soup any day." She raised her voice. "I said balché!"

A servant shuffled in from the now-unguarded back door with a barrel of the alcoholic drink. Once the container was breached and their mugs filled, she peppered Ziha with questions about their trip across the grasslands. It took a full mug to loosen the younger girl's tongue, but eventually, she was sharing the trials of leading arrogant and contentious scions across unknown lands with only the vague decree to get them all to Hokaia as quickly as possible.

"And what of Kuya?"

Xiala, who was carefully nursing her balché, recognized the name. Kuya was the woman who had harassed her and whose eyeball rested in her pocket even now.

"She deserved it." Ziha was defensive.

"I'm not saying she didn't, but be careful who you make an enemy." Terzha studied her sister. "I think Mother's wrong to leave you here alone with them. But Layat's only days behind, and he's to offer support."

Ziha's face fell.

"You'll survive it." She patted her sister's arm reassuringly. "Just take a few more eyeballs, if you must." She barked out a laugh. "Skies, where did you even get the idea?"

"Speaking of survival," Iktan cut in. Xiala noticed xe had not drunk from the mug. "The Shield captain is dead?"

Terzha swallowed. "You caught that, eh? That's why Mother's on a tear, among other things. They were lovers, you know. She's heartbroken."

"I don't know what's more disconcerting," Iktan said, "the idea of Nuuma fucking or the fact that she might indeed have a heart."

"It's the latter, trust me." Terzha took another drink.

"And who managed to kill him?" Xir eyes flicked briefly to Xiala, a reminder of the Odo Sedoh's murderous potential.

"She won't say. All I know is that she came back from meeting with the matrons raging about incompetence and something about 'that damned Sun Priest.'"

Iktan leaned forward, xir whole body suddenly alert. "What about the Sun Priest?"

"She wasn't clear, and when I asked later, she denied she'd said anything. But I heard her."

Iktan stayed primed another moment before relaxing. "Perhaps it was nothing."

Terzha shrugged, and Xiala could see the woman was well on her way to drunk. She felt conflicted that for once she was not the overtalkative fool deep in her cups.

Iktan stood. "You'll have to excuse me. If we are to leave at first light, there are some tasks I need to complete before then."

"I'll come, too." Xiala rose quickly.

"Stay!" Terzha reached for her, but Xiala had already moved away. The woman's hand flopped on the table. "I hate drinking alone."

"You have Ziha."

Ziha was quietly snoring, her head resting on folded arms.

Terzha sighed, disappointment wrinkling her freckled nose. "So I do."

They left the heirs of Golden Eagle behind and made their way back to camp. Iktan was unusually quiet on the walk, but Xiala had much on her mind, too, and did not disturb the ex-priest. They reached the edge of the camp, and Xiala murmured a farewell, thinking to go to her tent.

"I don't think it's wise for you to sleep alone tonight," Iktan said.

She turned, mouth in a scowl.

Iktan laughed, a low sound like the crackling of thin ice underfoot. "I mean, because you've made enemies, and you make an easy target without your Song, Xiala of the Teek."

She flushed, embarrassed that she had thought xe meant more.

Xe nodded. "It is a difficult thing to have a heart, Xiala. Do not think I do not see yours and where your affections lie. I have sympathy for your affliction."

Were her feelings for Serapio an affliction? Perhaps. "And yet you would use them against me." She remembered Iktan's casual offer to Nuuma to use her as a weapon against Serapio.

"You'll have to forgive me, but it was the only reason I could think of that would convince her you should accompany us to Hokaia. If she did not see you as a lever against her enemies, you would be useless. It is the same reason she tolerates me, after all."

Xiala folded her arms over her chest, suddenly chilled.

Iktan exhaled, xir breath fogging in the night air. "Who am I to accuse Nuuma of lacking the compassion I struggle to find in myself? Even I have a heart, although mine is well worn and inconstant. I am sure she does, too . . . somewhere."

"Terzha said something about the Sun Priest. Do you think she meant your friend? That maybe she's still alive after all?"

Iktan did not answer at first, and when xe did, it was like the wind through the canyons. "I don't know, Xiala, but if Nuuma is hiding something from me, I will find it. And if it has something to do with Nara, I will carve her apart until I reach her lying heart, and then I will take great pleasure in carving her heart apart, too."

CHAPTER 29

CITY OF TOVA (COYOTE'S MAW)

YEAR 1 OF THE CROW

> There is no question that the stars cannot answer save the one
> that goes unasked.
>
> —*The Manual of the Sun Priest*

Naranpa sat cross-legged in Sedaysa's hothouse garden, her tea
gone cold before her. Someone had brought her food earlier,
left it, and then come back later to take it away, untouched.
They had tried to feed her again in the evening, with the same
dismal results. Finally, they had given up and simply left her a
pot of hot tea, but even that failed to capture Naranpa's attention in time to be palatable.

They had not tried again.

Around her, flowers bloomed in glorious profusion. She
had found them beautiful once, enchanting even. But now they
seemed profane, gaudy in their unseasonal dress. They leered
at her, mocking her grief with their forceful gaiety. They possessed a rich fragrance that had once made her swoon. Now
they smelled like a dying thing, sweet with rot. They were false,
all of them. Little liars. They were a promise of life that ended
only in death. How dare they shine. What gave them the right?

326

"Naranpa."

Sedaysa's voice penetrated her haze. She had the feeling the woman had been calling her name for a while. There was the rustle of a skirt and the hushed tinkle of bells as the boss of the Agave sank to the cushion across from her.

Naranpa raised dull eyes and forced herself to focus. Sedaysa was still beautiful, but now Naranpa noticed the lines at her mouth, the brittleness of her silver hair, a dull patch of skin on her neck. The woman was dying already. Like the flowers.

Like Ochi.

Sedaysa folded her hands in her lap, concern pursing her lips. "It has been twenty-four hours since the others left, and you are the matron of Coyote's Maw. What would you have me do?"

Naranpa blinked slowly, waiting for the world to become something other than what it was. And when it did not change, the voice she had not used in hours rasped out, "No message from Okoa has come?"

Sedaysa shook her head.

After Denaochi's murder at the Lupine, the matrons and Okoa had removed to the Agave. Naranpa, Sedaysa, and Zataya had stayed behind to prepare her brother's body. It had been terrible work, the washing and the wrapping of the corpse. Naranpa remembered her mother performing the ritual once when she was a child and her uncle had died. Her mother had told her that people did it because it brought them comfort to care for the dead, but Naranpa found no peace in the practice, only a river of rage. By the time they had prepared his spirit meal and arranged for him to be entombed in the catacombs, Naranpa had been a singular seething current of fury. But fury was a privilege she could not indulge. The matrons and Okoa were waiting for her, so she had pushed her anger down, deep into the dark and cavernous places inside her, and in its place bubbled up an edgeless grief. She tried to hide that, too, but it refused to be contained, and it made itself known in ways big and small. The drag in her step, the waver in her voice, the way her mind would not fix on any given point. But she did her best, knowing people needed her, knowing Denaochi would disapprove of any weakness.

She and Sedaysa had arrived at the Agave to find Ieyoue, Peyana, and Okoa on cushions seated at a round table in Sedaysa's private quarters. Okoa nursed a wound Naranpa had not noticed before, and Peyana's right hand was thick with bandages. Someone was missing, and it took her a moment to realize the Shields of Water Strider and Winged Serpent were absent. Naranpa asked after them, thinking she may have overlooked their deaths while lost in the throes of her own sorrow.

"I sent Ahuat back to Kun, to put riders in the air." Peyana flexed her wounded hand. "I fear Nuuma will try to flee."

"And I the same with Water Strider," Ieyoue said. "If she leaves by river, we will find her first."

It was sound reasoning, but Naranpa was unconvinced. "Nuuma is clever and had likely already planned her escape before she came to the Lupine. If there is a way to elude your patrols, she will know it. We have likely lost our chance to hold her."

"Then we will find another way to make her pay for her crimes against the clans and the city." Peyana's look was dark, and Naranpa knew she meant it. But intent would not be enough, not against a woman like Nuuma.

Okoa cleared his throat. "Now that you are here, Sun Priest, there is news I must share."

The young warrior looked uncomfortable here on these opulent cushions in this house of decadence. He kept folding and unfolding his hands, and his broad shoulders hunched under his cloak. He was a boy, she realized. A man grown, yes, but young. Younger than he had seemed at his mother's funeral, where loss and pain had made their mark on him.

All is loss, she thought miserably. *Nothing stays. Even this man in the prime of youth will die, and sooner than he deserves. Can he feel it? Death, already tightening its fingers around his neck?*

Okoa glanced at her as if aware of her dark thoughts, and she did her best to shake them off. He gave her a hesitant smile, as if unsure of his welcome, even after the events of the evening.

She rallied. "I am glad you came, Okoa. I did not know how my message would be received. Last time we met, I thought you might kill me."

"You will have to forgive me." He hesitated, as if caught in a remembrance. "It was a different time."

"There is nothing to forgive."

"Then I am grateful for your trust."

"More hope than trust. I did not know, but I hoped, that the leadership of Carrion Crow might not have entirely fallen under the shadow of your dark god. I saw him, you know. On the roof of the celestial tower. He, too, wanted to kill me." She shivered at the memory. "I could feel it. But he was already injured and could not follow when I ran. He sent his crows after me. His arm . . . shattered . . . and became those black-winged birds." Her voice caught somewhere between horror and wonder. "They chased me through the tower until I found shelter in the kitchens. When I emerged, he was gone, and the flock was heading west." She was convinced he had let her go, but she could not say why. Perhaps his injury or some other reason she could not fathom. Whatever it was, it left her trembling all over again.

"It matches what we know." Okoa pulled a cloth bag into his lap. His hand slipped inside, but he did not pull forth the contents. His shoulders seem to settle in resignation, and he looked infinitely sad, as if whatever was in the bag had the power to break his heart. "I speak to you plainly now, as myself. I cannot speak for my matron or for the Odohaa, but I believe I act for their benefit. For the benefit of all of Carrion Crow, and for Tova as well."

Peyana leaned forward. "What is it?"

His expression was solemn. "We bear no ill will to the clans. The Watchers"— his eyes flicked to Naranpa—"we did not love, and the Knives least of all. We will not mourn them, although . . ."

He hesitated, as if his diplomacy had run dry.

"I walked that killing field on Sun Rock. I saw the bodies turned to ash, others left in strange contortions. And I have seen other deaths at Serapio's hands." His voice was quiet, intense. "As much as we Crow mourn those lost on the Night of Knives, one slaughter cannot justify another."

"Your Odohaa prayed for his coming." Ieyoue's reminder was a soft rebuke.

"They are but a small faction within the clan."

"I have seen what gathers at your doorstep, Crow." The matron of Winged Serpent was more blunt, her tone less forgiving. "They are not so small anymore."

Okoa's dark eyes brimmed with conflict, but determination set his jaw. "I think you have found the heart of the matter, Matron." He pulled his treasure from the bag.

Naranpa gasped. Her hand trembled as she instinctively reached for it, hovering just short of touching.

The Sun Priest's mask.

"I retrieved it from Sun Rock and have not known what to do with it. But I believe it can be used . . . as a weapon."

"No!" The denial was instinctive, and Naranpa regretted her outburst immediately, as they all turned to stare—Okoa surprised, Peyana curious, Ieyoue sympathetic. Even Sedaysa fixed her with an enigmatic look.

"It is sacred." Naranpa's protest was weak, and she knew it.

"A sacred weapon is even better," Peyana said.

"It can be forged, can it not?" His question was for Naranpa. "I believe the other Sun Priest broke off a piece here"—he pointed to a place where a ray of the sun had chipped off— "and used it to stab the Odo Sedoh. It is the wound he bears that still will not heal, the one you saw that pains him."

Peyana took the mask from Okoa, examining it more closely. "My people can work this metal. It is an ancient craft we practice, as our ancestors did. It is known to us."

Naranpa clenched her fists in her lap to keep from snatching it away from the Winged Serpent matron.

"What can be made from it?" Ieyoue asked, not without a compassionate glance toward Naranpa.

She, at least, understood the pain it caused her to see the mask out of her control, and for a brief moment, Naranpa wondered if they would give the mask to her if she commanded it. In her heart, she already knew the answer, so she did not ask. Only watched as they passed it around and speculated on the ways it could be transformed into something that might kill.

Peyana offered more than one. "A golden dagger, spear tips, even arrowheads."

Naranpa stopped listening after that. She let her mind wander as they continued to plan. Sometimes she found herself drifting through the images of her childhood, memories of her and her family she had not let herself revisit in decades. But mostly, her thoughts took her back to the look on Denaochi's face as he stepped in front of the blade to save her, and as he reached for her hand, and his low gasp, and her awful scream, as she realized she could not save him in return.

Finally, the gathered company came to the one element of the night they had not discussed: her powers. She roused herself from her waking nightmares to listen. But she could not answer their questions to anyone's satisfaction, including her own, because she did not understand her powers. She had only used them before to light her way, and to heal. To kill . . . she had no clear memory of how she had done it. She remembered the man's head between her hands, her moment of exultation as his flesh bubbled and popped. Only now it was revulsion, not triumph, that shivered her skin. The killing was like something she had witnessed from above, not something she had done. Yet she knew that if she allowed that river of rage within her to rise, if she gave herself permission to feel it again, the fire would come. So when they asked her about gods and sorcery and fire, she was vague and distant, until finally they stopped asking.

"Give me twenty-four hours to speak to my matron and devise a path forward," Okoa had said, his parting words.

But now it had been more than twenty-four hours, and no word had come. Perhaps the young man had failed to convince his matron to betray the Odo Sedoh after all. Perhaps the Odohaa had sniffed out his intentions and put an end to him, death tightening its fingers around his neck even sooner than Naranpa could have guessed. There were so many ways the earnest young warrior's plans could have gone wrong.

"And no word from Water Strider or Winged Serpent?" Naranpa asked Sedaysa.

"Matron Ieyoue sent word. Her clan saw no sign of Golden

Eagle on the river, but she sent a messenger to the Great House in Tsay, and they believe Nuuma, her advisers, and her direct kin have fled, likely to Hokaia."

It was what Naranpa had expected. "So summer will likely bring war."

"If not this summer, then surely the next. If summer comes at all."

"Ah." Here in this false paradise, Naranpa had almost forgotten about the eclipsed sun and the perpetual winter that squeezed the life from the city.

"What now?" Sedaysa reached over as if to hold Naranpa's hand, but she paused, no doubt remembering the death that had flowed from her palms. "You are our matron, and Coyote clan needs you."

"No." This much revelation had come to her. "Naming me matron was Denaochi's idea, and while it was a good one while he lived, I am not the woman who should lead Coyote clan. You would make a better matron, Sedaysa. You know this place, these people, more than I. The people will accept you, as will the Speakers Council. I am sure of it. You saw Ieyoue and Peyana talk with you as their equal."

"It was a surprising thing."

It was the right thing, and they both knew it. It would take some time for her to adjust to the role, but Naranpa could already tell Sedaysa was a good choice.

"What will you do, then, if you are not matron?"

She had been thinking about it for a while, and her voice was grieved but confident. "I do not belong here any longer. I thought I could come home, but with Denaochi gone, I have no home here anymore."

"If not the Maw, where will you go? Not the celestial tower?"

"No, I have no home there, either."

"Then where?"

"Where I should have been all along, but for foolish luck. I'm going to Sun Rock to face the Odo Sedoh."

Sedaysa startled. "Are you mad?"

Naranpa laughed. Now that she had said it aloud, she felt freer than she had in days. "Ochi asked me the same thing once, and I assured him I was very much sane."

"You counsel me to embrace a greater destiny, but I would advise you not to hasten your demise, Naranpa. You are still needed. Tova still needs you."

For once, she felt that was not true. "I think you are mistaken, Matron."

"At least wait until we hear from Carrion Crow."

"No. I do not know what has befallen Okoa, but I fear if we wait any longer, it will be too late. We have a narrow window of opportunity to strike at the Crow God Reborn, and I dare not squander it."

"Peyana promised us sun weapons. Is that not reason enough to hold? If you go to face the crow god now, you will go empty-handed."

Pasko's face, ruined by fire, flashed through her mind. "I beg to differ."

Sedaysa sighed. "I have seen those in the throes of grief do foolish things in the wake of a loved one's death, as if they seek to join them."

Now it was Naranpa's turn to be surprised. "Is that what you think I'm doing?"

"I don't know you well enough to know, but I fear it all the same." Sedaysa's look was that of a woman whose profession it was to understand a person's needs, sometimes better than the person themselves. "You are as stubborn as your brother, and I see there is nothing I can say that will stop you."

"I've made up my mind."

She took Naranpa's hands in her own, and held them tight. "Then burn bright, Sun Priest, and I shall mark your transit across the heavens."

• • • • •

Naranpa wore mourning white, a last gift from the matron of Coyote clan. The long sleeves clung tight to her arms, and a golden belt encircled her waist. Around her shoulders hung the white cloak Denaochi had gifted her, the one with the stars in the lining. Her hair was loose and tangled, and Sedaysa had washed it in gold dust.

"I once told you I was helping you only because of my love for your brother," Sedaysa had said as she ran amber-coated fingers through Naranpa's hair. "But this I do for you, Naranpa. You have earned it." And then she had touched her lips to Naranpa's own, briefly, intimately, before bidding her farewell.

The streets were blessedly empty, the city having developed a rhythm of morning and evening despite the absence of the sun to guide them, and Naranpa guessed it was a few short hours until a new day.

She had not gone far down the main road of the Maw before she saw what she was looking for. A crow, perched atop a ladder that leaned against an adobe wall.

"Go tell your master," she called to the corvid. "Tell him I go to Sun Rock, and we will have this settled between us."

She half expected the bird to speak back to her, to acknowledge the receipt of her message or to taunt her for marching to her certain death. But it only turned its eye to her and cried out before taking wing. *There*, she thought. *It is done. We will come to an end today one way or another.*

Perhaps Sedaysa was right, and grief made her reckless with her own life. Or perhaps it was the opposite, and the loss of her brother unearthed a bravery in her she had never known before.

She closed her eyes, turned her palm up, and let the barest trickle of rage breach her inner barriers. Flames rose to her hand, as bright and hungry as wildfire. It danced through her fingers, caressing her unblemished skin.

But I do not plan to die so easily, little bird, she thought. *Tell your master that, too.*

CHAPTER 30

CITY OF HOKAIA
YEAR 1 OF THE CROW

> It is no mystery to this traveler why Hokaia has grown into
> the Jewel of the Plains. It is well laid out, centrally located,
> and blessed with multiple riverways that stretch the length of
> the continent. It truly is the heart of the Meridian. Yet I can-
> not help feeling that it is thoroughly haunted.
>
> —*A Commissioned Report of My Travels to*
> *the Seven Merchant Lords of Cuecola,*
> by Jutik, a traveler from Barach

Xiala flew on eagleback over the Meridian plains. There were
fourteen of them among a dozen great birds of prey. Nuuma
rode alone at the front of the formation, on the back of a ma-
jestic creature named Suhtsee. She was flanked by three Shield
riders on each side. Behind Nuuma rode Terzha and Iktan, and
behind them rode Xiala, her arms wrapped around the waist
of a Shield woman who had introduced herself briefly and then
not spoken to Xiala again except to command her to hold on
and, when she had asked once about how far they would ride
that day, told her to save her words until they landed. *And how
long will that be?* Xiala had wanted to ask, but she had not,
choosing to simply endure.

Xiala had thought travel over land on foot had to be the most miserable form of travel, but she quickly amended her opinion once she was on the back of the great bird and the people below her reduced to the size of ants. She did not know how these Tovans withstood it, never mind preferred it. Insanity, all of it.

She could feel the muscles of the eagle moving beneath her, both powerful and incredibly fragile. Her rider had tied a rope belt around her waist and hooked the other end to her own belt.

"That way, if one of us falls, we both fall," she'd said with a grin that did not reassure.

Only when she had attached both belts to the saddle they shared did Xiala feel secure. But falling was only one of the worries of air travel. There was the chafe of sitting in a saddle for hours at a time, there were the high-altitude winds that made her nostalgic for Tova's comparatively balmy winter gales, and there were the bugs.

She had not anticipated the bugs.

Her rider also had a solution for that: a triangle of cloth to wear over her nose and mouth and a warning to keep her head down. Once again, insanity.

"If I ever make it back to the sea, I swear to never leave it," she muttered to herself at least a dozen times that first day.

But to her surprise, after the trials of adjustment, she began to understand the appeal of flight. They covered many miles, the landscape rapidly changing below them. Snowcapped mountains ceded to endless grasslands, the only variation the snaking flow of the Puumun River and its tributaries running ever eastward. They avoided fluctuations in the weather, noting growing clouds that portended storms and adjusting to avoid them. And once they flew over a herd of massive furred beasts that stretched across the plain and would have stopped Ziha and her march dead in their path.

They made camp on the banks of a river that night as the sun set. Nuuma and Iktan retired to a tent to talk privately, and Xiala found herself huddled around a fire surrounded by strangers, and soldiers at that. But someone had a flask, and they passed it around, and after she'd swallowed her share of the unfamiliar fiery liquor, the absurdity of her situation settled around her. She lay back, staring at the mass of stars overhead.

"A flying Teek," she whispered to herself. "Who would believe it?"

A figure dropped down beside her, and she glanced over to find Terzha stretched out, hands behind her neck, eyes on the night sky. Xiala knew she should be wary of this warrior woman, the matron's daughter, but the alcohol buzzed pleasantly in her head, and after a day of silence, she ached for company.

"What do you see when you look up there?" There was a slight slur in Terzha's voice.

"The way home." Xiala thought of the navigational houses of the Teek. "If we were on the sea, we could follow the stars and find our way."

"Show me."

She shifted, uncomfortable. "It is a Teek thing. It won't mean anything to you." She had a flash of memory, Serapio's hand in hers as she traced the star houses in his palm. *You study the stars, but I am made of the shadow between stars.* He had said that to her once, and the thought of it now made her ache. How many miles was he from her, how distant was she in his mind? His heart? She vowed again she would return to him as soon as she could find a way.

Terzha squinted. "I'll tell you what we say. See that constellation? We say it is the home of the ancestors of the clan Water Strider, and those trailing stars are beetle shit."

Xiala coughed.

"We don't say it to Water Strider's face, of course," Ter-zha amended. "So the way to Teek is there? Below the beetle shit?"

Xiala closed her eyes, ignoring the Golden Eagle woman's drunken jibes. Instead, images of her homeland overwhelmed her. The crystal waters, the warm breezes, the swaying palms. "There is a secret cove I visited as a child," she murmured. "That had the most beautiful shells."

"Shells?"

"Seashells. We harvest them. Wear them on our clothes, in our hair. Trade them for other nations' wealth."

"The detritus of dead animals."

She cracked an eye open. "You have a dark mind, Terzha of Golden Eagle."

"I attended the war college in Hokaia and trained with the spearmaidens there. They are a dark-minded people."

"I know someone who trained with a spearmaiden."

"Do you? The firstborn daughters of matrons rarely attend the war college. It is the secondborn's calling. Witness Ziha and her military ambitions. But Mother saw the wisdom in sending me. She knew war would come, and Golden Eagle would need me to lead not just as a matron but as a general."

"You mean she planned to start a war and trained her daughters accordingly." The words slipped out unthinking, but Xiala did not regret them.

"That's one way of looking at it." She rolled to her side to face Xiala. "The other is she prepared for the inevitable. Peace cannot last forever. Times change, and it is better to be on top than to be crushed at the bottom. Shells are pretty, yes, but they are already dead things when you find them. And they break so easily. And then they are dust." She rolled to her feet, looming over Xiala. "Careful not to break, Xiala, and leave behind only pretty dust."

And then she was gone, back into the night.

A foreboding rolled over Xiala, as real as a wave in deepening water. She pulled her blanket up around her shoulders, her back to the waning fire, and tried to sleep. But all she could think about were beaches scattered with the broken bodies of Teek, and Terzha standing triumphant over them, her heel grinding them into sand.

• • • • •

They were up before dawn, another day of riding before them. She managed to avoid Terzha, but Iktan tracked her down over a cold breakfast of corn cakes and dried strips of a meat Xiala didn't recognize.

"If all goes well, we reach Hokaia this afternoon," xe informed her, chewing at the meat as if it was a personal affront to breakfast itself.

She wanted nothing more than to get away from Golden Eagle. Terzha had unsettled her, and the premonition of Teek's destruction felt like a warning. She berated herself for even mentioning Teek navigation the night before, but a more reasonable voice in her head assured her that Terzha was no seafarer, and besides, she had not said anything that Terzha might use to find her homeland. Nevertheless, she worried.

Mother waters, she wanted free. Cuecola was not so far once they reached Hokaia. But Cuecola might not welcome her back. Lord Pech likely still held a grudge, and if not him, the tupile from the Kuharan jail. She did not know if she could count on Lord Balam to defend her. She had gotten Serapio to Tova as promised, but then she had lost a very expensive ship and crew. The jaguar lord might not look generously upon her. But there were other ports, other places along the coast she could hide until this war passed her by.

And what of Serapio? she thought. *Would you leave him to fight these vipers alone?* Never mind the treachery in his own clan that Iktan had alluded to. No, she had followed Iktan from Tova knowing that she could find a way to help Serapio by spying among his enemies, and she was determined to see it through. What she found in Hokaia would be what he needed most. And once she understood Golden Eagle's war plans, she would find a fast ship back to Tova. And if she could send a message to Teek, a warning that war was coming from the out-side world, she would do that, too.

They came in over Hokaia as the sun began to settle low on the horizon. The network of rivers that ran around and through the city sparkled in the setting sun, and the vast mound city glittered brightly along its wide avenues and waterways. She thought perhaps she had never seen a city so breathtaking. Tova was something out of a story, its buildings and banners clinging to the cliffside wreathed in clouds and held together by silky woven bridges. And Cuecola was the hot breath of the world, heavy with humanity and jungle sweat and the decadent memories of magic. But sunlit Hokaia blazed orange and red and joyful, a defiant splash of heat across the yellow winter grasslands, and she was thankful, if only for a moment, to experience it from a vantage point that no other Teek had likely ever seen.

The city itself was divided into four main plazas laid out along the cardinal directions, with a massive three-tiered mound in the north. Before it, a river ran neat along man-made banks to empty into a lagoon, and Xiala could make out boats docked at its shores. Her breath caught at the sight of black-hulled sailing ships, and she leaned over as if to get a better look.

"Careful!" her rider chided, and she immediately straightened.

They looked like Teek ships, the fast ones that made quick work of distance, the ones they called tidechasers, but surely there could be no Teek in Hokaia. Unless some had come to trade. Her heart sped up. Perhaps she could give her warning to these Teek and, at the same time, gather some news from home. It had been more than a decade since she had seen another Teek, and she knew return was an impossibility, but to even hear news . . . it would do her good. She rubbed at her legs. She suspected being back at sea would cure her land sickness, too, but she might also ask the visiting Teek if they knew a remedy. Suddenly, she felt a glimmer of promise at the prospect of getting to Hokaia.

The Golden Eagle riders spoke to each other in a series of complex hand motions to make themselves known, and together they descended toward the central mound. The top of the earthen structure stretched a mile long at least, the building at its top running the width of the back end. It looked big enough to house a thousand people, and Xiala wondered if it was temple or palace. Iktan's history lesson rose in her memory, and she knew this must be the place where the Treaty of Hokaia had been signed. *Palace and temple*, she thought to herself, as the great birds landed before it.

A woman approached, adorned in an antler crown and carrying a spear that she recognized as kin to Serapio's bone staff. She was flanked by a half dozen women with painted faces, carrying the same spear. She knew who and what they were.

Nuuma met the spearmaidens in the middle of the field, flanked by her own Shield. Xiala was too far away to hear their conversation. Minutes passed. Five, and then fifteen. The great birds flapped their wings in agitation, wind rippling across the mound top. She could see people gathering at the edges of the grounds, and behind the spearmaidens, through the broad open doors of the palace, figures moving in the interior shadows. Her rider had stayed behind, as had the two rear guards, and she could sense their tension, ready to strike and save their matron should the command come.

Finally, Nuuma turned and spoke their hand language, and Xiala felt her rider relax.

"They are well met," the woman told her. "All is at peace. The matron goes to feast with our allies now." She began to maneuver her eagle around.

"Are we not joining them?"

"We will house our mounts just there, over the river."

Xiala looked. "Just there" was at least five miles away. "Is that safe?" she asked. "I mean, it's so far. What if there's trouble?"

Her rider lifted a brow. "Do you expect trouble?"

"Always."

That earned her a laugh. "Suhtsee and the honor guard will stay here for now, but this mound is no place for an eagle. It is best to bunker them outside the city where they might roost." She eyed Xiala. "You are to stay with me."

Xiala watched the matron, Terzha, Iktan, and the majority of the Shield disappear within the palace, the grand doors closing behind them. She bit at her lip, unable to shake her concern but helpless to do anything about it. And then they were airborne again, and she was clinging to the woman's back, her worries reduced to not plummeting to the ground below.

· · · · ·

They arrived at their destination in a matter of minutes. What had looked distant from the mound was quick work on eagle-back, and that, at least, was reassuring. There were only four of them tasked with setting up camp and providing for the eagles, so Xiala offered to help.

"We have it in hand." This Shield was a man, as slender as a blade and half as friendly. "You can make yourself comfortable until you are needed."

In other words, get out of our way, Xiala thought. Well enough. She understood she was not one of them and should not confuse herself over it. She wandered away a bit, admiring the trees that surrounded them. She could hear the river rushing in the distance, the gurgle of water over stone, and a light breeze stirring through the giant elms. Unlike Tova, Hokaia was on the cusp of spring. No snow dotted the ground here, and the air smelled of pollen, not ice.

She found a shaded spot on the far side of a tree large enough to fit inside and sat down with her back against its massive trunk. She picked at a new blade of grass sprouting up between the winter yellow.

The Shield behind her worked at setting up camp, and she closed her eyes, listening to their chatter.

"What will happen?" the woman who had been her rider asked. "Will they give us soldiers to fight the Crow?"

"It is not just the Crow we fight now. All the clans have united under the Sun Priest."

The woman scoffed. "I could have told her Abah would fail to kill her. She was always overconfident, even when she lived in the Great House."

"She left at twelve. You didn't know her."

"I knew her enough. And her brother, too. That family is . . ." They moved away out of hearing.

Xiala huddled frozen against the trunk of the water elm. Iktan's suspicions had been right. Xir friend lived and, moreover, had united the clans of Tova. Surely that would change

Iktan's feelings about this impending war and xir commitment to Golden Eagle. No wonder the matron had kept the news from xir.

And what of Serapio? If the clans had united behind the Sun Priest, did that mean they had abandoned him? Or did it bode something even worse? She knew he did not need her to defend him physically. His crows and his god were guard enough, never mind his own fighting skills. But she knew Serapio bore a great wound of another kind inside, and she feared that when provoked, that wound would prove to be the more deadly of the two.

She could not aid Serapio against the Sun Priest, but she could find Iktan and tell xir what she knew. That might crack Golden Eagle from within and remove their greatest strategist. Then she would steal one of the tidechasers she'd seen in the lagoon. With a ship like that, she could be back at the mouth of the Tovasheh in a matter of days.

She left camp quietly, moving through the forest. She thought she heard one of the Shield call her name, and she hurried her pace. But no one followed, perhaps not thinking her valuable enough to chase, or assuming she would wander back on her own accord since she had nowhere to go.

But she did have somewhere to go, and she crossed a small wooden bridge and found herself at the outer gates of Hokaia. There was a steady flow of foot traffic, and she blended in easily. The city was more diverse than even Cuecola. Nevertheless, she kept her blue hood up, but no one looked twice at her. Perhaps Teek were not such a strange sighting on this side of the Crescent Sea, after all.

It was easy to know her destination; the great mound towered above all else. Her only hindrance was her legs. They still ached, especially after two days without her makeshift sea broth, and they made her slower than she liked, but eventually she came to the lagoon at the base of the mound that she had spotted from above. She passed near the black ships, and a mix of emotions flooded her when she confirmed they were indeed Teek. Longing, hope, a wild panic that she might be found out. She imagined herself at the helm of one of those swift beauties, and her heart sped up. She spied a woman lounging on the captain's bench, no doubt there to make sure no ships were stolen. She would have to get around her, but she'd find a way.

She reached the base of the mound stairs and looked up. Any joy she had felt at seeing the ships drained away. Her legs already hurt, and this would be torture, akin to Titidi's harbor steps. Someone bumped her shoulder, and she realized she was holding up traffic. She exhaled, braced herself, and climbed.

By the time she reached the top, her knees shook, and her breath came in short bursts. But she had done it, and that was all that mattered. She spied the great eagles still on the open grass, seemingly content and well trained enough to wait patiently for their riders to return. A curious resident approached one of the giant birds, hand extended as if to pet the creature, and almost lost his head to a snapping beak for his effort. She didn't see any Shield but circled wide anyway, looking for a side entrance into the palace. What she found was the outdoor kitchen.

It was half as long as the Grand Palace itself, and it bustled with activity, women bent over fires and boys hauling water, another woman butchering a four-legged beast with which Xiala was not familiar, and another slicing open great trout from the river. She kept her head down and her step assured, and she flowed into the controlled chaos, letting herself be buoyed along until she was inside the palace.

She followed the servants carrying trays of food down a long hallway that ran the length of the building. Doorways appeared at intervals, all leading into the same interior room. It was huge, a space that could host a thousand people. Massive tapestries hung from wooden walls bearing colorful geometric patterns. A thatched roof arched high above her head, its apex lost in the darkness above. To her right she spied what she was looking for. There was a feast in progress, one that had likely been going on since they had left Nuuma and her party here. Dozens were seated on benches around the largest table Xiala had ever seen. It looked carved whole from a single massive tree trunk and must have weighed as much as one of Cuecola's great canoes.

She ducked back into the hall and made her way closer to the table. As she drew near, she heard a woman speaking. Her tone suggested she was giving some sort of speech. Xiala had hoped to find them at the part of the feast where music and perhaps dancing reigned, but she dared not wait. If she was wrong about the Shield at camp and they guessed her destination, they could be on the mound to retrieve her in minutes. Not only would she be returned across the river, but she would also lose her opportunity for escape.

She peered into another doorway, this time searching for a distinctive face, one with a cap of black hair and quick, intelligent eyes. At the next doorway, she found xir. Iktan was seating with xir back to her, a man in a boxy headdress on xir right and Terzha on xir left. She did not see Nuuma from her limited vantage point but was sure she was near. The speaker droned on, something about an epic battle and glory won that sounded stultifyingly dull.

She pressed her body against the wall, as small as she could make herself, and crept forward, as close as she could get to the seated party.

"Iktan," she hissed.

She waited a moment, but xe didn't respond. Frustrated, she

tried again, this time louder. Still nothing. She needed something to get xir attention over the oration. She reached into her pocket, searching. Her hand closed on a hard pebble. She pulled it from her pocket and gagged. It was the eyeball, now dry and shriveled, that Ziha had given her, the wages of justice. She swallowed down her revulsion. It would have to do.

She threw the thing, striking Iktan in the shoulder. This time, xe noticed, as did the man in the headdress beside xir. They both turned.

The man next to Iktan, with a pinched, petulant face, was already annoyed, but when he spotted her, his jaw dropped.

"You!" The man's shout echoed around the high-ceilinged chamber.

Other faces turned.

Xiala could feel her world tilt. *No, no, no!* What were the chances? One in a million? A hundred million?

Lord Pech pushed up from his seat. He pointed a finger at her and declared in a voice that carried through the hall, "Sovran Naasut, this woman is a criminal! I demand that you arrest her and hold her in chains until she can be returned to Cuecola to stand trial for her capital crimes!"

Silence fell across the hall, all eyes on Xiala. She stood dumbfounded, unsure what to do. Her gaze scraped across the crowd. There was Iktan, looking more curious than concerned. And there, across from Lord Pech, was the familiar face of Lord Balam next to a dark-skinned woman with almost white eyebrows, and next to her—

Xiala's breath caught in her throat, and she swayed. *Blood at her feet. Bodies. The north wind blowing down across the island.*

The woman stood, the white shells in her long, thick hair ringing gently, but to Xiala they were as loud and damning as a funeral drum. Her storm-gray eyes narrowed, as dangerous as a shipkiller on the open sea, and familiar lips curled in dark acrimony. And in a voice Xiala had thought to never hear again, she said, "Hello, Xiala."

Xiala felt herself falling, but Iktan was there, keeping her on her feet. She could hear xir calling her name, but it felt like xir voice was coming from a great distance. And Lord Pech was there looming over her, waving his hands and screaming that she was dangerous and needed to be restrained immediately.

"You're supposed to be dead," she whispered, her words meant for the white-shell woman. Shock made her brain slow, her mouth thick and clumsy.

"What is happening here?" The spearmaiden in her antler crown and painted face added her voice to the chaos. "Who is this?"

Pech wrenched her arm, pulling her from Iktan. "A criminal!"

"You are mistaken," Iktan said. "She is a member of Golden Eagle's diplomatic envoy."

"How could she be Golden Eagle when she's clearly Teek?" That was the woman with the white eyebrows on the far side of the table next to Lord Balam. Balam leaned over and whispered in her ear.

Pech wrenched Xiala's arm again, and she felt her shoulder pop. Pain lanced through her side, clearing some of her confusion. "Let me go!" she growled, but the man dug his fingers deeper into her flesh.

She heard a laugh, cold and unsympathetic. *Stupid girl. Once again, you have made a mess of things. What will you do about it?*

And the dam inside her burst. She forgot about the bridge in Tova and the woman in blue and the green-eyed man. She waded willingly into the bloody sea. And she reached for her Song, recognizing it as an inheritance from her true Mother, a blade to wield as she must. No shame, no guilt. A gift for her use. And she used it now.

A single note, obsidian-sharp, burst from her lips.

Time stopped . . .

. . . and the room around her shattered.

Clay water pitchers cracked and flooded the feast table.

Men dropped to their knees, clutching their heads.

She saw the Cuecolan with the white eyebrows shout something, her lips moving, and the air around her and Balam shimmered. The spearmaiden in the antler crown yelled for her guards, terrified, but the woman in the shells only laughed.

As the note faded and time came rushing back, Xiala realized Pech no longer held her. She looked down at her feet. He lay dead, blood streaming from his nose and mouth, eyes open and staring. Horrified, she turned to Iktan. Xe had been on her other side.

Xe was bent over, blood trickling from xir nose. Xe straightened, wiping at the mess with xir hand, and a smile spread across xir mouth.

"Neither man nor woman," xe murmured, eyes shining in amusement. "But that was still unpleasant."

She sobbed in relief.

And then she was surrounded by spearmaidens. Rough hands forced a gag into her mouth, and the antlered queen stood before her, knife at her throat.

"Assassin!" she shouted. "Who sent you?"

"She's no assassin," the white-shell woman said. She stepped forward now, pressing a hand to Naasut's arm until she lowered her blade.

"Then who is she, Mahina?"

The Teek queen's laugh was thin. "My daughter."

CHAPTER 31

Rejoice! You go to battle now! A place of claw and tooth where there is no room for mercy.

—From the *Oration of the Jaguar Prince*
on the Eve of the Frenzy

Balam walked the hall of the Mole Palace with Powageh by his side. "And then the Knife says, 'I thought you killed your mother.' And the girl replies, 'So did I.'"

"Seven hells," Powageh exclaimed. "And then what?"

"Well, they had to arrest her. Pech was dead, after all, and we all saw that she did it. But he did pull her shoulder from the socket, and she is the Teek queen's daughter. Mahina claims it was self-defense, so Naasut is treading very carefully. I think she'd prefer if it all simply went away."

"And the other Cuecolan lords?" Powageh asked as they stepped out onto the open grounds that surrounded the palace. "Are they demanding justice for Pech?"

"I think we all know Pech was not particularly well liked. Sinik seems the only one who might protest. Tuun certainly won't, particularly if the Teek are willing to offer restitution.

In fact, I think she sees the opportunity in the Teek owing us a debt."

Powageh grimaced. "Not what we planned for."

"No," Balam admitted. "But chaos can only benefit us. Speaking of benefits, did you procure the thing I needed?"

"Do I ever fail you, Cousin?"

"Surprisingly, no."

"There's a thriving underground market here. All kinds of strange items claimed to be from the Graveyard of the Gods. But these I am assured are the true thing." He handed Balam a small fabric bag, dark rich dirt clinging to its slightly damp sides. "Godflesh. Not a great quantity, but it was all that was available."

"Ah." Balam quickly palmed the bag and secreted it away in an inner pocket of his cloak. "You'll have to watch my door tonight, Cousin. You're the only one I trust, and there's work to do."

"Naasut?"

"For one. And there's the matter of the spy in the cells below. He can't speak anymore, but I'd not leave him in such misery for his faithful work. And I'd like to get a look into Nuuma Golden Eagle's dreams. She's hiding something, that's clear, and I don't think I can wait for Layat's arrival to know what it is."

"Is there enough for that?"

His cousin's concerns about the godflesh were well taken. "I'll need more soon. It is a finite resource we must use sparingly, but our circumstances warrant the risk."

"As are you, a finite resource. I fear you are careless."

"You worry about the madness." He dared not mention the ever-growing blur between reality and his memory. Even now, he caught glimpses of burning corpses out of the corner of his eye. Images from the war, he was sure. "I am fine."

Powageh ceded the argument with a sigh. "We have made strange allies here, Balam."

"It is a new age. Alliances shift. We must anticipate the unexpected." He glanced at the sky. "And what of our comet? I had hoped for it to accompany our arrival, but it seems delayed."

"My calculations did not account for being farther north," Powageh admitted. "But it should be visible after sunset."

"And last how long?"

"Its transit will be brief."

"We do not need it to linger, only to grace the heavens long enough to make our point."

"Patience, Cousin. The heavens do not disappoint."

A young voice interrupted them. "Lord Balam!"

The two Cuecolans turned to find a Hokaia boy approaching at a run.

"Now what?" Powageh murmured.

"A message for you, Lord. The Princess Xiala of the Teek wishes to speak to you."

He exchanged a look with his cousin.

"She awaits you in the Otter Palace."

"And where is that?"

"Across the plaza, Lord, just opposite here. She said it was of some urgency, as she hoped you could speak in private before her mother returned from touring the city."

"Not in jail, then." He cleared his throat. "Then lead."

They started to walk, but the boy balked.

"She said only you, Lord. It is a private audience."

Powageh raised xir hands. "Please. Don't let me keep you."

"I will see you tonight, then?"

"I'll be there."

They exchanged an embrace, and Balam let the boy lead him across the plaza. It was bustling now, workers repairing the earthworks and servants hurrying between the Grand Palace, the smaller palaces, and the massive kitchen.

"Tell me of your house names," Balam asked idly. "Mole, Otter . . . what else?"

"The Grand Palace is there, Lord. That is where the Sovran and his"—he flushed under his brown skin—"her attendants stay. Honored guests may stay in Otter, Mole, Beaver, and Mink."

"And do they mean anything, these names?"

"They are animals, Lord." He said it as if Balam was a simpleton.

"Are they given according to favor or rank?"

The boy scratched at his nose, clearly confused by Balam's question.

"Never mind." He suspected the boy was playing the simpleton himself. "Just take me to the Teek woman."

"Princess," the boy corrected.

Ah, so the boy certainly knew what a title was and what it meant but played coy about the palaces, which suggested they did indeed mean something, and Mole, perhaps, was far down the pecking order. He made note.

Despite whatever rank each palace name might imply, the inside of the Otter looked much like the Mole. Two long outer hallways with interior rooms branching off and a vaulted thatched roof high overhead. Woven rugs in bright colors hung from the walls, and across from each thatch door was an alcove that contained a small ceremonial figurine. Here, fittingly, they were otters.

The boy led him to the last door in the hallway and knocked before entering. "Lord Balam of the House of Seven, Merchant Lord of Cuecola, Patron of the Crescent Sea, White Jaguar by Birthright," he announced, and Balam was impressed that he had taken the time to learn his address.

The room was dominated by a low table surrounded by sitting cushions, and through a doorway farther in, Balam spotted low reed bedding draped with fabrics, the packed dirt floors swept clean. A woman rose and came into the front room to meet him. Her deep plum hair coiled down her back, and she wore a sea-green robe wrapped tightly around the pronounced curves of her body. She carried a bottle of xtabentún in one hand and gestured to the table. He lowered himself onto a cushion, and she joined him, plunking the bottle down between them.

The boy hurried to a side shelf and retrieved two small clay cups and set them on the table.

She rolled dulled eyes to him. "You can go back to the Grand Palace to await my mother, but remember, not a word to anyone." She pressed a cloth bag that rattled with cacao into his hand. He bowed smartly before departing.

"So we meet again," she said, pouring Balam a drink. "And once more, I find myself in jail." She slid the cup toward him, her rainbow eyes taking him in.

"A much nicer cell than the one in Kuharan."

She laughed, the sound bitter. "Still a jail."

"A princess," he said, smiling. "You surprise me."

She made a face of distaste as she poured herself a drink, although it was apparent she had already been drinking directly from the bottle. "I don't know what game my mother is playing. The Teek do not have royalty. We barely have a government at all. Just village elders and grandmothers."

"And yet your mother comes claiming the title and the authority."

"To impress the likes of you," She downed the drink in a long swallow and poured herself another. "Lords and matrons and the Sovran. But her power is not unilateral. When she returns, they will argue her decisions in the listening house just like anyone else's."

Like most outsiders, Balam knew nothing of how the Teek governed. It was impossible to infiltrate their insular islands and floating cities. They had limited trade and no tourism and were notorious for killing anyone who did not respect their rules. Xiala, princess or no, had told him more in a few moments than he had been able to glean in a decade of spying.

"And so why did you call me here?" he asked. "It is not to renegotiate our agreement, I hope."

She blinked her large eyes at him.

He smiled. "Now I jest. I have heard that you successfully brought our mutual friend to Tova."

"To die!" She said it with such venom that he flinched, his fingers tightening involuntarily around his cup.

"It was his choice." He set his cup to the side and folded his hands on the table.

She pressed the meat of her palm against her left eye, as if her head ached. "It doesn't matter. He didn't die, or at least he was still alive two weeks ago when I left Tova. I do not know how he fares now."

It was nothing he did not already know from his own sources. "You still have not told me why you asked to see me."

"I need you to help me."

He raised an eyebrow.

"They're planning to ship me back to Teek."

"I would think you would want to return to your homeland after thinking yourself banished all these years. Particularly since your welcome in Hokaia is compromised."

She slammed her palm down, rattling the cups. The bottle tipped, splashing the table with liquor before she righted it.

"Get me out of this! I know your kind, Balam. You have a plan, something that benefits you."

"I hardly think—"

"Cut the shit."

He paused, mouth open. There was opportunity here, as there always was with the desperate. But he needed to find his advantage. "Very well. Let's say I do. Surely you know I am not an altruistic man."

"Spring me from my mother's tender care, and I'll sail your ships for you. Expand your trade. Whatever it is you need."

He sat silently, making a show of thinking, but he already knew exactly what he wanted.

"I cannot save you from returning to Teek. You and I both know that this is not the time to challenge your mother's authority."

"But—"

He raised a hand to silence her. "I propose a working arrangement of a limited duration."

She drank from her cup. "Go on."

"Return to Teek, and be my spy. We plan for war, Xiala, and I find this trusting of allies tedious business. I need someone who is close to the queen"—he stopped her again when she began to protest—"and when this war is over, I will give you whatever you want. A ship, no, a fleet of ships. Riches beyond your imagination." He leaned across the table, his voice low with promise. "I will give you Teek itself if that is what you want."

Her eyes flashed, and he felt the air shift, the same feeling he had gotten on the docks that first day they met, the same feeling that had preluded Pech's demise. He knew she drew her magic to her, but to what end? Had he pushed too far, asked too much? He half expected her mother and the Teek guard to burst through the doors and accuse him of treachery.

He pressed his long sharpened nail to his palm, ready to draw blood and call shadow.

"What you ask is treason against my own people," she said. "For that, I want something more than riches."

"Name it."

"I want you to save him."

At first, he did not know who she meant, but there was only one man they had in common. And the look on her face—he knew it well, for he had felt it himself, if only once.

"Ah, the heart is a terrible thing. You have fallen in love with him."

"He does not deserve to die."

"So seems to be the consensus." He thought of Powageh's similar protests. "Tell me, truly. What makes him so special? Ten thousand will die for this war. What is one more?"

She set her jaw. "That is my price."

He sat back. "Very well. I will spare him when we take Tova." He meant it not at all, of course. Serapio was too dangerous to let live, but if a small lie now would bring her to his side, it was easily made.

"Tell the truth!"

Her voice vibrated with power, the far roar of a coming wave. Her eyes swirled, pools of color that a man could drown in. He felt her power now, different from what had happened at the feast. This was compulsion, the yearning to splay his secrets out before her. He dug his fingernail deep into his palm. His mouth began to open, and he bit his tongue. He brought his hand up and slapped his bloody palm across his lips.

She Sang for a moment more, but his sorcery was already weaving around him, protection from her magic. She exhaled, the air rippling before her, and stopped. Her shoulders slumped in defeat.

"Sorcerer," she spat.

But it had been a near thing. He had thought himself immune to such magics, but twice in as many days, Xiala had almost overpowered him. Tuun's quick thinking had thrown a protective shield over him at the feast, and now his own magic saved him, but both instances were too dangerous for his liking. Perhaps Serapio was not the only one of this pair who was too dangerous to let live. Only when he was sure he could control his words did he release the protection spell. His hands trembled. "That was not nice."

"I am not nice," she shot back, unbowed. "Do not cross me on this, Balam. Or I will find you when you least expect and bind your blood in your veins and Sing the flesh from your bones and your bones to crack until there is nothing left of you but your name, and even then people will fear to speak it should I find them and do the same to them!"

"A shark after all," he said, after a moment. His drink sat untouched, but now he reached his unbloodied hand forward and took the cup. He sipped from it, and a steadying warmth suffused his body and calmed his shaken nerves. "Very well. We have an agreement."

"And one more thing."

"I am feeling disinclined toward favors at the moment."

"This one is simple enough. Find the Golden Eagle ambassador, the one named Iktan. I need you to pass xir a message for me. Two words only."

Balam waited.

"She lives."

He tilted his head. "That's it?"

"Xe will understand." She finished her drink. "How will I reach you from Teek?"

He took the small mirror he wore on his waist and placed

it on the table. His palm was still bloody, and he shook some of the blood onto the surface. It flowed with shadow. He murmured a few words to bind the passageway. "A drop of your blood on this mirror, and I will know it. When the mirror darkens, speak your tales to the shadow, and I will hear them and be able to speak to you. But only you. If you are discovered, shatter the mirror, and the shadow will aid you."

He did not say how, thinking of the spy who had swallowed his tongue, but she need not know that.

She reached for the mirror just as there were voices at the door. She looked up, listening.

"Mother!" She slipped the mirror into the pocket of her robe. "Hurry!"

He bolted to his feet and followed her as they raced into the adjoining room. There was a far door that exited to the parallel hallway that was no doubt used for air circulation in the summer months but was now blocked. Together they shoved the bed to the side, and he squeezed out. Before he was even through, she had run back to the receiving room. She took his cup and guzzled what remained before tucking it under a cushion. She flopped down onto her own seat and pulled the bottle close as if it would protect her.

Queen Mahina swept into the room. Balam pressed against the wall to listen, the narrow edge of the open door giving him a sightline. He saw Mahina's gaze rake over the room, taking in her inebriated daughter, the spatter of blood on the opposite edge of the table, the confusion of blankets and pillows.

"Drunk." It was a pronouncement of disapproval.

"What else have I to do since you locked me in here?"

"You're lucky you're not being dragged to Cuecola in chains. You killed one of the Seven Lords. Do you even understand the implications of what you've done? Of course not.

You always act without thinking and leave others to clean up your mess." She gestured to Xiala. "Is this what you've done with your life since you left Teek? Spent it in a bottle?"

"Left? I was fifteen, and they *banished* me."

Her mother tsked, tongue against teeth. "You were never banished. You ran. If you had stayed and faced the consequences of your actions, perhaps things would have been different."

"I thought I had killed you! I was a child!"

Her mother's look was arch and cutting. "Not too young to have a kahnay between your legs."

Balam did not know the Teek word, but he could easily guess. He could not see Xiala's face, but she lifted the bottle and drank directly from it.

"Mother waters," Mahina cursed. "What a mess you are! And I hear it's your association with another kahnay that's brought you here. Well, perhaps we should be grateful for that one, but did I raise you no better than this, Xiala? To become entangled with men? If you need love so desperately, there are so many women in this wide world. Teanni still speaks of you. She will be glad to see you again."

"Teanni was a dalliance."

Mahina took two quick steps forward and slapped her daughter. Xiala's head whipped to the side with the force of it. "Do not speak ill of that girl. She has shown you nothing but love."

"She never tried to find me."

"And where would she look? How would she go?"

Xiala said nothing. Mahina exhaled, crossing her arms across her chest. "You disappoint me, Xiala, but this"—she gestured around the room, at the xtabentún, at the woman—"can be fixed." She snatched the bottle up. Xiala did not protest. "The first thing you do is sober up, and then we'll see to the rest." She turned to leave, liquor in hand, but paused in the doorway. Her expression flattened, and Balam saw only one emotion on the Teek queen's face: fear.

And wasn't that interesting.

"It will all be better once you return to Teek. You'll see."

And then she was gone. Xiala folded her arms on the table and dropped her head. He could hear her sobbing softly.

He waited until he was sure Mahina was gone before he slipped out to return to his rooms.

CHAPTER 32

> Know now that Naranpa shall be my worthy successor. She
> will serve as a light against dark times, a symbol of reason for
> the world to see. Unto her very death.
>
> —From the *Oration of the Sun Priest Kiutue on the Investiture of*
> *Naranpa in Year 325 of the Sun*

He was waiting at Sun Rock for her.

Naranpa had crossed the Maw and the district of Titidi and
the bridge that spanned the width of the Tovasheh. This time,
there were no guards to question her, and she wondered if that
was Ieyoue's doing or if the city knew what was to come and
huddled behind its wooden doors and mud-brick walls hoping
to survive the deluge. Or maybe it was he that cleared her path,
and she would find ruined bodies lying in the depths of the
canyons below, drowned in shadow.

He was younger than she'd expected. The glimpse she had
caught of him on the roof had been brief, and he had been contorted with pain and his form half corvid. But now he looked
very normal. A man in his early twenties, shoulder-length hair
tied back from an almost delicate face. Tall and thin, dressed in

what looked like quilted black Shield armor from the waist up and an ankle-length skirt over bare feet from the waist down, a white staff in hand.

He did not look up at her approach but continued to walk in a strange pattern, curling and looping back on itself, as if he were tracing something in the dirt that only he could see. He was talking, quiet murmurs she could not discern, and occasionally he would stretch out his hand as if measuring the distance between his steps. Only when she had descended the stairs of the amphitheater and come to a halt in the center, no more than twenty paces away, did he stop.

As if on cue, the sun flared above them, just as it had on the celestial tower. Light broke across Sun Rock, the first dawn in many days.

He raised his face to the sun and smiled. "Ah . . ." His voice was easy, conversational. Nothing like the monster she had heard speak atop the tower. "It is as I suspected."

She shivered; she could not help it. The contrast was too startling, the contradiction disconcerting. She had come to face a nightmare and found this man instead.

"And what did you suspect?" She pitched her voice to carry.

He raised a hand, as if asking her to wait, and then, again as if expected, he winced in pain. His hand went to his side, and he gritted his teeth. She watched him swallow and come back panting. Then he straightened, and shadow flared around him. When he finally looked at her, his eyes were solid black.

She involuntarily took a step back before she felt her being respond, and she gasped as her eyes brightened and her body ignited. This was not the fire of her rage but something else. Something as warm and nurturing as the sun, akin to the healing power that had come over her in the Agave.

His laughter was a dark joy. "It seems our gods very much

want us to fight." He shifted his hold on the staff and spread his feet.

"I know what caused your wound." She spoke quickly, her words tumbling from her tongue.

He tilted his head. "So do I."

"But I can heal it." It was a daring thing to say, to promise when she was not sure it could be done, but it was what spilled forth.

"And why would you do that?"

"Because this is not you. This is not us." The truth of it came together all at once. The stories she had read in the tower books. Her visions. "As you said, it is our gods who compel us. Who puppet us through these motions. How many times have we fought before, Crow God? How many times will we fight again? It is an endless cycle, light and dark, fire and shadow. We, you and me, Serapio and Naranpa . . . we need not die for it!"

He was quiet for a very long time. "How do you know my name?"

She realized her mistake, but it was too late to take it back. "Okoa told me."

"Okoa . . ." Some emotion flashed across his face. "Funny. He has never called me by my name, even though it was something I wanted very much once." He smiled. "Is that what you came to tell me? That Okoa has aligned with the Sun Priest?"

"I came to sue for peace." It was not, in fact, the reason she had come. Sorrow had driven her. Exhaustion. She had come to win, or to die. But hope flared now, as new and promising as the sun above. "I have tried to do what is right for Tova, but I have only failed. The city was dying before you came, the Watchers corrupted, the clans too insular. We lay bloated and rotting under the sun as our people suffered."

"And now?"

"They suffer still," she admitted. "Too much darkness destroys as easily as too much light. We must seek the balance between us."

He seemed to turn inward, as if communing with a presence she could not discern. "My god does not think so. He has been bound for too long, kept from this place and his people by the greed of the sun god." He spread his hands. "He wishes to rule." He stood for a moment, arms still wide. A slow-creeping smile blossomed across his face. "He wishes you dead." Now she heard the god, the terrible voice like the dark shadows of the grave.

He began to run.

Toward her.

She only had time to turn, willing her feet to motion, before he was upon her. He slammed into her back, forcing her down. She hit the ground, face-first, ice cracking under her cheek. His forearm dug into the back of her neck, and his knee pressed against her spine. She sensed more than felt something sharp coming for her throat.

Terror drowned her. She fought to think, but her mind was gibberish. All she had was adrenaline and panic. She struggled, but his grip was stone. Desperate, her vision fading and her mind losing consciousness, she reached for that locked place inside her, her river of choler and grief. She ripped the dam free and let her fear explode in a torrent of rage.

Her body erupted.

He fell back with a curse as she unfurled her wings, twisting her sinuous body to rise.

His lips curled, amused. He lifted his arms, palms up, and exploded.

They collided in the air, firebird and the black-winged

flock. Naranpa felt the stab of a hundred beaks, the tearing of talons ripping across her stomach, and she screamed. Flames streaked from her mouth, searing corvids and driving them back. She gripped a bird between her talons and tore it in half. Shrieks shredded the air, and the crows fell. Suddenly, she was free.

She looked down to see the Odo Sedoh in human form again, cradling a bloody hand and wearing a murderous grin.

Flee! She thought but had no sooner conceived it than he shattered, and she was under attack again.

They struggled, light and shadow, fire and ice, each gaining advantage and then losing it. She struck, and he countered. He opened her flesh with his myriad claws, and she crushed a small body between her jaws. And on it went.

She could not last.

Exhaustion beat at her; the god magic that had transformed her was draining her to ash. He was faster, more deadly, well practiced. She was driven by instinct alone, and she was fading. She ducked a blow a fraction too slowly, and a talon slashed across her collarbone. She somersaulted back, losing her balance. Her body shuddered, and she plummeted to earth, a woman.

The impact knocked the breath from her body, and she lay helpless.

He landed heavily beside her, close enough that if she stretched her bloodied arm, she might touch his foot.

She expected him to leer over her, triumphant, to taunt her in that terrible voice. But he collapsed to sitting, fatigue bending his back. Tears of tar blackened his cheeks, and his body bore multiple burns.

Her smile was bittersweet. At least she had done that much.

He laughed, and it sounded like grief.

"Can you truly heal me?" It was the man again. Trembling, unsure.

Naranpa had always been someone who trusted, who believed in the best of people when others were willing only to condemn. Even her recent trials could not wholly destroy her humanity, and her humanity would not leave this man to suffer when she could help him.

Even if he was her enemy.

Especially because he was her enemy.

So she crawled to him. He was only an arm's length away, but it seemed to take an eternity. Plenty of time for her mind to scream at her to stay as far away from him as possible, to chide her for being a fool again, to remind her that Abah would laugh at her, that Denaochi would scold her for her recklessness. But they were dead, as were so many. If she could perhaps stop one more from dying, she had to try.

A gash in his armor exposed the wound in his side. It festered, but not with infection. With light. Her eyes met his, burnished gold and darkest shadow.

"It's beautiful," she whispered. Did he know? Did he care?

"It hurts."

His chest rose and fell, and she realized he was scared. She reached for him and paused, hand outstretched. Her nails had been ripped from their beds, and her second finger was warped and broken. "Skies," she murmured, no longer proud of the damage she had done to him, now revolted at the damage they had done to each other.

She pressed her mangled hand to his side.

Images flashed through her mind. The ancient fight above the lake at the Graveyard of the Gods, when her scales had been peeled from her stomach. Another battle between sun god and crow, this time as a woman in shadow armor and a man cloaked in fire. A third, and she thought she recognized the grasslands of the Meridian. The warriors were reversed, the woman's golden hair streaming down her back. And last, Eche, on his knees before the Odo Sedoh, breaking the mask and stabbing the crow god at this very place in his side.

"We are meant to be one," she murmured, but she could not say how. "Our battle is eternal and unwinnable."

She concentrated, the same way she had before when she had healed her brother. She thought perhaps it would not work, that her palliative powers were as spent as her rage, or that they would refuse to help her god's immortal enemy. But her hands warmed, and a glow spread along his skin.

She drew the essence of the sun god that had infiltrated his body to her own. Light and matter, and there, in her hand, a thin strip of hammered gold the size of her fingernail materialized. She recognized it immediately. It was the missing piece from the mask of the Sun Priest. It must have lodged in his side when Eche stabbed him.

She held it up to show him and realized something else had come to her hand. Shadow. It blackened her fingertips, crawled up her palm, encircled her wrist. She cried out, her hand suddenly icy with pain. The grain of gold tumbled to the ground.

The shadow ceased to spread and then dissipated, the cold retreating. But the healing glow had faded as well.

"The shadow feeds." He had opened his eyes, black pools that cut through her. "It always feeds."

This time, she was careful to wrap her hand in the cuff of her sleeve before picking up the piece of golden mask. "I think you will heal now."

He nodded, understanding. His voice was careful, thoughtful, and already he seemed refreshed. "All my life, I have been taught to hate you. Those who raised me spoke only of vengeance, but their vengeance ended always in my death, and they did not care. I was but a means to an end. They used my mother's grief against her, saying that I was meant to avenge Carrion Crow, when the truth was they cared nothing for me or my clan. But you, my enemy, care if I live or die. It is confusing."

He was quiet for so long Naranpa thought he did not mean to speak again.

She spoke instead. "Their end is war, and you are but a casualty in their war."

"Not simply war."

"What do you mean?"

"This eternal struggle you speak of. I feel it, too. Always before, the sun has prevailed, but I did not lie before. The crow god craves his rightful place."

"Tova's enemies plot against her, using your god's ascendancy as the excuse. They will come with armies, seeking to destroy the city and to claim her treasures as their own."

His smile was grim. "Let them come."

"You cannot defeat them alone. They will bring sorcerers and magic you have never seen." If Cuecola roused her sorcerers and Hokaia her spearmaidens, Teek her Singers, Golden Eagle their flock, and all their military might together on land and air and water . . . even the crow god would not be enough.

He tilted his head, studying her. "Then stay and fight with me. Surely they will tremble at our powers combined."

"I do not know that our gods would let us stay in the same city without willing us to try to kill each other."

"We could fight them, too."

"The gods? I do not think so, Serapio." She lay next to her enemy and confessed her plans. "I'm leaving Tova. You have lived with your god for a lifetime. I am new to mine and her power. I need to find a teacher, someone to show me how to master this new ability." Her firebird form still felt like a dream, so much like the vision in her mirror. But it had been real. She had transformed, and if she willed it, she was sure she could transform again.

"So next time we meet, you will be more adept at killing me?" His tone was wry.

She laughed. "No, Serapio. I do not think I want you dead."

He was quiet.

"I believe you are supposed to say you no longer wish to kill me."

A smile crooked his lips. "Where will you go?"

Her look was arch. "I do not think I will tell you, Crow God."

"Then I will not try to find you."

He was very alone, this man. Lost to grief and rage. She recognized in him a mirror of herself. As different as they were in age and temperament and gender, of all the people in the world, they probably understood each other the best. She would like it very much if they were friends. Not today, though. Today they were enemies who had fought to a truce. But another day, in the future.

But she did not tell him that.

"Beware of Carrion Crow."

His voice was hard. "So it seems."

She was unsure how much he knew, but at the very least, he understood Okoa had plotted with her against him. She thought to tell him of the matrons' meeting, but it felt perfidious to do so, and the matrons were still her allies. So instead, she said, "I see a side of you that is human. Show them that. Show them who you are, and perhaps you might sway them to your side."

His laugh was bitter. "You only see what you want to see,

Naranpa. As do they. As do we all. It is too late for 'human,' and I have done things Okoa will never forgive."

There was a bleakness in his expression that made her not press further.

"Perhaps you are right," she admitted, as much to herself as to him. "But perhaps unforgivable acts are what is required to save this city. I tried kindness, again and again, and failed."

"I do not begrudge the kindness you have shown me."

"I am not saying there is no place for mercy, but perhaps the Odo Sedoh's best weapon is ruthlessness. Ruthlessness and fear. Your coming bound the matrons to common purpose as they never have been before. And now it is you, a man of un-compromising will, who can keep them bound together. They are not bad people, but the matrons are too used to power, the Sky Made too rigid in caste and clan. They will not understand the danger until it is too late to stop it. Kindness will not win the war to come."

His voice was soft, a touch incredulous. "You *want* the crow god to rule them?"

Was that what she was saying? She didn't know. She only knew something had to change if Tova was to survive.

"Unite them as you must."

It was a dark fate she left for Okoa and her allies, but it was necessary. Their path to survival would be one of shadow and blood, but at least it gave them a chance.

He lifted his head as if hearing a voice she could not, and for the first time, she realized that in his human form he was blind. "You should leave, Sun Priest." His voice quivered, somewhere between the soft-spoken young man and the god.

She heaved herself to her feet.

"Farewell, Serapio."

"And you, Naranpa."

"May the stars guide you." It was an old Watcher parting, and likely out of place between them, but it seemed right to say, and she found that she meant it.

She turned inward and found the presence of the sun god. She drew from it and let it infuse her. She felt her exhaustion lessen, her breaks and bruises melt away. Her body ignited in transformation, and she took flight.

CHAPTER 33

> Make them fear you, and sometimes that is enough.
>
> —*On the Philosophy of War*, taught at the Hokaia War College

Serapio felt Naranpa leave. Heat flared against his face, and wind from the ripple of wings tousled his hair. He could not see in which direction she flew and decided that was for the best. He would not be tempted to follow.

"It seems I am of a purpose once again."

For the first time since he had awoken in the monastery, he felt at peace. Losing his god had broken him. He had been an empty hand, desperate to be filled again, bereft of direction if not a divine vessel. It had driven him to try to find a place within Carrion Crow, the people he had thought would be his home. But he had only confused and frightened them, and they had not recognized him as kin, no matter his haahan, his blood teeth, his mother's bloodline. His grief had morphed into shame and then resentment that settled into a quiet rage which he had cultivated like a hatchling fresh to the nest. Even the return of his god could not mend what had been broken by his abandonment.

The Odohaa loved him well, but it was not enough. They might love the Crow God Reborn, but they would never love Serapio, could not even see the half-Obregi boy separate from the Odo Sedoh. They wanted him only as their savior, only as a righteous killer. They cared not for the toll such a destiny took on him. They did not want to hear of his love of stories, or of the beautiful animals he carved from wood, or his preference for spice in his chocolate. If he died, they would rejoice as long as his death brought them glory.

And so he would use them accordingly.

All his life, he had sought destiny, and when it had played its course and he was left to be a man, he found himself unwanted. *Except Xiala*, he thought. *She would take you as you are*. And he would take her, gratefully. Desperately.

But in the end, he had lost Xiala, too, and all that remained was Tova.

A Tova he would make his own.

And a destiny he would shape to his needs alone.

If the clans would not open their doors and welcome him home, he would kick down their doors. Oh, he would be what Okoa had asked him to be, the bulwark and the blade, but not only for Carrion Crow. He would be the god over them all.

Serapio stood and walked to the place where he had been tracing patterns in the ice-crusted dirt before the sun god had come. He pressed tentative fingers to his wound and found it healed. Likewise the injuries the firebird had inflicted on him. Satisfied, he had turned his attention to his work.

The patterns were clear to him with his crow vision, lines of potential where the Odo Sedoh had left his carnage, where the shadow had eaten through and lay waiting below the surface. He took up his obsidian knife and cut across his arm. He let his blood fall, the blood that his old tutor had once coveted as an unimaginable source of power. And he fed the ground.

It started as a low rumble, like a great beast in its den, roused. He held out his hand, and the bone, sinew, and blood of dead priests and scions rose at his command. He shaped it like wood, spinning and chipping and refining as he went, and around him a fortress grew. Part Obregi keep, part Tovan Great House: rounded walls with turrets at the cardinal directions; rooms inside off a central courtyard, a great room at its heart; winding stairs that led to an aviary on the rooftop.

He exhaled, and the black walls smoothed and flattened. He turned his wrist, and red tiles patterned with interlocking crow wings spread across the floor. He dragged his foot, and blood formed and hardened into the steps to his throne room.

The throne itself he saved for last.

It was made of blackened sinew and white bone. The seat was round, supported by eight elongated X-shaped legs attached to a circular base. The back of the throne he wove from sinew and shadow, and wings that flared behind and above.

He left a hole in the ceiling above him so that the dark sun might shine through and cast its black light upon him. So that his small friends might come and go as they pleased. So that he could do the same.

And then he sat upon his throne and waited.

It did not take long for the crows to come. He told them what he wanted, and they scattered to do his bidding.

They returned within the hour, their cries heralding their return, and those they brought with them.

He had called twelve Odohaa to be his honor guard. Two for each direction, two for above, two for below, and he would stand in the center and make thirteen. Maaka and Feyou were among them, and he had asked each to pick five, the most faithful and loyal of their tuyon. He did not know their names yet, but he would come to know them as his own. They were imperfect vessels, but they would serve, and he would mold them into what he needed them to be.

"Odo Sedoh." Maaka's voice was breathy with awe. "What is this place?"

"This is our new home. The matron and her captain have proven themselves false. They have conspired with my enemies to kill me."

He heard gasps in disbelief. Even now, they clung to foolish hopes.

"So I give you a choice." Serapio stood. "You may leave the tuyon and return to Odo and no longer pledge your loyalty to the crow god, or you may stay and become my blood guard. Under my name we will unite the clans of Tova, and together we will rise under the crow god's banner, a power to make the Meridian tremble."

"We are loyal to you, Odo Sedoh!" That was Feyou. "Ask of us what you will."

This was the difficult part, but he needed to know they could be trusted. They would be his guard now, his knife hand when he could not be everywhere at once. He had to know.

"Take out your blades and open your throats."

Silence, and then a murmur of confused voices. He had expected it, but he was still disappointed. For all their bluster and sermons, they doubted. There was a time when if his god had asked him the same, he would have done it without hesitation.

"You pledged your lives to me. Promised me blood. Now I ask it, and you balk?" He leaned forward, hands braced against his knees. "If you are cowards, leave. But if you believe in me as you say you do, you will open. Your. Throats."

He heard the first body fall. A shriek, followed by a gurgling sound. He did not know who it was but hoped it was Maaka. Then the second, then another, and another. Until they were all broken and bleeding on the floor.

Serapio smiled and raised his arms wide.

He understood the wound in his side now. It had been power like any other. It had only hurt him because he had fought it, and he had only fought it because his god had rejected it. But when Naranpa had laid her hands upon him and the shadow had flowed to her in kind, he had understood. Shadow devoured, and light healed, and he had both at his command.

He drew the blood from the dying Odohaa just as he had from the blood-soaked earth of Sun Rock, and he carved. This time, he created armor, thick padded layers over chests and arms, torsos and legs, encasing the Odohaa from neck to ankle. He knit the seams with sinew and reinforced it with bone and formed helmets in the shape of a crow skull. When he was done, he healed their terrible wounds.

They rose before him, whole and remade.

"Maaka, come forward."

The man did as he was commanded.

"You are my first now, and Feyou my second. Swear your fealty."

"Until my death, and into the afterlife."

Feyou swore the same, and then the rest in turn.

When Serapio was satisfied, he spoke: "You are my Shield now called Tuyon, and we will unite Tova and become both weapon and wall, so that when the forces of the Meridian swarm at our gate, they will know their mistake. But first, we must meet the matrons. Go, gather the clan mothers to me. Let them tremble as you do, and we shall see who rules Tova now."

CHAPTER 34

Teek
Year 1 of the Crow

> Live as a Teek, die as a Teek.
>
> —Teek saying

"Land ahead!"

A cheer went up from the half dozen women who crewed the tidechaser, and one of them, a woman named Alani, nudged Xiala with her foot as she climbed over her to secure the boom on the triangle-shaped sail. Teek racing ships were small and crowded, built for speed and not comfort, and Xiala had found herself mourning the loss of her Cuecolan canoe that easily held fifty men. It was not fast, but at least a woman could stretch out.

The sky above her was thick with rain clouds, gray as the belly of a triggerfish, but so far they had avoided any spring storms. And with land sighted, it looked like their luck would hold and they would make it home dry.

Home.

The word curled tight in Xiala's belly. She had believed she would never see home again. And now that it was before her, she wasn't sure how she felt. She had longed to return, but not like this.

Alani leaned over and gave her a grin. "Come look."

"I can't." She lifted her foot, and the chain that held her secured to the deck rattled.

"Ah." The woman scrambled down and pulled a key from a string around her neck. "Mahina's not here to see. Just promise you won't try to get away."

"Where would I go?"

"You can swim, can't you? I hear you're good at running."

Xiala thought of the last time she had dived into the sea. Black scales that shimmered in the light, gills on her neck.

"Next time I run, no one will be able to catch me."

Alani laughed. "That's the spirit."

The chain fell off, and the woman beckoned Xiala to follow. She climbed after her until they both sat hunched in the bow. Wind buffeted their faces, sending their long hair streaming back behind them. Xiala tasted salt on her lips, felt the cold flecks of ocean water strike her face, and whispered a prayer to her Mother. Not the woman who had birthed her and had forced her onto the ship at knifepoint and in chains, but the one who kissed her now and welcomed her back into her arms.

"There she is." Alani pointed.

Xiala could just see it. A stretch of white sand, and just beyond it, thick green foliage she knew teemed with palms and mahogany, orchids and hibiscus, secret coves and endless waters. It was home, and for all she had not wanted to come, she could not help but be grateful she was here.

Teek.

The wind shifted, a flash breeze that rattled the sail and sent the crew into motion.

"Shit!" Alani shouted, and went to help.

Drops of rain bit at Xiala's face, the storm catching them

after all. She closed her eyes, and for a moment she was on a different ship on the Crescent Sea, sitting beneath the stars, drawing a sky map on the hand of a god.

"I'm sorry, Serapio," she whispered. "Just a little longer."

Thunder rumbled above them, and the sky cracked open, the rain falling in earnest.

CHAPTER 35

> Do not confuse your past for your future.
>
> —*Exhortations for a Happy Life*

Naranpa watched from atop the celestial tower as Serapio built his fortress. She could see the magic now, waves of shadow that inked the air around Sun Rock. She wondered how she had ever thought magic had no place in her life or the lives of the Watchers. It was all sorcery, her very being. So much potential throttled. So much power wasted.

She watched as the Odohaa came, and later as they left transformed into strange, disquieting warriors.

She watched as the clans came from their districts, adorned in their colors, their sigil banners raised. She smiled to see Coyote come, too, trailing across the bridge from Titidi.

She worried she had left them to a difficult future, but trial made one stronger. Tova was soft, spoiled. As they were, they could never survive against their enemies.

She thought of the young man she had met on Sun Rock, both god and human. He was not soft. He would break them and rebuild them into something that could withstand what came next. They would never thank him for it. In fact, they would hate him. But only he had the potential to save them.

She turned away, having seen enough.

The stairs wound below her one last time as she made her way to the library. She picked a handful of books, only the most important ones, and tucked them into a leather sack.

She went to the servants' quarters next and found a plain brown robe. She traded her tattered white dress for it. She left her hair golden and wild, for she still mourned her brother, but she traded the rich cloak he had gifted her for a plain one, tucking the precious star-lined mantle into a far corner of a shelf for safekeeping.

Her last stop was in the kitchens. She packed food, as much as she thought prudent. She hesitated over the resin lanterns. She lifted her hand, and her palm glowed. She curled her fingers, and the glow blossomed into flame. No, she no longer needed lanterns to find her way.

Once she had everything she needed, she went to the massive front doors of the tower. She had always thought those doors kept her safe from the outside world. Now she suspected they had done just the opposite. She dragged them closed and threw the bolt latch from inside. Someone stubborn could break them open, she supposed, but it would at least deter most thieves and the simply curious. The tower was still sacred. She did not want to see it desecrated or its libraries compromised.

She climbed the stairs to the tower one last time. The sun still burned black over Tova, but now there was a new presence in the sky in the north. A bright star trailing a smoking tail. A portent of change that seemed all too prescient.

She slung the leather bag over her shoulder, settled her cloak, and called the sun god.

Where Naranpa had once been was now a firebird. Her wings spread across the breadth of the tower. She considered going south to the region of the Meridian where sorcery had once thrived and still claimed a foothold, but south was Cuecola and the jaguar man. While the nightmares had lessened in their frequency, they still haunted her, warning her away from the fallen Jaguar Prince's city. Instead, she launched herself skyward, circling once before heading north, following the new comet's path to the Graveyard of the Gods. She hoped to find answers there. Perhaps a teacher.

She did not look back.

ACKNOWLEDGMENTS

I wrote a lengthy and detailed acknowledgments for *Black Sun* because it felt important for readers to understand the context and motivations of writing an epic fantasy novel inspired by the pre-Columbian Americas. But after surviving a difficult and challenging year, *Fevered Star*'s acknowledgments are all about gratitude.

I want to thank the team at Gallery Books/Saga who have continued to champion my work and this series. Bringing a book into the world is by no means a solo act, and it not only takes a village, but it takes a village of amazing and talented people who deserve my deep respect. First, thank-you to my editor, Joe Monti, who always saw the potential and pushed me to dig a little deeper and look a little harder with each iteration.

Thank you to Alysha Bullock, Senior Production Editor; Kaitlyn Snowden, Production Manager; Caroline Pallotta, Managing Editor; Michelle Marchese, Interior Designer; Allison Green, Assistant Managing Editor; Madison Penico, Assistant Editor; Jela Lewter, Editorial Assistant; Cordia Leung, Subrights; Sydney Morris, Senior Publicist; Kayleigh Webb, Senior Publicist and Marketer; Bianca Salvant, Senior Marketing Manager;

ACKNOWLEDGMENTS

Sally Marvin, VP, Director of Publicity; Jennifer Long, VP, Deputy Publisher; and, of course, Jennifer Bergstrom, SVP, Publisher.

Thanks to John Picacio for another stunning cover. You are an extraordinary artist and I am so glad you are on the team.

Thanks to my agent, Sara Megibow, who has gone above and beyond to support and nurture me, both as a human being and as a client. But most gratefully as a friend.

Thanks to my husband, Michael, for sitting through my late-night ramblings as I tried to work out plot and character arcs and your job was mostly to listen and nod at the appropriate times.

Thanks to my BFF of 30+ years, Anna Liza, who helped me with some of the initial brainstorming for what should happen in book two and for being a huge epic fantasy nerd along with me.

Thanks to my daughter, Maya. You brought your fresh imagination and anime sensibilities to the book and every time I was stuck, you imagined the most wild and unexpected solution. I didn't agree with all of them, but I like the way you think, kid.

I wrote *Fevered Star* during winter/spring of 2020–2021 during the height of COVID-19. Some days it felt impossible to write, other days all I wanted to do was escape into a fantasy world. I am grateful for all the authors whose books sustained and inspired me.

TURN THE PAGE FOR A SNEAK PEEK AT

MIRRORED HEAVENS

BETWEEN EARTH AND SKY

BOOK THREE

CHAPTER 1

Teek Territory

Year 1 of the Crow

May you die at sea.

—Teek farewell

Xiala was drowning.

Seawater, thick and salty, rushed into her mouth. Water weighted her limbs, saturated her lungs, and a growing blackness hovered at the corners of her consciousness. Her instincts screamed at her to resist, to fight. To do something!

But she did not.

Instead, she sank.

Willingly exchanged breath for brine until her feet struck the sandy bottom. She looked up, and her Teek eyes dilated, drawing in what scant light filtered down through the cold water.

Far above her, the hull of her small boat swayed as a figure leaned over the side. She could not see Teanni's expression, but she imagined her childhood friend's face contorted in concern . . . and expectation.

Xiala looked down at her legs—legs, damn it!—and slapped a hand against her neck. The skin under her palm was smooth.

This is not the way, she thought. *I'm forgetting something.*

But she was running out of time, the darkness closing in, her lungs compromised, her mind soon to follow. If she did not act now, she might never be able to.

With her last clear thought, she pulled a blade from the belt at her waist and sliced through the ropes that secured the netting—netting that held the stones that had sunk her to the bottom of the sea—and, with a powerful push, launched herself toward the surface.

She broke through the skin of the water, gasping. She sucked in air too quickly, and dizziness rocked her, made bursts of light dance in her vision. The sun slapped her face, blinding her too-wide eyes. Teanni's voice came to her, her words a jumble of alarm Xiala couldn't untangle in her deprived state.

She forced herself to slow down, to lay back and float, to trust the sea to hold her until she could get her bearings and convince her body that she was not dying. It took a moment, but finally her head cleared, and she scrambled aboard, Teanni hauling her up.

"Fuck," Xiala swore as she flopped onto the bench, coughing and spitting seawater from between her teeth.

"Nothing?" Teanni's expression mirroring Xiala's own disappointment.

"No. No gills, no tail . . . nothing." She hesitated. "Well, my eyes. I could see well enough, but . . ." She shrugged. "Well enough" wasn't enough, and she knew it, but it was something, at least.

"Did you try Singing?" Teanni asked.

"Of course." But had she? She couldn't recall. Almost drowning had scrambled her brain.

"Perhaps if you let the water into your lungs."

"I've swallowed half the Crescent Sea. That's not the problem."

"Then, what?"

Xiala's tone was crisp. "If I knew, I wouldn't be tying rocks around my waist and trying to drown myself."

Teanni hesitated.

"Say it," Xiala groaned.

"What if, and don't get mad, Xiala, but what if—"

"I imagined it?" Had Xiala not asked herself the same question a thousand times? And come up with the same answer again and again? If she closed her eyes, she could still see the wild storm, the rogue wave, Loob hanging loose-limbed from the rope, Baat leaving her behind to fend for herself after she'd saved him. And then, black scales, water sweeter than air in her lungs, the accusing stares of the crew. "It would be easier if I had, but I did not."

"A tail, gills. It is a thing only spoken of in the old stories. It would make you like a goddess."

Teanni's tone held a note of skepticism, but Xiala only laughed. How could her friend understand? Teanni had not seen a man who commanded crows as if he were their master, had not witnessed Carrion Crow clan pilgrims. She could not understand gods alive and working through human beings the way Xiala had learned to.

Teanni dipped her paddle into the water and began to push. "I admit that when you told me your secret, I thought . . . maybe. Maybe it meant the Mother had not abandoned us completely, if she still favored you. It's been hard these past years."

The Teek of Xiala's memory had always been a paradise. Warm sands, secret coves, plentiful food, and freshwater wells. And past the great island chain that marked the edge of their territory, miles and miles of Song-calmed seas where the Teek built their floating islands: platforms a quarter mile wide and half as long, fashioned from bulrush, a buoyant reed that grew in profusion where the sea touched land.

But that blessed place was no more.

The rains had not come for two seasons, and drought and disease had killed the marshy fields of bulrush. Without it, they could not maintain their floating homes. The Teek were land-bound, as they had been when the enemy had decimated them in the war hundreds of years ago. It was a sign, and it made Xiala's stomach knot to think of it. The parallels to the past were too stark, a harbinger that no one among them seemed willing to face. *Whoever said that one learned from the mistakes of history has never meet a Teek,* she thought. *Stubborn to a fault.*

"I know it is hard to believe, Teanni, but it happened. Many men saw it." Men who were now dead, although through no fault of her own. "And the Mother has not abandoned us. I still have my Song."

And that had been the greatest shock of all. The Teek had lost their Song, the very thing that marked them as the Mother's favored. Not all at once, Teanni had explained, but relentlessly and without mercy. First, the children, and then their mothers, and finally, even the elders. Many Teek had left for the mainland as their magic failed, others were so heartbroken they had simply walked into the sea. Song was the soul of the Teek, their very identity, and without it they were broken. It was desperation that had driven them to name Mahina their queen and rejoin the larger world. The elders had read the end of the Treaty as one last opportunity, willfully ignoring any danger.

Xiala understood why Teanni believed her return was a sign of changing fortunes rather than a twist of unpredictable fate. It was an unfamiliar weight to carry, this expectation that she might perform a miracle for a land and a people caught in a net of suffering, but Xiala would do what she could, help where she must. And the first step would be to find a way to awaken her powers, again.

"It's getting late." Teanni gestured toward the sun, well past its zenith. "We can try again tomorrow." She flashed Xiala a nervous smile. "Perhaps your aunt Yaala and the wise women's circle will have a better idea of how to wake your magic."

"No, no, no." Xiala felt her jaw tighten at the very idea. "We agreed on that. My aunt will never believe what she cannot see with her own eyes, especially from me. A little more time. I will find a way."

"I know. I'm just . . ."

"Impatient? I understand. But when has the Mother not worked in Her own time?"

"The Teek are dying. A little urgency would be appreciated," Teanni said, tone uncharacteristically tart.

Xiala laughed. "Feel free to tell Her. Let's see Her reply."

Teanni's eyes widened at the thought, which made Xiala laugh harder. She sobered as they paddled past an abandoned floating island. A dozen thatched reed houses still stood upon the mounded bulrush, but they were steadily sinking. Without more reeds to fortify each new layer of the foundation and the Teek to Sing the waters to kindness, rough tides had rotted the groundwork underneath and the artificial island sagged, salt-slicked and moldy.

It was a way of life now passing, and it broke Xiala's heart. Had the Mother truly abandoned them? And if so, why? Teanni had said the calamities began after Xiala left, but that could be coincidence. Other factors had to be considered. A generation of elders dying, fewer and fewer babies born each year, drought and disease.

Xiala could see the signs everywhere. If nothing changed, the Teek would be gone within her lifetime.

"Who's that?" Teanni asked.

"Where?" Xiala turned her attention back to the here and now.

A lone figure stood on land, arms raised and waving furiously to get their attention.

"It's Keala." Teanni tensed.

"Your wife? Why is she here?" When they were in Hokaia, Xiala's mother, Queen Mahina, had implied that Teanni may still hold affections for her. Xiala had dreaded their reunion, knowing her heart was firmly set on Serapio and had no room for another. But the concern was made moot when Teanni introduced her wife, Keala. Of course, Mahina had neglected to mention Teanni was married.

"There's something wrong," Teanni said, and they hurried their pace. As they pulled close, Keala waded out into the shallows to guide the small boat in. Xiala jumped out to help push from behind, and together they maneuvered the boat to shore.

"Ships are coming," Keala said without preamble.

"Sailors?" Teanni asked, hopeful. "It's been a long time since we've had men on the island." She grinned. "It could mean children in nine months."

Keala shared a brief smile with her wife. Xiala had learned that Teanni had birthed a son four years ago. A son given to the waves. Her friend had confessed it in a rush of shameful tears triggered by an innocuous observation about a cloud formation one day. Four years had past and a comment about the shape of a cloud had brought her to weeping. Teek were not supposed to mourn their lost sons, but how could they not? Were they not as much a part of their heart as their daughters? And with the population dwindling, every child lost seemed a tragedy.

"Yaala did not say what ships are coming," Keala said, "only that Xiala join her."

"Me?" Xiala asked, surprised. "Yaala hates me. Why does she want me there?" Her aunt had ignored her these past few months, preferring to pretend her long-lost niece did not exist. And when they did cross paths, their conversations were brittle, the past always an unspoken fence between them. Xiala had never forgiven her aunt for the part she played in driving her from Teek all those years ago, and her aunt had not forgotten how close Xiala came to killing her sister. So they tolerated each other on Mahina's orders, but at a distance, and often with malice.

"You are the queen's daughter," Teanni said. "It is only right."

Perhaps Yaala should remember more often that I am the queen's daughter, Xiala thought, *and that she is* not *the queen.* But she kept the words to herself and went with Keala and Teanni to the listening house.

Part of her still hoped she might find a way to steal a boat. The one edict Yaala had made upon Xiala's return was that she was not to be given a seaworthy ship. Her paddler, yes, but only for use on the far eastern side of the island. After all, her aunt could not keep her completely from the sea.

The handful of tidechasers had been under guard from the beginning with strict orders not to let Xiala near one. It hadn't stopped her from scheming, and she had considered Singing the guards to attitudes more amenable to a little thievery. But Xiala was not convinced that her Song would not kill, and she had no feud with the guards. She was not quite ready to become a cold-blooded murderer of her own people.

Yaala was waiting for them on the porch of the listening house. She sat straight-backed on a woven grass throne, arrayed in a wealth of shells. She wore abalone in a collar at her neck, moon shell in a crown around her head, and cowries woven through her long-locked hair. There was a small cluster of women sitting on mats around her. They were the Teek wise women, their circle of elders, and their hands worked as they stripped yucca leaves or ground corn, and their ears listened so that their tongues might provide counsel.

"Ships have been spotted on the horizon, coming from the north," Yaala said as Xiala approached.

"From Hokaia?" Xiala asked.

"They are too far yet to tell."

"Could it be the queen returned?" Teanni asked.

Yaala sounded relieved when she said, "Let us hope. She has been gone too long."

"You cannot be sure it is my mother," Xiala warned. "Whoever approaches could mean ill. Teek is poorly equipped to fight back."

"Enemies?" Yaala sounded dubious. "Mahina has made us allies in the great Treaty cities. Whoever approaches is surely a friend."

"It would not hurt to be cautious," Alani said, and Xiala shot the woman a grateful look. Alani was the sailor who had escorted Xiala from Hokaia. Over the past few months, they had become friendly despite their rocky start, and she was the only other Teek present who had been to Hokaia. She, at least, understood that sometimes those who called themselves friends wore false faces.

"What would you have us do?" Yaala asked, a touch of irritation in her voice. "Flee to our islands that no longer float? Gather sticks and rocks to fight off the foreigners? We cannot run, we cannot fight, and you and I both know we cannot Si—"

She cut off abruptly. In the silence, the wise women clicked their tongues, a sign of their disapproval. Everyone knew it, but it was still anathema to speak of the loss of their Song, and only a handful of women present were aware that Xiala still possessed hers. Yaala, because Mahina had sent a note explaining that Xiala had killed a Cuecolan lord with hers and that was the reason she was now returned to Teek. Alani, because she had escorted Xiala back. And Teanni and her wife, because Xiala had told them.

"No," Yaala said, "the arrival of these ships is a gift from the

Mother. We shall welcome whoever comes as our honored guests." She mustered her queenly poise and stepped from the porch.

The wise women put down their grinding stones and yucca leaves and gathered to join her. Xiala tried to catch Alani's eye, but the sailor avoided her and fell in with the other women, unwilling to challenge Yaala more than she had. Teanni took Keala's hand and smiled reassuringly at them both, but it did little to settle Xiala's worries.

"Walk with me, niece," Yaala commanded.

Xiala swallowed her foreboding and fell in beside her aunt. Silence stretched between them, until her aunt spoke.

"I know we have our differences," she said as they made their way to the shore, "but I need your support today."

"I have never challenged you."

"Not openly, but I know what you think of me." Her aunt's look was wry.

"And what you think of me."

Yaala acknowledged their animosity with a nod. "There is history between us. Wounds that have not healed. But perhaps tomorrow, once Mahina is home, we might find the time to mend them. All of us."

"Mahina will never forgive me, and I am not sure I can forgive her," Xiala said, thinking of their recent confrontation in Hokaia, and even older memories: her mother's betrayal, their dead lover, Xiala's desperate flight.

"You are her daughter, and she is your mother. This grievance has festered long enough."

Xiala did not think it was that simple, but she realized she wanted forgiveness very much, both to give and receive it.

"I would like that," she finally said. How could she not? Whether she felt the same tomorrow would have to be seen, but if her aunt was willing to offer her peace, she was willing to try.

By the time they arrived, a small crowd of the curious had already gathered at the edge of the water, all eyes on something farther out to sea, north-northwest.

"Has anything changed?" Yaala asked the nearest woman.

"No, and the setting sun obscures any identifying markings."

Xiala squinted into the distance. The woman was right. The ships were arriving just as the sun cut across the horizon, making it hard to see.

"Perhaps we should send someone out to greet them," Alani suggested. "Surely they would not see that as an insult."

"There is another way," Xiala murmured, and waded into the waves. She took a handful of deep breaths before she sank beneath the water. Here at the shoreline, the sea was calm and welcoming, and she greeted it as a relative. Unlike her earlier attempt at drowning, she only wanted it to speak to her, to tell her what it could see that she could not.

She opened her mouth, exhaled, and let the water hit her tongue. She did not swallow, only tasted. Salt and life, heavy in her mouth. And something else. Something bitter. She spit out the water, kicked up her feet, and dove to the bottom, not so far. She pressed her hands against the sandy floor. It was work to hold herself there, and she wished she had her net full of rocks.

She sought out the Mother's tongue, the language of the vibrations and reverberations. And she listened. For the smallest deviation, the barest confirmation in the movement of the waters. And the sea told her what she wished to know.

Satisfied, she rose. Water shed from her skin and hair as she made her way back to shore, her expression grim.

"Ships," she confirmed, "and not Teek."

"I have not seen someone speak to the sea in too long." Tears gathered in Yaala's eyes.

"Have the Teek lost the way of reading the waves along with their Song?" Xiala asked, caught between astonishment and dismay.

The wise women clicked, but Xiala didn't care. She looked at Teanni, who nodded. Mother Waters! It was worse than Xiala had imagined, and she had imagined terrible things.

"So it is not the queen, then," Yaala said, disappointment weighting her shoulders.

"That, I cannot tell. Only that they do not cut through the waves like a tidechaser, and that they sit heavy in the water."

"Heavy? Merchant ships?" Alani asked, and a buzz of excitement rolled through the crowd.

"Could be a merchant ship laden with goods," Xiala said, "could be a ship full of people."

"Maybe Queen Mahina has sent men back for us to make children," Teanni said, repeating her previous prediction.

"I don't think so," Xiala said, but the idea had already caught hold and the women practically trembled with the possibility.

"We should have prepared a feast," another woman said.

"Light the torches," Yaala commanded. "We will guide them in."

A cheer went up from the crowd.

"Better we wait," Xiala said, but she was not heard over the rising voices, an air of celebration already beginning. She leaned in to shout in Yaala's ear. "Let me Sing the ships back," she suggested. "Hold them at a distance until we know for sure."

Yaala faced her, took Xiala's hands in her own. "No, Xiala. Let them be happy. They need this."

"We have no defenses. We are like minnows in a pond here. You said so yourself. Easy pickings."

"Xiala." Her voice was gentle, but there was an undertone of exasperation. "Please. Not everyone is your enemy."

Xiala looked to Teanni, who was leaning into her wife and smiling. Even Alani was grinning. Yaala was right. The Teek needed something good, and perhaps she was overreacting, seeing danger where there was none. But she couldn't quite shake a sense of foreboding, and it shivered her shoulders like the first touch of winter.

Soon, the shadowy forms of the vessels drew near. Unlike the Teek, who stood on the beach under bright torches, the strangers' ships were dark; no resin lanterns illuminated whoever was on board. Figures paced on the deck, but none called out a greeting to the waiting women.

In the deep twilight, Xiala counted at least four hulking

canoes, Cuecolan if her eye for nautical detail served, although it was hard to tell in the dark. Four ships potentially holding fifty bodies each. That meant at least two hundred sailors. Why would two hundred sailors come to Teek?

A breeze whispered across the beach and sent the torches dancing. Xiala could hear the creak of leather, the shifting of restless feet against wooden decks. Light flared to life on the nearest ship. She caught a glimpse of animal skins, painted faces, and light reflecting against obsidian-tipped spears.

"Not sailors, an army," she murmured, and, as the realization sank in, "Move back!" and then "Run!" and louder, "Run!"

But no one heard her over the cheering.

Yaala stepped forward in her queenly attire, crown on her head, arms wide. And behind her, the wise women smiled. And all around, an enthusiastic crowd of those who had come to greet their allies waited, expectant.

Xiala heard it before the others did, or perhaps she was the only one who recognized the sound for what it was.

The huff of an exhale, the whistle of a spear cutting through the air.

It struck Yaala through the stomach.

The regent queen gasped, shock rippling through her body.

Her hands clutched at the weapon protruding from her belly.

Her mouth worked, but no words came out. Only a red-tinged cough, blood spattering the sand.

Yaala toppled over dead, and the sky broke open, obsidian-tipped arrows raining down around her.

The arrows struck the wise women. They fell, shafts jutting from throats and chests. Xiala watched, stunned, as an arrow pierced the eye of the wise woman next to her.

A wail cut through the shocked silence. Someone at the edge of the circle of the dead. Her cry was cut short by the thrust of a blade as soldiers stormed the beach.

Xiala opened her mouth to Sing, but she did not think she could stop two hundred warriors even if she wished to, and she might kill Teek, too, in the attempt.

So she did the only thing she could do.

She ran.

Bodies fell around her. Shrieks filled a night that quickly had begun to stink of death and betrayal.

Something hit her from behind.

She staggered, the impact throwing her to her knees.

Get up, Xiala. Get up!

She tried to stand.

But something struck her head, and this time when she fell, there was only darkness.